TRIVIUM

A SOOTHSAYER NOVEL

ALLISON SIPE

LIKE MAGIC
STUDIO

ALSO BY ALLISON SIPE

SOOTHSAYER SERIES

Soothsayer

Avalon: A Soothsayer Novella

Trivium

Le Fay: A Soothsayer Novella

Elysium

REALMS SAGA

Realm of Flames & Steel

Realm of Stars & Shadows

BOOK PLAYLIST

If you like to listen to music while you read, then you're in luck! We've created a playlist just for Soothsayer on Spotify and you can listen here:

To Jessica -
You are truly a writers best friend. Thank you for reading every
version of my manuscripts and putting up with the long wait in
between books. Your friendship and encouragement keeps me going.

"A sword wields no strength
unless the hand that holds it has courage."
-The Hero's Shade

CHAPTER ONE

His fist slipped past my jaw as I ducked out of the way and jumped into a defensive stance. He came at me again and I swung around and kicked toward the center of his chest. Without skipping a beat, he grabbed me by the ankle and pulled me off my feet. I hit the ground with an audible grunt as the wind escaped my lungs.

"That was better, but you need to make sure you have a clean shot or you'll just end up on your ass every time," Jake instructed.

"No kidding." I pushed myself off the blue padded mats and rubbing my butt and thigh. "Let's go one more round." I wiped the sweat off my brow with my forearm, doing my best to keep my panting in check.

The sun had long since taken its plunge beyond the horizon, but it was still unseasonably warm. The heat combined with the humidity made my skin slick with sweat and forced me to shower twice a day.

"Alright, when you're ready." He jogged in place as if training me wasn't a work out for him.

I grabbed a sip of water and when I was ready I chanced a swing at him while he was unprepared.

He blocked me with his forearm. "Fighting dirty, huh?" he asked, stepping back. "Bring it on, Miss Evans." He motioned with his fingers for me to advance.

I took a deep breath and shot forward, alternating my punches. Left, right, uppercut, right, uppercut, left. He effortlessly blocked all my blows, but I kept him on the defense and pushed forward. Taking another step, I swung around and planted a kick against his chest. He stumbled backward.

"There you go," he said, finding his balance and taking a swing at me. It was my turn to dodge and try to get the upper hand. My forearms were already red and sore, but he kept pushing forward. I ducked into a squatting position and swung out my leg, catching his feet and bringing him to the mat.

Applause came from behind us and caught my attention. Annabel and Brett stood watching us from the patio.

"It's about time someone put my husband in his place," Annabel laughed, and wiggled her fingers flirtatiously at Jake.

"You're coming along, kiddo," Jake said from the mats, resting on his elbows.

"It's all those kickboxing classes I used to take." I reached down to help him up.

"He's right, you're doing great," Brett said, stepping toward us.

"I'm motivated. I just wish my Magic was coming along as quickly as my self-defense."

Jake pat my shoulder as he stood. "Magic takes time and a lot of practice, but you'll get there."

"I hope so," I sighed. I had the ability to see the past, present, and future, but I still couldn't get a solid read on where Robert was or what had happened to him. I was slowly losing my sanity every time I used my ability to look for him and came up empty handed.

As a small measure of self-preservation, I threw myself into training. The hour or so I spent sparring with Jake every day was the only time Robert wasn't on my mind. When fists and legs are flying at you, it's hard to think about anything else.

"So what are you ladies up to?" Jake asked.

"Actually, I came out to talk to you," Brett said. She raised her eyebrows and tilted her head. Jake nodded slightly, and if I wasn't watching him, I wouldn't have noticed.

"And I just wanted to grab a quick kiss before heading out," Annabel stood up on her tiptoes to steal a peck.

"You're going somewhere?" Jake frowned.

"Just need to run to the store, I'll be back before you know it." She pressed herself to his chest.

"Hurry back." Jake smiled down at her and tapped her backside before she orbed out of sight.

Another careful lie. Annabel was doing some research for me in secret. She was the only one I'd opened up to about my parents besides Robert, and she was helping me search for answers. Her ability to orb in and out of hard to reach places always proved useful.

Annabel was also the only one on my side about Robert, which made her that much easier to be around and open up to. Sure, Jake wanted his brother back and believed Robert was still on our side, but he wasn't in a rush to look for him either. I think Brett was starting to wear him down. And who could blame him, with each day that passed, it was getting easier to believe that Robert was never coming back.

"Let's call it for tonight. We can practice more tomorrow," Jake said, wiping a towel across his face.

"Sounds good. Aunt Beth should be here soon to work on my Magic anyway." I wiped the sweat off of my forehead with the end of my shirt.

Over the last few weeks, I had gotten used to spending most of my time at the Maxwell estate. Brett and Annabel had helped nurse me back to normal after the battle at Pacifica Pier, and Jake was becoming more and more like a brother. Once I recovered from my near drowning, he began meticulously training me in the art of self-defense, while everyone else was helping me hone my magic.

I thought about how proud Robert would be of the progress I've made and my heart ached that he wasn't here to see it. He was my first introduction to Magic, and I'd fought him every step of the way. If only he could see how much I'd embraced the Magical world in the weeks since he'd been missing.

Leaving the changing room, I walked over to the pool and dove in. The cool water washing over my body was refreshing after a rigorous session of training. I did a couple laps, enjoying the feel of the water on my skin, and then rolled over and relaxed, floating aimlessly around the pool.

I moved my arms back and forth, creating ripples across the water as the rhythmic sloshing relaxed my mind. The stars above twinkled like diamonds against the black velvet of the sky. Propelling myself through the water, gently kicking my feet and using my arms to steer, I admired the cosmos.

My Magic squirmed inside me, begging for release as my thoughts wandered back to Robert. I wished I could see if he had betrayed us or not, I wished I could see if he was okay. The power inside of me hummed just beneath the surface, ready and waiting. There was something about the water that made my Magic flare up stronger and more robust than any other time. I always tried to reach out to Robert while I was in the water, hoping that extra boost would allow me to get a clear picture of him.

Taking a deep breath, I swished my hair back and forth, letting the strands float across my shoulders like seaweed. Magic soared inside me as I thought about the last time Robert and I were alone together, and a warm feeling bloomed in my chest and spread through my torso.

The stars swirled above me like Van Gogh's, *Starry Night* as a vision took hold.

Robert was fast asleep on a thin cotton mattress. He looked peaceful as his chest rose and fell with each gentle breath. Quiet footsteps made their way down the hall, and I peered through the bars to see who it might be.

It was Lila. She gazed over her shoulder as if to make sure the coast was clear and then waved her hand over the locked bars. They slid open with ease and she tip-toes over to where Robert was sleeping.

Oh god, what was she going to do to him, I thought.

"Robert, wake up," Lila whispered into his ear. She shook him until he opened his eyes.

He rolled over languidly and looked up at the woman hovering over him. His eyes widened at the sight of her and he jumped to his feet, saying, "What, what is it. What's wrong?"

"We have to go." She looked over her shoulder. "Now."

"We?" he asked, rubbing the sleep from his eyes.

"I promise I'll explain later, but we need to go." She held out her hand for Robert to grab, her expression deadly serious.

Colors and shapes swirled around me as the scene changed again and Robert and Lila were standing near the ruins of a castle arguing.

Before I could get a good look at the scenery, my vision went dark and a hotel room rose around me. Lila walked out of the bathroom, letting the yellow light flood the room with a healthy glow. She wore a towel wrapped around her and quietly padded across the carpet.

I looked around her and spotted Robert asleep on the oversized bed. The light from the bathroom touched his face, highlighting the dark circles under his eyes and stubble around his jaw. A hot branding iron seared through my heart and angry tears filled my eyes. How could he be with Lila after she tried to kill me?

Lila switched off the bathroom light and the room plunged into darkness.

My lungs burned as I coughed up a mouthful of chlorinated water. Two sets of hands dug into my arms and pulled me over the side of the pool, scraping my back in the process as they dragged me onto the concrete.

"Violet, are you okay?" Jake's voice rattled me to my senses.

"Yeah," I coughed again, "I'm fine." I waved him off.

"Any reason you were at the bottom of the pool?" Brett asked, un-phased and handing me a towel.

"My magic, it just took a hold of me." Another cough rattled me. My breath came out ragged as I tried to remember every detail of the visions I'd just seen. "I saw Robert."

"He's alive?" Jake grabbed me by my shoulders.

I nodded.

"So is he with them or us?" Brett asked with ice in her voice. She was still convinced Robert had betrayed us. And for the first time since he went missing, doubt crept into my heart.

"I don't know," I admitted, unable to meet either of their eyes.

"What do you mean, you don't know? What'd you see?" Jake helped me to my feet.

I shook my head and wiped the water from my brow. "Lila was helping him escape. I don't really know what to make of it."

Brett shook her head. "I knew he never fully let go of her."

Jake's eyes widen and his lips formed a hard line. "Brett, this isn't the time or place."

"What do you mean, never let go of her?" I looked between Brett and Jake.

"He and Lila used to be an item," Brett explained.

"Brett," Jake warned.

"She has the right to know," Brett shot back. "Robert left her when he realized he was meant to find you."

"How long ago was this?" I asked, dumbfounded.

"Five, six years ago," Jake confirmed.

"But I thought Robert knew about the prophecy since he was a boy?"

"He did, we all did. But William's journal was boxed up and

forgotten about. It wasn't until our grandfather died and we cleaned everything, that we found the journal and the second half of the prophecy."

"That Robert had to find me before it was too late," I added under my breath.

"Exactly," Brett agreed with a nod. "He walked away from Lila and his training to search for you."

"So you think he still has an attachment to her?"

"I think your vision speaks for itself." Brett crossed her arms over her chest.

"Can't we just be happy he's still alive?" Jake offered, trying to sound hopeful.

"When are you going to wake up and smell the coffee, Jake? Mark my words, Robert will be back for Violet." Brett scowled and pointed in my direction.

"You can't just write him off, he's our brother." Jake tried to reason with Brett.

"Can't I?" Brett's eyes shot daggers at Jake.

"Guys, let's not go down this road again," I pleaded as I put myself between them, placing a hand on each of their shoulders.

"Fine by me." Brett stormed off toward the house.

"And I thought I hated Lila," I huffed.

Jake shrugged and let out a heavy sigh as we watched Brett slam the French doors behind her.

"Brett has a hard time letting things go," he said.

Furrowing my brow, I looked back to him. "What happened? I mean, why does she hate Lila so much?"

"They used to be like sisters, inseparable even." Jake folded his arms across his chest. "Then one day they hated each other and Robert, in his infinite wisdom, sided with Lila."

I stared at Jake, eyes wide. The thought of Brett being inseparable with anyone was hard to imagine. Getting close to her was like trying to get near to a cornered animal.

"Ever since then," Jake continued when I didn't say anything.

"Her and Robert have had a shaky relationship." Turning to look at me, his lips curled up on one side. "It's been better since you came around though."

I chuckled. "Are you sure about that?"

"Absolutely." Jake clapped me on the back and I let out another shaky cough.

"What do you think about Robert and Lila?"

"I refuse to believe Robert would betray us."

"I hope not." I bit my lip and the corner of Jake's eyes crinkled as he appraised me.

"You two got pretty close, closer than you're letting on, huh?"

I leaned my head against his shoulder to hide my face. "I don't know," I hesitated. "Maybe."

Jake chuckled. "Don't worry. We'll get him back."

"Trying to beat the heat, I see." My aunt's voice carried across the yard.

"Trying would be the operative word." I coughed again.

"You sure you're okay?" he asked again.

I nodded. "You're going to start sprouting grey hairs if you don't stop worrying."

"Ouch. Point taken." Jake held up his hands in surrender. "I'll leave you ladies to it then."

Jake made his way back toward the house. I didn't envy him if he was going to search for Brett.

My aunt kicked off her sandals, sat down and let her feet dip into the water.

"How was your physical training today?" she asked.

"Good. I actually got one in on Jake. He went down like a ton of bricks." I snickered and sat down next to her, dipping my feet into the pool. "Training every day is starting to take its toll though. Jake isn't holding back as much anymore." I rolled my already sore shoulder and smiled.

"I'm glad things seem to be going well for you lately." Her

tight, sympathetic smile reminded me it had only been a few short weeks since I was fighting for my life.

"I wouldn't say things are peachy. My life's still on the line," I noted.

"Yes, but the next time a threat comes at you, you'll be ready."

The next time, I thought. There would always be a next time, wouldn't there? By now Aiden had to know I was still alive. They would be back. It was just a matter of when.

Sighing, I asked, "Should we get started?"

I was never ready for sessions with my aunt. It always left me feeling more depleted than my physical training. On the bright side, I was getting better at controlling my visions and that was the whole point. Getting sucked into a vision in the middle of a fight wouldn't end well. So it was my aunt's job to teach me how to block out my vision and only see them when I needed to.

"Ready when you are." She tucked one foot underneath her so she was facing me. I did the same and reached my hands out to her.

She placed her thumb in the middle of my palm and held the back of my hand with her finger.

"Now just relax and let your Magic flow in a steady stream like we've been working on." Her soothing voice made her sound wiser than her years.

I closed my eyes, took a deep breath and focused on letting my Magic course through me at an easy pace, instead of the burst of energy I was used to every time a vision took me by surprise.

Magic slowly spread from my chest into my limbs. Pins and needles pricked at my calves, then my toes, and I knew I was doing it right.

Over the last month, I'd become very intimate with how my Magic felt and now I couldn't imagine my life without it. I felt stronger now, more alive than I ever did before Robert healed me. I may not have been ready to accept all of this before, but this is who I am and I wouldn't have it any other way.

Taking a deep breath, goosebumps covering my skin, I said, "Okay, I'm there."

A warm breeze blew across my bare shoulders as I sunk deeper into my Magic.

"Alright, now clear your mind," Beth said and squeezed my hands.

I pictured myself in a room with no doors and no windows. Every thought, every feeling, was plastered to the walls from head to toe. A family photo of the Maxwell's hung on the wall closest to me. I touched the edge of the silver frame and it vanished, leaving a blank white space in its place as I pushed the thought of them out of my head.

I continued clearing the imaginary room, picking up items and letting them vanish from my mind until the only thing left was Robert. He stood in the center of the room, wearing the blue button-up shirt and jeans he wore the day we met, and he was watching me with a small smile.

Moving toward him, I tried to push him from my mind. The edges of him blurred a little, but he stayed in place. He was the one thing I could never scrub clean from my mind. The constant worry of what happened nagged at my subconscious twenty-four seven.

"It's not working," I sighed.

"You're almost there, what's blocking you?"

"Robert. He won't budge."

"That's okay, he's a part of you."

When Robert healed me, a part of his Magical soul infused with mine, making him forever a part of me and allowing me to come into my Magic.

"You have to stop thinking of him as a weakness and use him to strengthen yourself. Now take a deep breath and focus," My aunt instructed. She paused, allowing me to concentrate before she continued. "On your sixth birthday, what did I wear to your party?"

Images from my childhood started popping up around me, filling the white room with color. My sixth birthday started to take shape and then my aunt walked across the lawn, holding a large present.

"You wore a floor-length floral skirt and black strappy top," I said and smiled as the memory played out in front of me.

"Good," my aunt said. "Now, let's go to the night Robert saved you."

Just like before, I cleared my mind until the room was white and then focused on the memory of the night I was attacked.

Black asphalt rolled out like a carpet. The night sky formed above me, and Robert and I appeared on the ground at my feet. He hovered over me, panic radiating off his face as I lay there pale and still. Robert called my name and my eyes fluttered open. His hand moved to my torso and my body jerked as he began to heal me and change me forever.

This was an easy vision to pull up. I'd returned to this moment a million times when we were trying to figure out who had given the order to kill me.

"Come on, Aunt Beth, challenge me."

"Alright, let's see if we can get a read on where Robert is in the present," Beth suggested.

Damn, I cursed myself. I took a deep breath and tried to focus on Robert. He stood in front of me, his hand reaching out to grab my own, but I couldn't reach him. My heart started racing and my Magic became ragged instead of the smooth, steady flow it had been a moment ago.

"Violet, you have to focus."

Gathering my thoughts, I focused on Robert as he faded in and out in front of me.

Trees sprung out of the ground and he began to run through them like the devil was on his heel. Cold, damp air surrounded us as a bril-

liant blue light blinded me. The world turned upside down and my vision swirled around me, chaotic and violent.

My Magic flared to life, pulling at me with such force, the air was ripped from my lungs. I'd never felt the tug of a vision so strong before, so urgent, and I squeezed my aunt's hands to steady myself.

"Something's pulling me," I said, my voice shaking.

"I feel it too. Don't fight it, let this one take you," Aunt Beth encouraged.

Releasing the dam on my Magic, raw, hungry power erupted from every part of me.

As I opened my eyes, the blinding light subsided, and I saw a blue haze beginning to form. Heart pounding, I watched as the fog in front of me coalesced into an oval shape made of a thick, churning liquid.

Transfixed to the gentle ebb and flow of the oval, I noticed a shift in the ripples as a figure appeared in the center and stepped through the swirling blue. She was stark naked. Her long, dark hair flowing past her waist and her eyes a brilliant blue that stood out against her pale skin. She was undeniably beautiful, but there was something about her that made my blood run cold.

She wrapped a robe around herself and looked up as if she was seeing something far away. Her piercing blue eyes looked through me and a small wicked smile spread across her face. She raised her arm and pointed off into the distance.

Shaking and feeling like someone had punched me in the stomach, I was violently shoved from the vision back to reality.

"Who was that?" I asked the moment the vision released me.

Aunt Beth's eyes widened and her pupils dilated. "Morgana," she said, the word barely a whisper on her lips.

"Does that mean she's alive?"

"If she hasn't already been brought back from beyond the veil, she will be soon. The timing felt close."

"How, I mean, what was that?" I stumbled over my words. I

wasn't sure what to ask first. I'd never seen anything like that, never felt such raw power pull at me.

"Aiden must be opening the portal to the land of the dead. I always wondered how it would be done, but a portal, it's impossible," Aunt Beth rambled.

I grabbed her arm and pulled her focus back to me, "You need to explain to me what we just saw."

"Morgana will come through a portal, if she hasn't already, and rejoin the world of the living."

"Right, I got that part. What I'm not so clear on is how we can bring back the dead."

"No one in their right mind would. For every life you bring back, someone must die. In Morgana's case, an unthinkable amount of people must die in her name for her to escape the veil."

"Die in her name?" I watched my aunt's face carefully.

"Yes, a ritual must be performed, so the soul being sacrificed is counted toward Morgana's debt," she explained.

"So the spell Lila and Ian were trying to perform on me."

"Exactly. Had they succeeded, your soul would have been sacrificed in the name of Morgana and you would have become part of her re-birth."

"And this portal, how does it work?"

"You need very strong dark Magic. No one's dared to summon a portal in centuries." Beth rubbed her arthritic fingers nervously.

"Okay, well, we already know Aiden's psychotic. This seems pretty par for the course."

"You don't understand. Opening a portal is forbidden to the Magical world. Using that kind of Magic goes against nature."

"So what do we do?" I asked.

"You need to wake The Lady and you need to do it fast."

I gawked, overwhelmed. "Okay, but I don't know the first thing about waking her."

"We'll need The Pieces of Three. The Ring of Dispel, The Lufian Necklace, and Excalibur if you're to succeed. It won't be easy." She gave me a pained smile and squeezed my shoulder.

"And how do we find the Pieces of Three?"

"Talk to Matthew, he can help."

I scrunched up my face at the thought of telling everyone that Morgana was indeed back and the war for the Magical world was upon us.

"I guess we should tell the others," I said.

"Yes, it's time we start preparing for what's to come," Aunt Beth agreed.

"Am I going to talk like that one day?" I tried to lighten the mood. It's not that I wasn't taking this seriously, I just couldn't panic every time something bad happened, I'd be locked up in an insane asylum by now.

My aunt gave me a sideways glance. "Just warn the others."

"Wait, you're leaving?"

"There's someone I need to speak with now that Morgana's returning."

"Who?" My eyebrows formed a deep V at her sudden change in demeanor.

"It's none of your concern. Just make sure the Maxwells know what's going on."

"Okay," I said and nodded. I didn't want her to go, but I'd come to realize she wasn't just my aunt. She was a Soothsayer to the Magical community, and that came with certain burdens. Once I was able to master my ability, I'd be faced with the same sort of responsibility, so I let her go without another word.

Walking into the house, the air conditioner was on full blast and the towel Jake had wrapped around me did very little to keep me warm. I shivered as goosebumps covered my skin.

Jake, Annabel, Brett, and Matthew sat in the living room discussing the fact that I'd had a vision of Robert and Lila. Brett's face was as red as an heirloom tomato and Annabel's normally easy going attitude was nowhere in sight. Thankfully, Jake seemed to be keeping the peace between the two of them, while Matthew hid behind his laptop.

"I'll be in touch soon," my aunt said as she grabbed me by the shoulders and pulled me in for a hug. "Make sure Matthew helps you find The Tokens."

"I will and be safe," I said.

Her eyes reflected the sadness in my heart. Both of us knew how quickly things could change for the worse, so we did our best to never take our goodbyes for granted.

"I'll walk you out," Brett said. She motioned to Bethany, and they made their way to the front door.

"So, you finally got a good glimpse of Robert?" Annabel asked. Her expression was one you might see on a kid salivating over a Popsicle.

"I did." I shook my head in disbelief. "It wasn't like my other visions. I felt like we were connected somehow, like he was reaching out to me." I said, moving into the living room.

"And he's alright?" Annabel stood, untangling herself from Jake.

All I could do was nod.

"I remember doing some research on soul connections awhile back," Matthew began, "when you first started coming into your Magic." He flipped open his messenger bag.

"Soul connection? So, they're physically a part of one another?" Jake asked, laying his arm across the back of the couch.

"Well, yes actually. Because Violet was on the brink of death when Robert healed her, a piece of his soul latched onto hers and brought her back. We all know that's how she got her Magic. I wonder then..." Matthew paused and turned toward me. "If it's possible that you were able to see him from such a distance because he's a part of you."

"But why hasn't it ever happened before? I've been trying to get a read on him ever since he vanished. Why now?" I asked.

"I don't know, but if I had to guess, I'd say it's because of all the training you've been doing, physically and Magically. You're coming into your full potential," Matthew said, an easy grin plastered across his face.

I bit my lip and looked around the room. Somehow it felt bigger, emptier without Robert here.

"It's just..." I hesitated. I had gotten close to the Maxwell family since, but I was still hesitant about opening up to new people.

"What is it?" Annabel asked.

"My Magic, it felt different somehow," I admitted, shifting my weight onto my other foot.

"Different how?" Annabel asked.

"It was raw and urgent. Nothing like I've felt before."

"Here we go," Matthew interrupted, his laptop glowing brightly before him. "It was Graham who mentioned the soul connection. He's done a bit of research on the topic and thought I might be interested, given my proximity to Violet."

"Well, what's he say?" I asked, leaning against the back of one of the overstuffed chairs.

"He said that Arthur and Merlin are the only recorded account of anyone having a soul connection, and that's why they were so powerful. They were able to tap into each other's magic and join forces."

"So what, Robert and I are only the second ones this has ever happened to? I find that hard to believe," I scoffed.

"No, Graham said they were the only *recorded* account." Matty's smile grew as if he was about to let us in on a secret. "He's stumbled onto a few other pairs that he thinks may have had the soul connection, but it was during a time when Magic was banned, so digging up any information is proving to be difficult."

"Who were they?"

"He didn't say. He said he'd look into it more and let me know if he was on to anything."

"Alright, what does history say about Arthur and Merlin's connection?" I asked.

Matthew's eyes lit up with his smile. He looked thrilled to have a captivated audience. "We all know that Merlin saved Arthur's life because he knew Arthur would become one of the greatest kings of all time."

Everyone nodded in agreement.

"The reason Arthur was one of the greatest kings of all time is not because he had Merlin by his side, but because he and Merlin were able to tap into each other's Magic and make the impossible happen," Matthew continued.

"So it's possible that Robert and I have the same ability?"

"It's not only possible, it's the most likely explanation for what happened between you two. And it may be why they took him. To keep the two of you apart, so your Magic can't become something unbeatable."

"They thought I was as good as dead. Why take Robert if they've already eliminated the other half of the connection?"

"She's right," Annabel chimed in. "They'd have no need for Robert if they thought Violet was dead."

Matthew shrugged. "Maybe they knew there was a chance she would survive, and taking Robert was their insurance," he reasoned.

"Oh, come on, Matty, you can't actually believe that?" Brett asked. Her voice startled us all as she walked back into the room.

"You of all people know anything's possible when Magic's involved." His eyes narrowed on her. "And I refuse to believe Robert's a traitor," Matthew insisted. His last comment won him a glare that was probably meant to light him on fire.

I rolled my eyes, more than tired of this argument, and said,

"So back to the soul connection. Can you reach out to your contact and see if he can get any more information?"

"I'll email him right now and see if we can set up a meeting."

"Great. Thank you."

"It's getting kinda late. Should we head out?" Annabel asked.

"There's something else I need to tell all of you." I stood up straight and took a ragged breath. "While my aunt was here, we had a shared vision of Morgana." Fear, anxiety, and solace crossed their faces as I looked around the room. "Aiden's opened a portal to The Veil and brought her back, or will bring her back very shortly," I amended.

"You're sure?" Annabel asked, her mouth slightly open and eyes wide.

I nodded.

"So this is it, then. The war for the Magical world has begun," Brett concluded. She placed her hand on Matthew's shoulder and he looked up at her gravely.

"It's time to wake The Lady," I said. "But, first we'll need The Pieces of Three." I turned to Matthew. "Aunt Beth said you'd be able to help us find them, a ring, a necklace, and Excalibur."

"I'll put out a notice through the channels and see if I can come up with their whereabouts," Matty said.

"Are you ready for this?" Jake asked me.

"As ready as I'll ever be." I shrugged and chills that had nothing to do with the temperature ran all over my body.

CHAPTER TWO

An hour later, Annabel orbed us into my living room. I spent little time at home anymore. It was too lonely without Robert.

I chided myself at the thought of how quickly he'd become a fixture in my life. When he was here it felt safe, comfortable, like a home should. But without him, it was cold and lonely.

Brett had tried to convince me to stay at the estate. They had plenty of empty bedrooms, but I didn't want to give up every last shred of my old life. Instead, the Maxwells took turns staying with me, insisting that I couldn't be alone.

"Violet, are you alright?" Annabel asked, eyeing me as I dropped to the couch in a heap of sore muscles.

"Fine. Why?"

"Jake told me the history behind Robert and Lila." Her eyes drifted around the room. "He said you might need someone to talk to."

"Something doesn't add up." I ignored her mention of Robert and Lila's past relationship. "Why take Robert on the beach and then help him escape?"

It took all of me not to jump to conclusions since my heart wanted to scream at the thought of him trusting her, after everything she'd put me through.

"Do you want to punch something?" Annabel asked. She half smiled and shrugged.

I laughed and said, "No, I'm fine. I just don't get how he can align himself with her, you know?"

"What do you mean? You don't think he's just using her to escape?" Annabel crossed her arms, waiting for more of an explanation.

Turning to face her, I took a deep breath and closed my eyes before answering. Annabel and I had gotten close over the past month, and I was pretty sure I could trust her not to say anything. Still, I worried.

"Violet, you've got to tell me what's going on. You can't keep everything in all the time," she pleaded as she sat down next to me and picked up my hands in hers.

"I just don't know what to make of it, and I don't want to add any more fuel to the Robert fire."

Annabel chuckled. "I'm not Brett. I won't gather a hunting party based on one little vision."

I thought about it for a moment and then leaned against the back of the couch. "After they escaped, I saw them together in a hotel room," I began.

"Like, *together*, together?" Her eyebrows almost met her hairline as she looked at me.

"No, nothing like that. He was sleeping, and she had just gotten out of the shower."

Annabel's eyes shifted to the side, and she bit the inside of her cheek. "Do you think he's on her side now?"

"I don't know." Even to my own ears, my voice sounded flat. "I only got brief flashes of them, not much to go on." I ran my hand through my hair. "How can he be so relaxed around her after…" I trailed off and kept my eyes on the ground, unable to meet Annabel's gaze. "I know, it doesn't look good."

"That doesn't mean they're in cahoots." Annabel tried to sound optimistic, but I could tell it was getting harder and harder for her to ignore the facts.

"Do you think there could be an explanation for why he's with her that doesn't lead to him being a traitor?"

"I don't know. Maybe Brett's right. I mean, he is fraternizing with the woman who tried to kill you." She looked no more eager than I to think over the possibility of Robert being a traitor.

"There's clearly some level of trust between them. If there wasn't, he wouldn't have been fast asleep with her in the same room."

Annabel shifted and worried the hem of her shirt. She had to know I was right, but we both wanted to believe that Robert would come home and still be on our side.

"You may have the gift of Sight, but not everything you see comes with an explanation. What does your gut tell you?"

I huffed, my cheeks puffing out, and said, "I don't know if it's my gut or my heart, but something feels wrong about all of this. The pieces just don't add up."

"Alright, so until we know more, I say we cautiously hold on to hope."

"Thanks, Annabel." I gave her hands a gentle squeeze.

Pushing off the couch, I made my way into the kitchen and opened the refrigerator. The condo was still stuffy despite leaving the windows open all day. The carafe of sweet tea I'd made yesterday would be the perfect antidote for this hot, sticky weather.

"Want some?" I asked, holding up the pitcher.

"I'm good, no caffeine for me after three." She waved me off.

"I have to say, it's nice being able to talk to someone I don't have to lie through my teeth to." I took a sip of the sugary iced tea.

"You get used to it." Annabel shrugged and flipped through the book I'd left on the coffee table.

"I know. That's what everyone keeps saying. It's just been hard, not being able to talk to the people I care about."

"You mean Becky?"

I nodded. I hadn't seen Becky in a couple weeks, and it was taking its toll on both of us. Sure, we talked on the phone every couple of days, but I'd thrown myself into my physical and Magical training, and I was too drained to have a fake conversation with my best friend.

"Have you ever thought about telling her the truth?" Annabel asked.

I choked on a large gulp of tea. "Robert would die if he heard you say that."

"Robert's always had a stick up his ass about secrecy and rules." She rolled her eyes and dismissed the idea with a wave of her hand. "There was this one time, Jake and I orbed into his place overseas. He had a few people over playing cards or something, and when we popped into the room, he literally flipped the entire table." She snickered. "Apparently not everyone was Magical at the game and we got chewed out big time."

"How did he explain you materializing out of thin air?"

She shrugged and said, "He didn't. Everyone had been drinking and just assumed that Jake and I had come from the other room. They were more surprised by Robert's sudden outburst than anything else."

I shook my head and chuckled at the thought of Robert causing a scene over Annabel flaunting the rules.

Annabel waved her hand dismissively. "People don't believe in Magic. So when they see something unexplainable, they find a way to explain it with logic. Robert's just too old school sometimes."

"He kind of is, isn't he?"

It was nice being able to joke about him and reminisce. Annabel was great in that way. I think that's why I gravitated toward her more than anyone else. With Annabel, the pain of losing Robert didn't hurt as much.

"By the dreamy look in your eyes, I'd say you like that about him," Annabel noted, eyeing me as a secretive smile spread across her face.

"Anyway, back to telling the truth." I tried to hide my blush behind the glass of sweet tea.

"Changing the subject." She pursed her lips. "Did I hit a nerve?"

I nudged her leg and said, "I don't think I could drag Becky into all this." I mustered on, determined not to talk about my feelings for Robert. "Every time I turn around, someone's trying to kill me. I don't want to put her in harm's way."

Annabel sighed. "I hate to break this to you, but you can't protect everyone. You have to let people make their own choices once they have all the facts."

"I don't know. I just think keeping Magic a secret is better for everyone."

"Morgana's back from the dead and she'll be amassing an army to take over the Magical world. Do you think that's going to stay under the radar?"

"That's just one more reason not to tell Becky." I closed my eyes and rubbed the bridge of my nose. "Morgana is going to rain hell down on us. I don't want my friend getting caught up in the middle if I can help it."

Annabel raised her hands in surrender. "Alright, but for the record, I think having her in the know would help you more than you think."

"Duly noted." I tapped her on the knee and stood. "I'm going to hop in the shower and get to bed. Your husband exhausted me."

"Some women might take that the wrong way." She gave me a teasing grin.

I rolled my eyes. "You know what I mean."

"I do. Jake can be rigorous with his training." Annabel wiggled her eyebrows.

I shook my head and laughed. "Alright, see you in the morning."

Annabel stretched out on the couch and turned on the T.V. Unlike me, she was a night owl and would be up for another few hours binge-watching something on Netflix.

"Night," she called after me, already searching through the catalog of movies and TV shows.

I turned on the shower and ducked under the faucet while the water was still cool, letting the artificial rain wash away the sweat and chlorine from the day's activities. As I rinsed off, I could feel my muscles relax. Jake was kicking my ass, but I couldn't complain. I'd rather be ready for a fight than a helpless damsel in distress. After Pacifica Pier, I never wanted to feel helpless like that again.

As the water warmed up, I let it stream down my neck and shoulders, loosening up the tension of the day. I wish I could say my training was the only reason for the tightness in my shoulders. But, worrying about Robert, Aiden and now Morgana was wreaking havoc on my upper back and my nightly shower was my only reprieve.

With my eyes closed and the warm water at the base of my neck, I could feel a vision tingling just under the surface of my Magic. Dropping my walls, I let the vision take me.

Annabel was chained to a wall, grime and blood staining her skin as she screamed. A flash of green light shot from the shadows and her body went limp. Running toward her, the vision faded. As I reached her, a deep chuckle echoed through my bones.

The image of Annabel was replaced by the back of my eyelids. Heart racing, dread pooled in the pit of my stomach as water cascaded off of me. Swinging the faucet into the off position, I jumped out of the shower and ran down the hall, barely getting a towel around me as I stormed into the living room.

Annabel laid on the couch, her head propped up on a pile of pillows while Matt Damon jumped off of a building on the screen in front of her.

Letting out the breath I'd been holding, Annabel turned to look at me.

"Everything okay?

Unable to meet her eyes I said, "yeah, just grabbing a glass of water." I padded across the carpet to the kitchen, trying my best to act normal.

My aunt had taught me that the future can always shift and change based on free will. Sharing what we see with someone can have a direct influence on the vision, and sometimes, the knowledge can be the catalysts that creates the future we've seen. Until I had more to go on, there was no way I could tell Annabel anything. For now, she was safe, and that's all that mattered.

"Night," I said, taking my glass of water to bed.

"Night." Annabel's eyes stayed glued to the T.V.

Throwing on a pair of shorts and a t-shirt, I jumped into bed. With the soothing effects of my shower long gone, I picked up the journal Robert had given to me off the nightstand. Reading William's words helped me get to sleep sometimes. Cracking open to a random page, William's handwriting sprawled out in tiny neat letters.

13 May 1783

My heart is heavy after leaving Constance this morning, and not with sorrow but worry. Her betrothed appears to have a connection with Le Fay. How a person could choose to align themselves with Le Fay, I'll never know. Even now, drawing out each letter of their moniker makes me sick. To join them would surely be the death of one's soul.

My conscience pulls at me like a bridle in the mouth of a horse. I feel it is my duty to report him, no matter how small his involvement may be.

But alas, out of fear of betraying my promise to Constance, I shall say nothing yet. My only worry is that she'll get hurt or even killed if we wait too long. How can I keep her safe when I've been banished back to the shadows?

Letting the journal fall onto my lap, I stared at the ceiling.

Le Fay? Who the hell were they? I thought. I couldn't help but wonder if Robert knew anything about them. He was always the one with all the answers. How was I supposed to navigate this world without him?

I replaced the journal on the nightstand, turned off the light and rolled over on my side. Usually it was easy to fall asleep after reading through William's journal. But the vision of Annabel left me paranoid about the future, and William's words nagged at me as the name Le Fay danced around in my head. My eyes darted around the room, as I thought about how fast everything was changing. There was still so much more I didn't know about the Magical world.

My chest filled with doubt and before I could go down the rabbit hole of self-pity and anxiety, I pictured the ocean. Dark blue water, golden sand. The feel of a cool breeze on my skin as a wave crashes on the shore. Images floated around my head doing wonders to combat the darkness rising inside of me and slowly, I fell asleep.

Visions of Robert and Lila infiltrated my dreams. They boarded a train and lush green countryside rushed past them. They arrived in a bustling city, the buildings a mix of stone and steel. I watched them run across cobblestone streets and duck into a busy train station. Hundreds of nameless faces rushing passed them as Robert pulled Lila behind him. And last but not least, I saw the name of a hotel here in Pismo and a room number: 324.

My eyes shot open, and I stared at the ceiling with a heavy

heart and I knew without a doubt, he was back. Still exhausted, I looked at the clock on the nightstand. I'd only slept four hours. Groaning, I rolled over, wishing to fall back asleep.

I knew I needed to face him, but the thought of seeing him with Lila hurt more than I cared to admit. My heart didn't know how to reconcile what I felt for him now that he had returned to Pismo with the woman who had tried to kill me. It didn't matter that they had a history. He was supposed to protect me, to keep me safe, not harbor the woman who wanted me dead.

Closing my eyes, I let myself relive every moment with Robert. Falling asleep on his warm chest, his smile when I told him I wanted to learn how to use my Magic. A tear rolled down my cheek as I imagined his arms around me, his lips on mine and the warmth of his body pressed against me. I let myself feel the comfort of him one last time, and then I boxed him up and hid him in the darkest corner of my heart.

The path ahead wouldn't be easy, and I couldn't let my feelings for Robert get in the way. My mission was to wake The Lady, and if Robert and Lila were there to stop me, I'd make sure neither of them ever saw the light of day again.

Steeling my nerves for what needed to be done, I got out of bed and got dressed. I wanted to meet Robert alone, find out what he was up to before Brett and the others jumped to any conclusions.

Sneaking out of my house was easy compared to the Maxwell estate, and Annabel remained fast asleep. I went out through my bedroom sliding door, grabbed my bike and rode off into the early morning light to find out where Robert's loyalties truly lay.

Parking my single speed out front, I walked into the lobby of the Sandcastle Inn with sweaty palms and a pounding heart. The signs led me to the elevator, and I took it up to the third floor. The Magic inside me kicked up a notch as if it knew

Robert was close by. As the elevator moved between floors, my heart battered against my ribcage and Magic crackled on my fingertips. My hands shook as I tried to regain control of the power coursing through me.

The silence of the hotel made the prominent *ding* of the elevator seem much more menacing. The doors slid open, and I stood motionless, staring at the wall across from me. Chills ran down my entire body as an image of Robert and Lila sleeping peacefully flashed across my eyes.

As the doors began to close, I put my arm out, stopping them, then turned left down the hall. My eyes shifted back and forth as room numbers passed me by: *312, 313, 314, 316.*

At the far end of the hall, I found room number 324, and raised my hand to knock, hesitating for a moment. Sucking in a breath and steeling my nerves, my knuckled banged on the door. I waited a second, but not a sound came from the other side. Knocking again, I banged my fist against the pristine white door. Within a few seconds I could hear the distinct sounds of whispers and knew I had caught them off guard.

The door cracked open and a disheveled-looking Robert stood in front of me.

"Violet?" he said, exhaling with sleepy eyes.

A smile spread across my face at the sound of his voice. Everything I'd tried to bury, to extinguish inside me came to life at the sight of him. I missed him so desperately, his warmth, his comfort. I wanted to reach out to him, touch his face and feel his skin. I tried to move toward him, but my feet stayed rooted to the ground. The rush of seeing him again had taken over, but my subconscious still held onto the real reason I was here.

"It's really you." He took a cautious step toward me.

"It is," I said, pushing everything I felt for him back into the box I'd created.

A smile blossomed on his face. "It's such a relief to see you with my own eyes." He pulled the door open wider and allowed me to enter.

Standing with my back against the wall, I watched him retreat into the room. My heart reached out to him, but he was no longer the Robert I once knew. Lila had taken him and had somehow made him believe he could trust her.

Their room was large, even by hotel standards, but I shouldn't have expected anything less. Passing a spacious kitchen on my right, I edged into the living room. A door to what I assumed was the bedroom remained closed and the light from a TV flashed under the door.

"How are you?" Robert asked, watching me cautiously as if I was a snake ready to strike.

The sound of his voice tugged at my heart and threatened my resolve. I needed to get away from him and finish what I came here to do.

"Robert, who's at the–" a soft voice came from the doorway just to my right.

I turned toward the woman's voice and saw her, Lila. My resolve slammed into me and any notion of Robert fled my mind as blood boiled under my skin.

"How did you know where to find us?" Lila stared at me in complete disbelief.

"I have my tricks," I answered with a wicked smile. I enjoyed seeing the uncertainty in her eyes.

Raising my hand, my fingertips ached to release the Magic building inside of me. She deserved to die after what she put me through.

"No!" Robert yelled, putting himself between Lila and me. "Violet, don't. It's not her fault."

"Not her fault?" I narrowed my eyes on him. "She tried to kill me." Magic flared in my heart, ready to strike the second he let his guard down.

"Please, just let me explain," Robert pleaded.

"There's nothing to explain."

He raised his arms in defense. "Violet, let's talk this out."

"I will go through you if I have to." I held his gaze, daring him to challenge me.

"This isn't who you are." Robert took a step toward me as Lila recomposed herself and moved into a defensive stance.

"Don't you dare try to tell me who I am! You come back here with *her* and think you can just pick up where you left off?" I demanded, my voice laced with venom. All the hurt, frustration and anger I held in my heart burst to the surface.

"I knew it wouldn't be easy coming back here with Lila, but I know I can get you to understand if you just hear me out." Robert took another step toward me. His eyes held mine and the warmth I'd missed so much started rising within me.

I threw up my shield, blocking him from coming any closer. But what I felt wasn't something I could block out. My heart echoed with each step he took, making my Magic leap in excitement as it recognized its counterpart in his soul. Nothing could have prepared me for this. I knew how my Magic felt, but this was different. This was powerful in a way I'd never felt before. Standing frozen behind my shield, I tried to fight for control.

His features matched my anxiety, and I wondered if he was feeling the same Magical pull I was.

"Just let me explain before you do anything rash," Robert pleaded.

Looking past Robert to Lila, I watched her raise her hands in surrender. I could still feel Robert's warmth mingling with the Magic inside me, but I forced myself to concentrate just enough to glance into Lila's future.

Flashes of her filled my vision. She sat on the hotel bed, crying. As I moved closer, she wiped the tears from her eyes and huffed. "It's going to be okay, Lila," she told herself.

The room swirled around me, and Robert and Lila sat in the front seats of his Tesla. He held her hand reassuringly and said, "We're going to make it through this."

"How?" she asked, keeping her eyes trained on the windshield.

Robert's lips pressed into a hard line and he said nothing.

"They all hate me. I don't belong here," Lila continued.

"Don't let Brett get to you. She's difficult even on her best days, you know that," Robert said.

"It's not just her. Violet looks like she's plotting a million ways to kill me." Lila looked at him from under her lashes, eyes still blurry with tears.

"You don't have to worry about Violet. She would never purposely hurt someone."

"You underestimate her." Lila cracked a small smile. "But I guess you always see the best in the people you love."

Robert's worried expression came back into view and Lila watched me anxiously. I wasn't sure how I felt about seeing Lila in a vulnerable state, but I knew, for the moment at least, she wasn't a threat.

Letting my shield drop, I lowered my hand and nodded in agreement that I wouldn't attack.

"Thank you," Robert said, reaching out to touch me, but dropped his hand at the last second. He took a step back and I let out the breath I hadn't realized I'd been holding.

"Alright, go ahead, try to explain why you've allied yourself with *her*," I spat.

"I should apologize," Lila noted, stepping forward.

I shot her a look that should have killed her on the spot.

"Violet, she's on our side now," Robert insisted. "Once she found out the truth, she helped me escape and-"

"You wouldn't have needed help escaping if it wasn't for her."

"Look, I was just taking orders." Lila took another step toward me.

"So what? You don't think twice when you're ordered to kill

someone?" I matched her step. I wasn't helpless anymore, and I was going to knock her through the wall if she didn't back off.

"I was told you were a threat to my family, to the Magical world. As far as I knew, you were going to kill us all. What would you do in that situation?" she yelled.

My hatred toward her fueled the Magic inside me. How could I honestly sit here and have a conversation with this woman?

"Did you ever bother to think for yourself?" I yelled back. Anger pushed me forward and my Magic ached for release.

"Violet, calm down," Robert urged.

"Don't," I snapped at Robert and moved closer to Lila. "And don't pretend you and Ian didn't enjoy trying to kill me. You may be able to fool him." I motioned in Robert's direction. "But I was there, and you loved every torturous minute." Something inside me snapped and a wall of energy flew off me, tossing Lila across the room.

Lila bounced to her feet in a second, hot white light surrounding her fingers. Robert moved between us and grabbed her by the shoulders. "Don't do this," he demanded. "We knew this was going to be difficult."

"Fine," Lila seethed and threw the orb of energy she wielded against the back of the couch.

Robert let out a sigh of relief and his shoulders relaxed ever so slightly.

"I think it'd be best if I left you two alone." Lila nodded curtly at Robert. Something private passed between them and I felt a pang of jealousy deep in my stomach.

Lila walked to the door and paused as she grabbed her jacket. "I do hope we can move past this, Violet."

"Not likely," I replied without turning to look at her. I heard the door close behind me, and suddenly I was very aware that I was alone with Robert.

"Will you please sit down and let me tell you everything?" he said, motioning toward the couch in the small living room.

"There's nothing to say, Robert. You've made your choice. I don't care how well she plays the part, I will never trust her." I turned away from him and walked to the door as well.

I had to get out of here before my resolve cracked. With Lila gone, my anger dwindled and I couldn't afford to let Robert break through even the slightest bit, so long as he was close to her.

"Violet, wait." He grabbed my hand as I walked away.

His touch was like an electric shock and I froze mid-step.

"What?" I barked.

"I know you must hate me." He pulled at my hand, turning me to face him. "But you must know, I'd never put you in harm's way. Lila is a lost and lonely soul, always has been. I couldn't just leave her with Aiden. He would have killed her."

"Maybe she deserves to die." I pulled my hand free of his and tried to steel my nerves.

"You don't mean that." He shook his head and looked away from me.

"You sure about that? You have no idea what she put me through. What you put me through. I've been worried sick about you, whether you're alive, dead, being tortured. Instead, I find you all cozy and lounging around with the enemy."

"For God's sake, Violet. You want the truth, then open your eyes and *see* for yourself." He grabbed my wrist and our Magic exploded between us with such force it knocked the breath out of me.

My vision swirled and a small, dank chamber materialized around me.

Moonlight pooled on the floor at my feet and an older woman sat on the edge of her bed.

"Hello, Violet," she said, raising her head to look at me.

"You, you can see me?" I asked, taking a hesitant step forward. No one in any of my visions had been able to see me before.

"Yes, I can. I've been waiting for Robert to get back to you."

"Who are you?"

"Who I am is not important. I need you to listen. We have little time."

"Okay," I said, hesitantly. This was unexpected.

"They have modified our ability to see." She gave me a meaningful look. So she was a Soothsayer too. I wondered if all Soothsayers could communicate like this. I'd have to ask my aunt.

"You mean, he can block our visions?" I asked.

"Yes. You must be careful who you trust now more than ever, for you won't be able to see the danger until it's too late."

"Lila?"

A loud bang caught her attention, and she looked around anxiously. "I must go now," she said.

"No, wait. What about Lila?"

"Don't blame Robert. He did what he had to, to survive."

"But- "

"Good luck, Waker of The Lady."

Just like that, she disappeared, and Robert's hotel room materialized around me. Looking about, I realized I was on the floor and propped up against the wall. Robert knelt next to me with his hand on my shoulder to steady me.

"You alright?"

"I'm fine." I brushed his hand off of me and pushed to my feet.

"You're Magic's come along in my absence."

A sarcastic laugh escaped my throat. "I've been going through the Maxwell Magical boot camp."

"You've been training with Jake and Brett?"

I shrugged. "I wanted to learn how to protect myself so I'd never end up helpless again." It was so easy falling back into a rhythm with him.

"So can we move past all of this now?" He leaned against the wall, his arms crossed, his eyes searching mine.

As I looked back at him, I could hear the old woman's words in my head. *"Don't blame Robert."*

"I don't know if I can trust you," I said, sighing and stepping away from him. I did blame him for coming back with Lila. He chose to escape with her. He chose to come back to Pismo with her. And the whole time, he knew what she put me through.

"What did you see?" The sadness in his eyes almost broke me. I wanted to comfort him, but I wouldn't let myself, I couldn't let myself.

There was no way I would tell him about the Soothsayer who had just hijacked my vision, so instead, I told him what I saw when I looked into Lila.

"I saw Lila opening up to you, but it's just words, Robert. They mean nothing when you compare them to her actions," I explained, taking another step away from him. "I think you want to see the good in Lila. But just because you want something to be true doesn't mean it is." I shook my head and my heart broke as I took another step away from him.

"I know you don't believe she has any good left in her," he reasoned, closing the gap between us. "But I promise you, Violet, I would never have brought her here if I thought she would try to harm you."

He stopped our bodies inches apart. My heart raced and my lips fell open as I took a ragged breath.

"Robert, I..." he grabbed my arm and my words got stuck in my throat. The heat of his body engulfed me and I tried to take a step back to clear my head but ran into the wall. My back pressed against the cool plaster as Robert inched closer.

"Every day I was away, all I could think about was getting back here to my family, to you. This isn't exactly how I imagined the reunion would go," Robert lamented.

"Me either," I couldn't help agreeing. A lump formed in my

throat and the little box hidden deep inside my heart rattled. His eyes caught mine and for a moment and I thought he was going to reach out to me.

"I know it won't be easy, but I will earn your trust back. One way or another."

Swallowing the lump in my throat, I found the doorknob and opened the door. "We'll see about that," I said, stepping over the threshold.

"Will you do me one favor?" He followed right behind me and I could feel his breath on my neck. My heart sped up, and I had to fight the urge to turn around and face him.

"Depends."

"I'd like you to tell my family I want to see them. I need to talk to everyone, including you, and I think they'll handle seeing me better if you warn them first.

"I can't promise they'll want to see you."

"I know."

"I'll tell them."

He took a deep breath, and I could tell he was relieved. "I'll come by the estate later today."

Nodding once, I turned on my heel and left without another word.

The warm early morning air outside the lobby doors hit me like a ton of bricks. I knew I should call Brett or Annabel, but I was too furious with Robert to think rationally. Dialing Becky's number, I knew she would let me vent without question.

"Hey, what's up?" Becky answered, her voice crackling as she forced herself to wake up.

"Are you home?" My heart wouldn't stop racing as I made my way through the exit of the hotel.

"Yeah, is everything alright?"

"Fine. I'll be there in five." I ended the call and hopped onto my bike.

Luckily Becky's place was only a couple miles from the hotel so when I pulled up, she was already standing on the porch waiting for me.

"I thought you might like a warm cup of Joe." She handed me a hand painted ceramic mug.

"Thanks." I took a large gulp and the caramel-colored liquid warmed my chest and soothed my broken heart.

"So what's got you all worked up?" She rubbed the sleep from her eyes.

"Robert. He's back in town." I tried to keep the emotion out of my voice.

Her eyes widened and her mug froze halfway to her mouth. "How'd you find out?"

"I ran into him and this other woman," I lied. It was easier if Becky believed Robert had left me for someone else. My relationship with Becky had turned into careful truths and white lies. I didn't like it, but there was no way I could tell her there was a whole Magical world right under her nose.

"God, what an ass. What is he even still doing here?" she asked. "I thought he was just supposed to be here for the wedding."

I bit my lip. "I guess he's sticking around now."

"Yeah, well that was all fine and good when he was ogling you, but now he needs to go."

Releasing a heavy-hearted sigh, I closed my eyes and let my mind wander to a simpler time when I was sitting on this very couch with Robert.

"Are you okay?" Becky asked, setting her cup down.

"I just didn't think it'd be that hard to see him again," I admitted, this time a truth.

"You really cared about him, of course it hurts to see him with someone else."

"I just keep wondering if things could have been diff- "

"Don't start playing the 'what if' game," she cut me off.

I ran my hand through my hair. "You should have seen the way he looked at me. His eyes were so full of guilt."

"Don't do that to yourself. You deserve better and you know it."

"I know, it's just complicated."

"No, it's not, it's simple. He's an ass and not worth your time."

I laughed. "Thanks, Beck."

"Always." She smiled and retrieved her cup. We each took a sip of coffee. Becky was still my best friend but there was an awkwardness between us now. Like some part of her knew I was keeping things from her.

"I know things have been different since I've been spending so much time at the Maxwell estate. It's nice to know that some things will always stay the same." I kicked her foot with my own.

"You never have to worry about me bailing on you. And besides, Annabel's been trying to help you learn more about your parents. I would never stand in the way of that."

I smiled. Another half-truth. Annabel was helping me, just not in the way Becky thought. It was strange how easy living a lie had become. I used to chide Brett about it, but now I understood how necessary it was.

"I know," I said. "I just feel bad that I've been so preoccupied. What's new with you? How's work?"

"Work's been busy, actually." She rubbed the back of her neck.

"Anything juicy?" I asked over the rim of my mug.

She shook her head and said, "You know I can't tell you anything."

"I know, I know." I rolled my eyes. "So how's what's his name?"

She looked at the ceiling and bit her lip.

"Come out with it." I knew she had to be brimming with stories of her latest escapades.

Becky didn't disappoint. She launched into a story about the latest guy she was dating and if I didn't think about it too hard, I could almost pretend we were just two normal women gossiping about the men in our lives. Almost.

Unfortunately, the thought of Robert lingered on my mind in a way I couldn't talk with Becky about. I needed to tell his family he was back in town with Lila, which wasn't going to go over well. I knew Jake would be happy to see his brother alive, but no one would welcome him with open arms once they found out he'd brought Lila back with him.

Today is going to be a long day, I thought as I took another sip of coffee and nodded along to Becky's story.

CHAPTER THREE

Somehow mustered the strength to leave Becky's and face the rest of the day. I'd ridden my bike a million times between Becky's place and mine, but somehow the trip felt longer. The weight of Robert being back sat heavy on my heart and the warning in my vision gnawed at the back of my skull. If Lila was a danger to us, to me, why didn't the woman in my vision just say that?

Replaying my morning with Robert, I dissected his every word, hoping I'd find something that would make it easier to trust or even believe that Robert & Lila were on our side.

With each stroke of the peddles on the way to my complex, I grew more sure that no matter what the outcome; I was glad I'd gone to see Robert alone. I needed that face-to-face time without everyone's eyes on us. Knowing what to expect when I saw him again, I felt certain I could handle it better.

"Where the hell did you run off to?" Annabel's wind chime voice came from the front porch as I pulled up.

I shook my head and said, "Long story. We need to get to the estate."

"Violet, you're not supposed to go off on your own."

"Can we get to the lecture later?"

"Fine." She huffed and reached out her hand for me to take. "So why are we heading to the estate?"

Grabbing her outstretched fingers, I took a deep breath and said, "Robert's back and he brought Lila with him."

"Shit." Everything disappeared into a haze as she orbed us to the estate.

"What are you guys doing here so early? Is everything okay?" Jake asked as we appeared in the Maxwell kitchen.

"It's Robert," I said. "He's back. We need to gather everyone."

"Is he a threat?" Jake stopped pouring pancake batter onto the griddle and squared his shoulders.

"At the moment, no. He just wants to talk to the family."

Jake nodded, looking relieved. "Brett's upstairs." He dried his hands with a dish towel and threw it on the counter.

"I'll grab her." Annabel turned on her heel and left the room.

"And I'm going to call Matthew. I think he should be here too," I added and made my way out onto the patio.

I pulled my cell out of my pocket clicked Matthew's name in my recent call list.

"Violet, hey. Everything okay?" He answered on the second ring. I could tell I'd woken him up by his muffled voice.

"Everything's peachy." I was really getting tired of everyone asking me that. "How soon can you get to the Estate?"

"Bout twenty minutes. What's going on?"

"Robert's back and he wants to meet with everyone."

"I told you he'd make it back to us!"

"Yeah, well, don't go throwing him a party just yet." I paused. "He brought Lila back with him."

"Ah damn. What the hell's he thinking?"

"That's the question of the century. Just get here as soon as you can."

"Will do," he said dryly. "I'll see you soon." He hung up, and I made my way back inside.

"So he's back. You had a vision?" Brett asked the moment I walked into the kitchen.

"Yes and no." I shifted my eyes around the room.

"Why do I get the feeling that you aren't glad that he's back?" Jake asked with his brow furrowed.

"It's complicated," I sighed. "I did have a vision of him… and Lila last night, but I also went to their hotel- "

"Are you insane?" Brett shot off the barstool.

I shrugged and bit my lip. "I half wondered that myself as I rode to their hotel."

"You could've been hurt. Or worse, killed." Brett crossed her arms like a parent scolding a child.

"You think I didn't look ahead?"

"That's not the point!" Brett shouted.

"Can we save the argument?" Annabel interrupted before Brett could lash out again.

"Fine, tell us what happened," Brett said.

A crooked smile played on my lips and my eyebrow twitched with excitement. "I tossed Lila across the room like a rag-doll," I admitted.

"Damn right you did," Annabel said, all business.

"I didn't mean to. I mean, I wanted to, don't get me wrong, but my Magic just kind of bubbled over and exploded off me."

"I would have torn her head off," Annabel smirked.

"Yeah, well, she has Robert protecting her."

"That's it, I'm ending this when he gets here," Brett said through gritted teeth.

"Brett," Jake cautioned with the spatula as a warning. "Maybe there's an explanation."

"Get your head out of the sand!" Brett yelled at her brother.

Even I couldn't believe Jake would still defend Robert, knowing he'd come back to Pismo with Lila.

"Let's just see what he has to say before you play judge, jury, executioner, alright?" Jake pleaded.

"What could he possibly have to say?" Brett threw her arms in the air. I thought I was mad at Robert, but I had nothing on his sister's fury.

"I don't know," Jake snapped back. "But he's our brother and if he wants to talk, then we owe him at least that much."

I sat down as they argued, letting everything sink in. I'd had my chance to kill Lila, and I hesitated. Could I have doomed us all because I couldn't do what was necessary?

"Earth to Violet, you in there?" Annabel asked.

"Yeah." I rubbed my hands over my face. "I'm fine." The words were losing their meaning each time I said them.

"Don't worry," Brett started. "We're all on your side. He might be my brother, but you're The Waker. Sometimes blood isn't thicker than water." Brett stared at me like she was ready to go to war.

"You're also like family and we protect our family." Annabel grabbed my hand and squeezed.

"Thanks," I said with a tight-lipped smile.

"Hey guys," Matthew announced as he walked into the emotionally charged kitchen. Cautiously, he looked around the room. "Everything alright?"

"Just disagreeing with my ever-optimistic brother," Brett explained, putting on a fake smile.

Matthew and I shared a glance, and I hunched my shoulders in apology as he sidled up to Brett.

I finished the breakfast Jake made for everyone, even though I wasn't hungry. My nerves were getting the better of me and the pancakes sat in my abdomen like a stone.

The doorbell rang, and we all looked up as the *ding-dong* echoed through the house. This was going to rough.

"I'll get him," Jake said, rushing out of the room before anyone could argue.

"Try not to burst into flames the moment you see him,"

Annabel urged, giving Brett a pointed look as we all made the tense journey from the kitchen to the living room.

"I won't," she said with a smirk. "But I can't promise I won't turn him into a pile of ash."

"Brett," Matthew cautioned, putting his arm over Brett's shoulder as he whispered something in her ear.

I hung back from the group, taking my time moving across the house. I was still nursing my bruised heart from this morning's encounter and wasn't sure I was ready for round two.

Making it halfway through the living room, I stopped in my tracks. Robert stood across from me, one arm propped up on the mantle, the other in his pocket. He didn't look at me, but his shoulders tensed as I walked into the room.

"Do you really hate me that much, sister?" He asked and looked right past me to Brett. Hurt and anger were etched all over his features.

"That's the watered-down version," Brett stated. "If you really want to know- "

"That's enough. We're not trying to start a war." Jake put an end to their bickering.

Brett and Robert stared at each other, both daring the other to make a move.

"Speak for yourself," Brett said under her breath. She moved past me and sat in the chair furthest from Robert.

That's when he let his gaze fall on me. I still hadn't moved since laying eyes on him, and I wasn't sure I could. My mouth felt dry and my nerves danced under my skin. He had to know coming back here with Lila was going to be a hard sell, but he still looked crestfallen at Brett's words.

Robert's eyes searched mine. I'd missed him so much, but seeing him with Lila this morning made me sick. Clearing my throat, I crossed my arms and looked away from him. This was neither the time nor place to get lost in what I was feeling.

"You wanted to talk to everyone, so talk," I said, keeping my eyes averted.

He let out a heavy sigh and began, "I'm sure Violet informed all of you, Lila is with me."

Brett practically snorted and crossed her arms. "Yeah, we heard. So were you helping her the entire time?"

"How could you think that?" Robert recoiled at Brett's words.

"It wouldn't be the first time you sided with her," Brett said. "And she did miraculously escape when only you were there to defend Violet."

"You think I let her escape, that I wasn't trying to protect Violet?"

"Yes. I think your history with her clouded your judgment and who knows how deep that goes."

Robert closed his eyes and ran a hand through his hair. "Our past has nothing to do with this."

"Oh really? So did you bring any more of Aiden's henchmen back with you then?"

Robert gave her a pointed look but said nothing.

"I didn't think so," Brett scoffed.

"Alright Brett," Jake said and held his hands up. "We get your point, but he came here to say something, so let's hear him out."

Brett opened her mouth again, but Matthew put his hand on her shoulder and she reined in whatever she was about to say.

Jake nodded to his brother, who gave him an appreciative nod back.

"First and foremost, you need to know that Morgana is back," Robert began.

"We know," I stated.

The shock on his face was apparent. "So you *saw* her?" Robert looked like he just now realized I wasn't the same helpless woman he'd left behind.

"Yeah, Aunt Beth and I saw her come through the portal, but we weren't sure of the timing."

"I can say with certainty that she's back. We saw her come through before we left Avalon."

"And did you even think about trying to stop her?" Brett asked under her breath, just loud enough for all of us to hear.

"Of course I did. But there was nothing we could do. I was supposed to be the last sacrifice, but Lila saved me."

"She saved you, why?" Jake asked, eyeing Robert.

"I got her to see who her father really is and what he's up to."

"Ha!" Brett snorted "So what she cries about her daddy issues and you run to her rescue."

Robert looked like he wanted to blast his sister into next week.

"Aren't you worried she's playing you? That she just wants to gain your trust and get close to Violet?" Annabel chimed in.

Robert shook his head and said, "I'm not saying I trust her. But her father used her, lied to her. She didn't know what he was really up to."

"Even if we could believe that she still tried to kill me," I said, and paused. "Twice."

Robert rubbed his brow like he was starting to get a headache. "Yes, she tried to kill you. But only because she was told *you* were going to destroy the Magical world. She thought she was protecting everyone she loved."

"I'm sorry, but I can't sit here and listen to this," Brett blurted out as she got to her feet. "You want to play the hero in your little fantasy and rescue Lila again, go ahead. But do it without us."

"I hate to say it," Jake said, "but she's right. Lila tried to kill Violet. If you can't see how wrong this is, then we can't have you around Violet anymore." Jake looked away from Robert as he finished.

"Even if she is lying to me. She's still an asset," Robert

pleaded. Apparently, he was done trying to get us to see it from his side. Now he was going to play the rest of his cards. "She knows more about Aiden than we could ever hope to figure out on our own. She could help us stay one step ahead."

"Or send information back to them," Brett corrected him.

"And do you really think she'd be willing to trade in her own father?" Annabel asked.

"Yes," Robert said firmly. "She is on our side now and she'll do whatever she has to in order to prove it."

"Then why isn't she here now?" Brett asked. "Why isn't she making this case for herself?"

"Because you would have blown her into oblivion the second she walked through the door."

"Rightfully so." Brett shrugged.

"Violet, maybe you can- "Robert started.

"She can what?" Brett cut him off. "You want her to confirm that your girlfriend isn't a psychopath?" Brett's fury exploded and not even Matthew tried to reign her in. "Hate to break it to you little brother, but no amount of Magic is going to prove otherwise."

"If you don't want to have a productive conversation then just leave." Robert pointed out of the room. I'd never seen him this livid before. Sure, I frustrated him sometimes, but this was pure anger.

"You act like I ran off with her and joined Aiden and Morgana on their quest for world domination," Robert continued. "But they kidnapped me. I was kept in a ten-by-ten cell with no Magic, where I was beaten, tortured and experimented on." Robert took a step toward Brett. "You sit there on your high horse and act like everything's black and white, but life has grey areas, Brett." He took a breath. "Or did you forget that?" He shot a glance in Matthew's direction.

Brett stared at him, her cheeks flushed with a mixture of

guilt, anger, and embarrassment. No one ever went toe to toe with Brett like this.

"But go ahead, look down on me and pass judgment without all the facts," Robert finished. He stormed out of the room and slammed one of the French doors behind him. Everyone looked around, not sure what to say.

"I'll go talk to him, calm him down," Jake said to no one in particular.

"Let me." I waved him off.

He pat my back and smiled. Jake could keep a level head and calm Robert down, but right now Robert needed to talk to someone he couldn't be mad at and that person was me.

As I walked up to the French doors, I saw Robert standing about halfway into the yard, facing away from me. His arms were crossed and his head was leaned back. The early morning sun illuminated him in a soft glow, taking the edge off the hard set of his shoulders.

I steeled my nerves and walked into the backyard. He didn't turn as I approached, and I wondered if he'd heard me step across the grass.

"So you and Lila, huh?"

His head fell forward. "That was a long time ago."

I nodded. My heart was a bag of mixed emotions. He was never really mine, so getting jealous was pointless and there were more important things to worry about, but I couldn't help but wonder.

"If you're worried that my history with Lila is clouding my judgment, I assure you it's not," Robert continued.

"Well, there's definitely something clouding your judgment," I pointed out.

Robert looked at me and his eyes pierced right through mine. "I'm doing my best to keep everyone safe."

"I don't doubt you believe that, Robert."

"Then what is it?" He cocked his head to the side.

I felt silly and wasn't sure how to continue without sounding like a petty schoolgirl. "Based on what I've heard, you seemed to just turn off your feelings for her, but that's not how love works. You don't always have control over your heart."

He watched me carefully, and I hoped he couldn't see the true meaning behind my words.

"Superficial emotions are often easy to turn off, especially in the face of something much more important," Robert explained. His eyes fell to the necklace around my neck.

"You mean finding me?"

He nodded once and said, "Finding you was the single most important thing I've ever been charged with."

My heart doubled in speed and I hid my face behind the curtain of my hair. I knew he was talking about finding The Waker, but the way his eyes traced my face and landed on my lips told a different story.

"I've already screwed things up enough, and I swore to myself that when I got back here, I wouldn't let anything get in the way of helping you fulfill your destiny." His hand reached out and lightly brushed my hair off my shoulder. "So please don't worry about Lila or anything else clouding my judgment. You are my priority, and I will do everything in my power to make sure nothing ever happens to you again."

"I know you mean that, but coming back with Lila makes it difficult to believe," I admitted.

He sighed. "I know and I'm sorry, Violet."

"You've got your work cut out for you."

He shoved his hands in his pockets. "I know."

"You had to know this wasn't going to be easy." I stepped in front of him so he would have to look at me.

"True. But I didn't think my entire family would think I was a traitor." He pressed his eyebrows together and the shadow of betrayal crossed his eyes.

"You want us to see things from your side, but you haven't

tried to see things from our side." My heart crashed against my ribcage and I could hear the blood pumping through my body at the proximity to his warmth.

"Our side? So you feel the same as Brett, then?"

I looked away, ashamed. "Yes and no."

He let out a heavy breath and I could almost feel his heartbreak within my own chest.

"I never believed you betrayed us, but then you show up here with Lila, and I just- "

"I couldn't let Aiden kill her," he cut me off.

I stayed silent, unsure what to say. Did I hate Lila? Yes. Did I fantasize about her dying a gruesome death? Sure. But the notion that her own father wanted to kill her made me feel sick.

"All Lila ever wanted was to be close to the only family she had left. Aiden used that against her and made her believe she was fighting to protect her family," Robert explained.

"Robert, I hate to say it, but I think Annabel might be right. I think she's just telling you a sob story you'll believe so she can get close to me and finish the job."

"I'm not an idiot. I know that's a possibility. That's the other reason I brought her here, to keep an eye on her."

"Maybe you should have led with that."

The sound of someone clearing their throat made us both turn and look behind us. I was expecting Jake, but the two faces standing just a few feet away were unfamiliar.

"Ethan, how are you?" Robert's voice sounded calm and collected as he made his way over to the visitors.

"Can't complain, brother," Ethan said. He and Robert linked hands and shared a hug.

"It's good to see you," Robert said, pulling back. "And you too, Elodie." He gave the woman beside Ethan a kiss on the cheek.

"I hope we weren't interrupting anything." Elodie tilted her chin in my direction.

"How rude of me." Robert motioned for me to come closer. "This is Violet," he said with an edge of pride in his voice. "Violet, this is Ethan and Elodie. They're a brother and sister team of Promised Ones."

"It's very nice to meet you." Elodie shook my hand, and I noticed she had a tattoo running around her wrist and up her forearm.

"You too."

"It's a pleasure, Miss Evans," Ethan's handshake was firm and nearly crushed the bones in my fingers.

"Not that it isn't great to see you, but what are you guys doing here?" Robert inquired.

"We're looking into the disappearance of a P.O.," Ethan replied in a somber tone.

"We thought we'd check in with Matthew, see if he's heard anything," Elodie added.

"P.O.?" I asked.

"Promised One," Robert said off-handedly, keeping his attention on the two guests.

"It's got to be Morgana," I said under my breath.

"She's back? Already?" Elodie asked as her eyes shot to me.

All I could do was nod. The set of her shoulders and the fierce look in her eyes were intimidating.

As if on cue, the sound of glass breaking and a woman's scream came from somewhere within the house. Robert and I looked at each other for a fraction of a second, and then the four of us bolted across the yard.

CHAPTER FOUR

"*S*tay behind me," Robert ordered, putting his arm out to corral us as he peered around the open door.

I pushed past him and strode into the house, shield raised just as an explosion erupted from the living room. The blast tossed me like a rag-doll, and I hit the adjacent wall and crumpled to the floor. Splinters from the wood panels, along with plaster and dust, rained down on my shield as I got to my feet. A high-pitched ringing assaulted my ears as I slowly and cautiously moved toward the living room.

"Jake, secure the front end!" Brett yelled over the din.

A blurry figure ran through the smoke and I threw a stunning orb at the middle of his back. The overweight assailant toppled to the ground with such force that the painting hanging on the wall above him fell to the floor.

"Violet, you need to take cover," Robert yelled over his shoulder as he moved toward the living room. A bolt of electricity shot across the entryway, narrowly missing Ethan's and Elodie's head.

Summoning another stunning orb in the palm of my hand, I

rushed into the room. I hit another of the attackers before taking cover behind the overturned sofa.

Peering around the edge of the couch, I saw half a dozen faces I didn't recognize and one I did.

Ian.

He dodged every attack with little effort as he made his way to Lila, who lay in a heap of broken wood and glass. Blood dripped down her forehead and as Ian reached for her, an anger I didn't know existed erupted from my heart.

I ran toward the man who had beaten and kidnapped me, all of my attention focused on the slump of his shoulders as he pulled Lila from the rubble. A flash of electricity stopped me in my tracks as Lila lifted her shield and sent Ian flying across the room.

"I'm not going anywhere with you, Ian," she vowed as she stood and stalked toward him, the fury of a woman scorned etched across her face.

"Shouldn't you be taking cover?" Ethan's voice broke through the noise of the battle.

"I'll be fine, get Matthew out of here," I yelled, and turned toward Brett, who had summoned an electric storm. Black clouds rolled across the ceiling and the growl of thunder shook my bones as Ethan ducked behind a chair, narrowly avoiding a spell.

"Violet, watch out," Robert yelled over the roar of Magic and destruction.

Looking over my shoulder, I spotted another dark-haired attacker running right at me, a cinder orb raised and ready to strike. I smiled and raised my right hand in front of me, reciting the Magic siphoning spell under my breath.

"*Spolia auferte ab anima,*" I chanted, stepping toward him. A white-hot light burst from my fingertips. The attacker froze mid-step, cinder orb held over his head with a look of pure horror on his face.

The room stilled as I continued the spell, *"Spolia deminuerit de ossibus et sanguine."* The light jumped from my hand and disappeared into my attacker's chest. Saying the last line of the spell, *"Magicae quod vivit in cor tuum,"* Magic flared inside of me and the siphoning took hold.

Blood dripped from his eyes, nose, and mouth. His green eyes stared directly into mine as the cinder orb in his hand disappeared. Drained of his Magic, he crumpled to the floor at my feet.

As I raised my gaze from the body at my feet, cold blue eyes caught mine and Ian stalked toward me. The last time we'd met, my Magic was barely developed, and I'd been helpless against him. Not this time.

Raising my shield, I blocked the vibrant orange stunning orb he lobbed at me.

"Look who finally learned how to defend herself," Ian mocked from the other side of my golden safeguard.

A cinder orb flew toward him, but he raised his shield just in time and blocked the blow. Chancing a glance in the direction it had come from, I saw Lila, her teeth bared as she charged Ian.

With a flick of his wrist, Ian threw Lila's body into the air and she hit the wall with a loud, sickening thud.

"I've picked up a few tricks myself," Ian laughed. He smiled and his unnaturally white teeth made me shiver.

"Leave her alone." Robert jumped in front of me and pushed me behind him.

"Robert, I-"

He cut me off. "Ian's mine." The tone of his voice gave me pause and before I could say anything else, a piercing scream echoed through the room. I turned from side to side, searching for the source, when I saw two men dragging Annabel by a pair of green electric chains.

The vision of her being tortured and bloody flashed before my eyes as horror gripped me and I froze in place.

"Anna," Jake screamed as a red orb I'd never seen before materialized in his hand. He used it to incapacitate the woman he was fighting and then bolted toward Annabel. Another bolt of lightning flashed, forcing me to look toward Ethan and Elodie, who fought back to back. Using their weapons to deflect spells, they took their enemies out the old fashioned way, with brute strength. Robert raised his shield and blocked the freezing spell Ian directed at us.

Another scream tore from Annabel as she tried to orb. The chains wrapped around her wrist flashed a brilliant green, while her image flickered for a moment and then became solid once again.

"While I'd love to stay and finish this," Ian said in a casual, teasing tone. "That's my cue." A wall of fire blazed to life in front of us, blocking Ian and his few remaining men from the rest of our group.

Jake skidded to a halt and screamed, "Anna, no."

I could still see them through the flames. Annabel struggled for freedom, kicking and screaming, while Ian flicked his wrist, making a dark purple disk the size of a door appear next to him. Black and grey mist weaved in and out of the deep purple curtain, ebbing and flowing in an unseen current.

"You're not getting away that easy," Brett yelled over the roar of the fire. Summoning Devil's Flame, Brett set her sights on not one but two of the attackers in the room.

She threw her right arm toward the small, slender one, and the flames licked across the space between them, jumping over obstacles to find its target. To her left, the tall linebacker of a man holding Annabel's chains tried to block the spell, but he was too slow. The Devil's Flame stabbed him through the back, lighting him on fire from the inside out.

Annabel kicked at her other guard and was able to wiggle free for a fraction of a second before Ian grabbed her chains and yanked her back to the floor at his feet.

"Not so fast," Ian said. He clicked his tongue and dragged Annabel through the purple curtain, disappearing with the other men.

Jake ran after them, but whatever Ian had conjured dissipated only moments after he vanished through the plum-colored haze.

Fury propelled me across the room to Lila, who was still lying in a pile of rubble.

"You did this!" I screamed at her as she struggled to lift herself, blood dripping from her head onto the floor.

"Wait, just let me explain," Lila said, raising her shield in front of her.

Brett rushed across the room and stood next to me. "Your sob story isn't going to work on us. Annabel's gone because of you," she fumed. I could feel the wrath rolling off her.

Lila stood slowly, her shield still raised. "I was trying to warn you," she said through gritted teeth. She shifted her eyes around the room, looking for an ally. Dark red blood streaked her blonde hair, accentuating the growl in her voice.

"You really expect us to believe that? You led them here," Brett seethed.

"We have to go after them," Jake bellowed as he helped Matthew dig himself out of his hiding spot.

"We need to deal with Lila first." My words shook out of my mouth as fury rolled through me.

"Do you think maybe you could hear her out before you execute her?" Robert suggested. He took a step closer to Lila, glass cracking under his boot.

"She tried to kill me and you give her a pass. She leads an attack on your family, resulting in Annabel's capture, and still you want to hear her out? Brett's right, you're not on our side anymore." My heart hardened with each word I spoke.

The only indication my indictment affected him was the

slow, painful blink of his eyes and the tightening of his shoulders.

"I didn't lead the attack," Lila barked. "And I don't know if you were watching, but they attacked me as well." She clenched her jaw.

"I won't let you kill her out of revenge," Robert vowed. His voice was cold and hard as he placed his hand on Lila's shoulder and began to heal the gash on her forehead. "You may hate me and you may want to kill her, but you are not a murderer, Violet. I might not've been able to keep you safe, but I will save you from losing yourself."

"I'll give you one chance to move out of my way," Brett cautioned, her voice deep as thunder exploded above us.

"That's enough," Jake said and stood beside his brother.

Brett actually recoiled, and I felt the cold, hard stab of betrayal. "Jake, how could you? It's her fault Annabel's gone."

"She's our only chance of getting Anna back. She's been on the inside and whether she likes it or not, she will help us." Tears welled up in Jake's eyes as he swallowed the lump in his throat.

"So you're siding with her too?" Brett studied her brothers.

"This isn't about you, Brett, or your past with Lila." Jake squared his shoulders. "This is about getting Anna back and Lila can help us."

Brett's eyes settled on Lila, and then she stormed out of the room without another word.

"Anyone else feel like arguing or can we move past this?" Jake asked.

"I should go after Brett," Elodie whispered behind me.

"I'll stay here," Ethan replied. "I'll fill you in later. We've clearly been out of the loop." Ethan's hushed voice held an edge of scandal.

The air surged with an electric charge, but no one moved.

"Good," Robert concluded. He turned away and pulled Lila to the side.

"Not so fast," Jake insisted, grabbing Lila by the arm and pulling her away from Robert. "You're going to tell us how to get Annabel back." He stared at Lila with a fever in his eyes that made me take a step back.

Lila stuttered and said, "I don't know wh-"

"Don't lie to me!" Jake shouted. "You know what they do with prisoners." His eyes flicked to Robert. "You know where they take them, what they do with them. So talk, or so help me, I'll let Brett and Violet tear you to shreds."

Lila yanked her arm free and rubbed her bicep, where Jake's fingers had dug in.

The tension felt thick in the room as my eyes fell on the remaining Maxwells. A large part of me wanted to follow after Brett and leave Robert and Lila to cry wolf to someone else. But if my training had taught me anything, the more information you had, the better equipped you'd be.

"Looks like the floor is yours," I said, and motioned for Lila and Robert to take the lead.

Robert guided Lila away from Jake and made his way to the mantel. Lila limped on her first two steps, but as she walked across the living room, she righted herself and the cuts and bruises on her body disappeared. Catching Robert's hand on her bare arm, I had to fight the murderous anger building inside of me as he healed her.

"Avalon," Lila said, and let out a heavy sigh. "It's where we-they take prisoners," she corrected herself. "It's impenetrable, though. There are wards set up to detect Magic, guards crawling all over the island and a state-of-the-art security system. It'll be impossible to get in unnoticed."

"Nothing's impossible," Jake seethed.

"This is. We can't save her," Lila pleaded. "And even if we could make it to Avalon, there's no way of getting near the estate without Morgana knowing." She turned to Robert for support.

"She's right," he said. "Lila risked everything to get us off that island before it was too late. With Morgana in the picture, it's just too risky."

"I won't just give up on Anna. You need to figure out a way to get us past Morgana," Jake demanded.

"Jake, I want to help but-" Lila started.

"You want to help, then prove it and help us save Annabel before it's too late."

"If they wanted her dead, they wouldn't have taken her," Lila tried to reason with Jake.

"Is that supposed to make me feel better?"

Lila looked nervously around the room, spinning the ring on her finger. "Yes. It means she's still alive and at the very least, it's a start."

"It's not good enough, not by a long shot," I said.

"You can either help us or get out." Jake pointed toward the door.

Lila opened her mouth to protest, but then thought better of it and nodded. "Alright, I'll help you, but we do this my way."

"Fine," Jake said through gritted teeth.

"We're going to need Brett on board if we have any chance. We can't afford to let anyone sit out," Lila advised.

"Don't you worry about Brett. She'll be there when we need her." Jake gave Lila a sideways glance.

"Alright, then let's get started."

CHAPTER FIVE

ila and Robert briefed Jake on Avalon and the Patridge estate while the rest of us cleaned up the mess Ian and his men had left behind. Thankfully, with Magic and more than enough hands, we got everything back into its rightful place in a short amount of time. As I dusted off the last throw pillow and tossed it on the couch, exhaustion kicked in. Every muscle in my body ached, and I desperately needed to rest. Between a sleepless night and the fight with Ian, I had nothing left to give.

I sought out one of the guest rooms upstairs. While I'd rather have slept in my own bed, the attack and Annabel's capture had us all on edge and I didn't want to drag anyone away from the rest of the family. Turning on all the lights in the guest suite, I made my way to the attached bathroom in search of some painkillers and a glass of water. More than a few bruises had blossomed over the last couple hours and my body was stiffening up. I knew Robert would heal me if I asked, but I didn't feel right using him like that when we weren't on the best of terms.

The medicine cabinet revealed a bottle of Tums, B-complex vitamins and Advil.

Some hangover cure, I thought.

I shook a few Advil onto my palm when three dull taps knocked at the door.

"Who is it?" I called from across the room, popping the small round pills into my mouth and swallowing a gulp of water.

"It's me."

I froze halfway to the door. I didn't want to be alone with Robert, for more than one reason.

"Violet, please open up. I just want to talk to you without everyone else lurking about," he pleaded.

Against my better judgment, I open the door and my heart gave a gentle squeeze at the sight of him. Even with my feelings boxed up, he still took my breath away. He always did. But the man standing in front of me was not the Robert of my memories.

"So, what can I do for you?" I asked, trying to keep the conversation light.

Robert let out a heavy sigh. "I hate this, all of it," he said, running his hands through his hair and sitting on the edge of the bed.

I perched myself on the dresser across the room and kept a watchful eye on him. I wasn't sure if I was supposed to say something or if he was just letting off steam.

"I hate the way my family looks at me, Brett... if it was up to her she would have sent me to the gallows the moment I arrived in Pismo," Robert complained.

I scoffed, and he looked up at me. It was true. If Brett was in charge, Robert would have had a very different homecoming.

"But what I hate more than all the rest." He looked up at me through his lashes, "is the way you look at me now."

"Robert," I started, but he raised his hand to stop me.

"You can't hide from me, Violet. I know you better than the

rest do, and I know I've hurt you. Your mistrust goes deeper than this issue with Lila, I can see it in your eyes. I can't stand that I've made you feel like I'm the enemy. It's driving me mad."

"Is this what you came up here to talk about?" I could feel my heart breaking all over again and didn't want to hear his excuses. He'd made his choice when he brought Lila back here with him.

Looking up at me, his eyes burned into mine. I tried to break his gaze, but once again I couldn't find the strength.

He must have lost his courage because Robert looked away and said, "No. I need to talk to you about Avalon."

The blood in my veins froze, and I stiffened in response. "What about it?"

"Lila's right. You can't let Jake go after Annabel. He'll only get himself killed."

"So what, we just leave her with them?"

"Of course not, but we have to be smart about this. Avalon is a fortress, one Aiden built in honor of Morgana. We won't find any help on the inside like I did."

I wanted to hate him for siding with Lila, but the logical side of my brain knew he was right. Barging in guns blazing would only get us killed. "You won't be able to convince Jake to hold back."

"I know. That's where you come in." He gave me his best puppy-dog eyes.

"What do you think I can do to sway Jake?"

"I need you to look ahead," he said sheepishly. "To use your gift and stay Jake's hand or we'll lose him too."

"I'm not the Maxwells' personal oracle." I stood and took a couple steps toward the balcony doors.

"No, you're not. But you are a Soothsayer and you're meant to guide other Magical souls around you."

I crossed my arms, frustrated that he was willing to use my ability against me.

"Please, Violet. Look ahead and see that getting Annabel back will only result in more death," Robert pleaded.

"How can you just give up on her?" I asked, disgust lacing my voice.

He took a deep breath as if to steady himself. "Sometimes you can't save everyone. This is war, Violet, and we will lose people."

"The Robert I knew would never give up on those he cared about."

"I'm not giving up on Annabel, I'm just asking for your guidance. If you can see a way to save her that doesn't result in more loss, then I'll stand beside you, but I won't watch my family be ripped apart and killed."

"Lila really has changed you, hasn't she?" I turned to glare at him.

His shoulders slumped and his brow furrowed with almost permanent worry. Looking at him, I realized he was afraid. I almost laughed at the thought. Robert was the one who made me believe in my own strength, to believe in the people around me. And now, he was the one full of worry and doubt.

"This has nothing to do with Lila," Robert said, letting out an exasperated sigh.

"It has everything to do with her," I countered, and shot across the room, stopping in front of him. "The Robert I know wouldn't walk away from a fight. He wouldn't give up on his family." I was so angry at him for giving up, for giving into his fear. "You say she hasn't changed you, but you're not the same man who fought to save my life."

"She hasn't changed me." He stood up. "You have," Robert fired back and closed the gap between us. "Losing you... I won't risk it. I can't, not again." Heat rolled off of his body and I had to fight the shiver crawling up my spine.

My mouth fell open, but no words formed on my lips. I didn't know what to say, what to think or even feel.

"You may not like her, but you need to trust her on this," Robert continued. "Avalon is not a place you should ever wish to find yourself."

A short, sarcastic laugh escaped my nostrils. "You want me to trust her?" It took everything in me to keep my voice even. "Trust the woman who tied me up, beat me and tried to kill me?" I dared him to defend her again with a level, penetrating gaze.

"You have to understand. Things have changed." He held my eyes, his resolve returning.

"You're right, they have changed. You're in bed with the enemy now." I mustered as much control as I could so my voice wouldn't shake.

"Is that what you think? After everything?" He reached for me and I pulled away as his fingers grazed my arm. "Allow me to correct your perception. First and foremost, I'm not in bed with anyone. And second, Lila is no longer our enemy." His jaw flexed as his teeth ground together. Robert had never lost his cool with me, but I had a feeling I was tap dancing all over his nerves.

"She may not be our enemy anymore, but she is not our friend," I countered. Tension rolled off both of us, creating a charge in the room that threatened to ignite at any moment. "I've seen things, and I may not have all the information, but I have more information than you ever will."

The corners of his eyes narrowed. "What've you seen?"

"That's none of your concern." My voice came out hard and cold as I turned away from him.

"Violet, it could be important. You should tell me." He placed his hand on my arm.

Fire spread through me as his fingers brushed my skin and my Magic flared to life. When I pulled away from him, he looked as stunned as I felt.

"I'm sorry," he said. "I shouldn't have…"

"No, you shouldn't…" I hesitated. "I think you should go."

"No," he said with conviction. "I need you to listen to me, whether you want to or not."

"So help me, Robert, I will throw you out of here."

"This isn't about us, or you and Lila, or even me and Lila. This is about protecting the Magical world. You have a duty to use your gift to keep people safe."

"Don't you dare talk to me about duty. I never asked for any of this and I'm still here. I'm still fighting the good fight."

"Then look ahead and see for yourself. If we go to Avalon, we will lose more than we can ever hope to gain." He closed the gap between us and I could feel his breath on my face.

"Why is it so important that we trust her?" I asked. His insistence made me curious. Not killing her, I could understand, but trusting her? Why did it matter to him so much?

He sighed, and said, "Because I made a promise to her."

I crossed my arms. "And what was that?"

"That I would do everything I could to get everyone to understand that she is not our enemy. Not anymore."

"And why would you promise her something like that?"

"I owe her that much, at the very least."

"Owe her?" I balked. "Because she saved your life?"

"That too. But it's my fault she went back to Aiden in the first place."

"Robert, you can't take responsibility for her actions. She's a grown woman with the ability to think for herself."

Robert shook his head. "You don't understand."

"No. You don't understand. She made her choice. She's killed people. She tried to kill me of her own free will. Aiden may be a bad influence on her, but she chose to do those things."

Robert looked up at me, pain etched across his features. He really did blame himself for everything she had done.

"I just don't know how to make things right with her, with you, my family…" He trailed off.

"The first step would be letting go of this guilt you're carrying," I told him.

He gave me a secretive smile.

"What?" I asked, self-conscious.

"This life, your gift. It suits you."

I shrugged, unsure of where he was going with this thread of conversation.

"You've become comfortable, confident with who you are, who you're destined to be."

"If you can't beat them, join 'em, right?"

"I'm glad you've taken to this life. I know it was hard for you at first. I understand that now more than ever."

"Why's that?"

"My Magic. They took it from me." A flash of pain crossed his eyes. "For the first time in my life, I knew what it felt like to have my world and everything I've known ripped away."

"I'm sorry." I shifted uncomfortably. It was rare for Robert to let his defenses down, and I wasn't one hundred percent sure how to react.

"Don't be. It helped me understand what you were going through and what Lila is going through now," Robert shared. "She's been ripped from her reality, her only family. Everything she believed turned out to be a lie."

He was playing on my sympathy and I hated that it was working.

"I just want to help her start over and find a new place in this world. You can understand that, can't you?" Robert asked.

"Look, I get it. And I hope she can find a new way of life. But it's not with us. It won't ever work," I said.

"Never say never. There were some who believed you'd never grow into your Magic and look at you now." Robert smiled, but it didn't reach his eyes. "I get you don't want to trust her, or me for that matter. But trust your gift."

I sighed and closed my eyes. If Robert was right, and Avalon was such a danger, then I'd need proof other than Lila's word and his reassurance.

Focusing on an image of Annabel, I tapped into my Magic. Goosebumps covered every inch of my body as I tried to reach out and see something, anything that might confirm Robert's convictions. Nothing bubbled to the surface at first, not a single image, and dread filled my empty stomach. Trying again, I let my Magic course through me and cleared my mind like my aunt taught me.

Fuzzy images moved across my vision. An enclosed, concrete space formed around me and the smell of smoke sat heavy in the air. Ian's face came into view and I took a step back. Taken off-guard.

A sick smile spread across his lips as Annabel stepped forward to meet him. Her steps were deliberate and her eyes held nothing but hatred as she faced the man. Her hands were stained crimson and on the ground behind her, Brett lay on the cement in a pool of blood. Grey swirled around me in a rush and the three of them disappeared, giving way to four figures.

Jake stood across from a man and a woman, both of whom had cinder orbs burning in their hands. Another assailant came up behind him, electricity sparkling on his fingertips. As they raised their arms in unison, everything went into slow motion. I could hear my blood pumping through my veins, feel the wind moving each individual hair on my skin. A figured blurred past me and displaced Jake safely away from the orbs. Lila came into focus, standing next to Jake and helping him to his feet.

My vision blurred and the Maxwell house reappeared around me. Sorrow filled my heart at the image of Brett bleeding out. I couldn't lose another person in my life, I wouldn't, not when I could do something about it.

Opening my eyes, I found Robert watching me.

"Do you believe me now?" he asked with hope in his voice.

Exhaling, I met his eyes. "You're right, we can't let Jake go after Annabel. Not until we know more."

The muscles in Robert's jaw flexed as he recognized the pain in my eyes. "What is it?"

"Brett… she…" I shook my head, unable to finish the sentence.

"It's alright. Nothing's happened that can't be undone. You have the power to change what you saw." His fingertips grazed my shoulder.

"I just don't know how I'm going to convince Jake to wait. Annabel's his life, he won't leave her without a fight."

"I know the feeling well," Robert said, stepping toward me with a warm smile on his lips. "Just tell him the truth of what you saw. He may be grieving, but after he's cooled down a bit, he'll see reason."

"I hope so, but I have this awful feeling that no matter what we do, death hovers in the shadows."

Robert took a step back and sat on the bed. "And what of Lila? Did you see anything that might sway your opinion?"

"No," I lied. She may have saved Jake from being incinerated, but her motives had yet to be seen. If I told Robert what I saw, it would only ignite his argument that Lila had changed. Until I was certain about her, I was going to play my cards very close to my chest.

A soft knock interrupted whatever Robert was about to say, and he stood up to answer the door.

"Oh. I was looking for Violet," Matthew said, sounding annoyed.

Robert opened the door the rest of the way and motioned Matthew inside. "I'll leave the two of you alone," he said. Robert passed over the threshold and disappeared around the corner.

Closing the door, Matthew's eyebrows rose so high I thought they would disappear into his hairline.

"What was that about?"

"It's a long story. I'll fill everyone in later," I sighed.

Matty grimaced. "You shouldn't be alone with him." Matty

looked like he hated saying the words as much as I hated hearing them. Robert was one of us, and not trusting him was a hard pill to swallow.

"I'm assuming you wanted to talk about something?" I dodged any further conversation about Robert.

"Yes, actually," Matty said, taking the hint. "I wanted to tell you, I got a hold of my contact about The Pieces of Three. I set up a meeting for tomorrow, but, he'll only speak to us in person. So we're going to need to travel to him."

I gave Matthew a pointed look. "He can't answer a few simple questions over the phone or through email?" I asked, irritation plain in my voice. With everything going on, we didn't have time to be making house calls.

He shrugged and said, "He's kind of a hermit and wants to make sure he's really speaking with The Waker before he'll tell us anything."

"Perfect." I rubbed the bridge of my nose as a headache began blooming behind my eyes. "Just what we need, a loon with bogus theories."

Matthew's face scrunched up as he hesitantly added, "That's not all."

I leveled my eyes on him. "What?"

"Robert's presence has been requested." Matthew almost flinched at the words.

"Why?" What did Robert have to do with The Pieces of Three? And who was this guy to request that any of us be summoned to him?

"I'm just the messenger." Matty shook his head apologetically.

"Great, well this should be interesting," I grumbled. "Anything else?"

"That's all I have for now," Matthew said and reached out to give my shoulder a squeeze. "Get some rest, you look like hell."

CHAPTER SIX

Stiff as a two-by-four, I rolled onto my side as the sun rose to a new day. I'd purposely left the curtains drawn on the French doors so I could wake with the sunrise before everyone else. Sitting up, I stretched my arms and legs, feeling every bump and bruise from the day before. I was seriously regretting not asking Robert to heal me. Padding over to the bathroom, I grabbed a few painkillers and washed them down with a healthy gulp of water.

I studied my face in the mirror. I knew I needed to talk to Jake today, but I had no idea what I would say to keep him from going after Annabel. Robert seemed to think the truth would be enough, but in my heart, I knew nothing would stop him. So instead of using my visions as a warning, we would have to use my visions to skirt death. Robert wasn't going to like this one bit, but after tossing and turning all night, I knew we didn't have any other choice.

As much as I didn't want to admit it, Lila was our best shot at coming up with a plan that wouldn't end up with us dead. That was of course if she didn't betray us and lead us into a trap, which was incredibly likely in my opinion. So first thing this morning, I needed to pull her aside and get some information out of her.

With my resolve firmly in place, I threw on some workout clothes and grabbed my phone off of the nightstand. I had a text from Becky asking if I was available tomorrow night for dinner. More than anything I wanted to meet up with her, but life had gotten more complicated in the last twenty-four hours and it was only going to get worse with Morgana back.

As I made my way downstairs, wracked with guilt, I started to reply to Becky's text when I nearly jumped out of my socks from a very chipper, "Hey."

Looking up, I saw Robert seated on the blue mats Jake and I used for training.

"Hey." I paused mid-step and mid-text. "You're up early."

He shrugged. "Couldn't sleep."

"Where's Lila?" I scanned the backyard.

"With Jake and Matty. They've been up all night grilling her about Avalon."

"You sure that's a good idea, leaving her alone with them?"

Robert cocked his head to the side. "If I didn't know any better, I'd say you're concerned for Lila's well-being."

"Don't push your luck."

"Wouldn't dream of it." He gave me one of his heartbreaking smiles and clapped his gloved fists together.

"You feel like sparring? I was just about to wrap it up, but if you want to train a bit, I'd be more than happy to oblige."

Hesitating a moment, I leveled my gaze on Robert and returned his grin. "I guess kicking your ass isn't the worst way to start my day." I stepped onto the mats.

Robert shot forward.

"Let's see what you got," he said, barreling into me.

"Hey, wait a minute." I fumbled with my phone, and it hit the mat with an audible *smack*. "Jake normally lets me stretch first!" I shrieked, dodging Robert's advances.

"You think Aiden or Morgana will let you stretch first?" He threw a punch, and I felt the air rustle the tip of my nose as his knuckles barely missed my face.

Squaring my shoulders like Jake taught me, I raised my arms defensively and clenched my fists. Robert took a step toward me, a playful smile on his face. Turning on the spot, I kicked my leg out as hard as I could. My foot connected with his chest and he stumbled backward. Surprise lit up his face, and I had to admit, it felt good to get some of my aggression out on him.

"Jake's taught you well, I see." He gathered himself and we moved back into a dance.

Having put him on the defensive, I threw a punch, but he blocked it effortlessly. "Good thing too, since you brought a psychopath home with you." I swung again, but his forearm blocked my fist.

"Lila's not a psychopath." He took a swing at me and I ducked out of the way. Shifting onto the other side of the mat, I swept my leg out in an attempt to knock Robert to the ground, but he jumped clear.

Quickly getting back to my feet, I hopped from one foot to the other. Robert took another swing at me and I blocked him with the precision Jake had drilled into me. Robert pushed forward, charging toward me and throwing his fists at me as if he was a professional boxer. Not once did he break his form as he pushed me across the mats.

"Robert!" I yelled between breaths. He said nothing and kept pursuing me.

Letting my Magic boil to the surface, I summoned my shield and blocked his next punch. "What the hell?" I stared at him through the thin golden barrier.

A smile spread across his face and he looked me up and down. "Just wanted to see what you'd do if I didn't let up."

I shook my head and let my shield drop. "I'm not the damsel in distress you left behind." I charged at him, swinging, spinning and kicking until I pushed him back across the mats. He blocked me each time, but if I could take down Jake, who was bigger than Robert, I should have no problem knocking Robert on his ass. Throwing myself into another spin kick, I connected with his chest. Instead of stumbling backward, though, he grabbed my foot and threw me off balance. I hit the mat with a loud *thud,* my teeth rattling against each other as the air fled my lungs. Robert kneeled next to me, concern etched into his furrowed brow.

Anger that he'd gotten the better of me flared in my chest. Before he could move, I grabbed the back of his neck and flipped him over my shoulder, using my weight as leverage just like Jake taught me.

He hit the foam mat next to me and I pinned him to the ground. The look of surprise on Robert's face was priceless.

"You should never underestimate your opponent. Rule number one," I gloated over his prone body. The corner of his mouth turned up as he looked up at me. My heart doubled in speed, which was impressive since it was already elevated and I rolled off of him.

Robert chuckled, and I reached down to help him up. "Physically, I'd say you're up to par." His eyes scanned my body, making a full assessment.

I raised my eyebrows and cocked my head. "Is that right?"

He rolled his eyes and grabbed his water bottle. "But how much have you learned Magically?"

"I've been working with everyone on different things. Jake is defense," I noted. "My aunt is helping me with my visions, and Annabel and I mostly work on potions. William's journal has been very helpful with that. He has a ton of Magical recipes in there."

"I'm glad you're finding his words useful. He has a lot to offer." Robert took another sip of his water.

"It's been fun getting to know him. He's quite the character."

I smiled as I recalled a vision of William mixing herbs and humming along until he absently threw the wrong seed into the mixture. In his journal, he wrote about everything he saw during the thirty minutes of hallucinations, and Annabel and I spent the better part of that afternoon in a laughing fit.

Robert smiled, his eyes lighting up as I talked fondly of his relative. I knew how much the journal meant to him, and it was a nice change of pace to share a moment with him that wasn't tainted by Lila.

"I'm going to assume you've been working on offensive spells with Brett?" He threw the water bottle down and it rolled to a stop. "Let's see what she's taught you so far." He motioned with his hand for me to attack him.

"Are you sure?"

"I'm giving you a free pass to attack me. Most of the people in this house wouldn't hesitate."

"I'm not most people?" I placed my hands on my hips and stared him down.

"Oh, believe me, I know." He looked at me from head to toe and my heart rate sped up.

When it was just me and Robert, it was easy to forget about Lila and the rest of our troubles. It was like breathing in fresh air when I was around him, but I needed to remind myself he had changed just as much as I had over the last few weeks.

Summoning a stunning orb, I threw it directly at Robert's chest. His eyes held mine, and he summoned his shield without flinching a muscle. The orb dissipated as it hit the warm, red surface of his shield.

My heart raced as my Magic coursed through me with renewed strength. I felt stronger, more alive than I'd ever felt before. I wasn't sure if it was my training or if being this close to Robert made my Magic flare in recognition. Trying to take a deep breath, I struggled against the lump in my throat.

Robert's shield fell away, and he took a step toward me as

the hunger of a thousand fires flared to life in the pit of my stomach.

He took another hesitant step closer, studying me. Needing a diversion from the war raging inside me, I said the first spell that came to mind, *"Avertere animum."*

Small white lights went off like flashes around both of us. Robert's eyes broke away from mine and I summoned another stunning orb. Disoriented for a fraction of a second, he reacted a moment too late when the orb smacked into his arm and he fell to the mat.

"Don't lose focus. Rule number two." I stood over him again, shaking my head.

"Esrever," I said the reversal spell and his body unfroze.

He got to his feet and chuckled. "It's truly wonderful to see how far you've come in such a short time." He took a step toward me, his hand outstretched like he wanted to shake my hand and call a truce. I wasn't buying it. This was a game now, a game of who could trick the other with distractions and get them face down on the mat.

"You ready to go another round?" I eyed him and raising my fists in front of my face.

We spent the next hour and a half sparring and throwing spells at each other. I had to admit, it was the most fun I'd had in a while. More than a few times he landed me hard on the mats, but this was the type of training I needed. Robert didn't hold back, he was wild and aggressive. He pushed me much harder than Jake ever did because he knew what I could handle. And he was right about Morgana and Aiden, they'd be ruthless and we all needed to be prepared for whatever they had in store.

With my shirt soaked through with sweat and my body starting to ache, we called it quits.

"Do you want me to heal anything?" Robert asked as we sat down on the blue padded training mats.

"No, I'm fine. A few sore muscles never hurt anyone." I flinched as a sharp pain flashed down my shin.

Robert raised his hands defensively. "Just offering. You know where to find me if you change your mind."

"Thanks."

"I should probably make sure Lila hasn't been strung from the rafters."

I laughed harder than I should have. It was entirely possible that one of the Maxwell's would off her behind Robert's back.

Patting me on the shoulder, Robert picked up his discarded sweatshirt and water bottle, then made his way to the house.

I picked up my phone and padded along behind him.

"Robert," I called after him.

"Yeah?" He turned to look at me, and I couldn't fight the smile forming on my lips.

"Thanks. For training with me, I mean," I said, catching up with him.

"Anytime." The corners of his mouth turned up and a genuine smile touched his lips.

"Wow, everyone's up early today," I said as Robert and I stepped into the kitchen.

"Some of us haven't gone to sleep yet," Lila grumbled under her breath. She sat at a stool nursing a cup of coffee. From her disheveled look, I could easily believe she'd been up all night.

"I think we might have a solid plan for going after Annabel," Jake shared.

Lila cringed at the word solid, and Robert stepped to her side of the island.

"Jake, we need to talk about that," I said before he could continue. "From what I saw, we're going to need a better plan."

"You saw Annabel? Is she alright?" His bloodshot eyes searched mine.

"Yes, but we weren't. If we go now, some of us won't come back."

Jake let out a shaky breath. "Don't tell me I should give up on her."

"Not at all. I just think we need to wait until we can come up with a plan that doesn't end with half of us dead."

"Violet," Jake pleaded. "You can't ask me to let her go." He stepped across the kitchen and placed both of his hands on my shoulders.

"I would never ask you to stop fighting for her." I placed my hand over his heart. "But I need you to trust me. If we go after Annabel, we'll lose more than we gain."

Jake closed his eyes and flexed his jaw as his hands tightened on my shoulders.

"Then find a way," he muttered with as much control as he could manage before storming out of the room.

I felt my heart break as he let go of me, hating that I was keeping him from going after Annabel.

"It's for the best," Robert said after his brother walked out of earshot.

"If we're going to have any chance at this, I need to see Avalon from your perspective, Lila." I took a step toward her.

Startled at the sound of her name, Lila looked between Robert and me.

"Sure. I mean, I've gone into as much detail as I can think of with Matthew and Jake-" Lila shared.

"I don't need you to tell me," I interrupted, crossing the room to sit on a stool across from her and Robert. "I need you to show me." I placed my hand on the island's cold granite surface, palm up.

Lila's fingers touched my palm, and it was like being punched in the stomach. Gasping for air as my vision blurred, I saw Robert's face for a moment and then he disappeared.

A green field covered in fog took his place, the sound of a battle echoing all around me. And then there was Lila, laying in the grass, covered in blood. She was in my arms and as I looked down at the two of us, Lila raised her bloody hand and put it on my cheek.

The vision vanished just as quickly as it had come, and I found myself back in the Maxwell kitchen.

I stared at Lila, horrified as she looked back at me with a confused expression contorting her features.

"What did you see?" Robert asked. "I've never seen a vision take you like that before."

"I'm fine." I wrapped one arm protectively around myself. "Just startled."

"What was it?" Lila asked, and I saw the real question in her eyes. She wasn't sure if she trusted herself. She may have escaped with Robert and betrayed her family, but when it came down to it, she wasn't sure what her future held.

"I couldn't get a grip on any of the images," I lied.

Robert studied me but didn't say anything. If he knew I was lying, he would find a more appropriate time to ask me what I saw.

"Let's try again, shall we?" I took another deep breath and steadied my nerves.

This time I raised my walls in place and slowly let Lila in instead of all at once.

"I need you to focus on Avalon, so I can get a feel for the place," I said.

Lila nodded. She closed her eyes and slowly, like a door opening, I walked through. We spent the better part of an hour going in and out of the door as she showed me the place she had called home for so many years. Robert fetched me a pen and paper and in between each vision I built the Avalon, I saw in my head with ink on the page.

As much as I wanted to keep going and keep exploring, I was too exhausted. Between a restless night of sleep, training with Robert this morning and our whole world being ripped apart, I didn't have much energy left.

"That's a good start for now," I exhaled.

"I've never seen someone keep up a steady stream of visions like that before." Lila's voice was coy, like she was embarrassed to admit she was impressed.

"Violet's not just any Soothsayer," Robert noted.

"But you already knew that." I leveled my gaze on Lila.

Robert cleared his throat, attempting to break the tension. "Did Matty tell you we're leaving around three?"

"Umm, no. He didn't mention that. In that case, I need to head home. Do you know where Brett is?"

Robert shook his head. "I haven't seen her yet this morning."

"Alright, thanks." I went to search for Brett.

It didn't take long to locate her. She'd been attacking her hair with a brush in the bathroom and apparently hadn't gotten much sleep either. After a less than cordial "good morning," we were on our way to my place within the hour.

I needed to get some work done and was grateful to be heading home and away from the chaos of the Estate. With all the Magical drama in my life lately, my photography had been put on the back burner, which always left me feeling anxious. Just the thought of getting to work on my portfolio and enjoy something unrelated to Magic was soothing my nerves.

I made my way to the living room and opened a few windows to let some fresh air in. Brett plopped down on the couch and threw her legs up as if she had lived here her whole life. I always enjoyed when she was the one watching over me. We might not see eye to eye on everything, but we had grown close over the last few weeks and if I trusted anyone with my life, it was her. She was ruthless when it came to protecting the ones she loved, and fortunately for me, she considered me among them.

"So what's the plan?" Brett asked, watching me bustle around the room.

"I really want to make some progress on my Whitman port-folio. I've been slacking."

"Don't be too hard on yourself." She gave me a measured look. "You've had a lot on your plate and you've handled it amazingly well."

"Yeah, I just hate that *my* life has fallen away ever since I embraced Magic."

"You just have to find a balance. You'll get there, trust me. We all go through it at one time or another."

I gave her a half smile before making my way to the kitchen to grab a bottle of flavored water.

"So how was your training with Robert this morning?" Brett interjected.

The question seemed innocent enough, but the tone of her voice sent a shiver down my spine as I straightened from the refrigerator. Nothing got past her, even if she was nowhere in sight. Somehow she always knew what you'd been up to. I felt bad for any kids she might have.

Sighing, I sat next to her on the couch and propped my feet up on the coffee table.

"It was good actually, less controlled than Jake." I took a sip of my water.

She rolled her eyes at me but before she could say anything I said, "I know you don't trust him but I still believe there's good in him. He's changed, yes, but he still has a good heart. You have to try to see that."

Brett let out an exacerbated breath and let her head fall back against the couch.

"Look, I don't hate Robert," she started. "I know this is hard for him too. But Lila is a problem. She gets under his skin in a way I don't understand. She always has."

"She meant a lot to him, didn't she?" I pang of jealousy I had no right to shot through me.

"She was his first love and we all know how hard it is to kill first love. He may not've had a hard time walking away from the relationship, but she has a hold on him only you can compete with." Brett rolled her head my direction.

My eyes nearly popped out of my head and I choked on the sip of watermelon flavored water I'd just taken. "Me?"

"Violet, please," Brett scoffed. "We've all seen the way you look at each other." Her eyes caught mine and a warm smile formed on her lips.

I looked away, embarrassed that my emotions seemed so out in the open for everyone to see.

"If anyone has the ability to remove Lila's claws from him, it's you," Brett added.

"And how do you suggest I do that?"

Brett raised her eyebrows and shrugged. "I'm sure you could come up with some way of enticing him."

"Great, so not only do I have to wake The Lady and save the Magical world, but you want me to seduce your brother away from Aiden's evil spawn?"

"Don't act like I'm asking you to do something against your will. We both know it's gone through your mind more than once."

I threw my hands in the air and shook my head. "You've got a few screws loose," I said, my cheeks flushing.

"That's what I thought." She slapped my leg playfully.

"So let me get this straight. You're pro Robert now and you want me to wiggle my way between him and Lila?"

"As long as she's in his life, I can't and won't trust him. And believe you me, I will make his life a living hell for bringing that harlot back here."

"Duly noted." I raised my brows and reminded myself not to get on Brett's bad side.

"Shall we get to work?" She turned to face me, sitting up and throwing one leg under her to prop herself up.

"On Robert?" I gaped at her, mildly horrified. Seducing her

brother to our side was one thing, getting pointers from his sister was a whole other.

"No, on your portfolio," she laughed. "I want to help if that's alright."

"Of course." A sigh of relief passed over my lips. "Let me show you what I have so far and you can tell me what you think."

"Great." She wiggled to the edge of the couch.

I was my own boss, of course, but when Brett was around, I always felt like I had to answer to her. She commanded your attention in a way that best suited a military sergeant.

I pulled my portfolio from the bookshelf and handed the contents to Brett and said, "These are the images I want to use."

As she flipped the front page over, I grabbed the Walt Whitman book Robert had helped me pick out.

"These are beautiful." She flipped each photo over.

"Thank you." I ran my fingers nervously along the sticky tabs on the book. "I have too many poems, though. I need to narrow it down."

"Let's take a look." She reached for the book and sat down in the middle of the living room.

We spent the rest of the morning organizing the photos into an order that told a story I was pleased with. Turned out, I ended up telling the story of my life in Pismo. From the relaxed feeling that washed over me the first time I saw the beach, up until the day I learned the Magical world was real.

My stomach started rumbling by mid-afternoon and going through the rest of the poems was getting tedious. Needing a break and knowing that everyone would be there soon, I made my way into the kitchen only to hear a knock at the door.

"I'll grab it," Brett called from the living room.

Satisfied she'd take care of the visitor, I dug through my refrigerator and pulled out a jar of raspberry preserve Harriet had made me. Grabbing the peanut butter from the pantry, I laid two pieces of bread on the counter.

Spreading the preserve and peanut butter on each side of the bread, I mashed it together, licked the knife and took a bite.

Matthew and Brett were exchanging a few hushed words when I returned from the kitchen, and by the smile on Matty's face, it was clearly private. They shared a quick kiss and Brett curled her hair behind her ear before they both made their way toward me.

"Wha-er you ooing here al-reby?" I mumbled through the gooey jelly and creamy peanut buttery goodness.

"I found something I thought you should take a look at," Matthew explained. He motioned for me to follow him to the kitchen table as he plopped his bag down and started pulling out his data.

"I'll clean up the mess in the living room," Brett chimed "Holler if you need me.".

"We may need to get Bethany involved since this involves your timeline."

"Okay, first things first. What did you find out?" I asked.

"It all goes back to the original Prophecy. Do you have the Maxwell Journal?"

"Yeah, one second."

I rushed to the bedroom and grabbed the journal from my nightstand. As I headed back down the hallway, I flipped open to the page with the Prophecy and handed it to Matthew. He scrolled down the page with his fingers.

"Here we go," he said, pausing as he glanced at me before looking back down at the page.

"*There will be a woman named Violet. She will be the key to waking the Lady of the Lake and bringing an end to Morgana's war once and for all,*" Matthew read aloud and then turned the page, scanning for something else. "*Robert must find her before it's too late.*" Matthew stared up at me with an expectant look on his face.

My eyebrows shot up as I stared at him, puzzled. "And he did. But I'm not sure I'm following you."

"Only the people who've read this specific journal know about the second part of the prophecy. Belinda didn't tell the whole group," Matthew explained.

"Okay, but knowing that Robert was meant to find me doesn't really give us an edge."

"It does if Aiden doesn't know that it was part of the original prophecy." Matthew put the journal on the table. "You see, I don't think that *you're* the key to waking The Lady. I think your soul connection with Robert is the key."

"I see. And you think that's why I got my magic from him?"

"Exactly." Matthew removed a touchpad from his bag. "I've been doing a little research on The Lady." He pulled up a web page on the screen and said, "Read this."

As my eyes scanned the screen, the knot in my shoulders tighten.

O, wake once more! how rude soe'er the hand
That ventures o'er thy magic maze to stray;
O, wake once more! though scarce my skill command
Some feeble echoing of thine earlier lay:
Though harsh and faint, and soon to die away,
And all unworthy of thy nobler strain,
Yet if one heart throb higher at its sway,(1)
The wizard note has not been touched in vain.
Then silent be no more! Enchantress, wake again!
(1) First draft of the Poem stated two hearts throb higher at its sway

"What is this?" I asked once I'd finished.

"It's part of a Sir Walter Scott poem about The Lady. See the footnote?" Matthew pointed out.

"Yeah, two hearts. What about it?"

"That footnote was hidden by Magic. The published poem was changed to read *one heart* to hide the truth. You need two hearts to wake her."

"Yet if two hearts throb higher at its sway, the wizard note has not been touched in vain," I re-read the lines under my breath with the correct words.

"Do you see now? You're the key to waking her because Robert saved you. Your two hearts beat within a shared soul."

"And you're sure Aiden doesn't know about this?"

"I don't know how he could. I mean, it's probably safe to assume he knows that you and Robert are connected like Merlin and Arthur were. Most people have come to that conclusion since you didn't show signs of having Magic until after he healed you."

"That's not very comforting."

"I know, but the only way he can know that Robert is a part of the original Prophecy is if someone who's read this journal told him or if he has a Soothsayer working for him."

"How convenient then that his daughter is on *our side*," I said, using air quotes. "I'll have to have another chat with Lila." I still felt fatigued from that morning. The thought of having to use my Magic again left me feeling sour. "She should be able to tell us what Aiden does or doesn't know."

"Do you really think she'll be honest with you?"

"No, but Robert seems to trust her, so it's worth asking."

"About that." Matthew cleared his throat. "I think that maybe we should keep some of this back from him."

I eyed Matthew. "Brett's gotten to you, hasn't she?"

"I just think it would be safer to play our cards close to the chest. We don't know everything that happened while he was gone. And you have to admit, he's different."

I ran a hand through my hair and sighed as I remembered the look in his eyes when I showed up at his hotel.

"Something is definitely different. I'm just not sure it's Robert who's changed."

"What's that supposed to mean?" Matthew asked. He eyed me carefully, as if I had revealed that my mother was a unicorn.

"We've all been through a lot, and none of us are the same after the battle at Pacifica Pier. I'm not saying we should forgive him with open arms, but I do think he and Lila can be an asset."

"Agreed, but we can't let them in on everything. Lila might be feeding information back to her father."

"So what do we tell them?"

"Only what they need to know. It's Robert and Lila who have to prove to us they deserve to be trusted, not the other way around." Matthew put his hand on my forearm and gave it a gentle squeeze.

"You're right," I sighed and shook my head. "I don't know what's gotten into me."

"I do." Matthew smiled. "You care for him. It's hard to keep the ones you love at arm's length." He gave my arm another reassuring squeeze. "But don't worry, we'll figure this out."

I nodded in agreement. "Anything else?"

Matthew grinned and pulled up another website. "This will be on display in Los Angeles next week, and my sources say that Morgana is going to make a play for it."

"The Lufian Necklace?" I looked at Matthew, shocked. "You found it?"

"You know it." He winked, and the emerald green of his eyes seemed to shine a little brighter. "It won't be easy finding the other two. It's pure luck the necklace is even still in circulation."

"At least we know where to find one of the pieces. That's more than we knew yesterday."

Matthew shook his head. "You're telling me. I've been up to my eyeballs searching for any lead."

"Thank you, for all your help." I rubbed his shoulder.

He smiled. "It's all a part of the job."

"So what's the plan to get the necklace?" I scrolled on the touch screen to read the rest of the details.

"It's going to go on display at the Huntington Library a week from now."

"Okay, that's not much time to plan, but we can make that work, right?" I asked as I zoomed in on the necklace. It wasn't what I expected, not that I knew what to expect. The stone was crudely cut and as the light hit the opal, it looked like sunlight under water. The blue and green imperfections sticking out like seaweed against the milky blue stone

"I'm trying to nail down the arrival date so we can get inside before it goes on display. It's going to be tight, but I think we can manage."

A knock at the door startled us both. Matthew stepped across the entry and looked through the peephole. "It's Robert and Lila," he said. "I told them to meet me here around two-thirty so we could head out." He looked at his watch as he opened the door.

"You're early," he grumbled.

I closed Matthew's notebook and put his touchpad back in his bag.

"Can we come in?" Robert asked. He looked over Matty's shoulder and into the house.

"Sure, Violet was just saying that she wanted to speak with Lila," Matthew said and motioned them inside.

"She was?" Lila gave me a skeptical look.

"I have a few questions that I'm hoping you'll be able to answer," I shared, standing up to face them.

"I'm surprised you beat us here," Robert said to Matthew. "I thought you were still catching up on some much-needed rest.

"There were a few things I needed to discuss with Violet," Matthew noted.

"Anything you care to share?" Robert challenged.

"Not at the moment." Matthew's eyes danced over Lila and

the tension in the room thickened like the humidity of a coming storm.

"I see my sister's been whispering in your ear." Robert rolled his eyes.

Matthew shook his head and made his way toward the living room.

I turned my attention back to Lila & Robert and said, "Shall we?" I motioned for them to take a seat at the kitchen table.

Robert sat at the head of the table as Lila pulled out the chair across from me.

"You wanted to ask me something?" Lila's head cocked to the side.

"We were wondering…" I began. "Does Aiden have access to a Soothsayer or is he working with one?" I glared at her, hoping we could both cut to the chase.

Lila looked startled as she shared a worried glance with Robert.

"Yes, well, sort of." Lila stuttered like she was holding back.

"What does that mean exactly?"

"She doesn't have much of a choice," Lila admitted. "He killed her son, and daughter-in-law and took her grandchildren." She paused and fiddled with the ring on her pinky finger. "They live on Avalon with him and as far as I can tell, he's never hurt them. As long as she tells him what she can see, they stay unharmed. He even lets her see them every now and again."

"How sweet of him." Hatred toward Aiden settled in my chest and for the first time, I saw the broken woman Robert was so desperately trying to save. After everything she'd learned about her father, she was still justifying his actions.

"That's why they didn't restrain her," Robert said under his breath.

"Restrain?" My brow furrowed.

"Whenever they took me out of my cell, they put cuffs on me

so I couldn't use Magic. But with her, they never did. Some guards even seemed fond of her."

"No one's ever had a real problem with her, although she can get under your skin sometimes," Lila grumbled and her eyes became unfocused as if she was remembering a particular moment with the Soothsayer.

"In fact," she continued. "She chose to live on Avalon so she could be close to her grandchildren."

"So she just tells Aiden everything she sees?" I asked. Mixed emotions rolled around inside me like tennis balls in a dryer. On the one hand, I was furious that any Soothsayer would share their gift with someone like Aiden. But on the other hand, I understood she was trying to save what family she had left.

"I imagine she keeps some things to herself, but if he asks her a question, she always has an answer." Lila took a deep breath and exhaled. Her guilt seemed to ease a bit as she spoke.

"Our visions aren't meant to be abused that way." I let out a shaky sigh.

"She doesn't seem to mind." Lila shrugged.

"And what gave you that impression? Do you think she would be so inclined to serve your father if he wasn't holding her grandchildren hostage? Or was it the murder of her son that made her indifferent?"

Lila wouldn't meet my gaze.

"Yeah, I didn't think so."

Out of the corner of my eye, I saw a shadow move behind the curtains.

"Get down!" Robert yelled, throwing himself on top of me and Lila. The three of us flipped over as the couch was blasted onto its back. Shards of glass exploded toward us and the sick green electricity of a Galvin spell bolted over our heads.

Springing into action, Robert jumped onto the kitchen table and threw his shield up in front of us as Brett came running into the room, shield raised and ready for action. The Galvin spell hit the solid barrier and ricocheted into the bookshelf, sending books flying into the air.

"What the hell is-" Brett said, cut off by a Cinder orb roaring at her head. She ran at one of the assailants and let the orb explode against her shield. The smell of singed hair filled the room as Brett jumped over one of the chairs. Blue electricity flew from across the room, tearing apart her shield in mid-air. At that very moment, another spell smacked into her and she crashed into the couch at the far end of the room.

I was about to step forward and disarm the second attacker when another explosion erupted from behind us. Spinning around on my knees, I summoned my shield and stopped a fireball just in the nick of time. Two more men stood before me, and without thinking I ran at them full force, a distraction spell on the tips of my fingers.

The Magic flowed through me and the spell went off without a hitch, flashes of light blinding the two men in front of me for a split second, giving me the edge I needed. Keeping my shield in place, I swept my leg out and dropped one of them to the floor. Next to me, Lila started working on the other attacker. As my guy hit the floor, I smacked him with a Stunning orb and he froze in place.

Another fireball flew over my head and crashed into the wall in front of me, blasting plaster and dust into the air. Brett struggled with a lumberjack-sized man twice her size while Robert fired an Arcane spell at his sparring partner sending him through the TV.

Lila stepped in front of me, raising her shield as a man and woman stalked toward us.

"Stay behind me," Lila said.

I shot her a glance, I wasn't expecting her to step up and save anyone but herself. Stepping beside her, I generated enough Magic to take down an elephant, I let the Galvin spell wreak havoc on the two attackers in front of us as Lila finished them off with Cinder orbs.

On the other side of the couch, Robert moved headfirst toward his attacker as blue flecks of light flickered on the lumberjack's hands. As Robert came within reach, he pushed his hands through Robert's shield and tossed him backward like a rag doll. Robert hit the wall, his body making a sick snapping noise before he crumbled to the ground.

The assailant turned his attention on me and Lila, stepping toward us with a grin on his face. The blue light danced on his fingertips. Lila stepped up as the last line of defense and the lumberjack froze.

"Traitor," he snarled.

Lila raised her chin and squared her shoulders.

Pulling on my Magic, I summoned a Cinder orb behind my back and waited for my chance. The lumberjack took another step toward us and, just like before, he shot penetrating electricity from his fingers directly at Lila's shield. She took the hit and before she hit the wall behind us, I threw the Cinder orb directly at the lumberjack's chest.

His shield materialized, and the spell bounced off him, hitting the couch and leaving a scorch mark the size of a basketball.

"Like taking candy from a baby." His voice held an edge of humor that chilled me to the bone.

I kept my shield in place, bracing myself. The lumberjack's fingertips produced the sparks of blue light again as he took another step toward me. Coming to his full height, he smiled as he raised his hand to take me down like the others.

I took a deep breath, and thought back to my training, trying to figure out a way to outsmart him. Knowing I would have to jump out of the way, I needed to do something he wouldn't expect. Just as the electricity left his hand, I dropped my shield and rolled toward him, summoning a cinder orb. I popped up to my feet in front of him and pressed the cinder orb against his chest. His grin disappeared and his eyes caught mine just before he disintegrated into a pile of ash at my feet.

In disbelief that I'd actually succeeded, I felt relief wash over me as my Magic gripped me and I fell to the floor. The vision pulled at me strong and urgent.

Annabel was chained to a wall, grime and blood staining her skin as she screamed. A flash of green light shot from the shadows and her body went limp. Scrambling to get to her, a deep, chuckle burned through my heart.

"Violet, are you alright? What's wrong?" Robert's voice brought me back to the present.

"Annabel," I managed to squeak. "They're torturing her." Robert knelt in front of me.

The front door swung open and without thinking, I threw a stunning orb at the intruder. The orb missed Becky's head by a few inches and her shocked face stared back at me.

"Dammit," I cursed under my breath.

CHAPTER SEVEN

"What the hell was that?" Becky pushed the door open and stepped inside.

"Someone check on Brett." I nodded toward the heap of wood that used to be my kitchen table.

Without skipping a beat, Becky dropped her bag at her feet and rushed over to Brett, who was lying under an upturned chair.

Knowing Brett was being taken care of, I turned my attention back to Robert.

"Here, let me help you." Robert pulled me to my feet. "You alright?

"I'm not hurt." I brushed the dust off of my jeans.

"I don't mean physically." His eyes shot across the room to Becky, who was helping Brett up.

"Your vision," he whispered. "Annabel."

"I've seen it before… it just, took me off guard this time." I tried to play it cool, no one needed to know the gritty details.

"Did you see anything that might help us save her?" Robert's eyes scanned my face.

"No. There was nothing, just her and someone in the shadows."

"Is someone going to explain what the hell is going on?" Becky's voice was a mixture of irritation and worry.

"What're you going to tell her?" He nodded in Becky's direction.

"I don't know." I let out a heavy sigh and pushed my hair out of my face.

"A little help," Lila grunted.

"Is everyone alright?" Matthew asked, peeking his head from around the corner.

"We're all good," I answered, and he stepped into the room, immediately going to Brett's side.

Robert gave my shoulder a reassuring squeeze before moving around the ramshackle furniture and kneeling next to Lila. She had a large gash across her cheek and her arm was wrapped tightly around her middle as if she had broken a few ribs. Robert placed a hand on her shoulder and instantly I saw the tension melt from her face.

"Violet, where's your first-aid kit?" Becky asked, looking over Brett's superficial wounds.

"I'm right here," Robert said, leaving Lila's side.

The instant he placed his hand on Brett, the cuts on her arms and face disappeared before Becky's eyes.

"How'd'you... what'd you... that was amazing!" Becky exclaimed, smiling from ear to ear. "Did you know he could do that?" She looked back at me, her eyes as bright as a child's on Christmas morning.

Nodding, I said, "It's a long story."

"I'm listening." She shot upright and moved toward me.

I scrunched my nose at the mess. "We had a slight incident."

"I'll say. This place looks like the running of the bulls came through here." Becky looked around at the wreckage.

"Will you guys excuse us a minute?" I had no idea how I was going to explain everything to Becky, and I didn't need four extra sets of eyes on me.

"Sure thing," Matthew said and smiled.

"I should head back to the estate, let Jake know we were attacked again," Brett added.

"Are you sure you don't want me to help you explain?" Robert asked under his breath as he sidled up to me.

"I'll be fine." I took a step away from him. "It wasn't that long ago that I had to learn about all of this."

His lips turned up in a quiet smile. "We'll get rid of them and start cleaning up." His eyes fell on the crumbled bodies in front of us.

"Thank you." I squeezed his forearm in appreciation. "Come on." I reached for Becky's hand. "I'll explain everything."

I led her to my bedroom, the one place in the house that hadn't been destroyed, grasping desperately for some way to explain everything she had just witnessed.

"Alright, Violet. What's going on and why have you been holding out on me?" Becky leveled her gaze on me the moment I closed the door.

Sighing, I said, "I don't know where to start."

"Let's try from the beginning." She folder her arms across her chest, and her foot tapped away on the carpet.

"Alright." I sat on the edge of the bed. "Do you remember when I was attacked after the Maxwell wedding?"

"Yeah." Becky shifted her weight and furrowed her brow.

"Well, I wasn't mugged." I rubbed my forearm nervously. "I was attacked and left for dead."

"What?" Becky shot forward.

"Relax, I'm fine, Beck." I held up my hands in an attempt to keep her from jumping ship. "I made it out alive, but I've never been the same." I paused, choosing my next words wisely.

"When Robert healed me with Magic like he just did for Lila and Brett, it changed me in an irreversible way. I'm like them now. Magical."

"Wait, so Magic as in bibbidi bobbidi boo?"

A nervous chuckle escaped my throat. "Yeah, although it's not quite a fairytale."

Becky pursed her lips, her eyes moving back and forth as she tried to come up with something to say. "So you have, like, powers and stuff now?"

"It's a little more complicated than that. I'm destined to wake The Lady of the Lake and stop Morgana from enslaving the Magical world."

"You're screwing with me. This is all a joke, right?"

I bit my lip and shook my head.

Becky let out a shaky breath and began pacing again. "So let me get this straight. You were almost killed, Robert Magically healed you, and now you have powers that you'll use to jump into a folktale and battle it out with mythical characters?"

I couldn't stop myself from bursting into laughter. The way she put it made all of this sound so ridiculous.

"Don't laugh at me," Becky scolded. "I'm trying to understand."

"I'm sorry. I'm not laughing at you, I'm laughing at how asinine all of this is." Catching my breath, I started again. "The Lady, Morgana, Arthur, Merlin, they're all real, not just characters in a book."

Becky stared at me and for half a second I thought she was going to try to smack me over the head and drag me to a mental facility. Then she smiled.

"Seriously? The stories are real, all of them?"

I nodded. "You're handling this pretty well."

"It's a little hard to wrap my head around, but my best friend is Magical, that's pretty badass." Becky beamed.

"Maybe you should have been The Waker," I said under my

breath. Becky was taking all of this in stride, and honestly, I was a bit jealous that I hadn't handled it like her.

"The Waker?" Becky cocked her head to the side.

"It's what they call me since I'll be waking The Lady and all."

"Why you?"

I shook my head. "I'm not entirely sure what makes me so special, why it has to be me. But it's been prophesied for hundreds of years."

"All this time, you knew about this and didn't tell me?"

"Believe me, I wanted to. It's been so hard keeping everything from you, but I thought it was the best way to keep you safe. You've seen firsthand the kind of damage Magic can do." I gestured toward the rest of the house through the closed door.

"Magic did all that?" Becky scrunched up her face and for the first time since I threw a stunning orb at her, she looked nervous.

"That isn't even the half of it." I sighed as I thought over the last few months.

"What can you do exactly?" She sat down next to me.

"Well, for starters, I'm a Soothsayer. I have the ability to see the past, present, and future."

"Like a carnival psychic?" Becky rolled her eyes.

I smiled. "My gifts are a little more accurate."

"So what's my future then?"

"I'm sensing…" I said and closed my eyes. "That you'll be the victim of a blunt force trauma." I opened my eyes and punched her playfully.

"Come on, seriously. Tell me something."

I really didn't want to look into her future. I worried about what I'd do if I saw something I didn't like. Deciding it was better to stay in the past, I pulled up a picture in my head of Becky as a child and smiled as the vision of Becky materialized before my eyes.

"Alright, something from your past," I started. "You wore a cupcake dress to your first day of school when you were five."

"I hated that dress." She shook her head but smiled despite her thoughts on the dress. "What else?" She rotated to face me. "Can you heal people too?"

"No, that's just Robert. From what I'm told, every Magical person can learn most Magic, but some people like Robert and myself have abilities above and beyond the norm."

"You should have told me sooner." She crossed her arms.

"I know, I was just trying to protect you."

"When are you going to learn? Your problems are my problems." She draped her arm over my shoulders.

A knock at the door interrupted us and we both looked up.

"Come in," I said.

"I don't mean to intrude," Robert said as he opened the door.

"Yes, you do," Becky challenged. Her voice caught me off guard and when I looked at her, her eyes were shooting daggers at Robert.

Robert hesitated a moment and looked to me for some sign of what he should do.

"You may have saved her life, but don't you dare think I'm okay with you betraying her."

"Beck," I said, and shot up from the bed to stare down at her.

Robert started backing out of the room. "Maybe I should-"

"Oh no you don't." Becky started after him. "Where do you get off disappearing for weeks on end and then showing up here with that blonde tart?"

"Perfect, so I'm on everyone's shit list, then?" Robert sighed.

"Becky, it's not like that. It's way more complicated than I let on." I tried to explain.

"What do you mean?" She turned her attention back to me.

"He's not with Lila. At least not that I know of."

Robert cleared his throat, but I ignored him and continued

on. "She tried to kill me, but then she saved his life and now she's here trying to prove that she's on our side."

Becky stared at me for a pregnant moment, blinked, then turned on her heel and slapped Robert across the face. Shocked just as much as he was, my hands flew to my mouth.

"She tried to kill my best friend, and you brought her here, into her home?" Becky fumed, unleashing her fury on Robert.

"I'm not going to defend myself." He squared his shoulders. "Violet can explain if she cares to." He held Becky's eyes, waiting for a response. When she didn't answer, he looked up at me. "Brett's going to leave soon and Matty wants to head to Grahams when she heads out," he said as politely as he could with Becky's handprint still red on his cheek before he turned and walked away.

Becky looked over her shoulder at me. "Well, I guess he told us," Becky snickered.

I shook my head and chuckled.

"So what's the deal with you two then?" She closed the door and leaned against it.

"I don't know. It's complicated." I pulled a duffel bag from my closet.

"I've heard that before." She eyed me as I began packing.

"I'll explain everything when I get back." I shoved anything that touched my hand into my bag without looking.

"When you get back? You're going with him?"

"Like I said, it's complicated."

"When will you be back?"

"Honestly, I don't know. A couple days maybe?" I shrugged and felt bad for leaving just after dropping the Magic bomb on her. "Beck, you can't say anything about all this, to anyone." I put my bag on my shoulder.

"I won't."

"I mean it. This isn't just small town gossip. It's life and death."

Becky locked her lips and threw away the key. "You've got my word."

"Thank you." I gave her a quick hug, then held her at arm's length. "If you need someone to talk to, I'm just a phone call away. I know this is a lot to process."

"I'll be fine." She patted my hand. "And don't think you're getting off the hook. I still have some questions for you when you get back."

"I'll answer anything you want, promise," I said, giving her a tight hug.

An hour later, Matthew, Robert, Lila and I were heading north on the one-oh-one freeway. Guilt ate away at me for leaving Becky after dropping a bombshell on her, but I really didn't have a choice. Matthew sat beside me in the driver's seat, focusing harder than normal on the road ahead. He wasn't thrilled that Lila was joining us and he definitely wasn't happy that I'd agreed it was a good idea she accompany us to Graham's.

It wasn't that I trusted her now that she'd fought alongside us. In fact, the reason I wanted her along was because I didn't trust her on her own. Keep your friends close and your enemies closer. And with Robert along, I doubted she would try anything too stupid.

The drive took longer than expected and by the time we pulled off the freeway the sun had long since continued its course beyond the horizon. I was exhausted. The battle had left me drained Magically, but having to keep my walls up around Robert was a whole other kind of emotional exhaustion. Not falling into a comfortable rhythm was proving to be harder than I'd ever imagined.

Turning down an unmarked dirt road, Matthew drove cautiously as the car jostled back and forth on the uncivilized path. Massive pine trees rose out of the ground on either side of us, guiding the way ahead. The further down the road we went, the narrower it got. Anxious, I fidgeted in my seat at the thought of being stuck out in the woods, when out of nowhere a break in the trees and the soft glow of lights illuminated a large cabin. Matthew pulled into the clearing, parked, and we all stretched our tired limbs.

"You sure this is the place?" I asked Matthew as we walked up the steps to the front door.

"Of course," he said, giving me a warm smile, then looking over his shoulder at Robert and Lila. "He's not going to be too pleased that she's here, though." He sighed and rang the doorbell.

A distinguished looking gentleman opened the door, wearing a red smoking jacket and holding a glass of some sort of amber-colored liquid. His appearance came as a bit of a shock. For some reason I was expecting an old and half-broken man, like Billy Crystal's character in the Princess Bride, to greet us, not a handsome older gentleman.

"Matthew, it's so good to see you, lad," Graham said. His British accent boomed through the empty trees as we all followed him inside.

"You too, Graham. How've you been?"

"Can't complain. What about you, staying out of trouble?"

"Never." Matthew laughed.

Graham turned right into a large study. Books lined the walls all the way to the ceiling, and the dark wood reminded me of the Maxwell estate. A heavy, overstuffed couch sat across from the large fireplace with embers crackling and popping gently as we entered.

"That's my boy. So what can I do for you?" Graham sat in the plump leather armchair adjacent to the couch and motioned for us to take a seat.

"Like I said in my email, we wanted to find out more about their soul connection. And since we're here, I thought we could ask you about The Lady's tokens." Matthew motioned between me and Robert. "I've reached out to a few of my contacts, but its radio silence mostly."

"Of course. But may I ask why you're traveling with Aiden's daughter?" His eyes shifted in Lila's direction.

Lila looked surprised at the mention of her father's name, but didn't look away from Graham.

"Yes, my dear," he cooed. "I know exactly who you are and the only reason I haven't turned you to dust is because of the company you keep."

I liked this guy already and did nothing to hide the smile forming on my lips.

"She helped Robert escape Aiden and Morgana." Matthew cleared his throat. "And now she's trying to make amends." His words dripped with insincerity.

"So, I'm to believe that you've betrayed your father to help them?" Graham motioned between me and Robert, addressing Lila like she was a stain on a white rug.

"You can believe whatever you want about me. I have nothing to prove to you," Lila said, crossing her arms.

Graham let out a short, sarcastic laugh. "Don't you though?" His eyes grazed over her like she was something truly distasteful.

"Anyway," Matthew cut in. "This is Violet Evans, The Waker." Matthew motioned toward me.

Graham inclined his head and said, "The pleasure is mine."

"Not at all." I shifted on the couch, uncomfortable. I'd come to expect this kind of reaction when people found out who I was, but it was still hard to get used to.

"And this is Robert Maxwell." Matthew nodded in Robert's direction.

"Yes, of course," Graham added. "We met once or twice back home when you were mentoring under Felix."

"We did. I didn't think you'd remember," Robert said and smiled.

"The memory of an elephant." Graham tapped his head absentmindedly. They shared a look that made me wonder what their connection was.

Turning his attention back to Matthew, Graham said, "Now that we're through the introductions, shall we get started?"

"Like we discussed," Matthew began. "Violet is a Soothsayer and Robert, as you are well aware, is a Healer."

Graham swirled the amber-colored liquid in his glass as he nodded along, then took a delicate sip.

"I think they might be Bonded." Matthew paused for dramatic effect. "You see, Violet didn't have any Magic until June when Robert healed a fatal wound in her abdomen."

Graham sat up straight and said, "Quite right, and you believe that because Robert gave Violet her Magic they're Bonded?"

"Exactly. I was hoping you could confirm it for us." Matthew shared a satisfied smile.

Graham stood and crossed the room, kneeling when he reached Robert and me on the couch. "May I?" he asked, hands outstretched.

He placed my hand in Robert's and cupped them with his own. Closing his eyes and inhaling deeply through his nose, he mumbled an incantation under his breath. A slight tingling started building in my palm where my hand met Robert's. It was the same feeling that coursed through me every time Robert was near, like my Magic was waking up and reaching out to him.

Graham glanced at our joined hands and smiled up at us. I locked eyes with Robert and the tingling sensation spread, turning into a hungry fire surging through my entire body. Everyone fell away. Graham, Matthew, Lila, they all became a blur. My eyes fixed on Robert as the fire built inside me. Somewhere in the back of my mind, I heard the delicate *click* of the padlock on my heart coming undone. Flames licked at my skin and begged to be released. I'd never felt so powerful, so full of raw energy.

Graham pulled our hands apart, and I felt as if the sun had been plucked from the sky. Confusion and a sense of deep loss filled my heart as I stared at Robert.

CHAPTER EIGHT

"*D*id you feel that?" Robert whispered, sounding a little out of breath.

"Mmhmm." I nodded, stunned. "What was that?" I turned my attention toward Graham.

"I tapped into your Magic." Graham gave us a smug smile.

"I've never felt anything like that before," Robert sighed.

"That's because you've never experienced *Artognou-Magic* before," Graham pointed out, standing up and moving across the room to a large desk piled with books.

"So they're really Bonded?" Matthew chimed in.

"Your suspicions were correct," Graham mumbled under his breath while moving books around on his desk. "Ah, here we go." He lifted a book from the table and slipped a pair of reading glasses on.

"*Artognou-Magic* is a very powerful and complicated form of Magic. First, one person must be non-Magical, which you were," Graham explained. He flipped through the pages of the book, coming to a stop about halfway through. "Second, a healer must save the person's life through Magic, which you did." He pointed to a paragraph in the book. "But most importantly, one person must be from Merlin's bloodline and the other must be from Arthur's bloodline."

"So that's what makes my blood different from the other healers," Robert said, more to himself than the room.

"Other healers?" Graham's eyebrows rose as he looked at Robert over the rim of his glasses.

"When they held me prisoner, they took my blood and had me use my Magic." Robert paused and laced his fingers together. "They were trying to find a way to replicate my ability to transfer Magic through healing. None of the other healers Alyssa had worked with could complete the transfer."

"Interesting. So Aiden is unaware of what gives *Artognou* life, then."

Robert nodded. "It would appear that way."

"Do you think it's possible that my father could recreate the *Artognou-Magic* with just Robert's blood?" Lila asked from the corner of the room.

"I'd keep my eye on that one if I were you." Graham's eyes met mine.

"Answer the question," Lila barked.

"Lila," Robert said in a warning voice.

"Looks like he's already got her on a leash." Graham smirked.

Lila rolled her eyes and added, "We're not here for a lesson on genetics. We need to know if my father can recreate *Artognou-Magic* in another pair."

"Yes, it's possible if he has all the right pieces. But I doubt he'll ever figure it out." Graham gave Lila a once-over.

"I wouldn't underestimate him." Lila held Graham's eyes.

"Aiden Patridge doesn't scare me, child. He's an over-zealous, pompous prick and he'll get what's coming to him," Graham returned in one breath.

"What if he does figure it out?" I asked. "How would we stop another Bonded pair?"

Graham swirled the amber liquid in his glass and took a

healthy sip. "It's not likely, dear. There've only been a dozen or so pairings throughout history. As a matter of fact, the last pair on record, had it stripped from them and almost all knowledge on *Artognou-Magic* was destroyed. There are less than a handful of people left in the world who know the secret behind *Artognou-Magic*."

"Who were they?" I asked. "The pair that had their Magic stripped from them?"

"Ah, that's a very interesting story in and of itself." Graham got up and searched for another book among the many shelves. He soon found what he was looking for, a small leather-bound book with no discernible title or markings, and rejoined the group, handing the book to me.

"About 800 years ago," Graham began, "there was a young woman and her adopted son who lived in a small Magical village. Once the *Artognou-Magic* took hold, they were unstoppable, a force of pure brute power. They climbed the social ladder, so to speak, and eventually rose to the throne. At first, they helped defend their people from Viking invaders and kept the kingdom safe and prosperous. Then one day, everything went to complete and utter hell." He let out a heavy sigh, as if the tragedy weighed on him.

"They ordered the massacre of their Danish allies out of paranoia. They believed they were plotting against them in order to take the throne for themselves." Graham recited the story from memory as if he had experienced the event firsthand. "It wasn't just Magical people they slaughtered in that church, but humans too. They had become delusional, driven mad by power. The irony is, after that, their own people did plot against them and stripped them of their Magic."

"What happened to their Magic once it was stripped from them?" I asked.

"It's all in there." Graham motioned to the book in my hands. "The man who took in their Magic sacrificed his life when he did so. No one person can harness that kind of raw power."

"Aiden must be trying to create *Artognou-Magic* to use as a weapon against us," Matthew suddenly spoke up.

"They'd be unstoppable," Robert said, and by the hush in his voice, I knew he could still feel the crackle of Magic between us.

Graham moved closer to Lila as if he was inspecting a curious looking painting.

"Not unstoppable," Graham clarified. "With the proper training, there isn't a soul alive who could combat you."

"I don't know about that. Morgana's back," Lila shared.

Graham paused mid-step and for a fraction of a second, his face paled. "You're sure?"

"We saw her come through the portal with our own eyes." Lila looked at Robert, who nodded confirmation, pursing his lips.

"And I had a vision when she came through. She's back, I'm sure of it," I added.

"We always knew they would find a way," Graham said under his breath.

"Which brings us to the Tokens. Do you know where we can find them?" Matthew was doing his best to keep the conversation on track.

"Unfortunately, no. They went missing ages ago."

"Then how am I supposed to wake The Lady?"

"You'll find a way. You're The Waker, it's your destiny," Graham said with confidence.

"There has to be some trace of them somewhere, in a story, a history book, something," Matthew pleaded.

"Indeed, there is a lost tale of a necklace that's said to have mysterious powers. It's possible that it's The Lufian Necklace."

"What's the story?" I asked.

"It's been said that the necklace has a heartbeat of its own, that only the person wearing it can hear. Once you put on the necklace, it matches the rhythm of your heart and feeds on your fears and desires until it consumes you, leaving nothing but an empty shell."

We all stared at Graham in silence.

"There is a limerick, I believe," he continued, "about a stone that carried the hearts of everyone who wore it."

Graham closed his eyes and pinched the bridge of his nose.

"The spark of life beats across your surface,

Each imperfection, a desire from which I cannot part,

You hang from my neck with a secret purpose,

Your beauty ensnaring me and capturing my heart," he recited, then looked at each of us.

"If it wasn't so terrifying, that would be beautiful," I said with my mouth half open.

"The necklace is the one token we have a lead on." Matty's voice was gruff with frustration.

"Really?" Graham asked and cocked his head to the side as he looked at Matty.

"A wealthy Moroccan family donated the necklace to some charitable organization, and it's going to be on display in Los Angeles," Matty explained.

"Interesting. Do you recall the name of this family?" Graham asked, placing his thumb under his chin and his index finger over his lips as he contemplated Matthew's words.

"Yeah, it's the uh… Per, Perrin Family," Matthew recalled.

"Hmm. It's possible," Graham said to himself.

Matthew and I shared a look while Graham mused over his thoughts. When it was clear he wasn't going to elaborate any further, Matty cleared his throat.

"And the Ring of Dispel?" Matthew inquired.

"Ahh, the ring has changed many hands over the years. I have an old friend who used to track its whereabouts. He may be able to locate the ring." Graham kept his eyes on the ice in his glass. "I'll reach out to him in the morning."

"What about Excalibur?" Robert chimed in. "There has to be a record of the sword somewhere."

"I've been working with Michael Ainsworth on tracking down the sword," Matthew admitted.

"Michael Ainsworth?" Robert cocked his head like a curious bird.

"Michael's ancestor attended the same gathering yours did, Robert. The gathering where Belinda first spoke of The Waker and prophesied Morgana's return," Graham shared.

"Right. I remember the mention of a Thomas Ainsworth, but what do they have to do with Excalibur?"

"Can you guess what profession Thomas held?"

"No."

"A blacksmith," Matthew said proudly.

"Right you are." Graham lifted his glass in salute to Matthew's contribution to the conversation. "While the black-smith trade is no longer viable, they adapted and now they run an auction house specializing in antique weaponry. If anyone has a lead on Excalibur, it'll be Michael and his family." Graham polished off his glass. "Good work, Matthew, my boy."

"So that's it?" Lila asked, breaking the silence. "We drove all the way out here just so you could give us some vague leads? I thought you were supposed to be helpful."

"He has been helpful," Matthew spat.

"Everything he told us he could have put in an email. Why make us come all the way out here?"

Matthew stood and faced Lila. "I would've gladly left you behind," he said through gritted teeth.

"Alright, that's enough you two," Robert huffed, trying to keep the peace. "I'm sorry," he added, looking at Graham.

Graham pursed his lips. "There's no need for apologies on my behalf."

"She does have a point, though. Why not tell Matty all of this through email or over the phone?"

I hated to admit it, but Lila had a point. Nothing we learned so far had been too sensitive for email. So why did Graham insist we make the drive to him?

Three pairs of eyes settled on me.

Lila chuckled. "Hell must have frozen over if we're in agreement on something."

I rolled my eyes at her. "Seriously, Graham, why insist we meet you in person?"

Graham gave me a small smile. "Matthew, do you mind if I speak with Violet and Robert alone for a moment?"

"Sure, no problem." Matthew moved around the couch, directing Lila out of the room.

"There's something I wish to speak with the two of you about." Graham paused and moved across the room to pour himself another glass, waiting for Matthew to shut the door behind him. "A few rumors have reached my ears."

"Rumors?" I leaned forward.

"Another prophecy has made its way to me."

Dread crept into my heart. The last prophecy I'd heard changed my life in an irreversible way. "What is it this time?" I wasn't entirely sure I wanted to know.

"That," Graham said, pausing to clear his throat as he put his hand on my shoulder. "That The Waker will lose herself to The Lady."

"But that can't be," Robert blurted out. "Violet has to live." The pain in his eyes took me off guard.

"The prophecy didn't say that she would die, only that she would be lost."

I sat there stunned, unable to think of anything to say.

"Lost? What does that mean?" Robert demanded.

Graham shrugged. "Your guess is as good as mine."

"So you're saying there's a chance we can save her." Robert looked over at me, pain and fear etched across every line of his face. He had lost me once and promised it would never happen again. The thought that he might lose me to the destiny he helped create seemed to add salt to the wound.

"It's possible, yes. But I must warn you, The Lady is a force to be reckoned with. Morgana is a monster, yes, but The Lady, she's another being all together." Graham's eyes looked full of sorrow as he glanced between me and Robert.

"Violet, try to see something. Maybe you can see a way out, a loophole that'll save you." Desperation laced Robert's voice. It was so unlike him, it scared me.

I closed my eyes and focused on Graham's words. The Magic inside me stirred and as I let my guard down, I could feel the vision slowly start to form around me.

The amethyst eyes that haunted my dreams filled my vision. A small smile that was not my own spread across my face. It was her, I knew without a doubt that it was The Lady smiling back at me. Her crystalline eyes moved away from me and Robert appeared in front of her like he had before.

"Violet, are you alright?" Robert asked.

"You're Bonded to this one? How fascinating," said The Lady. Her lips didn't move, but instead, her voice echoed inside my head.

Returning to the present, like I'd been shoved out of a dream, Graham's study swirled back into view. As my eyes refocused, I felt Robert keep his hand on my shoulder.

"What did you see?" Robert asked, his voice full of anxiety.

I looked at Graham and his eyes searched mine. "Nothing," I lied. "I couldn't see anything."

Recognition flashed across Graham's face before he cleared his throat and quickly said, "It would have been impressive had you been able to see into your own future, but even a Soothsayer as powerful as you, has her limitations."

"The prophecy didn't say anything else?" I asked meekly.

"I'm afraid not." Graham gave me a small reassuring smile. "But you know how prophecies are. They often have a double meaning."

"I need some air." I turned away from them both and padded across the hardwood floor as quickly as I could.

"Violet, is everything alright?" Matthew called after me as I made a beeline for the front door.

Footsteps follow behind me, but I didn't turn to see who it was.

Bursting through the front door, I welcomed the cool night air on my face. It was too warm in the house, too suffocating. I rushed into the night, my shoes grating against the dirt and pine needles as I ran toward the trees.

I soon reached a large pine tree about fifty yards from the house and placed my hand against its rough bark, letting my head fall back. Breathing heavily, I slammed my fist against the tree trunk.

I tried to find peace in the stars twinkling through the trees. Watching the night sky had always been peaceful for me, the knowledge that no matter how much things changed, or how bad things got, the stars were always there watching over us.

The few I could see above me shone like jewels and I tried to divine some meaning out of them or my own life. How could something with so much power and raw energy burn within each star, only to be fated to darkness?

Sadness washed over me as I realized that many of the stars lighting up the velvet darkness above me had already exhausted their fuel and died out thousands if not millions of years ago. Like them, I too was fated to darkness and my light would burn out just the same.

Twigs snapped in half as someone approached me, but I didn't turn to see who it was.

"Violet," Robert called out, breaking the silence.

I sighed at the concern in his voice. "Yeah?"

"Are you alright?" His boot crunched in the brush as he took a cautious step toward me.

"Just peachy." I folded my arms across my chest and looked

up at the stars above. What I wouldn't have given to escape to a far corner of the world where I could just live my life in peace.

"Can we talk about what just happened in there?"

"What's there to talk about? No matter what I do, in the end, I'll be lost to The Lady." Her amethyst eyes flashed across my vision, taunting me.

"You can't think like that," Robert insisted. I heard him take another step but still couldn't bring myself to look at him. "That prophecy could mean anything."

"I wish I could believe that, but we both know prophecies aren't made lightly. I've learned the hard way that you can't compete with destiny."

"Will you look at me, please?" The hard edge to his voice made me turn around and face him.

"I've been fighting most of my life to find you. I'm not going to let any prophecy determine what happens to you in the end."

"I thought you lived and breathed destiny and prophecy." I placed my back against the trunk of the pine tree and propped my leg against it.

"I realized there are other things to live for." He took a step toward me and my heart kicked up a notch.

"Like saving Lila?" I tried to keep the wall up between us.

"I don't know what you think you saw-"

"I saw enough," I cut him off, shifting my weight against the bark digging into my spine.

"Care to enlighten me?" He tried to keep the emotion from his face, but I could see the hurt in his eyes.

I shrugged and looked away from him. "Not really."

"I know you saw something when you were looking into Lila."

"I already told you, it was nothing."

He took another step toward me. "Yes, I know you said you weren't sure about what you saw but you forget who you're talking to. I know you. I know that when you brush your hair behind your ear, it's because you feel embarrassed. And I know that when you bite your bottom lip..." He lifted my chin with his thumb and forefinger, forcing me to look at him. "It's because you're hiding something." He released me but didn't back away.

"Robert, there's nothing to tell." I bit my lip and instantly regretting it.

He smiled. "Told you."

Sighing, I actually smiled. "Look, when I have more information I'll share, but for now what I saw isn't anyone's business."

"Alright, I'll drop it... for now. But whatever it was, I hope it's not too late by the time you decide to trust me again."

I thought about the vision of Lila in my arms and her blood dripping from my fingers.

"I guess we'll have to wait and see."

Robert smiled and began to turn away from me, but I didn't want him to go yet. I'd missed being alone with him.

"Robert, wait." I pushed off the tree.

He looked over his shoulder. "Yeah?"

I searched my brain for any legitimate reason to keep talking. "Umm, you said something about a woman taking your blood and making you heal her?"

He nodded. "Alyssa. What about her?" He turned toward me and placed his hands in his pockets.

"When you healed her, did you feel..." I broke off, unsure of how to finish my sentence.

"Feel what?" Robert took a step toward me, and I could see a faint glint of hope in his eyes.

"I mean, do you think you shared any of your Magic with her?"

"No." He shook his head and tucked my hair behind my ear. His finger's grazed my cheek and flashes of Robert filled my vision.

Robert was sitting in the corner of a dark, wet cell, his arms draped over his knees and his head bent forward. I crept toward him, taking in what little I could of the room. There was a small window about ten feet up that left a spotlight of sunshine on the floor. I moved closer to Robert and knelt down to see if he was awake or sleeping.

"Is someone there?" Robert asked. His head shot up, and it scared the living daylights out of me.

Robert was barely recognizable. One of his eyes was swollen shut. Blood caked the side of his face and his neck was covered in red, angry welts.

My vision shifted again. Lila and Robert were in a small bedroom talking. The bruises were gone, but the dark circles under his eyes stood out against his fair skin.

"How'd it go?" Lila asked. She put her hands on Robert's shoulders, comforting him.

"Fine," he said and moved away from her touch. "She's going to tell my family I need to speak with them." He didn't look at her.

"Is everything okay?" She turned the ring on her pinky finger as her brows furrowed.

Sighing, Robert rubbed the back of his neck and said, "This is going to be much harder than I thought."

I let out a shaky breath and the Robert of the present came back into focus.

"Welcome back," he said, searching my face.

Seeing him in pain, learning what he's been through, I felt all of it at once. I wasn't sure what to make of it. Did I forgive him for Lila? No, but I was starting to understand why Robert did what he did. He cared to a fault. About me, his family, and even though I didn't want to admit it, he cared about Lila. How could I stay mad at someone who chose to only see the good in people?

I sighed. "What were we talking about?"

Robert studied my face, an internal war waging in his dark brown eyes.

"Alyssa," he finally said. "And how I don't think I shared any magic with her."

"Right," I said, picking up the train of thought. "How can you be so sure?" A cool breeze touched my skin, and I shivered.

"Because I've healed superficial wounds on people plenty of times, and it's never resulted in a transfer of Magic. Besides, what are the odds of me coming across another one of Merlin's descendants?" He closed the small gap between us and I could feel the heat coming off his body.

"True." My eyes caught his and my heart leapt in my chest. "That's a relief then." I shifted from side to side. "I mean, we don't have to worry about you being Bonded with anyone else."

"You heard what Graham said. What happened between us, when I healed you, it was the perfect storm."

Our bodies remained inches apart as my heart began to thrum against my ribcage. Pushing myself closer to the tree, I tried to regain some of my composure before I did something really stupid.

"I won't let anything happen to you. I promise we'll get through this." He reached for my hand.

My fingers were already frozen from the cool night air, and the warmth of his hand came as a welcomed reprieve.

"But how?"

"With *Artognou*." He brushed my hair back and gave my hand a squeeze. "We'll learn how to control it and we'll get out of this alive."

I smiled and searched his eyes. "I forgot how reassuring you could be."

A smile played on his lips and he moved closer to me. "I know things are different now." His arm found its way around my waist and he pulled me against his chest, away from the tree. "But I won't lose you again."

"Robert, I'm fine. I made it out of there alive." My breath

caught at the feel of his body pressed against mine and my words came out in a whisper.

"I know, but I failed you." He cupped my cheek and his eyebrows turned down in pain.

I wrapped my hand around his to push him away, but as my fingers laced around his wrist, I couldn't find the strength to remove his hand from my face.

The heat from his body pressed against me, inviting me closer. "I was supposed to keep you safe." His hand snaked itself around the back of my neck.

"You tried," I said, a little breathless. My blood sang with anticipation. Somewhere in the back of my mind, I knew I shouldn't give in to him, but every part of my body responded to his touch.

"You have no idea how glad I am that you're alive." He rested his forehead against mine and breathed a sigh of relief.

Closing my eyes, I moved my hand from his wrist to his chest. His heart beat with a fever that matched my own. This was my Robert, the man I'd lost that day on the beach.

"The feeling's mutual." I chuckled and opened my eyes.

He pulled back ever so slightly, keeping our lips just a breath apart, and smiled.

"I've missed you more than I can put into words," he said.

"Robert? Are you out here?" Lila yelled from the house.

Her voice broke through the bubble of warmth and safety, and we practically jumped apart.

"Guess we should go back inside." I cleared my throat and put some distance between us.

"There you guys are. Robert, Graham wants to speak with you," Lila said. She looked between us, noticing the tension. "Is everything alright?"

"Just fine." My voice came out cold and distant as I stomped back to the house.

Part of me was glad Lila had interrupted us. As much as I

wanted to believe he was still my Robert, he wasn't. Lila had gotten under his skin, and no matter how much I wanted to trust him, I couldn't bring myself to forgive him for siding with the woman who'd tried to kill me. We'd both changed in the weeks he'd gone missing and although I still had feelings for him, there was no way things could work between us now that Lila was in the picture.

"Everything okay?" Matthew asked as I stepped through the front door.

I let out a heavy sigh. "As much as it can be."

Matthew's lips twisted to the side as Robert and Lila walked in behind me.

"I see," he said, appraising the look on Robert's face. "Why don't I show you where we'll be sleeping. Graham was kind enough to offer up the spare bedrooms for us tonight." Matthew hooked his arm around mine and pulled me toward the stairs.

"Thank you," I mouthed to him.

He patted my arm, and we made our way to the second floor.

"I hope you don't mind being bunkmates," Matthew said as we reached the landing.

"Not at all." I gave him a warm smile, and we stepped into the first room on the right.

Two twin beds sat against the wall closest to us. Moonlight spilled across the floor from the one window in the room, a loveseat carefully placed beneath it.

"I know it's none of my business, but are you really okay?" Matthew asked as he closed the door and flipped on the light.

"Yeah, I'm fine. It's just a lot of new information to process."

Matthew gave me a knowing look but didn't press the issue. I guess I wasn't fooling anyone.

CHAPTER NINE

Staring at the ceiling, I listened to Matty saw wood louder than anyone I've ever heard in my life. Even if I was tired, there was no way I'd be able to fall asleep with him snoring like that. Throwing the hand-knitted blanket off me, I decided to head downstairs and see if I could find some tea.

I tip-toed out of the room, closing the door behind me with a soft *click*. Each step groaned as I made my way down the stairs to search for the kitchen. Graham hadn't given us a grand tour, so I was going to have to snoop around.

Holding out my hands out on each side to guide me through the darkness, I passed the den where we'd all gathered earlier.

Up ahead, a door stood open and moonlight pooled on the floor in front of me. Peeking inside, a quiet kitchen came into view. The stainless steel appliances glimmered in the soft moonlight, and the wooden bar stools around the island invited me to take a seat.

"Bingo," I said under my breath.

Searching for a light switch along the wall, my fingers brushed against a dimmer switch and the overhead lights gently came to life.

The soft yellow glow illuminated the kitchen like candlelight as I moved across the tiled floor.

I opened one of the large pantry doors, feeling a little intrusive as I dug through Graham's kitchen.

It wasn't hard to find a box of tea bags, and a kettle was already sitting on the stovetop. *Thank god for the English and their obsession with tea,* I thought as I filled the kettle and turned on the burner.

Waiting for the water to boil, I went back to the pantry in search of something to nibble on. Each shelf was piled high with health food, but on the top shelf, I spotted a familiar blue package.

I reached up and could feel the three rows of cookies under my fingertips. My mouth salivated.

The package *crinkled* as I peeled the wrapper open and plucked one of the cookies from its tray. Twisting the two black circles in opposite directions, I split the cookie in half and licked the cream filling.

Someone chuckled from the doorway and looking up, the cookie still pressed against my tongue.

"You found my guilty pleasure, I see." Graham smiled as his eyes moved between me and the cookies.

"Sorry, I couldn't sleep." I started packing the cookies back up.

"Enjoy yourself, my dear." He waved off my concern and joined me at the island.

"What're you doing up so late?" I asked as he plucked a cookie from the package.

"I don't sleep much anymore. A couple hours a night is all I need."

"Must be nice." I popped the chocolate half of the cookie into my mouth.

"Was there something, in particular, keeping you up or just

the weight of the world?" Graham's smile widened and I couldn't help feeling comforted.

There was something warm and welcoming about Graham that I just couldn't put my finger on.

"It's a little of everything, I guess," I admitted. "I don't know how much you know about me, but this is all new and as much as I try, it's still overwhelming sometimes how much my life has changed."

"Life is change, Violet. Without it, we'd never grow into the people that we're meant to be."

"I know." I looked down, embarrassed. "But sometimes I just wish I didn't have all this responsibility on my shoulders."

"From where I was sitting tonight, it didn't look like it was all on your shoulders." He gave me a meaningful look.

"Robert, you mean?" I guessed. It was hardly a secret that Robert took on the burdens of everyone around him.

The tea kettle started singing, and I pulled it off the burner.

Graham moved around me and took two mugs from one of the cabinets. "It seems to me that he would gladly share the weight of your burden."

"Yeah, well, it's complicated," I huffed as Graham placed the mugs on the counter next to me.

"It always is when matters of the heart are involved."

"Are you speaking from experience?" I eyed him carefully as I poured the hot water over the tea bags he placed inside the mugs.

Graham laughed. "Haven't we all been there a time or two?" His eyes ventured toward the ceiling like he was remembering an affair from long ago. "It doesn't help that you're Bonded. You're much more in tune with what the other is feeling. Have you not noticed?"

I thought about the way my Magic felt every time I was around him, how my emotions were heightened when he was close by. "I guess things between us have been a little more amplified." I shrugged. "But I really don't have anything to compare it to."

"Honey or milk?" he asked, walking back to the pantry.

"Honey, please."

"Your *Artognou-Magic* will get stronger once you start training together and everything you feel will intensify." He handed me the honey. "It's what makes the two of you so powerful, to be able to feel one another like a sixth sense." His eyes glassed over and I couldn't help but wonder if Graham had ever been Bonded in his life. The way he spoke about it wasn't something you could pick up and convey just by reading about it.

He shook his head slightly, coming back to the present. "Arthur and Merlin trained for hours every day to perfect their control over their *Artognou*. It's how they were able to accomplish so much in such a short amount of time."

"Do we have to use our *Artognou-Magic?*"

Graham raised an eyebrow and cocked his head to the side. "No one can force you to use it, no. But without it, you won't stand a chance against Morgana."

"Isn't that why I'm supposed to wake The Lady of the Lake? So she can take down Morgana?"

"I have no doubt you'll wake her, but that doesn't mean she'll cooperate in the way you expect. You have to be ready for whatever this world throws at you, and your Bond with Robert is your best chance."

"I see." I took a sip of my tea and let the warm liquid sooth my frazzled nerves.

"I must say, for being a novice you do handle yourself quite well."

"Not that well, I'm afraid." I ran my fingers through my hair and sat my mug down.

"What is it that worries you? The prophecy we spoke of?"

I laughed sarcastically. "If only that was my only problem."

"Then what?" Graham asked, taking one of the cookies for himself.

I bit my lip and said, "I used Magic in front of a friend of mine. She took it well, but now I don't know what to do. I don't want to alter her memory, but I also don't want her to be in danger."

Graham put his hand on my arm and I stopped rambling. "Like I said before, change is a part of life. If your friend took it well, then celebrate the small victories. I can't tell you how often people take the news poorly."

"You've told people about Magic?" I stared at him with a mixture of shock and excitement.

"Of course. It's human nature to want to show off, especially in young men." He elbowed me and we both laughed. Talking with Graham came easy, and he felt like a warm father figure. One who never judged you and always had a small lesson to teach or a bit of advice that would change the way you looked at the world.

"I just never thought it was possible. Robert always made it seem like keeping our secret was life and death."

"Sometimes it is life and death, and Robert knows that. He's been a part of the Magical world his whole life, and I'm sure he's seen his fair share of death from Magic. We all have. But that doesn't mean you should live in fear."

"But once someone knows about Magic, don't they become a Promised One like Matty?"

"No. The ones who are Promised descended from the Knight of the Round Table. Merlin performed a ritual that tied their blood forever to the Magical world."

"Are you saying Matty is a descendant of one of the Knights from the Round Table?"

"Yes"

"I guess I shouldn't be surprised."

I took a sip of tea, letting the warm, smooth liquid relax the tension that had been building since we got here.

"You're very wise," I said, eyeing him over the rim of my cup.

Graham chuckled and said, "There are some who might argue that sentiment." We shared a smile, but I got the sense that he was hiding something from me.

"Well, I supposed I should get to it then," he said finally and placed his cup on the island before reaching into the pocket of his smoking coat.

"Get to what?" I froze with my own cup, half raised to my mouth.

"You asked earlier why I insisted that you make the trip out. I did have a reason, but you ran out before I could explain to you and Robert."

"Okay." I eyed him and the little hairs on the back of my neck stood up.

"There's something I want to give you." He pulled out a small piece of jewelry. "The Ring of Dispel." He held it up to the light, then placed it on the counter between us. "It's yours now." He nudged it with his fingertips.

"But I thought you didn't know where the ring was?"

"A careful lie. This ring contains unimaginable power. I couldn't risk anyone, but The Waker taking possession of it."

"Where'd you get it from?" My voice was barely a whisper as I reached for the ring.

Inspecting the intricate pewter design, a crown encircled a cloudy blue and white stone which sat atop a skull. The sunken eyes drew me into their empty darkness as the stone reflected the moonlight, making the ring seem alive. I rolled the band between my fingers, the cool metal sending a bolt of excitement through me and bringing my Magic to the surface.

"Old family heirloom. It's been with me for years." Graham shrugged.

I turned the ring over and found an inscription inside.

Graham noticed my gaze and said, "It's one part of the spell you'll need to wake her."

A nervous laugh escaped my throat. "You said it was powerful. How so?" I kept my eyes on the ring as if it might jump up and bite me.

"It's in the name. Dispel comes from the Latin word *Dispellere*, which literally means *to drive apart*. The ring has the ability to drive one's soul apart from their body. It's how they were able to send Morgana's soul beyond the veil the first time."

"So why can't we just use the ring again? End this here and now." A renewed sense of hope had me balancing on the end of my stool.

"It's not that simple. When The Lady and Merlin drove Morgana's soul out of her body, they needed someone to escort her essence beyond the veil so that she wouldn't linger in the land of the living." He motioned around the room with his hands as he talked.

A shiver ran across my skin as understanding started to blossom in my heart.

"No living person can cross over to the other side," Graham continued, inclining his head as his eyebrows rose up on his forehead. "The Lady had to give up her own corporeal form as a sacrifice."

"She had to die to stop Morgana." Cold, unrelenting dread settled in my bones. "But then who am I supposed to wake, if she's beyond the veil?"

Graham chuckled. "The Lady cannot die, my dear, for she is immortal. She's been in a slumber, waiting for someone to call on her so that she may return."

"How do you know so much about all of this?" I studied his features.

"I've always had a hunger for knowledge. Even as a boy, I couldn't get a hold of new books fast enough." His voice was light and playful, but the stiffness in his shoulders told a different story. He was keeping something from me.

"So the ring is used to part someone's soul from their body," I said matter-of-factly. "But how is it supposed to bring The Lady back?"

"There's a charm on the ring, necklace, and sword," Graham explained.

"The inscription?"

"Yes. When all three are read together by someone who bears the mark of Merlin's blood," he said, motioning toward my necklace. "The Lady will wake and be brought back to this world."

"Matty said something about needing two hearts to wake her. He thinks that my connection with Robert, that the *Artognou* is really what will wake The Lady and not just me."

"He's correct, you need two hearts within one soul to create enough Magic to wake her. Had Robert never saved you, the Bond between you never would've formed and you wouldn't be able to wake, The Lady.

"Does Robert know all this?" I looked up from the ring.

"No." Graham sat back. "I was planning on telling the both of you before you walked out tonight."

"I'm kind of glad you didn't tell him," I said, my voice hesitant like I'd swallowed a rock.

"Because of Lila?" Graham guessed.

I nodded. "I want to trust him, but with her underfoot, I just can't."

"Can't or won't?" His eyebrow shot up on his forehead.

"You think I *should* trust him?"

"As a Soothsayer, you should trust your intuition, of course," he said matter-of-factly. "But, your connection to Robert, your *Artognou* should have the final say. From what I felt, he has nothing to hide from you."

"Maybe. But things aren't always what they seem." I tried to reason.

"True, but if you can't trust the ones around you, then Morgana's already won." He stood and poured himself another cup of tea.

"And you wonder why I can't sleep at night." I leveled my eyes on him. Every time I thought we'd gotten a handle on things, another puzzle piece made itself known.

"I have faith that you'll make the right decision." Graham's smile was probably meant to be reassuring, but the fear in his eyes spoke volumes.

"I wish I could say the same." I undid the latch on my grandmother's necklace and slipped the ring around the chain. Fastening the necklace back in place, I concealed the ring and pendant beneath my shirt.

"There's one more thing," Graham added, squinting his eyes in an apologetic expression.

"Yes," I said through mostly gritted teeth.

"You'll want to direct The Lady to me when the time comes."

"I thought you said I'd be lost to The Lady?"

"I can't pretend to know what the prophecy means, but we both know you're stronger than anyone gives you credit for." He gave me a warm smile. "And in case you manage not to lose yourself, I'll be able to help."

CHAPTER TEN

I dragged myself out of bed and made my way downstairs. For the first time in my life, I understood why people needed coffee in the morning.

"Do you think you could spare another day?" Graham asked as I sat down and joined everyone else at the table for breakfast.

Robert eyed me, his brow furrowing in concern. I was always the first one up and ready to take on the day, but today I wished I could stay in bed for a week.

"I'm fine with staying. I actually wanted to do a little more research in your library, if that's alright with you," Matthew replied with more than enough enthusiasm for all of us. Clearly he had gotten a good night's sleep.

"Of course," Graham said, lifting his coffee mug in consent.

"If Matty's staying, then I don't see why we can't." I shrugged innocently and poured myself a cup of coffee.

I was actually hoping we'd get to stay a bit longer. After the midnight rendezvous with Graham, I was a little suspicious of him. Sure, he was incredibly helpful and acting like a perfect gentleman, but he was hiding something. Staying would allow me to try to get a read on him.

"Fine by me," Robert said, taking a sip from his mug.

"Wonderful. I can teach the two of you how to tap into your *Artognou-Magic*," Graham concluded. He sat up straight and smiled from ear to ear.

"And what am I supposed to do?" Lila huffed.

Graham gave her a pointed look.

"You can make yourself useful by helping me with research," Matthew chimed in.

Lila shared a look with Robert, who nodded once. "The library it is," she sighed.

Narrowing my eyes, I watched Lila and Robert silently communicate. *And Graham wondered why I had a hard time trusting Robert?* I thought.

"When you're ready," Graham interjected before the tension in the room exploded, "I'll be out back." He patted my back twice, and I almost spilled my coffee.

"You up for this? You're looking a little worse for the wear," Robert whispered, leaning in close to me.

"Why don't you just drink your coffee." I was in no mood to be coddled, especially by Robert. Grabbing a piece of toast off the ceramic plate at the center of the table, I took a bite and made my way upstairs to change into something more suitable for Magical training.

I finished the buttered toast and coffee while I changed, then met Graham outside. The backyard looked much like the front. There was a small open space covered with red, orange and yellow leaves that had already begun to fall for the winter. Large trees sprung out of the ground at intervals, though there didn't seem to be any discernible fence or property line.

"I trust you slept well after our conversation last night," Graham began.

"Hardly. Matty snores louder than a 747 during take-off," I lamented as I threw my hair into a ponytail. "What did you end up doing the rest of the night?"

"Just some light reading." He waved his hand casually.

"Something tells me you weren't reading a Danielle Steel novel."

"Don't knock it until you've tried it," he laughed.

"Until you've tried what?" Robert asked as he lightly jogged to where we were standing.

"Nothing," I said with a chuckle.

"Right, shall we get started?" Graham rubbed his hands together in excitement. "You have very powerful Magic between the two of you. The first step is learning how to tap into that Magic. Then we'll work on control."

Robert studied Graham carefully. "I thought there wasn't much knowledge on the topic."

"There isn't. But from my extensive research, I believe I can guide you in the right direction," Graham replied quickly.

"How do we start?" I chimed in. The coffee was starting to kick in and I was antsy to get moving.

"You're surprisingly okay with all of this," Robert noted and turned to look at me.

"And you're surprisingly cranky," I shot back.

He pursed his lips, let out a heavy breath. "Alright, how do we do this?"

"You're going to need to join hands. Until you've learned how to connect and control your *Artognou*, you'll have to have a physical connection to one another," Graham explained.

I reached out my hand and Robert took it. Even though it was cool outside and my own hands were freezing, his hand felt warm as he laced his fingers through mine. A hunger stirred inside me that I wasn't entirely sure had anything to do with Magic.

"I'll get the connection started." Graham lifted our joined hands in his own and closed his eyes.

The rush of Magic almost knocked me to the ground. It was like drinking an entire pack of Redbull. The blood in my veins hummed just beneath my skin, leaving me feeling resilient and uniquely alive. My heart accelerated and my Magic ached to be released as a vision started pulling at me. Putting up my wall, just like my aunt taught me, I hoped that I could block out whatever was trying to break through. I'd only ever succeeded once, but now was not the time to get sucked into another time or place.

Focusing on the here and now, I let the barrier in my mind surround me and to my surprise, I was able to keep the vision at bay. Making a mental note that there might be something to see later, I pushed the thought to the back of my mind.

"Right, I need you to focus on the *Artognou*. How it feels, where it's coming from within and how it flows through both of you," Graham instructed.

Between my training with my aunt and the Maxwell's, I was able to pinpoint exactly how the *Artognou* felt different to my own Magic. It was deeper, ancient. My Magic felt uniquely a part of me, but this felt bigger, like I was somehow linked to the stars and every living thing all at once. My limbs felt heavy and electric as the *Artognou-Magic* pulsed under my skin. My head spun and my heart beat against my ribcage with the force of a jackhammer.

"I'm going to let go now. I want you to try to hold on to the Magic," Graham said.

He gave our joined hands a final squeeze, then released us. Within half a breath, the *Artognou* faltered inside me. Digging deep, I was able to grab onto a few threads before it receded into the darkness. Keeping a hold on our Magic as tightly as I could, I focused on the connection running through every nerve in my body.

Standing side by side with Robert and practicing Magic with him reminded me of the first time he'd showed me how to summon a shield. I smiled at the memory. So much had changed from that moment to this one. I held onto the feeling of that first memory and used it to tether the *Artognou* to my own Magic like a lifeline.

Robert let out a small gasp and said, "I can feel you, your Magic. It's different from my own." His voice startled me.

"Good." Graham's voice was filled with pride.

A strangled grunt escaped Robert's throat and he let go of my hand.

"Are you okay?" I asked as his features crumpled into a pained expression. I stepped toward him and reached out to touch his shoulder, but he flinched away. I recognized immediately what had just happened.

"You had a vision, didn't you?" I said.

Robert looked between Graham and me. "Is that what that was?"

"Now I know why you always looked so concerned when I first started having them. You look terrible." I laughed.

Robert took a deep breath and gave me a sarcastic grin.

Turning to Graham, I asked, "How is that possible?"

"The *Artognou* connects you. It allows your Magic to flow through one another freely. What you're feeling isn't some other form of Magic altogether. It's the counterpart to the Magic that's already inside you."

"So does that mean I have the ability to heal?"

"If Robert really did just have a vision, then I'd say it's safe to presume you can heal when you're connected."

I turned to Robert, excited. "What did you see?"

"Do you remember when you first asked me to teach you Magic?"

"My shield," I said under my breath, and chills ran up my arms.

"It's like I was there, watching it happen right before my eyes."

"I was actually thinking about that day. I must have triggered the vision."

"But why didn't Violet get pulled into the vision with me?" Robert asked Graham.

"I've been learning how to control them with Aunt Beth."

Robert ran a hand through his hair and said, "It's much more violent than I would have thought. Being pulled away from the present like that is unnerving, to say the least," he ruminated.

"Now you know why I was so freaked out when it first started happening."

Robert gave me an apologetic smile and nodded.

"Wonderful, shall we try again?" Graham said as he clapped his hands together and smiled from ear to ear.

"Yeah, let's give it another go." Robert turned to face me and grabbed my hands with his own. The corner of his lips turned up in a half smile as his eyes melted into mine.

Graham stepped forward and placed his hand on ours once more. I could feel him searching for the connection before he brought it to life inside of us. It was like being struck by lightning. My hands shook in Robert's. Adrenaline pumped through me and I fought to stay in control.

Graham lifted his hand off ours, and the *Artognou-Magic* wavered like a leaf on the wind. Reaching after it, I couldn't quite grab hold. As it slipped through my fingers, I felt something different for a fraction of a second. A warm and inviting presence swirling in the pit of my stomach. It reminded me of what being healed felt like.

I let go of Robert's hand and he sighed, looking defeated.

"I think I felt you that time," I said.

Robert's head snapped back up at me.

"It was the same warmth that spreads through me when you use your ability," I added.

"You didn't hold the connection very long this time," Graham interrupted us. "Let's try again."

Again Graham helped bring the *Artognou-Magic* to the surface. Once he was certain we had a handle on it, he let us go.

Gripping Robert for dear life, I was already starting to feel drained, but it was important that we learn how to use our Bond. Without it, we'd never be able to wake, The Lady and defeat Morgana.

This time we held the Magic between us until Graham told us to let go.

Despite the cool air, I was starting to sweat with exertion. Using Magic still didn't come naturally to me, and this was a whole other level of difficulty.

"Now that you're able to maintain the connection, I want you to try to bring it to the surface without my help," Graham instructed.

"Maybe we should take a break," Robert suggested. Looking him over, he seemed just as spent as I was.

"Do you think Morgana is taking a break?" Graham's eyebrows rose unnaturally high on his forehead, making him look like a caricature of himself.

"Right." Robert turned to me with his hand outstretched. "Ready for another round?"

Hesitantly, I reached for his hand. I'd never seen Robert bend so easily to someone. Of course Graham had a point, but the fact that Robert didn't push back at all made me look at him differently. I'd always seen Robert as an authority figure, but now he was a student, just like me.

Lacing our fingers together again, I faced Robert and said, "I'm going to have to let my walls down if we want any chance of doing this on our own." He nodded in acknowledgment. "I don't know if anything will come through, so just be prepared." I shifted from one foot to the other and he smiled.

"Don't be nervous, we've got this," he said and shook my arms.

"Here we go." I looked between Graham and Robert, then closed my eyes to focus.

I pictured the walls I used to keep visions at bay and let them fall away, piece by piece. Summoning my own Magic was easy. It bubbled to the surface in seconds. Searching deeper for the *Artognou,* for Robert, came much more difficult. Briefly, I felt something tug at my torso.

"Robert," I whispered.

"I felt it too," he replied.

We gripped each other's hands a little tighter. I felt the tug again and this time my body reacted and I jolted upright.

"What is it?" Graham asked, sounding concerned.

"I don't know. It feels different. Like something's pulling at me," I explained.

"I can feel it too," Robert added.

The *Artognou* flared to life like a wildfire inside me and took my breath away. I held onto Robert as tightly as I could for support as the Magic built inside me.

Robert exhaled heavily, and it took all of my concentration not to give in to the Bond. The Magic wanted to be used and just like with my own Magic when I first got it, the untapped energy started bubbling over.

"Open your eyes," Graham instructed. His voice was soft and held an edge of pride.

Lifting my eyelids, I looked at Robert. His eyes burned with the same fire I felt inside of me. I grasped the connection with everything I had and took a step toward him. I'd never felt so energized, so powerful in all my life. Heat rolled off my skin and electricity crackled around us, making the hair on my arms stand on edge.

Robert's eyes left mine, and I followed their path above our heads. We were surrounded by white, swirling lights. Like shooting stars, the lights swirled around us impossibly fast, leaving a shimmering streak imprinted on the back of my eyelids.

"What is it?" I asked, mesmerized.

"It's a manifestation of the *Artognou,*" Graham explained.

"It's beautiful." I watched the tiny orbs of light fly around us and disappear like fireflies, blinking in and out of existence.

As the last one faded, so did my strength, and I locked my knees in place to keep from falling over. I was exhausted and every muscle in my body hurt. My hands shook as I let go of Robert and braced myself by putting my hands on my knees.

"Okay, now it really is time for a break," I huffed.

"That was amazing," Matty said from the back door on the deck.

Robert and I looked up at Matty, who was smiling down at us. Lila stood close by, and she looked like I'd just killed her kitten.

"Since they need a break, do you have a minute? I think I may have found something, and I wanna run it by you," Matthew said to Graham.

"Of course." Graham waved his hand, dismissing us. "Help yourself to the kitchen," he said as he walked passed us. "And great work. You'll make a fine Bonded pair." He smiled, but I saw ghosts in his eyes.

I couldn't help but wonder again if he had been Bonded at some point. But if he was, what happened to his other half? Several scenarios played through my head, none of them pleasant. Looking at Robert, I smiled at how exhausted he appeared and a lump formed in my throat. What if something happened to one of us? What if I really was fated to be lost to The Lady? Would Robert end up like Graham, alone and haunted by his past?

"Penny for your thoughts?" Robert's eyes caught mine, and I had to admit, it was frustrating that I wore my emotions on my face.

"Just wondering if there are any more Oreos," I said, trying to evade further questions.

"Mmhmm." Robert's lips formed a hard line, and he crossed his arms. Clearly he wasn't buying it.

Shrugging and climbing the porch stairs, I made my way to the kitchen. I didn't have to answer to him and if he wanted to stand outside and pout that was his business. Searching the pantry, I made it my mission to hunt down the bag of cookies and finish what was left of them.

I heard Robert shuffle into the kitchen behind me as I wrapped my fingers around the cookie package.

"Would you like something to drink?" Robert asked as he opened the refrigerator.

"I'll take a glass of milk if there's any," I answered.

"You know, you really should eat something a little healthier."

"Maybe so." I took a bite of one of the cookies. "But I figure I've only got so much time left, might as well enjoy the finer things in life." I smacked my lips.

"Violet, you can't think like that." Robert poured me a glass of milk.

I shrugged. "Just being realistic."

"So that's it, you're just going to give in without a fight?" He handed me the glass with a little more force than necessary, and some liquid spilled onto the floor.

"Of course I'm going to put up a fight, what do you think I'm training my ass off for?"

"You can train your body all you want, but if your mind isn't in the game too-"

"What're you getting so upset about?" I set the package of cookies on the counter, getting frustrated. Robert had no idea how hard I'd been working to get up to speed both physically and Magically. Who was he to judge my state of mind?

"This isn't a game, your life's at stake. Your life, Violet," Robert scolded.

"You think I don't understand that? You think I don't have nightmares about your little girlfriend tying me up and trying to kill me?"

He flinched at my words and his hands clenched into fists.

"This has nothing to do with Lila," he said, raising his voice. "This is about you and your fight. You think kickboxing and learning a few Magic tricks is going to save-"

"Oh, get off your high horse, Robert. You think now that you're back, things are just going to go back to the way they were? I don't have to listen to your every word. In fact, I've gotten on just fine without you."

I could feel my frustration bubbling to the surface and I knew I was letting things get out of hand. But I couldn't help myself. The *Artognou-Magic* had left my nerves fried, and Robert was really starting to frost my cake.

He scoffed and said, "When did you ever listen to anything I said?" He threw his hands into the air in frustration. Robert hardly ever lost his cool, so our Bond must be having the same effect on him.

"Are you kidding me? I gave up every ounce of privacy so you could protect me just because you deemed it necessary."

"Everything I've done has been an attempt to keep you safe."

"Keep me safe or keep me alive long enough to fulfill your precious prophecy?" The second the words left my lips, I regretted them. I knew Robert cared about me for more than just the prophecy and that his goal had always been to keep me safe and alive. It was a low blow, and I knew it.

He looked at me with glassy eyes. "You really believe that, after everything?" Every emotion was etched on his face like a map. Pain in his eyes, frustration in his jaw, loss in the high set of his brow. It was the first time since I'd met him that he truly looked vulnerable and my heart broke.

Taking a step toward him, I opened my mouth to apologize, but he closed the gap between us in one stride and pulled me into his arms. Our bodies pressed together and his lips came crashing down on mine. A bolt of lightning shot through me like an arrow and fire tore through my core. The *Artognou* had left our emotions raw and exposed, which only served to intensify the inferno building inside us.

Unable to keep my feelings at bay, I melted into him as his hand found its way into my hair. His lips felt soft against mine and as he deepened the kiss, every bone in my body melted. Giving into the desperate need that had broken loose when I let my walls down, I pushed myself closer to him. I didn't fully realize until that moment how much I missed the intoxicating comfort of his embrace.

Robert pulled away from me and held my chin in his thumb and forefinger. We were both a little breathless as he said, "Still think I'm in this just to fulfill the prophecy?" One side of his mouth pulled up in a smile and I had to fight the urge to kiss the smirk off his face.

Nodding was the only thing I could manage at the moment, which felt robotic and automatic after the heat of our embrace.

The sound of someone's knuckles on wood brought me back to reality. Robert took a step away from me and broke our gaze.

"Always playing with fire, aren't you?" Ethan asked. He looked me over and then punched Robert playfully.

"It's not like that," Robert said stoically.

"From where I'm stand-umph."

Elodie, standing next to her brother, elbowed Ethan in the ribs and said, "Will you behave for once. Whatever's going on, it's none of our business."

"Thank you," Robert said with a nod.

"Why ya always gotta take his side?" Ethan asked, eyeing Elodie.

"Because I actually like him." Elodie smiled, her bright white teeth contrasting with her warm complexion.

"Did you find any other leads on the P.O. you were looking for?" Robert asked, changing the subject.

"That's why we're here," Elodie started. "He was doing some research with Graham before he disappeared."

"You think Graham has something to do with this guy's disappearance?" Robert balked. I had to admit. I'd be surprised if Graham had anything to do with whatever happened to the P.O. they were looking for.

"It's more likely that it has something to do with Morgana," Ethan chimed in.

"We're just here to get some answers. Graham was the last person to have any contact with him," Elodie added, picking up where her brother left off.

"Things are starting to get bad, aren't they?" I asked.

On paper, I knew how important it was to wake The Lady and stop Morgana, but in practice, I was just starting to understand the devastation Magic could have on the world. All the attacks, the disappearances, they were starting to pile up. Each one a hammer blow to my heart. I was responsible. I was the one who needed to fulfill my destiny and end this war once and for all.

"Things have been better, but they haven't even begun to get bad yet," Ethan admitted, giving me a sideways smile.

"Morgana and Aiden are just warming up and it'll only get worse until we get you to The Lady," Elodie explained. She placed her hand on my shoulder in an attempt to reassure me, but the pit in my stomach only grew larger.

Robert looked me over and cleared his throat. "Why don't I help you find Graham?" he suggested. "I think he's with Matty in the library." Robert wrapped his arm around Ethan's massive shoulders and started toward the front of the house.

"You and Robert look to be on the same page again," Elodie told me once they'd left.

"Not quite."

She smiled. "You sure about that?"

"That," I started, referring to the kiss she and Ethan had walked in on, "was just emotions bubbling to the surface. We're still a long way from being on the same page."

"For what it's worth, I've known Robert a long time, and he's always been loyal to his heart. If you can't trust anything else, trust that."

"Thanks." I shifted uncomfortably.

"I should catch up with the guys. Lord knows they can't focus without me to keep them in line." She rolled her eyes, and I laughed as she bounced out of the kitchen.

Taking in the silence, I grabbed the bag of cookies off of the counter and propped myself up on the bench by the window. I popped another cookie in my mouth and ruminated on Elodie's words. I realized it was honorable that Robert always followed his heart. I just wasn't sure where his heart was leading him at the moment. My Magic nagged at me again and I recalled that I'd blocked a vision when Robert and I first tapped into our *Artognou.*

Letting the Magic take me, I closed my eyes, and the room began to swirl around me and morph into another place and time.

CHAPTER ELEVEN

"**R**obert!" I yelled as I ran down the hall toward the library.

"What is it?" Robert stepped into the hall. Arcane Magic flickered on his fingertips. Elodie and Ethan flanked him, weapons drawn, and Matthew and Graham froze mid-sentence.

"Morgana she… there's been an attack." My voice cracked as images of bodies and people screaming in terror flashed across my eyes.

"When?" Graham asked as he shot forward.

I tried to recall how urgent it felt. "It feels close, maybe a couple hours ago, although it might still be happening."

"Do you know where?"

I nodded. "Hurst Castle."

"Why would they lead an attack on a tourist destination?" Matthew wondered aloud.

"Because it's not just a tourist attraction." Graham's eyes widened in horror. "It's where the Ainsworth family operates. All the weapons they collect, the armor…" Graham searched the room for a moment and his eyes stopped on Robert. "Where's Lila?"

"I… I don't know." Robert hesitated. "She wouldn't have," he said, putting the pieces together.

Graham rushed out of the room, making a B-line for the backyard where Lila was last seen. We all followed, running down the hall.

Lila was still on the porch, leaning on the banister and staring off into the backyard, apparently lost in thought. She either didn't hear us coming or didn't care.

Graham grabbed her by the arm and whipped her around to face him. "You little snake. I knew they shouldn't have brought you here," he accused. Anger rolled off of him as he stared down at Lila.

"What're you-" Lila stuttered. Her eyes bounced to each of us as a mix of confusion and fear pulled at her features.

"Graham, she didn't do this." Robert tried to reason but didn't dare step in Graham's way.

"It was only hours ago that we discussed the Ainsworth family and now they've been attacked by Morgana and her men," Graham accused, tightening his grip on Lila as he pulled her closer to him.

"I… I had nothing to do-" she stammered.

"We'll see about that." Graham raised his other hand. Wisps of blue and green smoke formed on each finger as he reached toward Lila.

"Graham, stop this," Robert commanded as he took a step forward.

Reaching for Robert, I stopped him from getting between Graham and Lila. I wasn't sure what Graham was about to do, but the murderous glare in his eyes frightened me and I realized my intuition had been right. Graham played the fun father figure well, but there was a dark side to him too.

"If she didn't betray us, then she should have nothing to fear from, *ad veritatem,*" Graham reasoned. The coils of smoke edged closer to Lila as his fingers danced in front of her.

"It's fine." Lila put her free hand up to stop Robert from arguing further.

"Did you tell anyone about the Ainsworth's and their connection to Excalibur?" Graham asked the smoke roamed over her like snakes exploring their prey.

"No." Her voice sure and hard. The smoke pulsed over her body as we all watched in silence.

"Well? Is she telling the truth?" I asked, not sure how the spell worked.

"Yes," Graham conceded and released Lila's arm.

"You're not the only ones looking into The Tokens," she sneered. "It's entirely possible that Morgana figured it out for herself. It's not as if the Ainsworths are a family of nobodies. Everyone in the Magical world knows of their connection to the original Prophecy."

"It's possible, but the timing is suspicious, to say the least." Matthew eyed Lila like he didn't trust the *ad veritatem* spell.

"So it's safe to assume they have Excalibur now, right?" I crossed my arms to keep the hole in my chest from completely engulfing me. If they had the sword, there was no way we'd be able to wake The Lady.

"Yes, it would appear that way," Graham concluded. He looked away from Lila and made his way back inside.

I followed after him and he walked into the living room and turned on the television.

Every station was playing the same footage. The headline at the bottom of the screen read, *12 dead, dozens more injured at Hurst Castle.*

We watched the footage in horror. Smoke billowed from the castle grounds. Helicopters, firemen, police all converged on the scene trying to get a handle on the situation.

"It is unclear whether this was a terrorist attack or a robbery gone wrong. At this time, police are asking those in the area to stay inside while the search for the suspects continues," the stern male broadcaster announced.

"Why didn't you see this coming?" Lila turned on me.

"I don't always get to pick and choose what I see," I said through gritted teeth, even though I knew exactly why I didn't see it. The Soothsayer in my vision had warned me that our visions were being blocked.

"That's not good enough. We could have prevented this. We could have been there." Lila's anger bubbled over.

"Well, there isn't much we can do about it now, can we?"

Lila scoffed. "So they get the sword and kill a dozen- "

"Since when do you care so much about innocent lives?" I snapped at her.

"There's no use in arguing about-" Robert tried to cut in.

"Everyone is so quick to crucify me, but Violet doesn't see something this big and everyone's just fine with it?" Lila asked.

"A Soothsayer's gift is not for you to question," Graham scolded. "Visions are bestowed upon them when they are meant to-"

"But- "

"No. The fact that Violet didn't see this happening until after it occurred means she wasn't meant to."

"That's bullshit." Lila threw her hands in the air.

"Actually, there's something I should tell everyone," I admitted. Anxiety and guilt swirled in my chest as each second ticked by.

"What is it?" Graham asked, studying my face.

"When Robert and Lila first returned, I had a vision, or conversation through a vision, with another Soothsayer."

"Is that even possible?" Lila sneered.

"Soothsayers have the ability to communicate through visions, yes, but it's a difficult feat," Graham explained.

"She warned me," I continued. "That Aiden had found a way to block our visions."

"Why didn't you say anything?" Matthew asked.

"I wasn't sure I believed her. She was really cryptic, and for all I knew she was working with Aiden to get in my head."

"But how is it possible to block a Soothsayer's visions?" Robert asked. He moved to my side and placed his hand on my back, reassuring me.

"Haven't you learned by now that anything is possible? With Morgana back in the game, all bets are off. You're going to have to out think her if you're to have any chance of beating her," Graham warned.

"If she knew where to find the sword, then she'll go after the necklace too," I said and met Matthew's eyes. "Any news from your contact on the arrival?"

"Not yet," Matthew admitted.

"Then find out. Now." It was the first time I was giving an order as The Waker.

Looking back at the T.V., one of the helicopters was doing an aerial shot. White sheets lay in front of the castle, covering the deceased, and I felt like I was going to be sick.

"Be ready to leave within the hour. We need Jake and Brett's help if we're going to come up with a plan to get the necklace before Morgana," Robert ordered.

"You're going to need all the help you can get." It was Ethan who spoke up. "We'll come with you."

"I can't ask you to risk your lives," I argued.

"With respect, it's our lives, our decision," Elodie said matter-of-factly.

Everyone's eyes lingered on me as I nodded, accepting their help. Robert had wanted me to embrace being The Waker from the moment he saved my life. Finally, I was ready.

No more death would be in vain. There would be no more

loss because we were ill prepared. This was war, and we needed to start acting like it.

"Matty, reach out to the Ainsworths and see what the damage is," I said.

"Got it." He turned and left the room without another word.

Everyone turned their attention back to the T.V.

"Do you think they're alright?" Ethan whispered to his sister as they stared at the carnage.

"We can only hope." She laced her arm through her brother's.

"Something's not right about this." Robert looked away from the T.V. "Why would Morgana cause such a scene?"

"What do you mean?" Lila asked, her brow furrowed.

"Wouldn't it be better to steal the sword without any of us knowing about it? Why create a public spectacle?"

"Fear," I said without breaking my gaze from the screen. "She wants us to know she's five steps ahead of us."

"You think all that," Lila said, and waved her hand at the T.V. "was just to rub it in our faces?"

"It makes sense. I've only *seen* a couple visions of her and when you look at them together, she's telling a story. *I'm back and nothing will stop me, not even The Waker.*"

"It does send a stronger message than sneaking off into the night with Excalibur," Ethan chimed in. "If I was an evil genius, I'd make as much noise as possible to keep you on your toes."

"That's a lovely sentiment." Elodie elbowed Ethan in the ribs.

"As morbid as it sounds, he has a point. Another death in her name is nothing when you compare it to the list of people who died to bring her back," I noted.

"Lila, are you able to cook up some more of those potions you used to get us off of Avalon?" Robert asked.

"What are you thinking?" she asked without skipping a beat.

Studying Robert, I wondered what potion he was talking about.

"With Annabel out of the picture, we're going to need to get in and out of places quickly," he explained.

"What kind of potion are you talking about?" I asked, looking between the two of them.

"It mimics Annabel's orbing ability. It's not as precise and we'll need a full moon or another powerful natural occurrence."

"And you can make this potion quickly?" I asked, my forehead wrinkling with anticipation.

"With the right supplies, I can have it done in twenty-four hours." Lila nodded eagerly.

"I might be able to help in that department," Graham said and switched the T.V. off. "Come with me."

"Violet, try to get a glimpse of something, anything that might be useful," Graham added as he and Lila left the room.

"I'll try." I nodded.

"What do you need us to do?" Elodie asked, flipping a dagger in her hand with deft fingers.

"Get whatever info you came for and get ready to go," I told her.

"You got it, boss," Ethan replied.

Elodie and Ethan concealed their weapons and left the room, leaving Robert and me alone.

"We'll get the sword back," he said and placed his hand on my shoulder.

"I hope so," I replied, giving his hand a gentle squeeze before he walked away, phone in hand.

Needing some alone time, I dragged myself up the stairs. My feet felt sluggish as I climbed up to the guest bedroom and laid down. I felt like a cinder block had been laid on my chest as a wave of anxiety rolled through me. The only solace I took in any of this was the fact that I had the ring. Graham was right to keep it a secret from everyone else. Whether I could trust Robert or not, the fewer people who knew about the ring, the better.

~

Matthew decided to stay with Graham to do some more research and said he would meet us back at the estate in a day or two. Which left Elodie, Ethan, Robert, Lila and I to share one car all the way back to Pismo.

Robert exited the freeway at the first sign of a gas station and pulled in to fill up for the trip home. As he got out of the car, an awkward silence settled over the rest of us.

"I'm going to grab a bottle of water, do you want anything, Violet?" Elodie asked as she opened her door.

"I'm good, thanks," I said and gave her a small awkward smile.

"I'll help ya, sis," Ethan said, practically knocking Elodie over trying to get out of the car.

If I thought the silence was uncomfortable before, being in the car alone with Lila felt almost painful. I'd had dreams of what I'd do to her if I ever got her alone, and sitting quietly in a gas station was not one of them.

"I was hoping we'd get a chance to talk alone," she broke the silence.

"Oh, what about?" I asked, staring daggers at the back of her head.

"I feel terrible about the things I've done to you."

"So attempted murder doesn't sit well with you anymore?" I looked out the window at Robert, who was placing the nozzle into the gas tank and watching the horizon. I had a sneaking suspicion he was deliberately leaving Lila and me alone.

"There was a lot I wasn't aware of." Her voice cracked, and I wondered if she was actually upset at her father.

"So I've heard," I grumbled, and crossed my arms.

"But I want you to know, the second I found out what my father was really up to, I left." Her left arm rested on the center console and she twisted the ring on her pinky finger over and over again as she spoke.

"You and Robert both seem to think that your ignorance should give you a free pass." I adjusted my legs and shifted in my seat.

"I'm not saying that." She looked over her shoulder at me.

"Then what is it you're trying to say exactly?" I looked her straight in the eye. I was no longer the woman she'd tied up on the beach, and I would not back down from her.

"I don't know what you saw when you looked into my future." She dropped her eyes from mine as she adjusted the strap on her seatbelt.

Lila's limp body in my arms flashed across my eyes and I looked at my hands in my lap.

I sighed. "I don't fully understand what I saw in my vision, but I do know you're here to stay."

"I am. I have nowhere else to go."

The sadness in her voice struck a chord inside me. I knew what it felt like to have nothing left in the world.

"Even if you did have somewhere else to go, there's no way we would let you out of our sight now."

"Believe me, I know." She rolled her eyes and chuckled in an attempt to lighten the mood. When I didn't share in her laughter she continued, "And I know you won't believe me, but I really am on your side." She tried to look earnest, but I could tell she hated groveling.

"You don't have to bullshit with me, Lila." I looked up at Robert, who was still pretending to ignore us. "He's the only one who cares if you've changed."

She turned back around and looked out the windshield. "You don't give him enough credit."

A clipped, humorless laugh fell out of my mouth. "I don't need you to play peacekeeper between me and Robert."

"You may not like it, but he did what he had to so he could

get back to you." She took a deep breath. "He would have served as the last sacrifice to bring Morgana back, and I would have been collateral damage for speaking against my father." Her voice hardening with each word. "You may prefer that fate for me, but we both know it would cause you a great deal of pain if you lost Robert."

"Of course it would. I care for all the Maxwells," I said, giving her a pointed look as Robert circled around the front of the car.

"Don't bullshit a bull-shitter," Lila said as the driver's door swung open and Robert slid behind the wheel.

"Alright, we're ready to go then?" He tried to break the tension.

Lila turned in her seat and stared out the window as Elodie and Ethan climbed into the back next to me.

"So did you guys find out anything new on your missing P.O.?" I asked as Robert exited the gas station and made his way toward the freeway.

"Possibly." Ethan shared a look with his sister. She nodded once. "Annabel actually came up. Between her and the missing P.O., we think there might be a connection."

"Like what?" I asked.

Ethan shrugged. "I don't know. It's possible that Annabel is privy to something we don't know about."

"Our missing P.O. was researching lineage with Graham and Annabel's family came up in the data," Elodie said, clearing her throat as she removed a book from the bag at her feet and flipped to a bookmarked page.

"How so?" I asked, furrowing my brow as I tried to decipher how Annabel could be connected to this Promised One.

"It was just a mention of a distant relative, but it can't be a coincidence that she and the P.O. have gone missing in the span of a couple weeks," Ethan added, finishing his sister's thought as they often did.

"Do you have any theories yet?" Robert asked as he pulled onto the freeway toward Pismo.

"Not yet. But we're going to follow up on the family connection," Ethan replied.

"Alright, you keep working on it. Dig up everything you can on Annabel's family and the P.O."

"You got it, boss." Ethan gave Robert an excited smile as we made a left onto the one-oh-one south.

We spent the rest of the ride back to Pismo in silence and, personally, I was fine with that. It gave me time to think about Annabel, Graham, the ring, and Morgana. Things were starting to move quickly and as ready as I thought I was, Annabel being taken and the attack on Hurst Castle proved that none of us were ready for how serious things were getting.

Morgana had returned, and she was wasting no time. We needed to stop being petty with each other and start forming a plan. Fingering the ring Graham had given me under my shirt, I was thankful we were at least even with Morgana. She had the sword, but we had the ring.

I caught Robert's eyes in the rearview mirror, and a part of me wanted to tell him about the ring. But if people were able to operate outside of my visions, then I was blind to the truth and I needed to be careful who I trusted. The Soothsayer's words from my vision played in my head again as I leaned my head back and closed my eyes, *"You won't be able to see the danger until it is too late."*

Somewhere between dreaming and falling asleep, a vision snaked its way into my subconscious.

Moonlight illuminated the stone floor that formed under my feet. Annabel was still chained to the wall, her normally perfect blonde hair matted with blood and sweat. My vision moved in and out of focus like I'd been drugged when a scream echoed through the small space. Holding onto the wall, I tried to focus on the scene playing out in front of me. A flash of green light shot from the shadows and Annabel convulsed without making a sound. Running toward her, the vision tipped sideways, and I had to fight to regain control of my balance. This time, as I reached her, the figure in the shadows stepped into the pool of moonlight. Her piercing blue eyes shot through me as she cocked her head to the side.

"Had enough?" she asked and smiled right at me.

Kicking the seat in front of me, I was brought back to reality.

"Violet?" Elodie watched me like a wounded animal.

"What is it?" Robert quickly looked over his shoulder.

"Annabel." I forced her name from my lips.

Lila turned around in her seat and asked, "Is she-"

"No, she's still alive," I said, guessing what Lila was about to ask.

"But it's bad though, isn't it?" Lila asked.

All I could do was nod.

"Did you see anything useful, anything that could help us save her?" Robert asked.

"No, Morgana… she's taunting me. She isn't going to let me see anything that could help us."

Robert banged his fist against the steering wheel, making me flinch.

"Hey." Lila touched his shoulder. "She's still alive, hold on to that."

Robert pulled off the freeway and turned left toward the Maxwell estate.

"I'll talk to Jake, see how he's holding up." Robert let out a heavy breath. His eyes met mine in the rearview mirror, and I could feel the anger and frustration simmering inside him.

"And I'll get to work on the potions," Lila noted.

"What do you want me to do?" I asked, feeling helpless.

"We need you to try to have another vision." Robert turned in his seat to face me as he put the car in park. "If you can see something, anything…"

I nodded in agreement and said, "I'll do what I can."

CHAPTER TWELVE

e all filed into the house, Robert and I picking up the rear, and it was déjà vu all over again. His hand found the small of my back in the tight, dark hallway as he guided me into the estate's main hub.

Everyone disbursed, and I watched as Robert climbed the stairs to find his mourning brother. We all had our orders and now was not the time to reminisce and get sentimental.

I thought the pool would be a good place to relax and try having another vision, so I made my way to the backyard. But everything felt too quiet, too calm for the turmoil raging inside me.

Bending down, I let my fingers dance in the water. The normally heated pool felt cold and uninviting. There was no way I could find my center while shivering to death. I paced across the backyard and sat down on the swing bench. It creaked under my weight and again I found myself thinking about times gone by. A vision of Annabel in her wedding dress smiling as Jake leaned down and kissed her filled my head. So much of my life contained memories of the Maxwells now. They were like family and one of them was missing. Unable to focus on anything other than my own grief, I needed a surefire way to clear my head.

A pair of seagulls flew over me and dove toward the ocean. The waves crashed on the rocks and threw water into the air before receding and repeating the pattern again. Just watching the water move back and forth started calming my frazzled nerves and eased the pain in my heart. I needed to be down there. I needed to feel the force of the water pounding against the shore.

Heading to the gate set in the far corner, I made my way down the stone stairs. Kicking off my shoes, I ran down the steps two at a time. As my feet touched down on the cool sand, I dug in and made my way to the shore. The salty air assaulted my senses and as I neared the water, the spray of the waves crashing in front of me reached the tip of my nose. Taking a deep breath, I sat down and faced the vast Pacific Ocean.

You'd think I'd fear the ocean after almost drowning, but I still found something inviting about the sea. The constant ebb and flow, the fresh humid air. It grounded me and I felt the heaviness in my chest lighten.

"Violet," Brett yelled over the roar of the waves. "Thought you might like some company." She jogged up to me.

"Sure, thanks." I pat the sand beside me. "How'd'you know I'd be down here?"

She sat down next to me and handed me a mango flavored water. "I saw you bolt down the stairs, thought I'd check on you."

"Thanks." I nudged her with my shoulder. "How's Jake doing?"

"Honestly, he's not holding up too well. He needs something to do soon or he'll go after Annabel on his own."

"Well, he just might get his wish."

Brett tilted her head to look at me. "What's that supposed to mean."

"Morgana has Excalibur." I was unable to look her in the eyes.

"That would explain everyone's dour mood."

"I don't know what we're going to do." I kept my eyes on the waves rolling toward the shore.

"Violet, it isn't your fault she beat us to the punch." She squeezed my shoulder to reassure me.

"I know it isn't, but I'm supposed to stop her. I'm supposed to put an end to her reign."

"And you will. This isn't over yet."

I looked up at the sky, closed my eyes and sighed. "I just wish there was more I could do. Annabel's being tortured, people are dying and we're learning Magic tricks in the forest."

"Man, you and Robert really are cut from the same cloth." Brett shook her head. "Give yourself some credit. You can't take the world's problems onto your shoulders alone."

Letting out a heavy sigh, I felt the guilt ease a bit. Of course Brett was right, but being objective and level-headed wasn't one of my strong suits.

"So, now that we have that out of the way, what's really eating at you?" Brett asked in a more leisurely tone.

I looked up at her and bit my bottom lip. The ring around my neck felt like a ten-pound weight and I felt the urge to tell her, even though I knew I should keep it secret.

"I have information." I let out another heavy sigh, "but I'm not sure I should share it with anyone just yet."

"Well, I don't know what it's like having your gift, but I know Bethany is very cautious when it comes to sharing anything, with anyone. Maybe you could talk to her about it."

"She won't help. She's all about trusting your intuition and learning to hone your gut feeling." I rolled my eyes and Brett chuckled.

"I know that look. When I was in training, my mentor used the same sort of line on me and it drove me mad."

"If I ever start sounding like that, slap me, please," I laughed.

"It's a deal." She gave me one of her rare smiles. "And whatever this information is, trust yourself. You're more in tune with your Magic than you give yourself credit for."

"Maybe you're right." I thought about the old woman and her warning about trust, but looking at Brett, I knew I trusted her with my life and if I could put my life in her hands, then I could trust her to keep this secret.

"Graham gave me the Ring of Dispel," I blurted and pulled the ring from its hiding place. I knew I had to tell someone, and right now Brett was one of the few I trusted more than anyone.

Her mouth fell open and her eyes widened in shock. "The others don't know?" It was more of a statement than a question, and I shook my head in answer.

A wave crashed on the shore as I swallowed my nerves.

"You're sure it's *the* ring?"

"Yeah, I can feel it." Chills ran down my skin and I pulled my knees against my chest.

"Why are you trusting me with this?"

I shrugged. "Through everything that's happened, since I was attacked after the wedding to the battle on the beach, you've always fought to keep me safe. And when I thought about telling you, the words just sorta spilled out. I guess my intuition thinks it can trust you."

A nervous chuckled escaped her throat. "I don't know whether to be glad or frightened to be in cahoots with you."

"Gee, thanks." I snorted and felt the mood lighten. Telling Brett made me feel like I wasn't alone in this. It might be my destiny to fulfill, but doing it alone was never going to work.

"I promise I won't say a word." The ocean breeze tossed her hair and a secret smile crossed her lips.

"No pillow talk either," I said, knowing it would be difficult for her to keep something this big from Matty.

"My lips are sealed." She mimicked zipping her mouth shut and throwing away the key.

Leaning back on my elbows and closing my eyes, Brett and I sat in a comfortable silence. The sound of the tide rising and falling washed over me, making me feel lighter and less burdened.

It had been awhile since I'd been able to sneak away and enjoy the beach without being reminded of what was at stake. With each break of the salty seawater on the sand, a layer of tension rolled off me.

Tiny dust motes danced behind my eyelids. Each time I tried to follow their path they would jump at the movement of my eyes until they began to swirl abnormally and the darkness, giving way to images. A huddle of men formed before me and I realized that someone, somewhere, wanted me to see this.

"The time has come to embrace who we are and flee from the shadows," Morgana said, her voice rising above the crowd of spectators surrounding her.

"No longer will we hide our Magic. No longer will we be afraid of who we really are."

A few people in the crowd clapped as concerned grumbles made waves through the men.

"You sir." She pointed one long finger toward a gentleman in a black t-shirt and jeans. Dirt and dust covered his clothing and stains ran the length of his pants. He looked from side to side and then pointed at his chest.

"Yes, you." Morgana smiled as she walked toward him. The crowd parted and circled around the two of them. "Tell me, what is your name?" She placed a finger on his chest and made a design down his torso.

"Anthony," he stammered.

"And Anthony, aren't you tired of working so hard with your hands when you could use Magic?" Her head fell back, and she looked directly up at him.

Anthony licked his lips nervously. "I mean, I guess so." He shrugged. "Yeah." He rubbed the back of his neck.

"Then what's stopping you?" She almost purred and pushed herself a little closer to him.

His Adam's apple bobbed up and down. "Well, uhh..." He looked from side to side. "It's not allowed."

Morgana stepped away from him with a wicked smile on her face. "Oh, and are you a good little pet and always do what you're told?" She batted her doll-like lashes over her big blue eyes, a move the men seemed to fawn over.

"I'm no one's pet," Anthony growled and puffed his chest out like a proud pigeon.

"Then prove it. Show everyone you're not afraid to be who you are." Morgana rushed back to him in a few short steps. "Show them you'll no longer play their little game of hide and seek."

She was working them up and twisting them to her will. One man yelled out, "Yeah!" and started clapping. Another threw his fist in the air and said, "I'll show them!" And then they all started cheering.

Morgana stood in the middle of the circle of men, arms crossed and a deadly smile on her maroon lips. They were hers with just a few short words. Whether she was bewitching them or just providing them with a message they could stand behind, I couldn't be sure.

Morgana's expression changed and as if on cue, the men simmered down and waited with bated breath for Morgana to speak again.

"Will you fight with me, then?" she cooed and stepped toward one of the men, an innocent look in her eyes and a flirtatious pout on her lips.

He nodded, and all the men cheered.

Morgana squinted and a dark mischievous expression replaced the damsel in distress look she'd been wearing so well. "Will you fight to free the Magical world?"

A thunderous roar exploded from the men.

"Who among you will step forward?" She swung her arms open wide, gesturing to all of them, "And claim their place in history?"

Anthony, the dusty, tall man she had coaxed into obedience, stepped toward her and said, "I will," with a ferocious growl.

Morgana pulled a crude- dagger from the inside of her boot. Holding the dagger with one hand and pressing the tip of the blade against the index finger of her other, she stepped toward Anthony and said, "Take off your shirt." She bit her lip, and a breeze rustled her skirt as she looked him up and down.

Anthony lifted his shirt over his head, revealing a muscular torso, and threw the wad of cotton into the dirt. His thick muscles made it clear he was used to working with his hands. Morgana pressed the tip of the dagger near his collarbone, then dug in and began to brand him.

Anthony's jaw clenched, but he kept his gaze glued to something off in the distance. Not once did he make a sound as blood dripped down his chest and collected at the hem of his jeans.

Stepping to the side to get a better look at what Morgana was carving into Anthony's skin, it took me only a fraction of a second to recognize it. It was the same symbol my parents bore when they were killed. And it was the same symbol that brought Morgana back from the dead.

Morgana placed the palm of her hand against the bloody wound. "Hoc est corpus," she began, reciting a spell. The sound of skin sizzling filled the air. "Et ad sanguinem." Her voice rose as she finished the incantation and removed her hand from his chest. Where a fresh wound had been moments ago, now just an angry red scar remained.

"Who's next?" Morgana looked around the circle. As each and every one of them stepped forward, the scene in front of me pitched sideways and disappeared into a blur of red, until I was staring at the back of my eyelids again.

Sitting up and putting my head between my knees, I took a few deep breaths to get rid of the dizzy spell that followed my vision.

"Are you alright?" Brett put her hand on my upper back.

"Yeah, just a little dizzy," I lied.

"What was it, Morgana?"

"She's gaining support in large numbers."

"Did you see Annabel at all?" Brett's voice sounded eager and filled with hope.

"She wasn't there." I shook my head. "It was just Morgana recruiting more people to her side. She wants us to see her gaining strength."

"A game of chess it is then." Brett's eyes narrowed and her jaw tightened. "We need to get one step ahead of them and stop reacting."

My phone rang, interrupting us. "It's Matty," I said, glancing at Brett. "Hey Matty, you're on speaker with me and Brett. What's up?"

"We have a date and time to swipe the necklace," he said through the phone.

"Really? When?" Finally, we could take action on something and get ahead of Morgana.

"Two days."

"That doesn't really give us a lot of time to plan." Brett echoed the words in my head.

"We'll be fine. I've already mapped out a plan for us," Matty reassured us. "And we'll have almost a full moon. It's not perfect, but it should get the job done."

"What exactly do you mean when you say 'us'?" The tone in Brett's voice was one only a significant other would use when they didn't agree with the other.

"We're not arguing this again, Brett. I'm the only one who's been there before, you'll need my help to get in and out quickly."

"But if something goes wrong."

"It won't," Matthew said with a degree of finality. Brett backed away from the phone in response.

"I'm going to head down shortly and then we'll all head out," Matthew continued. "I have a friend in L.A. who owns a hotel close to the library. He's already set a few rooms aside for us."

"Sounds good, we'll notify the others. Anything else we should know?" I asked.

"Keep your guard up. The closer we get to gathering all the tokens the messier it's going to get."

"Will do. Travel safe and we'll see you soon." I hung up and turned to Brett. "I guess we should get a move on then." She looked like she wanted to shoot fire out of her eyes.

Some part of my brain wondered if she could actually set someone on fire with just one look. Maybe the Magical world was where that expression came from.

"We can't let Matty come with us," Brett practically growled.

"Brett, you can't-"

"You don't understand," she interrupted. "If anything were to happen to him..." Her voice changed from the drill sergeant I had become accustomed to, to a woman worrying after her man. It was a side I had only seen glimpses of, and it took me off guard.

"You know he's our best chance of getting the necklace, why are you against him helping us?" My brow furrowed as I studied her.

She looked me over and then hugged her knees to her chest and said, "I lost someone." She bit her lip and kept her eyes on the water. "He thrived on learning old Magic. The kind of spells that hadn't been used since Merlin, but one day it backfired."

"Oh, I'm so sorry." I placed my hand on her knee.

"He and Lila were working on a potion together," she continued, and the puzzle pieces started falling into place. "They kept it secret, knowing it was dangerous, and I'd force them to stop."

"That's why you hate Lila so much," I uttered. "She could have warned you."

She nodded her head. "They overestimated one of the ingredients and... he died almost instantly." She sat motionless as I waited patiently for her to continue.

"Robert tried to save him, but he was too late, he was already gone." She ran her fingers through her hair and took a deep breath. "Lila tried to apologize a million times," she scoffed. "But I couldn't forgive her."

"Jake said that Robert took Lila's side, but I don't understand how he could-"

"Because of Lila. She warps his sense of reality. He argued that I should forgive her, that it wasn't her fault and they both knew the risks."

"I'm so sorry, Brett." My heart broke as I watched her lip quiver.

"If they'd just told me... I could've-"

"You can't play the what if game."

"It was a long time ago, but I still miss him from time to time." Shaking her head, she squared her shoulders and her moment of vulnerability began to recede. "That's why I can't let Matty come with us. It's too dangerous and I won't risk losing him." Her voice was stern once again.

Standing up, I reached out my hand to help her up. "You have to believe in us. Believe that we're going to make it through this."

"I believe that you'll wake The Lady, but that doesn't mean Matty has to be in harm's way to do it." She stood and dusted the sand off her jeans.

"You know as well as I do, Matty is our best chance of getting in and out of the Library as fast as possible."

"I know," she sighed. "But maybe there's another way."

"Maybe, but if not, you have to let him come with us."

She nodded once, and we started walking back toward the house.

The truth was, she was right to worry about Matthew. Any of us could end up dead or captured. Annabel's imprisonment was proof that none of us were safe.

Walking back to the estate was a quiet affair. I was lost in my thoughts and by the set of Brett's shoulders, she was lost in hers. As we climbed the stairs, I paused and took in the view one last time before heading off to L.A. A nagging feeling in the pit of my stomach told me that nothing would be the same after this.

As we made our way into the house, the familiar sound of the kitchen sink running and pots and pans banging against the counter filled my ears. If I closed my eyes, I could almost pretend I was still at Annabel and Jake's wedding and all of this had been a dream, almost.

The kitchen was a sight to be seen. Lila stood at the helm directing Robert, Jake, Elodie, and Ethan with perfection. Robert was going through a pile of herbs overflowing on the counter, creating a sea of leaves and twigs. Selecting only tiny bits and pieces requested of him, he handed them off to Elodie, who mixed and ground everything with a pestle and mortar. Jake was at the stove, always the cook, mixing the ingredients into a large pot, a wooden spoon in one hand and a sifter in the other. While Ethan was bottling the muddy green liquid as it finished boiling down.

"Well, aren't you all the perfect little team," Brett said with condescension.

"Don't start, Brett," Jake growled, apparently not in the mood for another one of her attacks on Robert and Lila. "We all need to work together if we're going to have any chance of getting through this without losing someone else."

Brett opened her mouth to say something, but the words seemed lost on her tongue.

"Matty's on his way down," I said, changing the subject.

Robert looked up at me, a million questions in his eyes. "Everyone needs to be ready to leave when he gets here," I said. "Matty tracked down the date and time for the necklace."

"If Matthew was able to nail down specifics, then my father won't be far off either. We should expect company." Lila sounded hesitant, like she didn't want to bring up Aiden.

"Is that a warning or a threat?" Brett narrowed her eyes at Lila.

"It's a promise." Lila squared her shoulders and held Brett's gaze. "He wants the tokens just as badly as you do, and if you think he hasn't been keeping tabs on you, you're just being foolish."

"She's right. We need to be prepared." Again, I was shocked to be agreeing with Lila. But she had a point. We'd be idiots to think this was going to be easy.

"What should we be watching out for?" I asked Lila, but my eyes drifted to Robert for a fraction of a second and a small, quiet smile played on his lips.

Jake was right, we needed to work together, all of us, if we were going to make it out of this in one piece. I wasn't happy about Lila being here and I knew I would never fully trust her, but I was finally willing to use her skills and knowledge as an asset.

CHAPTER THIRTEEN

Matty spread out the map of the Huntington Library on the mahogany hotel desk. There were a few buildings clustered towards the north end of the property, but most of the grounds were landscaped gardens by the looks of it. We all huddled around the small table as Matthew went over the plan. We were going to enter from the west in groups, Jake, Lila and Elodie, Robert, Ethan and myself, with Brett and Matthew leading the way. Coming in from the west was probably the furthest away from the research library where the necklace was being held, but it also gave us the most cover.

"Alright, everyone knows their roles?" Matthew asked when he was done going over the plan.

We all nodded in acknowledgment as he distributed walkie-talkies to each of us, and we tuned them to the correct frequency.

"Let's do this," Brett said with determination and linked her fingers through Matty's.

Out of the corner of my eye, I saw Robert glance at their shared hands. I understood now why he was so cautious and wary of Brett and Matty's relationship. Just like Brett, he was stuck in the past.

"Ready when you are." I nodded.

We all joined hands and drank the green potion Lila and the others had made earlier. It tasted like dirt and rotten eggs, and a small part of my brain wondered if this would work.

Under her breath, Lila recited the spell and the hotel room lurched from under us and disappeared. Every part of me felt like it was being ripped apart, and I fought to hold on to Brett and Ethan's hands as we swirled through the darkness.

I hit the ground and my stomach rolled. I had to fight the urge to throw up, no part of me wanted to find out if the potion tasted just as bad coming up as it did going down. Taking a couple of deep breaths, my head between my knees, I regained my composure before opening my eyes.

"I think I prefer orbing." I wrapped my arm around my stomach.

"Sorry, I know it's a rough ride," Lila said, breathless herself.

"Everyone ready?" Robert asked, looking over our group.

"Let's do this." Ethan pulled his sword from its sheath. He may not have had Magic, but he was still a force to be reckoned with.

"Alright, everyone pair up and follow the plan exactly," Matthew ordered.

"Try to keep to the shadows, and if you see or hear anything, use the walkie-talkies," Robert barked.

The others followed their course toward the Research Library as I made my way toward Robert. "Ready?" I asked, sidling up to him.

"As I'll ever be." He nudged me with his shoulder and our eyes lingered a second longer than they should have. There was still so much unsaid between us. The kiss we shared in Graham's kitchen was like a ghost with unfinished business.

"Do you guys need a few minutes?" Ethan asked, his jovial

voice popping the fragile bubble holding Robert and me. As I turned to look at him, Ethan wiggled his eyebrows suggestively.

"Shut it, Ethan." Robert's his voice was laced with venom.

"Just saying, we could all die tonight. Might as well enjoy life while your heart's still beating," Ethan whispered as we moved through the shadows like creatures of the night.

"No one's dying tonight." Robert looked over his shoulder, his eyes narrowing at Ethan's words.

"Just trying to lighten the mood, brother. Relax." Ethan swung the blade in his hand and placed his arm over my shoulders, walking in step with me.

I shook my head. "You're just gonna piss him off."

"I know. It's half the fun." He smiled, and I couldn't help but chuckle at Ethan's easy nature.

The trees gave way, opening into a clearing. The moonlight illuminated the grass like a high school football field on a Friday night. We all shared worried looks, and then one by one made a run for it. It was too late to turn back, and we hadn't seen any signs of another living soul. Even our own group had disappeared into the night without a trace.

We soon made it under the cover of trees. A few buildings loomed up ahead at the top of a small hill. There was an asphalt walkway that I assumed took tourists on a marked path from one location to the next, but we were taking a less traveled route through the desert garden.

Every kind of cactus imaginable surrounded us. Some were on the ground, long and tubular or round like beach balls with spikes. Others were tall, looming over us like prickly scarecrows. Some had flowers blooming off of them in odd directions. I had to admit, it was beautiful.

Pausing for a moment, I leaned in to get a closer look at the delicate red flower growing off a sharp and crude cactus. The contrast reminded me of Lila, prickly and not something you wanted to spend much time with, but the flower was her softer side, the side that saved Robert and helped us get here tonight.

"This isn't exactly the time or place to stop and smell the roses," Ethan whispered in my ear and nudged me along.

Stumbling, I scraped my arm against a cactus and little pricks of blood popped up on my skin.

"Ow." I muffled a yelp.

"Come on, we're almost there." Ethan pushed past me and took the lead.

I grumbled, catching up to Robert as stealthily as I could. He looked down at me as I wiped the blood off of my arm. Without skipping a beat, he laced his fingers through mine. The warmth of his touch washed over me, stirring my heartstrings as goose-bumps crawled over my skin. His Magic poured into me and healed the tiny pinpricks left by the cactus. Giving my hand a gentle squeeze, he released his grip on me.

"Thanks." I cleared my throat before we continued on behind Ethan.

As I took my place beside Robert and Ethan, we scanned the perimeter of the research library. Not a single leaf was out of place. Everything looked calm, perfect. Too perfect. The prickling sensation of a vision crawled down my spine and even though I couldn't *see* anything, the feeling it left behind was unmistakable. Dread crept through my veins as I steadied myself. Something was wrong, and I was helpless to *see* anything.

Robert took a step forward, and I grabbed his arm.

"What is it?" he whispered. He searched the building in front of us, looking for something he might have missed.

"Something's not right." I did my best to keep my voice even despite the cold chill that had settled in my chest.

Ethan twisted his sword in his hand, making it arc in a fluid, almost invisible circle next to him.

"Did you *see* something?" Robert asked.

"Not exactly. It's more of a feeling. I don't think we're alone," I shared, letting my hand drop from his arm.

"You don't have to be afraid. The plan is solid."

"This isn't about fear," I snapped. I couldn't believe he was trying to pass off my apprehension as anxiety instead of intuition. "Take a look around. It's too quiet," I said, keeping my voice low. "Where are all the security guards?"

Robert opened his mouth to argue, but hesitated as he looked over his shoulder at the research library. I was right, and he knew it.

"She's got a point. I thought this place was supposed to have pretty tough security," Ethan agreed.

"It's supposed to." Robert searched the shadows again. "We need to proceed with caution. If you're right and we're not alone, this could get ugly."

"What's the plan?" Ethan asked, itching to get moving.

"See that door there?" Robert pointed to a set of double doors hidden half in the shadows. "That's our entrance. I'll go first. Once I'm inside, you and Violet follow behind me."

"Got it," he agreed.

"Make sure to keep to the shadows." He pointed out a path to the building that led away from the door and circled back around.

Ethan and I both nodded. Without further hesitation, Robert disappeared into the night. I kept my eyes on the door, waiting, hoping he would make it without a problem. My anxiety grew with each passing second and I wished I could get a glimpse of something, anything that might tell me how the night would pan out. What was the point of being a Soothsayer if I couldn't *see* anything when I needed to most?

I was ready to go after Robert when I saw the door crack open just enough to let him squeeze through.

"Let's go." I pulled Ethan along before the thick metal door sealed Robert inside.

Sticking to the path, we stayed well hidden until it was time to step into the floodlights surrounding the building. Looking for anything out of place, I squared my shoulders and made a run for the double doors half hidden in the roof's shadow. I twisted the knob, and it turned over easily, but as I pulled the door open and slipped inside, I found the darkness blinding.

Holding the door open for Ethan, we both snuck into the building. Robert grabbed my arm the moment the door *clicked* closed and pulled me behind a large crate. I heard Robert knock on the speaker button on his walkie-talkie to signal that we weren't alone.

"What is it, what did you see?" I whispered as my eyes adjusted to the darkness.

"Someone's here." He pointed ahead. A tall figure stirred in the shadows, too big to be Matty or Jake.

Wrapping his hand around mine, Robert pulled me toward the far wall into the shadows with Ethan trailing behind us, watching our back.

Two distinct knocks sounded from the walkie-talkie at my waist, signaling that someone in our group had the necklace.

Letting out a sigh of relief, I started taking a step backward when a ball of fire came flying towards us and blew the crates into a million tiny fragments. Wood rained down as a cloud of dust filled the room.

"Move!" Robert yelled, as a bolt of blue electricity shot toward us.

"Jake, get Matty out of here," Brett shouted, her voice exploding through the walkie-talkie.

"Watch out!" Lila warned from the other side of the warehouse. Robert and I both turned in the direction of her voice as a flash of green exploded just seconds after Matty jumped out of the way.

"Dammit, the potion," Matty cursed, and I noticed the broken glass and fluid at his feet.

"Matty, stay down and out of sight," Robert yelled.

We both made a run from our hiding place in the shadows.

"Robert, look out!" I yelled just as a man dressed in black combat attire jumped from a crate above us and landed on top of him.

Time to put my training to work, I thought. Taking one more step, I spun and kicked the guy off Robert. He tumbled and sprang to his feet, but I was quicker. Jumping in front of Robert, I threw my shield around us as Robert stood up and shot a stunning orb at the attacker. He flew backward and slammed into a concrete support beam, his body crumpling to the floor like a sack of bones.

My magic tingled inside of me and curled up in my chest, begging to be released.

"Let's go." Robert grabbed my wrist and pulled me toward Lila's voice.

Navigating through the stacks of crates wasn't easy. I felt like we were in a maze going round in circles. We turned another corner, and a bewildered looking man ran right into us. He fell down and threw his hands up in defense.

"Please, don't," his voice cracked as tears streamed down his face.

The warehouse shook under our feet.

"Guys, we could use some help," Brett called over the sound of concrete being torn apart.

"*Somnus.*" Robert waved his hand over the sniveling man, and he instantly fell asleep.

Sparks flew in unnatural directions like gravity was pulling them to a central location. Coming upon Brett, I realized that she was pulling the electricity from the air and forming a sphere of charged sparks above her head.

"I've almost got it. I need you to hold them off a bit longer," she said through gritted teeth.

Letting my Magic take hold, my shield rippled off of me and

wrapped around Brett with little effort. The energy humming through my body leapt in strength as Robert drew near. I looked over my shoulder as he brought up the rear of our group, and he nodded in acknowledgment. He could feel it too. The *Artognou* was bubbling to the surface in both of us, waiting to be unleashed.

Wind swirled around us as more and more people moved out from the shadows. We were outnumbered.

"If you're planning on doing something, I think now would be the time," I yelled over the crackle of electricity.

The sparks under Brett's control froze for a fraction of a second, vibrating in place as they waited for their commander to give them an order.

A shadow moved to my right and without hesitation, Robert threw his arm out. A cold blue light shot toward the attacker, but he jumped out of the way like a gymnast and smirked as he landed back on his feet.

Neon purple light exploded somewhere in front of me, drawing my attention away from Robert and his fight. The tangy smell of electricity and burnt wood clung to the air and made it hard to breathe as the hairs on my arms began to rise.

"Brett, what're-" I tried to say.

The warehouse shook with a force only Mother Nature could compete with. The sphere of electricity Brett had been collecting exploded in every direction and threw me off my feet. My back slapped into something solid as concrete and wood crumbled around me. A high-pitched ringing filled my ears, making it impossible to hear anything else as dust and debris clouded my vision. Something heavy fell on top of me, knocking the stale air from my lungs.

Laying in the pile of rubble, I tried to get my bearings and focus on standing up. Strong, gentle hands pulled beside me, lifting the heavy weight off my chest. I took a deep ragged breath, coughing up dust and smoke.

Robert's face came into focus above me as he helped me to my feet. His lips were moving, but I still couldn't hear anything. The ringing in my ears muffled out the rest of the world. He rested his hands on my shoulders and I winced.

As my eyes caught his, I could feel his warmth spread through me, healing my injured shoulder. How I ever got along without him always healing me, I'd never know. The pain in my shoulder eased until it wasn't there at all, and the ringing in my ear gave way to the sound of a building alarm. The place would be crawling with police in a matter of minutes.

"Thank you." I took a tentative step, unsure whether my legs would hold me.

A pile of rubble shifted on the floor next to me, and Brett appeared. "That's not quite what I meant to do," she admitted.

"You think?" Robert seethed as he reached out a hand to help her up.

"Like you were any help," she said, getting up on her own. Blood dripped from her hairline, but she didn't seem to notice the superficial wound.

"We should get out of here while we can," I advised. The warehouse had been destroyed. Every window was blown out, every crate shattered into a million pieces.

"Where's Matty," Brett replied as she dug the orbing potion out of her pocket.

I started to do the same when I noticed we were missing a few people.

"Last I saw him, he was over there." Robert nodded his head in the direction we'd come from.

"You left him?" Brett yelled.

Turning in a circle, I searched for anything that resembled a body.

"Matty? Where are you!" Robert yelled, an edge of fear in his voice.

"Robert, stop yelling, we have to go." Lila pulled at his arm.

Piles of rubble were beginning to shift as our attackers slowly got back to their feet.

"I'm not leaving him." Brett's eyes pierced right through me

I couldn't let her die alone looking for Matty. I started lifting pieces of wood off the floor and kicking debris out of the way. A hand grabbed my ankle, and I fell backward.

"Over here!" I yelled.

Brett lifted another couple pieces of wood off Matty's body as I got to my feet. Together, we hefted the last pieces of debris off him and I gasped. He looked like a victim in a horror movie. His face and shirt were covered in blood. His arm was twisted in an unnatural way and the veins in his neck looked purple and swollen against his pale skin.

Robert placed a hand on his chest, careful not to touch any of his wounds, and I could feel him pull on his Magic to heal him.

High heels echoed against the concrete, making all of us turn and crouch behind whatever we could find. Robert pulled Matty along with him. Only half healed but able to walk, he joined Robert hiding behind a fallen concrete pillar.

The crunch of pebbles under a boot clattered nearby, and I held my breath. A tiny gap in the rubble showed a black flowing skirt.

Morgana, I thought. Every muscle in my body tightened as I tried not to move.

"I want the necklace!" Morgana yelled.

She turned, scraping the balls of her shoes against the debris and searching for an answer. No one said a word.

A guttural scream erupted from her mouth and the sounds of a freight train smacking into a wall boomed somewhere ahead of us. The tinkling of dust and rocks rained around us like heavy snow.

"Fine. Bring out the prisoner." Morgana sounded amused as

she took a couple languid steps away from me, her heels *click-clacking.*

The sound of someone whimpering and breathing heavily echoed across the room.

"If you won't speak up to save yourselves, maybe you'll answer to save her life," Morgana offered in a stern voice. "Bring me the necklace or so help me I will send her beyond the veil." Morgana snarled as she shoved a haggard-looking Annabel into an upturned crate.

"Show yourself, Waker," Morgana commanded. She barely looked human, hunting the room with predatory eyes.

Annabel screamed as her knees buckled and she fell at Morgana's feet.

"Don't test me."

I wanted to give myself up, to trade places with Annabel, but as I was about to step out from my hiding place, I caught Brett's eyes. Annabel wasn't the only person in this room I had to protect. I had to think about the others. I had to find a way to get all of us out of there in one piece.

"Fine," Morgana growled. "Boys." The shuffling of feet and rocks echoed around the room. "String her up." A low laugh resonated within her and she hurried away, her boots bouncing against the destroyed warehouse.

"No, please," Annabel cried out as several men dragged her to her feet and my resolve almost broke. How Jake managed to stay quiet, I would never know.

"Your callous actions, your missteps have led all of us here tonight," Morgana's voice boomed. "Like children, you play without knowing the real consequences of war." The sound of chains clanking together filled my heart with ice.

"Please, no!" Annabel screamed, struggling against her captors.

"But are you truly ready for the consequences?"

"Don't do this, please. I'll do anything!" Annabel cried out as two men pulled her arms above her head and tied her to the chains dangling from the ceiling.

"Too late." Morgana smiled like a school girl playing with a doll.

"Oh God," Annabel whimpered, the chains jingling as she struggled.

"Last chance," Morgana announced. "Come out or have her blood on your hands."

I couldn't let her do this. It was me she wanted, not Annabel, and I couldn't stand by and watch as Morgana tore her apart.

"Stop this, Morgana!" I yelled. My voice echoed in the silence, making me feel more alone than I'd ever felt in my life. I knew my allies were all around me, but when all was said and done, this fight was between Morgana and me.

"Show yourself and maybe I'll reconsider your friend's fate," Morgana offered.

I spotted Annabel dangling from the ceiling through the cracks in the debris above me, her body wrapped in chains.

"Violet, don't!" Annabel screamed through tears. "She's going to kill me no matter what."

"Silence," Morgana howled. Annabel swung slowly above us and as much as I wanted to help her, I knew she was right. There was no way Morgana was going to let her go, and I wasn't powerful enough to stop her. "What'll it be, Violet? Are you really willing to let her die for you?"

Swallowing the lump in my throat, I held my tongue.

"Fine. A game of hide and seek it is."

The shelving and plaster hiding all of us began to rise off the ground. I hesitated for a moment as the debris moved toward the ceiling, then rolled into what used to be an aisle. Large chunks of plaster, shelves, and crates all hung in the air effortlessly. Looking around for the source, I spotted Morgana in the rafters, her arms raised with a wicked smile on her face.

Slowly, everyone emerged from the rubble. Robert and

Matty's eyes were glued to Morgana. Ethan stood straight, searching for something or someone. Brett got to her feet next to me and Jake and Lila stood a few feet away, staring at Annabel, who still hung from the ceiling like a rag doll.

"There you are," Morgana cooed. Her eyes caught mine for just a second and then she threw her arms down and everything came flying back to the ground. Everyone jumped out of the way and tried to take cover.

"Now hand over the necklace or she dies."

I looked between Morgana and Annabel, trying to figure a way out of this.

"You can't have it, Morgana," Robert said, holding his ground.

Morgana moved her head from side to side like a bird watching a worm squirm. "How heroic of you to try to stand up to me, but it's the necklace I want and nothing else."

"I won't let you have it," I spoke up, forcing myself to make an impossible decision. No matter what happened here tonight, I had to leave with the necklace or I'd never be able to wake The Lady.

"Then the girl's death is on you." Morgana waved her hand at Annabel and my friend screamed out in pain. Her clothes tore and large lacerations appeared on her arms, legs, and chest as if someone had taken a dagger to her skin. Blood dripped from the open wounds and Annabel let out a whimper before passing out, hanging limply in the air. My stomach lurched.

Jake moved toward me, his face white as a sheet and his eyes so round I thought they might actually pop out of his head. Grabbing my hand, he placed something heavy and cool in my palm. I looked down at the necklace in my hand and then up at him. He couldn't want me to give it up, could he? I knew he loved Annabel, but would he really give up our only chance at stopping Morgana to save her?

"Trust me," he whispered, and his jaw flexed as he tried to keep his composure.

"Last chance before I finish her." Morgana pressed her lips together. She looked frustrated, like she thought it would be easy to manipulate us into giving her the necklace.

I searched Jake's eyes and saw no guilt, no hesitation, so I decided to trust him, hoping I wouldn't regret it later.

"Fine. You can have it." I took a step forward, holding out the necklace to show Morgana.

"Was that so hard?" Morgana batting her lashes and the corner of her mouth pulled into a grin that turned my stomach.

"First let Annabel go."

Morgana looked like I'd sucker punched her. "Do you take me for a fool?" She gripped the railing and pressed herself against the bars.

"Let her go and the necklace is yours."

Only a few feet separated our entire group. If I played my cards right, I might be able to get the rest of us out of here alive.

Morgana studied me for a long moment. Her crystal blue eyes tore into my soul, probing and searching for what my real plan was. I held her gaze, daring her to give in to my demands.

Without looking away from me, she waved her hand and Annabel began to plummet. Jake rushed to catch her and as Annabel reached his arms, invisible fingers plucked the necklace from my open hand.

"Now!" I yelled as Jake moved toward us, cradling Annabel. Lila threw Matty another vile and began reciting the spell as we each grabbed onto the closest person and downed the orbing potion.

CHAPTER FOURTEEN

"Put her on the bed," I said, throwing Matty's research to the floor.

I circled around the other side of the bed to make room for Robert. If he was going to have any chance of healing Annabel, he'd need to connect with her fast.

"You did this, didn't you? You told them we'd be there tonight," Elodie charged Lila.

"I had nothing to do with what happened." Lila held her ground with a ball of green electricity on the tips of her fingers.

"That's enough," Robert demanded.

Lila withdrew her Magic and stepped aside as Matthew made his way across the room toward us.

"How could you give her the necklace, we were so close!" Matty yelled.

"I had to. Did you want Annabel to die?" I snapped back.

"It wasn't the real necklace!" Jake yelled over everyone, silencing us all.

Before Jake could explain, a blood-curdling scream erupted from Annabel and she began to convulse under Robert's touch.

Blood stained her teeth and dripped from her mouth as Robert tried to soothe her.

Annabel's head lulled to the side unnaturally as Robert placed a gentle hand on her forehead. Closing his eyes, he tried again, and she screamed out in pain, her back arching up off the bed.

"Let her go!" Jake yelled at Robert. "You're making it worse." He pushed his brother aside and fell to his knees beside Annabel.

"If we can't save her with Magic, we're going to have to do it the old-fashioned way." I met Robert's eyes, and he nodded in agreement.

Turning to Elodie, I said, "Get down to the front desk and see if they have a first-aid kit."

She stared at Annabel, stunned.

"Go!" I yelled.

This broke Elodie out of her reverie, and she stalked toward the door and disappeared.

"Jake, I need you to get a bucket of ice and as much water as you can carry." I pointed toward the door. If anyone needed a moment to catch their breath, it was Jake.

"I'm not leaving her." He didn't bother looking up at me. His entire focus was on his beaten and bloody wife.

"Jake-"

"It's fine," Lila said, putting her hand on my shoulder. "I'll get it." She eyed Jake and Annabel thoughtfully and limped out of the room.

"Grab a glass too," I called after her.

"I don't understand." Robert kept his voice low as his eyes roamed over Annabel.

"We can't worry about it right now. We need to make sure Annabel's stable. Matty, I need you to get in touch with Harriet. There's this tea she made after I was attacked that helped with the pain and the rest of my bumps and bruises."

"Got it." Matthew nodded and moved without hesitation.

"Brett, go with him. Morgana and her men might not be far off," Robert said and glanced over his shoulder at his sister.

"Right, let's do this quickly. I don't want to be gone too long," Brett replied, all business.

"Lead the way." Matthew reached for Brett's hand.

"Maybe you should clean up first," Brett suggested.

"Right," Matty replied, looking down at his blood-soaked shirt.

As Matthew got changed, Elodie rushed in the room, a large plastic box tucked under her arm.

"Here you go." She handed me the kit before sitting on the edge of the second bed. "Is she going to be okay?"

No one answered. What could we say? Without Magic, Annabel might not survive what'd been done to her. As brutal as Morgana was tonight, it paled in comparison to how Annabel had been treated while being held hostage.

"Be back as quick as we can," Matty yelled as I heard the door open and close again.

Tearing into the emergency kit, I searched for gauze, tape, pain meds and alcohol. I gently rolled Annabel's head to the side, and she coughed, spitting up the blood filling her mouth and throat.

Lila returned with a bucket of ice, towels and several bottles of water.

Sorting through the medicine, I found a couple packets of pills marked *Pain Reducer* and emptied all of them onto the nightstand. I was about to grind them down with the bottom of one of the water bottles when Robert reached out to stop me. Picking up the pills, he closed his hand around them and hot blue light pulsed for half a second. He opened his palm, and I saw that the pills had been turned into a powder.

I cracked the seal on one of the water bottles and poured some around the corners of Annabel's mouth to wash away the blood. Looking up at Robert, I nodded, and he gently pulled her bottom lip down and let the powder coat her tongue, while I poured a little water in her mouth.

She wasn't swallowing on her own, so Robert had to coax her throat to get the concoction to slide down her esophagus. She started coughing and spitting up water, so Robert held her mouth closed and forced her to swallow the medicine.

We gave her a minute's reprieve as I got my gauze and tape ready.

"Where did you learn how to do this?" Robert asked as he watched me tear the gauze into strips.

"When I was a girl scout, we joined a few other troops and did a big survival skills trip every summer."

A small smile pulled at the corner of Robert's mouth.

"Hold her head up for me?" I said.

Robert gently placed his hands around the nape of Annabel's neck and lifted her head from the bed. There we found a large open wound filled with debris. I didn't even want to think about the kind of torture she'd endured. Rage boiled in my blood and I made a silent promise to myself that I would tear Morgana apart for putting Annabel through hell.

Pouring the rest of the water bottle onto the open wound to flush it out, blood, plaster, and water spread across the bed and seeped into the white bedsheets. I dabbed around the wound with the coarse hotel towel in an attempt to clean her up.

"Give me the alcohol." I motioned to the bottle next to Robert.

"Be gentle," Robert advised. "If she can feel anything, it's going to burn like wildfire."

Nodding, I unscrewed the cap and tentatively poured a couple drops on the wound. Not a sound came from Annabel, and somehow her silence was worse than all the screams in the world.

"Please don't give up, Annabel," I pleaded, my words barely a whisper.

Packing the wound, I wrapped a bandage around her head to stop the bleeding and keep the gauze in place. Robert placed her head back down, removing the damp crimson pillow that had served as our surgery table.

With her head wound out of the way, we set to work on the rest of her body. Robert and Jake cleaned and wrapped the gashes across her arms and legs while I spread antibacterial cream on her chest and bandaged the angry laceration.

Once we'd finished doing everything we could for her, I pulled my duffel bag from the closet and stared down at a pile of clothing. Riffling through my t-shirts and jeans, I found an oversized shirt I liked to sleep in and a pair of sweats that would allow Annabel's injuries to breathe.

"Violet?" Elodie whispered, leaning against the closet.

"Yeah?" I looked up at her while I stuffed everything back into my bag.

She nodded toward the bathroom.

I looked around the room. Jake was using one of the towels to clean the dirt and grime off of Annabel, and Robert was making himself busy cleaning up the large amount of trash we'd accumulated.

I nodded at Elodie and we went into the bathroom. Closing the door behind us, she leaned against it so no one could barge in.

"I was wondering, well, I don't really know how to put this," she whispered.

I turned on the faucet to cover up our voices. "Put what?" I asked. She kept her eyes on the ground like she was ashamed of what she was about to say.

"Elodie, what is it?"

"I don't mean to question your judgment, but do you really

think that Lila should be here? She could be the reason we were ambushed tonight." Elodie choked on the last word.

I sighed. "I really hope not. We have enough on our plate without having to worry about Lila."

"Can't you *see* anything?"

"I can't get a clear picture of anything right now," I said, anxiously wanting to get back to Annabel.

"Do you think maybe we should separate her from the group? Try to get some answers out of her?" Elodie crossed her arms, a shadow of determination settling across her features.

"Tread lightly. Robert isn't going to take too kindly to anyone tearing into her," I warned.

Part of me felt the same way Elodie did, but I couldn't shake the feeling that tonight had nothing to do with Lila. Sure, she was dangerous and could very well be the reason Morgana knew exactly where to find us. But the Soothsayer in me didn't buy it. Something bigger than Lila was going on, and it scared me more than I cared to admit.

"Noted." Elodie pushed off the door and slinked back into the other room.

"Robert, why don't you let us get Annabel changed." I made my way back to her bedside.

"She's going to be alright, isn't she?" Jake asked. He wanted me to reassure him, not as a friend but as a Soothsayer.

I smiled. "She's gonna be fine," I said with as much reassurance as I could muster into my voice. I didn't have the heart to tell him that her injuries were substantial and that whether she was going to pull through or not remained to be seen.

Gently, Jake and I peeled her torn and bloody clothes from her bruised body and slipped the t-shirt and sweats on. There wasn't much more we could do for her until we had Harriet's recipe.

"Thank you," Jake said and clasped my shoulder.

"You don't have to thank me. It's the very least I can do." I gave his hand a gentle squeeze. He released his hold on me and sat down next to Annabel. Keeping his eyes on her like he was afraid death would sneak up from the shadows and take her if he wasn't paying close enough attention.

Exhaustion set in the moment I finished tending to Annabel's wounds and my own bumps and scrapes began to throb. I grabbed a random bottle from the mini bar and downed it in one shot. The clear liquid burned my throat and warmed my chest as I padded to the bathroom to wash my face.

Robert followed close behind me and said, "Thank you, for everything." His voice sounded uneven and when I looked up in the mirror, I noticed he had blood dripping from behind his ear.

"You're bleeding." I touched my own ear to indicate where he was injured.

He tapped the wound and his fingers came away bloody.

"So I am," he sighed.

"Can't you heal yourself?"

"I'm spent. I used everything I had left trying to heal Annabel."

I grabbed a towel from the rack and wet it under the faucet. "Go grab the rubbing alcohol."

Robert turned sluggishly back to the bedroom. Now that the adrenaline had subsided, Robert looked as drained as I felt.

I looked myself over in the mirror. I had a few cuts and what looked to be the beginnings or a gnarly bruise on my shoulder.

"Here, take a load off," I said, tapping the edge of the sink as Robert limped back into the bathroom.

He leaned against the counter and sighed heavily. Placing myself between his legs, I turned his head to the side. The wound wasn't too bad, but there were a few splinters protruding angrily from his skin.

As gently as I could, I pulled the bigger splinters out with my fingernails and threw them in the sink. Using the end of a towel, I squeeze some water into the wound and Robert flinched as the cool liquid washed away the dirt and sweat. His hand flew to my hip and gripped me tightly as I wiped some of the debris away.

"Sorry," I said under my breath.

"I've made it through worse." He exhaled and loosened his grip on my side, though he didn't let go.

I reached around him and grabbed the bottle of alcohol.

"This is going to burn." I looked him in the eyes and the flame between us flickered in my chest.

"Just do it." He leaned his head to the side and held onto me with both hands.

Tentatively, I poured the clear liquid onto his skin and felt his grip tighten on me.

"Son of a…," he cursed through gritted teeth.

I leaned around him and wet the other end of the towel in the sink.

"Almost there," I said, trying to sound reassuring as I cleaned up the blood that had dripped down his neck and wiped the wound one last time. "Done."

"Thanks," he said, taking a few deep breaths.

I tried stepping away from him, but he held me in place. My body only a few inches from his as he looked up at me with heavy lids. The fight had drained us all, Magically and physically. Robert was no exception.

Logic warred with my heart, telling me to pull away, but this wasn't a fight that could be won with reason. My chest ached with the need to feel his arms around me. We could've lost each other tonight, and he would've never known how I truly felt. I leaned into him, the heat of his body engulfing me, warming not only my skin but my soul.

"I don't know what I would've done…" I started to say. My voice was barely a whisper as I placed my hand on his chest and picked at a piece of dirt on his black t-shirt.

He wrapped his fingers around mine, holding onto me like a lifeline. "I'm here," he promised.

I leaned my forehead against his and let out a shaky breath. "We can't lose Annabel."

"Can't you *see* anything?" he asked gently. Robert knew me well, and the fact that I was worried about Annabel's fate spoke volumes to him.

I shook my head.

"It's what Morgana wants, to weaken us." His breath felt warm on my face and I had to fight the urge to press my lips against his as our Bond stirred deep within me. "You're stronger than you think. Don't let her defeat you." His hand made its way down my spine to the small of my back and he pulled me closer.

"I'm doing the best I can," I sighed and lifted my head.

"I know you are, but you can do better. We both know you're stronger than you give yourself credit for." His eyes bore into mine and a small secret smile played at his lips. My heart began to race, matching the thrum of his under my hand.

Some might take his words as a slight, but I knew he only wanted to remind me of my strength, to remind me of the woman he saw when he looked at me.

"Always the optimist."

"One of us has to be." He tucked a loose strand of hair behind my ear and traced my jawline. My lips parted in anticipation as I melted into his touch.

The bedroom door slammed closed, making me jump in Robert's arms.

"Violet?" Matthew called from beyond the closed bathroom door. Every part of me wanted to stay where I was, safe and warm. But for Annabel's sake, I unwrapped myself from Robert's embrace.

Sighing, he pushed himself off the counter, seeming just as disappointed as I was that we were interrupted. It sent a thrill through me.

I reached for the handle, but Robert stopped me before I could pull the door open.

"I don't know what I would have done either, if I'd lost you tonight." He slid his hand into my hair and kissed my forehead.

Opening the door, he left me standing in the bathroom, the feel of his lips lingering on my skin.

"Did you get in touch with Harriet?" Robert asked, his voice all business as I followed him into the other room, trying to slow my racing heart

"Yep. This is everything we need." Matthew held up two bags of ingredients.

"Do you know how to make it?" I asked.

"It'll be difficult with just the coffee pot to work with, but as long as I can get it to boil we should be fine."

"Since no one needs me, I'm going to hop in the shower," Lila announced and limped toward the bathroom.

"Make it quick," Matthew called after her.

She waved in acknowledgment and closed the door behind her.

"I'm going to try to hunt down some food for everyone," Ethan said and looked around the room awkwardly.

"I'll go with you." His sister jumped to his side, and they rushed out of the room.

Matthew and Brett started unpacking the ingredients on the coffee table, speaking in hushed voices.

Not sure what to do, I walked over to Annabel and took her pulse.

"How is she?" Robert asked, leaning against the wall.

"Her heart rate is still pretty high." I really hoped that Annabel would pull through. I couldn't imagine what it would do to the Maxwell family if they lost one of their own.

"What about you?" Robert asked. The shower turned on and the muffled sounds of the curtain being drawn back came through the wall.

"I'm fine. Exhausted but otherwise unscathed." Laying down on the other bed, I finally let myself relax. Every muscle in my body screamed as they unclenched and I felt the full force of what had happened.

The bed dipped as Robert stretched out next to me. He sighed heavily and I could feel our connection pull at me again.

"It's been a long day." I threw my arm over my eyes.

"I should have been able to heal her," Robert lamented as his shoulder brushed mine.

"Maybe it's a new kind of Magic or something."

"I don't think so. I could feel my Magic pouring into her, but instead of healing her, it was tearing her apart."

"You could feel it?"

"When I'm connected, I can feel everything. It's what drains me more than anything."

"Maybe this all has something to do with what happened to you on Avalon?"

"Alyssa," he whispered her name like a curse.

"Right, you said she was trying to replicate your healing ability." I turned onto my side and propped my head up to look down at him.

"Yes, but instead I think they may have reverse engineered my ability…"

"But you've healed more than one of us since you've been back."

"They must have done something to Annabel, made it so my Magic works against me."

"We have a big problem if they figured out how to stop you from healing."

"That's an understatement," he scoffed and ran a hand through his hair.

He sat up fully on the bed, swiveling around so he was looking down at me. His eyes held mine, and I knew he could see the unbridled panic bubbling inside of me.

"We shouldn't get ahead of ourselves, there could be a dozen other reasons why I can't heal her."

"It isn't a coincidence that they were testing your ability and now Annabel, who's been imprisoned by the same people, can't be healed," I reasoned and sat up, putting our bodies only a few inches apart.

"Right, well, if they did find a way to block my ability, that means we'll just have to be more careful until we figure this out." He pinched my chin between his thumb and forefinger.

I took a deep, shaky breath. Tonight's events coupled with exhaustion were making my walls come tumbling down one after the other.

"You mean, try harder not to die." I leveled my eyes on him.

"Exactly." Robert moved his hand around the back of my neck.

"It does no good to worry about things that are out of our control," he continued. "All we can do is keep moving forward." His thumb moved back and forth on my cheek rhythmically, soothing the waves of anxiety building in me.

"When did you get to be so wise?" The corners of my lips turned up in a half smile.

"I always have been. You're just now starting to realize it." He gave me a cocky smile and released his hold on me.

I rolled my eyes. "This room isn't big enough for your ego."

For the first time in a long time, Robert's smile reached his eyes, and it warmed my heart.

Reaching for him, I placed my hand on his as his eyes held mine. I saw a sadness deep in his soul that hadn't been there before, and I realized that the time we'd spent apart had left its mark on both of us. His smile faded and his expression matched the heartbreak I felt beneath my ribcage.

I had wished for this moment a thousand times since Robert disappeared, but I never thought I would feel so much loss as I looked into his eyes. My heart lurched forward as Robert leaned toward me and the room blurred out of focus.

William laid in bed next to Constance, both of them naked and covered only by a sheet.

"What is it, my love?" William asked

She smiled and broke their gaze, "I'm worried about Colin." William did his best to keep his face neutral but I could see the edge of his eyes crinkle at the sound of another man's name. "He's up to something."

"What ever could he be up too that has you so worried?"

"I found this, hidden among his dirty clothes." She leaned over him, opening the bedside table and pulling out a folded piece of paper.

"What is this?"

"Open it." She held the square piece of paper gingerly between her fingers.

William sat up, leaning against the headboard as he took the note and unfolded it twice. His face paled, and he looked between the sheet of paper and Constance.

"He's a Le Fay sympathizer?" The look of horror on his face sent a chill through my spine.

I moved across the room to get a better look at the piece of paper, but I was stopped short when he laid his hands on his lap and the symbol I'd become so familiar with caught my eye.

Morgana. I seethed. Even in William's time, she was wreaking havoc.

"You have to report him."

"It's not that simple, Will. I can't go to the council without implicating myself."

"I know, Constance, but you can't pretend you didn't see this." He practically shoved the piece of paper at her. "Colin's an alchemist they could be recruiting him to mix potions based on the old ways."

"You think I'm blind to what they're trying to do?" She got out of bed, a sheet wrapped around her like a Greek goddess.

"I didn't mean- "

"Of course you didn't." Her features soften slightly.

"Constance, if he's already mixing potions for Le Fay, you could be in danger. There's no telling the kind of damage he can do."

"Promise me you won't do anything about this, not yet."

He began to shake his head no. "Please, if you really love me, let me get to the bottom of this first."

"Alright." William agreed, but he wore the same expression Robert did when he was placating me.

It felt like a long time before I heard Robert say, "There you are." His voice was soft and welcoming. "What did you see?"

"What do you know about the Le Fay sympathizers?" I asked, shaking my head back to reality.

"Le Fay?" he balked. "They were a small uprising who believed in Morgana's mantra."

"William and Constance were arguing about them. Something about Colin being an alchemist and joining the cause."

"Hmm," Robert ruminated. "Odd that you should have a vision about Le Fay."

"Why would it be odd?" I cocked my head to the side and watched Robert's brow furrow as if he was trying to work out an equation in his head.

"Why now? Why would your Magic be drawn to them?"

"I don't think it is drawn to them. William pops up from time to time showing me bits and pieces of his life."

"Interesting. Maybe his connection to the original prophecy connects him to you in some way."

"Is that even possible? To be connected to someone in another time?"

Robert leveled his gaze on me, a small smirk playing at the corner of his lips. "Haven't you learned yet? Anything is possible."

"Right." I shook my head at the insanity of being connected to a man who lived hundreds of years ago.

"We can ask Graham about Le Fay when we get back. He

may be able to decipher the meaning behind your vision." He placed his hand on my thigh and gave it a gentle squeeze.

The flame that had been building inside of me since our training with Graham flickered to life at Robert's touch. His eyes caught mine and for the third time in the space of twenty minutes, I found myself inexplicably drawn to him.

The soft click of a key sliding into the door announced the return of Ethan and Elodie. Both of their arms were full, and they looked like they'd cleaned out every vending machine in a hundred-mile radius.

"Can't a man have a moment of peace," Robert grumbled under his breath and pulled away from me.

"You two really should get a room," Ethan noted.

"Shut up, Ethan," Robert and I said in unison.

"I'm just stating the obvious." Ethan dumped the hoard of snacks on the small round table next to the window.

"One of these days, he's going to blow your ass into next Tuesday," Elodie mocked, giving her brother a not so gentle shove with her elbow as she dumped her portion of the foil bags onto the table.

"Anyway…" I said, trying to conceal my coloring cheeks.

"You know, I wonder…" Robert said, recovering himself quickly.

"What?" I turned my head to look at him. His eyes were on the ceiling and he wore a confused look.

"How did they know we were going to be there tonight? No one was supposed to even know that the necklace was coming in early."

"Someone had to know it was coming in tonight, otherwise how did it get there?" Elodie asked. She glanced between me and the bathroom where Lila was still hiding out.

"Everyone involved in the shipping was vetted. It wasn't them," Robert reasoned.

"Well, there is one obvious person," Elodie commented and looked over her shoulder toward the bathroom.

"She had nothing to do with this," Robert insisted, an icy glare replacing the warmth that had been in his eyes just a moment ago.

"You know, now that I think about it, no one from their side even went after the necklace. They came after us," Ethan noted as he slipped between Elodie and Robert, trying to break the tension. "It's like they were waiting for us, not the necklace."

"But that doesn't make any sense. Why wait for us when they could have grabbed the necklace and stopped us from ever getting our hands on it?" I asked, forcing myself to look away from Robert and turning toward Ethan.

"My thoughts exactly." He grinned and puffed out his chest in satisfaction. "The necklace was a consolation."

"If they could take Violet out of the picture, then the necklace wouldn't matter. We wouldn't have anyone to wake The Lady," Ethan finished.

"Smart, even for a Promised One," Lila chimed as she padded out of the bathroom in a fresh pair of jeans and a white t-shirt. "It's what I would have done. Kill The Waker and the tokens don't matter anymore."

"Comforting that you and Morgana share the same twisted logic," I hissed through my teeth.

"Anyone with a half a brain would come to the same conclusion." Her eyes darted to Ethan. "We need to be better prepared next time or we won't be so lucky."

"Lucky?" Jake's voice startling us all. I'd almost forgotten he was even there. He moved away from Annabel's bedside and marched toward Lila, a menacing glare warping his features into something I'd never seen from him before: pure, unaltered anger.

"Annabel is fighting for her life. We can't heal her and you think we got lucky," Jake growled.

"We all made it out alive, so yes, we got lucky this time," Lila said. She didn't back down or bat a lash at Jake's tone.

"I should have let Violet finish you when she had the chance," he snarled and moved to my side.

"Jake, that's enough," Robert snapped, and I recoiled at his tone. Jake, however, stood tall, unphased by his brother's command.

"What if it was Violet laying in that bed? Would you still trust your little harlot?" Jake asked.

Robert's eyes flicked to me, an apology written on his face, and I realized that he would still trust her. It didn't matter what any of us thought. It didn't matter what she had done in the past. Robert had given her a clean slate and trusted her with everything he had.

An odd feeling stirred in my heart, and the words spilled from my lips before I could think twice. "I don't think Lila betrayed us."

Everyone turned on me and Jake took an unconscious step back like my words were a physical punch to his gut.

"Thanks?" Lila furrowed her brow as if she couldn't believe I was defending her.

"So what, you've forgiven her now? Now that it's not you fighting for your life?" Jake spat. His words cut through me like a knife, and my heart ached at the look of betrayal in his eyes.

"I haven't forgiven anything. I just don't think Lila had anything to do with what happened tonight." I kept my voice as even as possible while summoning courage I didn't know I had.

"Then who?" Elodie asked.

"I don't know." I rubbed the back of my neck and my muscles tensed. My entire body was starting to stiffen up, and all I wanted to do was sleep. "And honestly, I'm too exhausted to try to come up with anything."

"It's possible that no one betrayed us," Ethan chimed in. "Ian got close to Violet on more than one occasion without us knowing. Maybe they found a way to keep close to one of us again."

"We're not living in one of your spy-thriller movies, Ethan," Elodie scoffed.

"It's not out of the realm of possibility," Robert ruminated.

"We could discuss this until we're blue in the face, but speculation gets us nowhere. We need to come up with a plan, get ahead of Morgana," Lila advised. Apparently, by letting her off the hook for tonight's events, she had found her confidence.

We all stared at her, wanting to find fault in her words, but the fact of the matter was, she was right.

Sighing, I said, "First, I need a shower. Then we can come up with a plan."

"Make it quick. We shouldn't linger here too long," Robert said with an edge of warning.

"You want to leave? With Annabel in her condition?" I balked.

"They could track us here and finish what they started," Robert replied.

"The hotel is protected against Magical detection," Matthew chimed in. "They won't be able to find us here."

"That may well be, but I'm not waiting around to find out."

"How are we supposed to get Annabel home?" I crossed my arms, challenging him.

"Robert's right, we need to get home," Jake growled from Annabel's bedside.

After the death stare he had given me for defending Lila, I wasn't about to argue with him.

"Whatever you guys want. All I ask is fifteen minutes." I grabbed a towel off the bed.

"Don't hog all the water," Ethan chuckled and ripped open a bag of Doritos.

"Do you ever take anything seriously?" His sister chided him.

"Oh, I take *Cooler Ranch* very seriously." He popped a chip into his mouth and crunched loudly.

"You're insufferable sometimes." Elodie sneered.

Shaking my head, I made my way to the bathroom as Elodie and Ethan continued harassing each other.

"Violet, wait," Lila called behind me as I rounded the corner to the bathroom.

"Yes?" I stopped short.

"Thank you, for defending me. I know that couldn't have been easy for you." Her eyes fell to the floor, and I got a glimpse of the broken girl Robert was so determined to defend. Her sharp, hostile edges had been chipped away, just like the flower blooming on the cactus. This was not the same woman who had tortured me and left me for dead.

"Don't mention it," I said, keeping my voice indifferent. I slipped into the bathroom and closed the door, not waiting for her response. I might have defended her to the others, but I was certain that placing my trust in Lila would bring my downfall.

CHAPTER FIFTEEN

he sound of muffled voices arguing stirred me from my sleep. Rolling onto my side, the cool sheets felt good on my sticky skin. The curtains were pulled back, revealing deep maroon clouds with streaks of greyish-blue sky as the sun started to rise in the distance.

The ride back from L.A. had been thankfully uneventful. Annabel still hadn't regained consciousness by the time we arrived, but Harriet's tea seemed to be helping a bit. Her heart rate was growing steadier by the hour, and her wounds were starting to show early signs of healing. I could only hope Harriet's tea would perform a miracle since Robert's ability was clearly out of commission.

Sliding out of bed, I moved toward the French doors and pulled them open. The cool ocean breeze tossed my hair back and refreshed my skin. It feels good to be home; I thought as I took in the Maxwells backyard and sweeping ocean view.

The voices in the hall grew louder, shattering any hope of being able to ignore them. I recognized Robert's argumentative tone almost instantly and could feel the Bond pulling at me, aching to find its other half. Wiping the sleep from my eyes, I left the peacefulness of the balcony behind and stepped into the hall.

"What's all the noise about? Is Annabel alright?" My voice cracked slightly from disuse, and I realized I must have been asleep longer than I'd thought.

"She's alright," Jake replied, keeping his eyes glued to his brother.

"We didn't mean to wake you." Robert turned to look at me.

"It's alright. What time is it?"

"A little after six in the morning." Robert narrowed his eyes as he scanned the cuts and bruises on my skin.

"Have either of you gotten any sleep?" I rolled my head from side to side, stretching out the sore muscles in my neck.

"No, and I'm glad I didn't. He..." Jake jabbing a finger into Robert's chest, "was gonna try to heal Annabel again. But after last night, I don't want him anywhere near her."

"I don't want to hurt her, Jake, believe me," Robert growled. "But we need to find out if she's immune to my Magic or if whatever they did to her has worn off."

"How stable is she?" I asked, knowing Jake wouldn't be happy that I was entertaining Robert.

"I don't know." Jake let out a heavy sigh and ran his hand through his hair. "She still hasn't woken up, but her vitals seem to have leveled out."

"Why don't we wait until she's awake?" I glanced at Robert. "That way if there's something going on inside of her, she can tell us."

"The longer we wait-" Robert tried to say.

I cut him off by placing my hand on his arm. "I know, but it won't do you or Annabel any good if your Magic backfires again." I gave his arm a reassuring squeeze. I knew how hard it was for him not to have answers. The fact that this might stem from him being on Avalon was clearly eating away at him.

"Fine," he conceded and walked down the hall toward the stairs.

"Thank you." Jake stopped me before I could follow Robert. "I know I shouldn't be so hard on him, but it's Anna. I'll do anything to save her from any more pain." His eyes glistened, shrink wrapped with tears.

"Hey, she's gonna be okay and we'll figure out what's going on with Robert's Magic." I reached out to him and he pulled me in for a hug.

"I don't think it's Robert's Magic that's the issue."

"What'd you mean?" My brow furrowed in confusion as Jake held me at arm's length, a guilty expression crossing his features. If he didn't think anything was wrong with Robert's ability to heal, then why not let him try to help Annabel?

"I think they did something to her. Changed her somehow so he can't heal her." Jake's voice was barely a whisper and the blood in my heart turned to ice.

"Whatever this is, we'll figure it out, okay?" I met his eyes and my lips pressed into a thin smile. A part of me hated saying the words that everyone repeated to me over and over again, but what else could I do?

Three resounding bangs came from the knocker at the front door. Jake and I looked at each other for a moment, confused by who would be here at such a late hour.

"This can't be good," Jake said under his breath, and we both made our way down the staircase. The knocker sounded again as Robert's footsteps tapped across the wood floor. Jake and I were halfway down the stairs when Robert pulled the door open to get a glimpse of the visitor.

"Is this the Maxwell residence?" A small woman's voice spoke. Out of the corner of my eye, I saw Lila's fingers spark to life from the shadows. Everyone was still on edge from the night before and ready for another ambush.

"Yes," Robert answered. He held the door open about a foot

and his body blocked my view of the visitors as I hesitantly moved down the last few stairs.

"Ambrosius," the woman at the door said with a shaky breath.

Robert's back went stiff and then he swung the door open, saying, "Of course. Come in, please."

A woman in her mid to late thirties and two young boys walked past Robert into the grand entryway. Her eyes swept the room as she looked at each of us in awe. I smiled at the memory of the first time I'd walked into this house.

"What is it that brought you here?" Robert ushered the small family into the living room.

"Is there somewhere the boys can go?" The woman asked. She looked nervous but seemed to trust that we were on her side, or that we would at least help her.

"Of course." Robert looked around the room and Jake immediately stepped up.

"You two want to check out the pool?" Jake asked with more enthusiasm than I had left in my pinky finger.

"Yeah," the older of the two boys said excitedly and ran toward Jake while the smaller child held onto to his mother's leg with a death grip.

"It's okay, honey, go with your brother." She nudged him along.

Jake guided the boys outside as Robert ushered the woman toward the living room. We had no idea who this woman was and for all we knew she could be working for Morgana. Lila and I both followed and shared an anxious glance.

"What does Ambrosius mean?" I whispered to Lila.

"It's Merlin's Magical name," she replied. "Whenever another Magical person is in trouble, all they need to do is evoke Ambrosius' name. As long as their heart is true, the name will act as a sanctuary." Her words hung in the air as we moved into the living room.

Guiding the fragile woman to the sofa, Robert helped her take a seat. By the light of the fire, I could make out her features a little better. Dark crescent moons hung heavy from her eyelids, and her thin lips were turned down at the corners. Her clothes were singed at the ends, as if flames had licked at the material.

"I've forgotten my manners," Robert apologized. He pulled a blanket from a trunk behind the sofa and wrapped it around his guest's shoulders. She pulled the corners of the knit blanket toward her like a lifeline. "This is Violet and Lila." Robert motioned between the two of us. "And my name's Robert."

"Gwen." She gave us a half-hearted smile.

"Do you mind telling us what brought you here seeking refuge?" Robert sounded kind and warm. I recognized the tone well. It was the same voice he used with me when I first found out about the Magical world.

"Morgana," she snarled. Robert and I exchanged a glance. "She's gathering followers. Those who don't answer to her call, die. My husband..." She broke off and her bottom lip quivered as she tried to hold back tears. She took a deep breath and continued. "He held them off so I could escape with the boys." Tears filled her eyes and spilled down her cheeks.

"Lila, can you get some water and a box of tissues?" Robert asked.

She nodded and left the room.

"How far have you traveled?" I asked.

"We came from Los Angeles."

My body went stiff and Robert and I shared a worried glance.

"You're safe now. You and the boys can stay as long as you'd like," he reassured her.

"You said her name's Violet," Gwen said and looked at me. "As in The Waker?"

I gave her a small, nervous smile. "Guilty."

"Thank Merlin's beard. You'll save us all." The reverence in her eyes made me anxious, and I had to look away.

"That's the plan," Brett said, removing herself from the shadows.

"Here you go." Lila returned to the room with a glass of water and a wad of tissues. She handed everything to Gwen, who graciously took the water and blew her nose.

"You said that Morgana was gathering followers?" Brett asked all business.

"Brett, not now," Robert said under his breath.

"What would bring her to your house seeking support for her cause?" Brett continued, ignoring her brother.

"I... I don't know," Gwen admitted. She pulled the blanket closer, as if trying to shield herself from Brett's questioning gaze. "We've always been supporters of The Waker."

"That may be true, but it is my understanding that Morgana is reaching out to all known members of Le Fay."

"What are you rambling on about? Le Fay was wiped out hundreds of years ago." Robert dismissed the accusation.

"No, they weren't." Matthew followed behind Brett, looking disheveled and exhausted. "They just got better at hiding themselves."

"Why haven't you mentioned them before?" My brow furrowed in accusation.

Matthew shrugged. "I didn't know. It was Graham who tied the pieces together."

"And you think her husband may have been a part of Le Fay?" I tilted my chin in Gwen's direction.

"He wasn't. I swear he was a good man," Gwen insisted.

I moved across the room and sat down next to Gwen, placing my hand on hers. "I'm sure he was." Searching for the Magic within me, I tried to conjure up a vision of her husband. "What's his name?" I wanted to keep her calm and to give me something to latch onto.

"David," she sniffled.

The room swirled, and I was pulled into the middle of an inferno. The entire house was ablaze. I turned in a circle, looking for anything that would confirm David and Gwen's allegiance. Voices caught my attention and as I moved toward them, a family portrait toppled from the mantel. Glass shattered and the heat from the fire made the photo curl in on itself. The patriarch's face, whom I assumed was David, was the last one to disappear into ash as another scream echoed over the fire.

Breaking into a run, knowing the fire wouldn't hurt me, I burst through a closed door. Gwen and her two boys were sneaking out a back window as a man's voice roared again. Gwen climbed her frail body over the window sill. She took one last look, pain and regret etched into her features before she disappeared.

It didn't take long to find David on his knees in the kitchen, bloody and sweating from the heat of the fire.

"Tell me," the burly man standing over David snarled and slapped him across the face. "When will the necklace arrive?"

The necklace? So David was the one in charge of delivery. He was the one who'd helped us get to the necklace first.

"Just kill me. We both know I'm not going to tell you anything." David spat and a wad of dark ruby blood smeared across the floor.

"We'll see about that." The burly man smirked. Fire danced on the attacker's fingertips and moved toward David as if it was a puppet on strings.

Back in the Maxwell living room, the fire crackled and made me flinch.

"She's telling the truth. David isn't a part of Le Fay," I announced.

"I've never been read by a Soothsayer before." Gwen looked around anxiously.

"I only looked at David through your eyes." I paused, seeing the pain in her expression. "You did the right thing, saving your boys. If you'd stayed, they would've killed all of you."

Tears filled Gwen's eyes, and she nodded. I knew my words wouldn't ease her guilt, but the need to reassure her overwhelmed me.

"Your husband was a very brave man. Don't ever forget that," I encouraged her.

"I won't." She sniffled and her lips quivered ever so slightly.

"Why don't you get some rest?" I suggested. "You and the boys have been through a lot."

"My boys. What am I supposed to tell them?"

"Tell them that you're safe now. They can't reach you here, I promise." I knew I shouldn't make promises, but this woman had just lost her husband and her home in the space of a few minutes. I knew firsthand what that kind of loss could do to a person and giving her hope was the only thing that would keep her moving forward.

"Brett, do you mind showing Gwen to one of the empty rooms?" I asked.

"Sure, right this way." She motioned for Gwen to follow her.

"Matty, can you grab the boys? They're outside with Jake."

"No problem," he said with a nod. "We'll be right behind you," he told Gwen, who still looked hesitant to follow Brett.

"What did you see?" Robert asked once Brett and Gwen were out of earshot and put his hand on my shoulder. "You look a little pale."

"Her husband wasn't being recruited. He was targeted because he helped us," I said without preamble.

"Who was her husband?" Lila stepped forward.

"David was in charge of delivering the necklace."

A tense, quiet moment passed.

"Do you think Gwen and the kids will be alright?" Lila asked no one in particular.

"They'll keep moving forward, but it'll be a long time before they're alright again." The tone of my voice sounded off even to my own ears, and I caught Robert's worried eyes

The death of Gwen's husband, Annabel fighting for her life, all those people dead at Hurst Castle. It was all starting to chip away at my carefully constructed exterior. I did my best to not let it show, but each and every loss cut me deep.

After my parent's death, I let very few people into my life, out of fear of losing them. But now it was too late. The Maxwells had worked their way into my heart and become family. Terror I hadn't known in a long time settled into my abdomen like lead. There was a very real possibility that I was going to lose more people I loved.

"Well, I guess we know how Morgana found us," Lila sighed.

"We have to end this before anyone else gets hurt," I pleaded.

"We will," Robert reassured me.

I looked into his eyes, wanting to believe that we could stop Morgana, that we could save the ones we loved. But for the first time since I learned my destiny, I no longer believed we would all make it out of this alive. I could feel it deep in my bones. I could feel it bubbling in the core of my Magic. There would be losses on both sides.

"I'm going to check on Annabel," I said.

"We'll come get you if we need you," Robert offered. I didn't know if he could feel helplessness through the Bond or if he could read it in my eyes, but he must have known I needed my space.

Heading back up the stairs, I quickly made my way to Annabel's room. I wouldn't have much time alone with her once Jake turned the kids over to Matthew. I opened the door slowly, afraid I might disturb her. As I stepped into the room, the smell hit me like a ton of bricks. The earthy aroma of the tea assaulted my nose, but it was the sweetness in the air that had me rushing to Annabel's side.

I propped her head up, and she sighed and made a few grumbling noises, but otherwise stayed unconscious. I carefully pulled at the makeshift bandage at the back of her head, only to have my suspicions confirmed. The wound was infected. The skin all around the gash was swollen and had turned an angry shade of red. Small pockets of white goo clung to her scalp and as I pulled the bandages away a bloody, yellowish film coated the strips of gauze.

"Dammit," I cursed and wrinkled my nose.

Laying her head back down with the bandage still half attached, I made my way to the bathroom. I found a small first-aid kit and a bottle of hydrogen peroxide in the cabinets. Next I checked the medicine cabinet with fingers crossed for some antibiotics. There were several bottles of medicine, one for allergies, another for acid reflux and a couple half-empty bottles of various painkillers but no antibiotics.

Letting out a heavy sigh, I pulled a chair up to Annabel's bedside.

"Come on, Annabel, you can pull through this," I said to the quiet room as I rolled her head to the side and carefully peeled the used bandages off her head.

"If you can feel this, I'm sorry. It's going to sting a bit." I looked down at her peaceful face, but she didn't respond.

I poured some hydrogen peroxide on the wound and it immediately started foaming like a school volcano project. Pouring a little more on the rest of the gash, I let it do its work while I grabbed a towel.

"You know, Jake's pretty worried about you." I dabbed at the wound with the towel and let it soak everything up. "I've never seen him like this." I poured more of the clear liquid on her head and watched it foam up again, but not as furiously as it had the first time. "He snapped on Lila, wanted to kill her for what they did to you." A dry chuckle escaped my throat.

"And Robert," I continued and sighed. "He's hiding it pretty well, but he's torn up about not being able to heal you." I dabbed the wound again with a dry portion of the towel. "You know how he is, always blaming himself for everyone else's problems."

I opened the first-aid kit and meticulously pulled on the latex gloves, then took out the gauze and anti-bacterial cream. It wasn't nearly enough, but it would have to do until I could get Annabel some decent medicine to fight the infection.

"He kissed me, you know. When we were at Graham's," I admitted as I opened the tube of cream, squeezing it onto my finger. "I'm sure you'd have something wildly inappropriate to say about that." I smiled at the thought. "And Lila, she's… I don't know. I still don't trust her, but I don't think we have to worry about her." As gently as I could, I smeared the opaque cream onto the gash, trying to make sure I covered the entire wound.

"I know, you'd probably yell at me and remind me that she tried to kill me. But as weird as it sounds, I think she's on our side now." I exhaled wearily as I finished off the rest of the cream. "We need you, Annabel. I need you." I placed a few strips of gauze against the back of her head, trying to create a barrier. "I know it's selfish, but I can't lose another person in my life. You've become like a sister to me and I just can't…" A single tear rolled down my cheek and dropped onto her shoulder, leaving a tiny wet spot on her cotton shirt.

I finished wrapping her head in silence. I'd been so busy worrying about everyone else that I hadn't realized how broken my heart was at the thought of losing Annabel.

I rolled her onto her back to make sure she was in a comfortable position and collected all the trash from my makeshift surgery. I wasn't quite ready to face the rest of the world again, so I fidgeted with the comforter and busied myself with tidying up the room.

"Now I know how you guys must have felt when it was me fighting for my life," I huffed and ran my hand through my hair. "Just keep fighting, okay?" I gave her hand a gentle squeeze and left to find the others. If Annabel was going to have a fighting chance, then we'd need something stronger than Magical herbal tea.

Taking the stairs two at a time, I made my way back into the living room. Lila lay on the couch, curled up and fast asleep. Robert sat across from her in a plump armchair, his head leaned back and eyes closed.

"How is she?" Robert cleared his throat as I stepped into the room.

"She needs medicine," I said, facing him and leaning against the wall.

"The tea isn't working?" He stood and walked toward me, guiding me outside so we wouldn't wake Lila. We'd all had a rough twenty-four hours, and it was only going to get worse.

"It is, I just don't think it's meant to heal something this bad. Her wounds are starting to get infected."

"We'll get her some medicine then." Robert placed his hand on my shoulder.

"Thanks." I nodded, trusting he would find a way to get Annabel what she needed.

The sun began to banish the darkness as we made our way across the yard, giving way to a perfectly clear, blue sky. The air was still cool when we reached the fence overlooking the water. Leaning on the railing, I wished I had my camera. The deep blue ocean below reached the cliff side and exploded in a fury of white foam that churned between each set. The black rocks below glistened in the early morning sun. Pelicans circled about fifty feet off the shore, searching for their breakfast. I watched one of the birds coast over the water. Suddenly its left wing turned toward the sky and he dove, disappearing into the ocean.

"Beautiful, isn't it?" Robert's voice was barely a whisper.

"It must be so freeing, being able to fly wherever your heart desires," I said, watching as another pelican lifted its wing and dove into the water.

"Feel like running away?" He leaned on his forearms, watching the pelicans beside me.

"Can you blame me?" I looked over at him, watching his eyes scan the water. I had a feeling he wanted to fly away too.

"After the library, I'd be surprised if you didn't feel like heading for the horizon."

I sighed and looked out over the water. "You should get some sleep."

"Who needs sleep?" He nudged me with his shoulder. He was in a surprisingly good mood for it being so early. "Come on, let's sit down." He pushed off the railing and walked toward the swing.

The hinges *creaked* as I sat down beside him, the swing moving back and forth. His fingers reached mine and fell into place as we watched the sunrise. His skin was warm as always, and it was comforting to have Robert close again.

"Tell me more about this Le fay group," I prompted without looking at him.

"Honestly, I don't know much," Robert admitted. He traced a circle on the top of my hand with his thumb. "Like I said to Matty, they were taken care of a long time ago."

"But who were they, exactly?" I turned my eyes from the horizon and looked at Robert.

"They sympathized with Morgana's ideals. She gave otherwise voiceless people something to cling to, something to fight for."

"How could anyone side with Morgana?"

"Well, the idea of not hiding in the shadows, living up to our full potential, it's intoxicating." If I didn't know any better, I'd have said Robert was bewitched by the idea as well.

"Okay, but how can they justify killing so many people just to prove their message?"

"Because for Le Fay, it wasn't about any message. They wanted to change the world, convert people to their way of thinking. If you disagreed, then you were simply part of the problem," Robert explained.

"So how were they stopped?" My brow furrowed at the thought of living in such a cut-and-dry world, us and them.

"Like I said, I don't know the whole story. But William was involved, or around at least when the last Le Fay supporter was killed. Or so we thought."

"Do you really think Morgana is calling them out of the woodworks?"

Robert sighed. "More likely Morgana is recruiting new supporters and reusing a moniker that carries weight in the Magical world. But then again, anything is possible. Morgana's living proof."

I wasn't sure what to say. My thought's ping-ponged around my head like an Olympic match. Could Le Fay really be back and helping Morgana gain support? How on earth were we supposed to win when our enemies were willing to kill anyone in their way? Watching the sun slowly float higher and higher, I thought back to the entry I'd read in William's journal and the vision I'd had last night. I wondered what William did about Colin and if he or Constance ever came forward about their suspicions.

Resting my head on Robert's shoulder, I closed my eyes and tried to force a vision of anything relating to Le Fay.

CHAPTER SIXTEEN

My stomach growled, breaking the silence between us.

"When was the last time you ate?" Robert chuckled.

"I had a bag of chips in the car last night." I tucked my hair behind my ear.

"When are you going to listen to me? You need real food, Violet." Robert stood and pulled me with him.

I gave him a lighthearted smile. "Chips are real food."

He gave me a pointed look. "You've been spending too much time with Ethan."

The smell of bacon and cinnamon hit me as I walked into the house. "Damn, that smells good." My mouth watered, and I inhaled deeply.

"Morning, Jake," Robert said as we walked into the kitchen. Jake was standing at the stove, a towel over his left shoulder and a spatula in his right hand, flipping a piece of French toast.

"Morning," he said curtly. As he turned to face us, his eyes immediately went to our joined hands. Looking up at me for a brief moment, his lips parted into a small smile that quickly disappeared.

"Why aren't you with Annabel?" I let go of Robert's hand and put some distance between us.

"I needed to do something useful. Watching her, hoping she'll wake up, it's just… Brett's with her now." He kept his eyes on the French toast in the pan.

Matty dragged himself into the room and shuffled over to the coffeepot. "Does no one ever sleep around here?" He poured himself a healthy cup.

"What's sleep?" Robert grabbed a cup of coffee for himself.

"Matty, I wanted to ask…" I hesitated as he shot me a glance over his coffee cup. "Do you know where we can get medicine for Annabel?" I felt guilty for asking even more of him since he looked as drained as the rest of us.

Taking a large sip of coffee, he lowered his mug. "Robert still can't heal her?" He glanced in Robert's direction.

"I haven't had the opportunity to try again," Robert admitted and took a sip of his own coffee.

"Haven't had the opportunity? She's lying unconscious upstairs." Matthew scrunched his eyes together.

"What he means to say," Jake said before he turned around and plopped a plate of French toast onto the counter. "Is that I won't let him try again."

Matthew's shoulders relaxed. "Oh, do you think he can't heal her?" he asked, taking another large gulp of coffee.

"I don't know, but I'm not willing to put her through more torture. You saw firsthand what happened last night."

"To be fair." I plucked a piece of French toast from the plate. "We really don't know what happened when Robert tried to heal her."

"It was enough for me to know that his ability can't help her." Jake let out a heavy sigh.

"If we're not going to let Robert help her. There are a few people I can reach out to for meds. What are we looking for?"

Matthew said, his chipper attitude starting to peek through the haze of exhaustion.

"She needs antibiotics. The tea can only do so much. It can't fight off the infection without help," I explained.

"That'll be easy." Matty waved his hand dismissively as he started turning away.

"Oh, Matty?" I tried to make my voice sound as apologetic as possible.

"Yes, Violet?" he cooed playfully without turning around.

"How are Gwen and the kids?"

He shrugged. "Still sleeping as far as I know. I wanted to talk to everyone about them, actually." He ran a hand through his unkempt golden locks. "I don't think this is the best place for them to stay."

"Is any place safe?" Jake mumbled.

"The estate's already been attacked once and with Annabel on the mend, we can't easily defend them."

"Any suggestions?" Robert asked. He sounded all business, and I was surprised that he wasn't arguing against Matthew's point.

"Caltome. The cavern I showed you, that's used as a wine cellar," Matthew looked in my direction. "Doubles as a bunker. They'll be safe there and no one will be looking at the winery."

"You can't have kids staying in a wine cellar," I reasoned.

"There are a few quarters setup that will give them privacy and safety," Matthew amended. He looked around the room, waiting for one of us to argue against moving the family, but no one did.

"It's a plan then. Brett and I will move them this afternoon," he said with finality and left the kitchen, presumably to lay down.

We spent the rest of the day constructing a plan to get Annabel the medicine she needed and making arrangements for Gwen and her kids to stay at Caltome. Everyone was still exhausted from the previous night's events, and by late-afternoon, the sleep deprivation was really starting to take its toll.

I made my way back upstairs and threw myself on the bed. I felt like I'd been pulled through hot coals, and the simple act of being alone soothed the ache in my bones. Stretching onto my back, I relished in the solitude as it began to recharge me mentally and emotionally as each second ticked by. My whole life I'd grown accustomed to being alone the majority of the time, but the Maxwells stormed into my life like a hurricane. The only private time I ever really had was while I slept or showered.

Curling up under the covers, I turned the light off and rolled over. Exhaustion from the last 48 hours pulled at me and I fell asleep almost instantly.

Waves crashed on the shore in front of me, churning and throwing a mist into the air so forcefully I could feel the weight of the water under my feet. I could hear voices, like someone was stranded out in the water, screaming my name. The ocean rose impossibly high, then swirled around me like smoke, revealing an entirely different scene.

Annabel was chained to the wall in front of me, grime and blood staining her skin as she screamed my name.

Streaks of tears streamed down her dirty face as she yelled, "Violet, please. You have to save me, don't-"

Her words were cut off as the chains wrapped around her came to life. Yellow smoke and electricity coiled around her as she convulsed and fell silent.

The thunderous rumble of a freight train smacking into a wall woke me up. Blurry-eyed and my heart racing, I jumped out of bed. A flash of light erupted through the room and without hesitating I raised my shield. The constant roar of water slamming against the roof slowly brought me back to my senses. Looking around the room, I realized I wasn't under Magical attack, it was just Mother Nature.

Heart still pounding, I couldn't shake off the dream about

the beach and Annabel. It didn't feel like a vision, but there was something about it that made my skin crawl. Taking a deep breath, I reminded myself that Annabel was home, and she was safe.

Another extraordinary rumble churned overhead, followed by a loud crack reminiscent of a gunshot. My bones rattled inside my body as lightning struck nearby, illuminating my room so brightly I had to close my eyes. As the spots in my vision cleared, I got a glimpse of the sky outside my window. The dark, rolling clouds hung low, threatening to press down and envelop the world. Raindrops the size of dimes splattered the window, and the ocean outside rumbled as a wave connected with the solid rocks.

Unable to tell the time by the sky, I looked over my shoulder at the clock on the nightstand. The normally neon green lights displaying the time were dark. *Great,* I thought. The lightning must have taken out the electricity.

A soft tapping on the door caught my attention. Had I been asleep, I probably wouldn't have heard it. Wiping the sleep from my eyes and clearing my throat, I opened the door half a foot.

Robert stood in the dark wearing a sheepish expression. "Happy Birthday," he whispered. "I have something for you." He held up a poorly wrapped package.

"Birthday… How'd you…" My mouth fell open in surprise as I opened the door wider, letting him pass over the threshold.

I had no idea he knew when my birthday was. I'd never mentioned it to him, or anyone else for that matter. I wasn't big on celebrating when I didn't have a family to celebrate with. And never in a million years did I think Robert would get me a gift, even if he did know.

"When you spend the better part of your life learning about someone, the details tend to stick."

"That's not creepy at all." I laughed, and he shifted uncomfortably. "Joking. So what is it?" I moved closer to him, careful to keep a small distance between us.

"You'll have to open it." Excitement danced in his eyes as the corners of his mouth turned up and my heart stuttered.

He stood a few feet away from me, but in the darkness, it felt like we were inches apart. My heart raced, trying to keep pace with the rain thundering down on the roof. I could feel his eyes on me. I could feel the heat of his skin as I reached for the small package wrapped in newspaper.

"I know, it looks like a fifth grader wrapped it." He rubbed the back of his neck nervously. "Brett was always the one who was good at wrapping gifts."

"It doesn't need to be pretty if I'm just going to tear it apart." I moved to the bed and flipped the switch for the lamp on the nightstand, but the bulb stayed dark. *Right, no power*, I reminded myself. I peeled the newspaper away from the corner, tearing the *Archie* comic in half, and a dark suede material brushed against my fingertips. Yanking free the rest of the paper and flicking a rouge piece of tape off my finger, I realized it was a journal.

"I thought you might like one of your own. Some place to write your own story to pass on one day," Robert said in a soft, shy voice as he sat down next to me on the bed.

The mattress dipped under his weight and I had to keep myself from turning to him. This close together, in a bedroom, in the middle of a thunderstorm. It was what romance novels were made of.

"Thank you." I cleared my throat and shifted on the bed to put some distance between us. "It's beautiful." I let my fingers trace the embossed design on the front cover. Swirls of vines and knots formed an intricate design that wrapped around the spine and disappeared.

"It isn't much." He touched the corner of the journal. "But I wanted you to have something that would hold meaning to you."

I placed my hand on his, touched by the gesture. "It's perfect." Looking up, I realized the distance between us had disappeared and our lips were inches apart. Light blossomed through the window again, followed by a slow rumble. The lightning flashed across his face and a softer, less guarded Robert looked back at me.

"I hope you don't mind," his voice was like a purr. "I took the liberty of writing a little something for you." His eyes fell from mine and now I understood why he was being so coy. "To get you started, of course."

Letting go of his hand, I flipped open the front cover. Like William's journal, the inscription was simple and heartbreakingly beautiful.

To Violet,

With all my love and devotion.

– Robert.

A swell of emotions overwhelmed me. I wanted to kiss him and never leave his side. I wanted to run from the room and let the rain wash everything away. Instead, I turned the first page over. Written in small black ink was a letter in Robert's handwriting.

I wanted to read it right then, to soak in each and every word, but I was too self-conscious with him sitting next to me. Closing the journal, I wrapped my arm around his neck and pulled him close to me.

"Thank you. It means the world to me."

"You're welcome." He pulled away from me and kissed my forehead before standing and making his way to the door.

"Oh, and Robert?"

He turned to look at me, his hand on the doorknob.

"If you tell anyone else that it's my birthday, I'll be forced to use my Magic against you."

He laughed and his eyes crinkled at the corners. "Your secrets safe with me."

I nodded once. "Thank you though, really."

"Anytime." His eyes trailed up from the journal in my hands to my face and a longing that matched my own radiated off of him before he disappeared back into the hall.

Glued to my place on the edge of the bed, I traced my fingers along one of the vines on the front cover. Flipping to the page with Robert's perfectly scrawled writing, I began to read.

September 23, 2016

Violet,

First and foremost, Happy Birthday. You of all people deserve to be filled with love and joy on the day of your birth. May it be spent with the people who are nearest to your heart.

I've spent the better part of an hour staring at this blank page, wondering what I could say freely to you now that our worlds seem to have altered yet again. I suppose there isn't anything I can write that will repair the damage I've done by returning with Lila. Only my actions and time can heal those wounds. Still, I hope what I have to say might not be a waste in soothing the ache of your heart.

When we first met, I told you I wanted you to trust me. That rings true now more than ever. These are uncertain times and after everything we've been through, everything we've learned, in the end, I can only hope that you'll look at me with trust in your eyes as well as in your heart. Though it may not seem like it, everything I've done since the moment I healed you, has been in service to you. Not just as The Waker, but as my Violet. The stubborn woman who wouldn't listen to reason, the woman who fought me every step of the way, the woman whose strength and perseverance impresses me to this very day. It's all been for you.

You've worked your way into my heart and I fear that I have worked myself out of yours. I could fill this journal with a thousand words, and it would still never be enough to express how much you truly mean to me. Instead, I think it best that I end this letter here, with a salute to you, an extraordinary woman.

Yours Truly,

Robert

A single tear rolled down my cheek as another round of thunder rumbled overhead. My heart ached with his words and my hands shook as I closed the front cover. Never in my life did I think I could feel so much love and frustration toward one person. He was right, he didn't deserve my forgiveness for bringing Lila back, but every cell in my body, every beat of my heart ached to forgive him.

I was glad I hadn't read the letter in front of him. Surely if he was still in the room, I would've fallen into his arms without a thought to the consequences. Instead, I set the gift down on the nightstand and opened the window.

Cool, refreshing air touched my skin. As I listened to the even patter of raindrops, I let myself feel each and every single one of Robert's words. Another tear fell from my eyes as lightning flashed across my closed eyelids. My heart swelled as I took a deep breath. The clean, earthy smell of rain filled my nose and made its way into my chest, healing the broken pieces of my heart. Another deep breath and I opened my eyes.

I couldn't allow myself to be vulnerable like this. As The Waker, I had a job to do and letting my heart rule my emotions would only end in disaster. Watching the rain fall in sheets, I took another shaky breath and pushed my feelings for Robert aside. Maybe when this was all over, we might have a chance at something real.

Another crack of lightning bounced off every reflective surface, followed by a deafening round of thunder that trembled through the house. Squinting, I closed the window and made my way downstairs to the living room.

As I moved through the house without the aid of any light, I saw a slim figure folding blankets in the living room.

"Morning," Lila trilled. She seemed to be in a good mood.

"Morning," I sighed. "Are all the lights out down here too?"

She moved around the couch and flipped the knob on and off. No lights.

"Damn," I said under my breath.

"*Inlihtnes*," Lila recited the spell with little effort. Tiny spheres of light flew around the room, lighting up the space in a soft candle-like glow. "Unlike the rest of your neighbors, we don't have to live in darkness." She smiled.

"What are those?" I asked. One of the little globes floated just a few feet away from me, bobbing up and down like a jellyfish and giving off just enough light to brighten a small radius.

"Illuminator orbs. It's a basic spell. Most people don't use it very often, but it's incredibly handy for situations like this." Lila's casual tone made me feel inadequate, like I should have known such a simple spell.

"Matty called," Robert said, coming out of the kitchen holding two mugs. "They're on their way back from Caltome and should be here in about ten minutes." He handed the chipped mouse ear mug to Lila.

"Hopefully they didn't run into any issues," I said, making my exit into the kitchen.

Searching for something to settle my grumbling stomach, I found a box of granola bars in the pantry. The cranberry almond bar wouldn't be nearly as good as Jake's pancakes, but it would do for now.

"I don't know what we're going to do if my father finds the ring first," Lila lamented as I walked into the middle of her and Robert's conversation. "With the sword already-"

"Let's not get ahead of ourselves. We'll talk with Matty when he gets here and we'll come up with a plan to find the ring," Robert reasoned.

"My father's been searching for the tokens much longer than Matthew has."

"We found the necklace, didn't we?"

I took a healthy bite of my granola bar, idly wondering if Robert ever got tired of being the optimistic one.

"Great. One out of three." Lila rolled her eyes.

"Please try to stay positive," Robert urged, touching her shoulder.

"Something's been bothering me." I took another bite of my snack.

"And what might that be?" Robert turned to look at me, his left eyebrow cocked.

"Why would Aiden, or Morgana for that matter, care about the Tokens?"

"Why wouldn't they," Lila furrowed her brow and crossed her arms.

"If the tokens are meant to wake The Lady, then what reason would they have to collect them?"

"To keep them out of your hands," Lila suggested.

"See, I'm starting to think it's more than that."

Robert nodded his head. "Maybe, they want to harness the Magic somehow."

"It does seem like something Alyssa would be into," Lila said.

"What made you think of this all of a sudden?" Robert asked.

I shrugged. "I don't know. Ever since I had that Vision of William and Le Fay, I've felt like we're missing something, something important."

Jake stumbled into the room, holding up a pale, albite healthier looking Annabel.

"What're you doing out of bed?" I rushed to Annabel's side and helped Jake ease her down onto the couch.

"I'm fine, really," Annabel insisted with a voice raspy and deep from disuse.

"You're not fine," Jake seethed. "You should be resting."

"He's right. You shouldn't be out of bed, you need to save your strength," I advised.

"I'm telling you…" Annabel struggled to say. She winced as she adjusted herself. "I'm much better. Whatever miracle drug you guys dug up, worked."

Leaning forward, I picked at the fresh bandages around her head. The gaping, infected wound that was there last night had almost healed. Pink scar tissue blossomed across her skull and the bruising had all but disappeared.

"I don't understand how this is possible." I meant it as a statement of fact, but the inflection in my voice tilted up at the end as if I was asking a question.

"I'm fine, really. A little tired, but I'll make it through," Annabel reassured us.

I wanted to push her to lie down and take it easy, but having been in her situation before, I left her alone. I hated it when everyone fussed over me, especially when all I wanted to do was train and get back into the fight. I couldn't fault Annabel for feeling the same. If she said she was healthy enough to be there, then so be it.

"Do you remember anything from your time away?" Lila asked, making an effort to sound soft and gentle like she was afraid of scaring the skin right off of Annabel. Never in a million years did I think she could summon any kind of compassion, let alone concern for someone she hardly knew.

Annabel looked at her lap and wrung her fingers. "Yeah, I remember quite a few things." She bit her lip and refused to make eye contact with anyone but Jake.

"You don't have to do this right now," Jake said. He folded into a squatting position in front of his wife and held her fidgeting hands.

"I do, it's important." She nodded and her eyelids closed like weights were hanging from the edge of her lashes.

"Lila, while I do not harbor any sort of compassion for you, I do not envy you in this moment," Annabel began.

Lila adjusted herself and started turning the ring on her pinky finger at Annabel's cryptic words.

"Your father…" Annabel said. "Aiden, he's dead."

Lila froze, her ring facing upside down as her bottom lip fell open.

Robert moved his hand over hers and everyone's eyes fell on Lila.

"How?" Robert asked. His jaw clenched and his eyes flared with the same intensity I used to look at Lila with.

"It was Morgana. I overheard the guards talking about it. She took him out of the picture the first chance she got," Annabel replied.

"Good riddance," Lila spat, composing herself. "He may have fathered me, but he was far from a loving parent. He got what he deserved." She sounded angry, but her glassy eyes told a different story. She might be mad at Aiden for everything he'd put her through, but he was still her father and it was never easy to lose family.

"I still can't believe she killed him after all the trouble he went through to bring her back," Jake said, giving Annabel's shoulder a gentle brush with his fingers.

"I can," Annabel said, her voice cold. "Aiden's men are her followers now. They all know they're expendable. If they don't fall in line behind her, she'll get rid of them in the blink of an eye, just like Aiden." Annabel's eyes slowly rose to meet mine. "You have to wake The Lady and end this before it's too late."

I nodded, chills running down my arms at the harshness of her voice.

"Anything else?" Robert asked, redirecting Annabel's attention.

Annabel sucked in a sharp breath as she adjusted in her seat. "Morgana's gaining strength," she continued. "I couldn't see how many supporters she had, but I could hear them. At night, she'd hold rallies outside and the roar of the crowd… it still gives me goosebumps." Annabel paused to catch her breath. "There was one day, after they… when they were trying to get me to talk. They thought I'd passed out." Her eyes lingered on the floor and the room fell silent except for the steady thrum of rain and the occasional bout of thunder. "They didn't realize I could hear them when they started talking about Le Fay."

My eyes met Robert's as my heart turned cold. So it was true then. Morgana's supporters were never defeated, they just went into hiding.

"They're doing raids, imprisoning people with strong Magical abilities who won't fight for the cause and killing the rest," Annabel went on.

"Imprisoning them? Why?" I asked.

"Alyssa," Robert said through gritted teeth.

Annabel nodded.

"How many?" Robert asked, leveling his eyes on Annabel and crossing his arms.

"From where I was, I only saw a couple dozen," she answered. "But I don't know if there are other cells or not."

"We *need* to help them," I interjected. I had no idea what Avalon was really like, but after everything I've seen in my visions, I knew we couldn't leave people there to suffer.

"Hello, hello," Brett's voice rang through the house.

The front door slammed closed with a bang and a rush of cool air wafted through the room.

"What's will the Illuminators?" Matty asked as he and Brett joined us. The orbs floating around the room bounced out of the way like little jellyfish, making room for our two late arrivals.

"Power's out," I said.

"How was Caltome?" Robert's voice boomed through the room.

"Good morning to you too," Brett snapped.

They both looked like they hadn't slept in days. In contrast to Matty's normally infectious personality, he was subdued and muted as he walked across the room and the slump of Brett's shoulders spoke volumes.

"While we were dropping Gwen and her kids off, we ran into Michael Ainsworth and a few others from Hurst," Matty explained as he switched on the fireplace.

"How's everyone?" I asked.

"They lost a couple people," Brett revealed. "And a handful of others are pretty badly injured."

"I should head up there," Robert remarked in a business-like tone.

"I told them you would. The Deardon's are doing their best, but they need help that a first-aid kit can't provide." Some of the edge in Brett's voice disappeared as she addressed Robert.

"Michael also confirmed that Morgana got away with Excalibur." Matthew let out a heavy sigh.

"So we go get it then," Jake said matter-of-factly as thunder rolled ominously overhead.

"It's not that easy, Jake. If she's taken over Avalon, which I assume she did when she usurped my father, it's going to be very hard to reach her, let alone get the sword," Lila explained.

"No one ever said any of this was going to be easy," Annabel said, doing her best to show strength. "But it's a risk we have to take."

"You don't understand. The whole island is protected. We can't get within a hundred feet without setting off every alarm in the place."

"I may know someone who can help disable the alarm systems," I chimed in. I didn't want to drag her into this, but now that Becky knew about the Magical world, she could be an asset.

"It isn't just a physical alarm. There are Magical wards, patrols, and who knows what else, now that Morgana has taken the helm," Lila explained.

"Well then, it's a good thing we have someone who knows the ins and outs of Avalon, isn't it?" Brett said, cocking her head like a bird inspecting her prey.

Lila shrugged. "I'll tell you whatever you want to know, but that doesn't mean we'll get very far."

Everyone fell silent as Lila's words hung in the air. A flash of lightning and the deep rumble of thunder rolled over each of us.

"It's settled then," Matthew chirped. "Once we have Excalibur, all we have left is to find the ring."

Brett's eyes caught mine, and she nodded toward the hall.

"Do you have any leads?" Jake asked as Brett moved across the room.

Robert's eyes followed his sister and then glanced in my direction as I moved after her. I gave Robert a short, tight shake of my head and walked away.

"What is it?" I whispered, practically running into her as I turned the corner.

"I know this isn't my place, but you should tell them about the ring." Brett was unable to meet my eyes.

"Are you crazy?" I asked, feeling betrayed. I'd wrestled with the idea of telling anyone about the ring and decided I could trust Brett, and now she wanted me to tell everyone else?

"Hear me out." She held up her hands defensively. "The ring is the last piece of the puzzle. Once we have Excalibur-"

"If we get Excalibur."

"Once we do," she amended. "There's nothing stopping you from waking The Lady. Don't you think they have a right to know that we're this close?" She held up her thumb and index finger, indicating the distance between us and the finish line.

"Brett, what this ring can do..."

"It's your call, of course, but I just think if they're going to go up against Morgana they should know we have a real chance of ending this."

"Maybe, I'll think about it." I tucked my hair behind my ear before making my way back into the living room.

"Everything okay?" Robert whispered as Brett and I returned to the others.

"Peachy," I said, giving him a smile.

"Violet, you said you know someone who can help us get past the physical alarm?" Matty thankfully jumped in before Robert could stick his nose any further into my business.

"I'll shoot her a text right now." Grabbing my cell from my back pocket, I scrolled to Becky's name and sent her a quick message.

Need your computer skills, asap.

I wasn't expecting a response from her since it was still fairly early, so I was surprised when my phone *dinged* with her reply.

Just tell me when and where.

And HAPPY BIRTHDAY! <3

CHAPTER SEVENTEEN

For the first time since Becky found out about the Magical world, I didn't dread her knowing the truth. Instead, I thanked my lucky stars that she might be able to help us get Excalibur back.

"Becky will be over soon," I announced, and sat down next to Annabel.

"Becky?" Annabel's eyes narrowed. "Did you finally tell her the truth then?"

"In a roundabout way." I bit my lip. "After you were captured, there was another attack at my place and Becky showed up at the tail end. I may or may not have thrown a stunning orb at her."

Annabel burst out laughing. "I wish I could've been there to see her face. How'd she handle it?"

"Honestly, better than I did when I first found out."

"Don't sell yourself short, kid." Jake squeezed my shoulder as he made his way around the couch. "You handled it better than most."

I let out a short, sarcastic laugh. "I'm sure Robert would

disagree with you." I glanced up at him as he moved to Matthew's side.

"I plead the fifth." Robert gave me a crooked smile.

"You would," Brett remarked, and we all laughed.

"I told you she'd handle it better than you thought," Annabel said. She playfully slapped my arm as I watched Robert and Matthew lay out all his research on the coffee table.

Robert's letter replayed in my head and echoed in my heart. Even without his beautiful words, it was getting more and more difficult to keep myself in check around him. Not only did my Magic flare up when he was near, but my heart ached every time I had the chance to reach out to him and didn't. I bit the corner of my lip as he picked up one sheet in particular and ran a hand through his hair.

"You might want to wipe the drool off your face," Annabel whispered, leaning closer to me.

"Huh, what?" I muttered, pulling my eyes away from Robert.

Annabel raised her eyebrows suggestively. I flushed.

"Am I that obvious?" I asked under my breath.

"You're about as subtle as a gunshot," she chuckled.

I sighed and glanced back up at Robert for a brief moment.

"Something happened between you two, didn't it?" Annabel squealed.

"Not now." My eyes widened in horror at the thought of gossiping about Robert right in front of him.

"I take it you finally gave him a proper homecoming?"

"Knock it off. It's nothing like that." I rolled my eyes but couldn't help smiling. I'd missed Annabel's playful, easy-going banter more than I'd realized.

She raised her hands in surrender. "Hey, I'm not judging you. Everyone knows you care about each other, there's nothing wrong with expressing it."

"Maybe when things cool down." I nodded, but the words felt hollow.

"There's never a right time or place for love."

Annabel glanced in Jake's direction and a small, secret smile pulled at the corner of her mouth as he left the room to pour her another cup of Harriet's tea.

The large knocker resounded twice through the house, interrupting our conversation.

"I'll get it." I jumped to my feet.

Opening the door, Becky stood under the portico, sopping wet.

"Thanks for coming so quickly," I said, as she stepped inside.

Peeling off her jacket and wiping her feet on the mat. "It's like apocalyptic rain out there."

"Sorry for dragging you out of bed so early," I said as we made our way toward the others.

"Don't be silly, I'm happy to help." She waved her hand, dismissing my guilt. "How was your trip?"

I let out a heavy sigh. "There's a lot to catch you up on."

"It's nice to see you again, Becky," Annabel incline her head.

"You too." Becky looked between Annabel and me. Her eyes widening at Annabel's appearance.

"Like I said, there's a lot to catch up on," I said under my breath and gripped her shoulder.

"Clearly," Becky said, looking around the room. "It's Jake, right?" She pointed in his direction.

"Hello again," Jake replied, "Welcome to the fold." He extended a hand toward Becky.

"You might remember Brett from the wedding as well." I motioned in Brett's direction. She and Becky shared a secret look.

"That's Matthew." I pointed in Matty's direction and he gave Becky a warm smile. "Anything and everything you could ever want to know about Magic, he's your guy," I went on. "And of course you know Robert and Lila"

"Why is she here?" Becky asked, looking down her nose at

Lila. I'd only given her the highlights on who she was, but it was enough for Becky to harbor a ball of hate fire for the woman.

"Don't start." I leveled my gaze on her.

"And who are you exactly?" Lila asked with a cold tone.

"Is she being serious right now?" Becky shot me a glance like she was ready to brawl.

"Beck, it's safer with her around," I explained.

"Oh, of course, it's always a safer tactic to share a cup of tea with your would-be murderer."

"Alright, Beck," I said, pulling her by the arm. "There's a lot you don't understand."

"Whatever you say." She plopped down on the loveseat and riffled through her bag. Becky was always good at dropping a topic in the heat of the moment, but I knew I would hear about this later.

"So, what do you need help with?" she asked a little more aggressively than necessary.

"We need you to take a security system down," I replied.

Becky pulled her laptop out of her bag and flipped the screen open. "Okay," she said hesitantly. "What exactly are you trying to accomplish?" She fired up her laptop.

"We need to get into a compound, steal Excalibur and get out without raising any flags," Lila offered.

I shifted my eyes from side to side. When Lila put it that way, it sounded terrible. Becky was still new to this world, and she had no idea how important getting Excalibur was. I cringed internally as I waited for her response.

"Excalibur, as in the sword in the stone?" Becky asked. She turned her head slowly and looked up at me, excitement filling her eyes.

I nodded. *Becky was made for the Magical world.* I thought.

"Alright, first I need to know whose system we're breaking into, and the location," Becky pressed on, unwavering, though her smile lingered.

"His name is, was, Aiden Patridge and Avalon is located in the Scottish Isles," Lila explained.

"Do you happen to know the name of the system he's using?"

Lila shook her head.

"Alright, let's dig up everything we can. I need three unique identifiers, birthday and I'll take either a social, driver's license, passport number?" Becky readied her hands over the keyboard.

"Aiden Patridge, November 14, 1956, and I don't know his social or anything like that," Lila shared, leaning against the mantel.

Becky's fingers flew over the keys as her search into Aiden began.

"Okay, how about place of birth?" Becky asked, trying to narrow her search.

"Inverness, Scotland," Lila answered.

Becky typed the location, and we all waited, watching her like the sword would Magically pop out of her computer screen.

"Parents were Lilian Mackay and Dorian Patridge?" she asked.

"Yes," Lila replied.

"Alright, let's see what I can dig up." White letters flew across the black little box she had opened at the top of her screen.

I knew very little about Becky's work since most of her assignments were classified, but I did know that she was extremely good at what she did.

"And bingo," Becky said and smacked her lips. "It looks like he had quite a few accounts open with different security companies. Hmm." She began typing again.

"What is it?" I asked as Becky sat up and leaned closer to the screen.

"It looks like he recently made a large wire transfer to one of the companies. We'll start with them. I just need to find a backdoor into their system and I should be able to look up individual accounts."

"She's pretty good," Brett said and nodded in approval.

Becky finished typing and said, "Now we wait." She leaned back in her chair and watched the screen.

"How long's this going to take?" Lila asked, eyeing Becky.

"This isn't some spy thriller where the good guys hack into someone's system in thirty seconds. The program has to run in the background until it finds a way in and downloads all the data we need."

Becky stared Lila down like she wanted to light her on fire. Lila was the first to break eye contact and whispered something to Robert.

"In the meantime, I brought something for you, Violet," Becky continued, picking up her bag and pulling out a rectangle wrapped in brown paper. "It's from me and Brett."

"Brett?" I looked between the two of them, both smiling like children. "You guys didn't have to do this."

"I know, you say that every year, but just open it." Becky clapped her hands eagerly.

Self-conscious, I ripped the paper and exposed a smooth black surface. Opening the front cover, I realized it was my Walt Whitman photo album. My mouth fell open, but no words came out as I turned the page. Each landscape was printed on thick cardboard, allowing the photo to span across the seam without interruption. The poems and quotes that Brett and I had worked on together were perfectly paired and exactly as I'd imagined them.

"I know how important it was to you to finish the portfolio," Becky began.

"And with everything going on," Brett picked up where Becky left off. "We just thought you might like to see the finished product."

"How long have you two been working on this?"

"Not long. After we paired all the photos, I contacted Becky.

There was a lightness about you when we were working and I wanted to capture that memory."

"I told her you wouldn't mind if we finished putting the portfolio together. You already did the heavy lifting," Becky explained. She gave me a warm smile, and I had to fight the tears shrink wrapping my eyes.

"Thank you, both so much. You have no idea how much this means to me," I said. Running my fingers across the dedication to my parents, the memory of my dad reading Whitman to my mom filled my heart with joy.

Becky's computer beeped and her eyes flicked to the screen.

"Dammit," she grumbled, and her hands went flying across the keyboard again.

"May I see?" Robert sidled up next to me and held out his hand for the portfolio.

Smiling, I handed him the book. As I did, a memory cropped up of him standing in front of me, holding out a book for me to take. It felt like a million years had passed since that moment in Frank's bookstore.

As he flipped to the next page, a small smile touched his lips and his eyes met mine. Looking down at the photo in his hands, I recognized the landscape immediately. To everyone else, it was just a beautiful photo of the beach, with a grouping of rocks. The sun had all but disappeared beyond the horizon, which allowed me to keep my shutter open long enough to make the water have a soft, almost airy quality. It was magical even if you didn't know that it was against those rocks, I learned that I was a Soothsayer.

"It's beautiful," Robert said, flipping to the next page.

"It's exactly as I imagined it."

"I was wondering if you wanted to join me over at Caltome?" I looked up at him as he idly flipped to the next page. "I know the Deardon's would love to see you again and it'll help morale if you were there," Robert said, keeping his tone light.

"Sure, if you think it'll help."

Robert flipped the book closed. "Wonderful, we should head out then."

"Right now?" I searched his eyes.

"People need my help. The sooner we get there, the better." He brushed a rogue strand of hair over my shoulder.

"But what about forming a plan to get Excalibur?"

He leaned closer to me and whispered, "I think they're on it."

When he nodded toward everyone else, I realized that the rest of the group was working together without hurling insults at one other. Lila and Annabel were speaking in hushed tones, while Jake and Matthew were going over the pile of notes and research. Brett stood behind Becky, looking over her shoulder as she furiously typed on her keyboard.

"It kind of feels like the kids have all grown up," I said with a chuckle.

"Shall we then?" Robert cocked his head to the side.

Nodding in agreement, I took the portfolio back and moved toward Becky and Brett.

"We're going to head over to Caltome," I said to Becky. "You'll be safe here with them." I looked at the rest of my makeshift family.

Becky barely acknowledged me when I gave her a quick one-armed hug. "And thank you for the portfolio," I said and gave Brett a hug too. "Both of you."

"Take your time," Brett smiled and glanced at her brother. "We've got things covered here."

"All set?" Robert asked.

"Wait," Lila called after us. She jumped off of the couch, rifled through her bag and rushed over to us. "Take these just in case. It's the last of it." She held out two little bottles containing the putrid tasting orbing potion. "The moon is starting to wane, but it should still do the trick in a pinch."

"Thank you." Robert plucked the bottles from her hand,

sloshing the liquid back and forth, making my stomach roll. I crossed every finger and every toe, hoping we wouldn't have to use them.

"Be safe, both of you." Lila held out her hand for me to shake.

"You too," I said, and gripped her hand firmly.

Morgana might be trying to rip us all apart, but somehow we'd become stronger, more aligned. Never did I think Lila and I would be fighting on the same side, and I certainly didn't think Becky would be sitting in the Maxwell's living room, trying to help us steal Excalibur.

The whole world might have turned upside down, but for a brief moment, I felt at peace knowing that all the people I cared about were under one roof, and safe.

CHAPTER EIGHTEEN

As we walked toward the garage, Robert smiled like a kid on Christmas.

"What's your deal?" I eyed him suspiciously.

"I'm glad you decided to move on from your past with Lila." His hand fell to the small of my back, guiding me forward like he always did. I wondered if it was an unconscious habit since he never seemed to notice.

"I wouldn't go that far. She's an asset, yes, but I'm still not going to be making B.F.F. bracelets anytime soon."

"Whatever your reason, I'm just glad you're not at each other's throats anymore."

I sighed. "Honestly, it just takes too much energy to keep fighting the both of you when she clearly isn't going anywhere."

"Even if she wanted to, she has no place left to go now."

I couldn't quite pin down what Robert really felt about Aiden's death. On the one hand, he seemed to empathize with Lila, but every time Aiden was brought up, Robert's shoulders tightened.

"How do you think she's handling the news?" I asked as we approached Robert's car.

Robert ran a hand through his hair. "Lila's complicated. She doesn't like to share what she's feeling."

"I can relate," I mumbled under my breath, and slipped into the passenger seat.

"Whether she wants to admit it or not, she's in pain and in the past..." He paused as if remembering another life. "Grief can be a powerful thing. But allowing her to help us, it's what she needs right now."

"You're not worried about her walking us into a trap, are you?" I asked as he pulled out of the garage.

"No. At this point, she has nothing left to lose and everything to gain."

"What could she possibly gain from all this?"

"A second chance at life. Under her father's thumb, she never had the opportunity to think for herself, let alone live a life by her own rules." We stopped at a stop sign and Robert turned to look at me. "I know it's hard for everyone to understand why I brought-"

"No, actually I kinda get it," I admitted. "I don't like it, but I get it."

"Really?" Robert raised an eyebrow.

"It fits with who you are." I shrugged. "You take the world's problems on your shoulders and make it your mission to solve them.

"I do my best to see the good in people," Robert clarified. "We aren't born with hatred in our hearts and Lila's no exception. She's a good person once you put the broken pieces back together."

"And what about Morgana? Do you apply the same philosophy to her?" I asked as Robert turned onto the freeway and we sped off toward Caltome.

"Yes and no," he ruminated. "I don't believe she was born a bad seed. I believe her environment made her into the monster she's become."

"And so you think she can be made whole again?"

"The problem with taking the world on your shoulders is knowing that some people can't be saved and having the strength to do what's necessary." He sounded as if he was speaking from experience, and I was reminded of what Graham had said about death and loss in the Magical world.

I laced my fingers through his in an attempt to soothe his heart. Surprise flickered across his features as his eyes met mine for a brief moment before returning to the road.

"Are you worried at all that you won't be able to heal anyone?" I asked.

"Yes." His grip tightened on the steering wheel. "But I have to try. We need to know if it's just Annabel that they've made immune to my ability or if they've branched out."

"Whatever the case may be, we'll figure this out as a team." I squeezed his hand to reassure him.

We spent the rest of the ride in companionable silence. Even without words, I sensed a warmth with Robert that always made me feel safe and content. It was a sweet treat getting to spend an hour wrapped up in his presence without the rest of the group hovering around.

Too soon, it was over and as we pulled into the winery. Meredith and Scott Deardon were already waiting for us.

"It's so good to see you again, dear," Meredith said and gave Robert a big hug, her bright orange hair blowing in the breeze.

"I wish it was under better circumstances." Scott rubbed the back of his neck.

"And Violet, how are you?" Meredith pulled me in for a hug like I was her daughter returning from college.

"I'm good. How's everyone? Gwen and the kids?"

"They're alright, far better than some," Scott answered. He motioned for us to follow him as he swung himself up into the Gator.

"How many are injured?" Robert asked, holding his hand out for me.

"About twenty or so. Only a handful are critical," Scott reported.

"Right, let's go then." Robert hopped into the back of the Gator next to me.

Jostling back and forth on the hard surface, Scott drove the four of us through the vineyard. I assumed we would enter through the same little shack that Matthew and I had used, so I was surprised when we came to a stop next to a door set into a hillside.

The large iron entrance nestled into the dirt and weeds looked like it'd been there for hundreds of years. Scott lifted the latch with a loud *clunk* and pulled the door free. Robert and Scott took the lead, with Meredith and me following.

The cement floor echoed with each of our footsteps, making it sound like an army of people were walking along the corridor. Large metal lamps hung above us at intervals, giving off a soft yellow light that lit the way to the cellar and sparkled across the dark glass of the wine bottles we passed.

"We ran out of private space a few days ago and had to make room." Meredith motioned to the crates lining the walls. "Matthew arrived just in time for Gwen and her kids. They got the last room."

"How long have people been showing up here?" I asked, surprised this was the first time we were hearing about it.

"About a week or two."

"I'm sorry. We had no idea."

"Don't be. You're doing your part, we're doing ours," she said as the corridor opened to the massive wine cellar I remembered. Instead of racks of wine stretching as far as the eye could see, a makeshift village had sprung up. The large racks and barrels had been pushed off to the walls, allowing pockets of people to congregate around the cavern. Children played with a few toys off to one side while another group of adults talked in hushed voices. In the corner to our left, cots had been set up for the injured. Makeshift bandages helped to address some wounds, but others needed a doctor or, in this case, Robert.

A deep sadness settled in my heart after seeing all the people Morgana had already hurt.

"What can I do?" I asked, needing to help these people.

"She can help the ones who are better off. I won't be able to help everyone in one pass," Robert called over his shoulder as Scott led him to the people who wouldn't make it much longer without him.

"Are you squeamish at all?" Meredith asked, handing me a pair of latex gloves.

"Not really." Though my heart started to race. I was good at first aid, but I'd never been faced with bandaging battle wounds.

"Good, I need help re-dressing their wounds. Some of them got burned pretty badly at Hurst."

I nodded and turned to the person closest to us.

"Hey, I'm going to help you with some fresh bandages," I said to a boy who couldn't have been more than seven.

He nodded and pushed himself into a sitting position. His right shoulder and chest were wrapped with gauze, and little spots of blood had begun seeping through.

"Here you go," Meredith said. She dropped a first-aid kit on the bed and made her way around to the others, checking on each one and stopping to look over an older woman.

"What's your name?" I asked, turning my attention back to the kid.

"Zan." He kept his eyes on his lap as I unwrapped the first layer of gauze.

"Are your parents here?" I asked, hoping for his sake they weren't among the injured or dead.

He nodded and looked toward the group of whispering adults.

"You're The Waker, right?" he asked.

"What gave me away?" I replied, trying to keep my voice light and easy.

"Robert. Everyone knows he's been protecting you." The boy looked over at Robert, who was kneeling over a prone body.

"Is that right?" I nodded as I peeled the last gooey layer of gauze off his shoulder.

"What's he like?" Zan asked. He flicked his head so his jet black hair flipped to the side.

"Robert?" I asked, inspecting the burn. It wasn't too bad. The skin on his shoulder was pink and angry, but it was nothing life threatening by any means.

"Most the time he's a pain in my butt," I mumbled, and Zan's face lit up. "But I guess he's alright." I shrugged dramatically as I applied some more burn cream to his skin.

"Is it true you got your Magic from him?"

I looked up at his wide, excited eyes and couldn't help but feel a sense of wonder. Robert was a hero to Zan. I'd never thought of it like that before, but what Robert did was nothing short of a miracle.

"I did." I glanced over at Robert as he moved to heal the next person. "When he saved my life, he made me Magical."

"Cool." Zan beamed.

"It kind of is," I admitted.

"Ahh." Zan twisted from my grasp as I began wrapping his shoulder.

"Sorry. We're almost finished, I promise." Gently lifting his arm, I finished spinning the gauze around his shoulder. "Alright, you're all set, Zan. Try to take it easy, okay?"

"Waker?" Zan's voice came out soft, like he was afraid to ask what was on his mind.

"Yeah?" I turned to look at him as I pulled my gloves off.

"Do you think you could introduce me to Robert?"

"Of course. I'll bring him by in a bit." I brushed Zan's hair out of his eyes as he smiled up at me. "Now get some rest and relax, okay?"

He nodded furiously and curled up on his side.

Moving around the room, I knelt to help the next person in line. It was a woman, much worse than Zan, and heavily sedated on who knows what. I dressed the burns on her legs and cleaned the large gash across her forearm. Guilt ate at me as I silently finished wrapping her wounds with fresh bandages. I hated that I couldn't do more for her, that I couldn't do more for all of them.

Searching the room for Robert, I noticed he was sitting on the floor, his head leaning back against the wall and his eyes closed. I wasn't sure how many people he'd been able to get to before he needed to rest. I recalled the memory of the night he saved me and remembered he was near exhaustion when I came to, and I was just one person.

The desire to go to him pulled at me, but there were others who needed my help much more than Robert. Moving through the room, I knelt next to a guy about my age. His hands and arms were both heavily wrapped in gauze, and his mouth was turned down in a frown of utter defeat.

"Do you mind if I change your bandages?" I asked, kneeling next to him and his makeshift cot.

He shrugged and held out one of his arms for me to take. I gently unwrapped the dressing, not sure what to say. Waves of hostility rolled off of him, and again I wished there was more I could do.

Once I'd finished with the gauze, I gingerly held onto his arm. His skin was red and angry from the tips of his fingers all the way to his elbow. Pockets of bubbles disfigured his flesh, and I had to fight the urge to look away.

"It's a thing of nightmares," he said, holding up his arm and turning it from side to side.

"It won't be like this forever," I reassured him. "Once Robert-"

"I don't want to be healed." He finally looked up at me. "I don't deserve it."

As softly as I could manage, I pulled his arm closer to me. "How can you say that?" I began to spread some burn jell over the tender skin with a feather's touch.

He looked away as his eyes became glassy and I realized that he felt guilty. That he was taking some sort of blame on himself.

"Whatever happened, it wasn't your fault. Morgana's the only one with blood on her hands. Do you understand?"

"She wasn't even supposed to be there." His voice was barely a whisper.

"Who wasn't?" I lowered my voice and started winding the fresh bandages around his hand.

His eyes met mine as he let out a shaky breath. "Ava."

"Is she here somewhere?" I looked around the cellar. "Maybe Robert can-"

"No." He shook his head. "She didn't make it."

"I'm so sorry." My hands faltered as a tear ran down his cheek. "But this isn't your fault." I gripped his shoulder lightly in an attempt to get through to him, but he looked away and clamped his mouth shut.

I knew all too well what it felt like to take the blame onto yourself, the pain and anger that congealed in your heart. Even if this man did accept Robert's help, it would be a long time before he would ever truly be healed.

It took the better part of an hour to finish his left arm, and then I moved to the other and repeated the process. Neither of us spoke as I finished wrapping the gauze around his arm. There wasn't anything I could say to ease his pain and as much as I wanted to tell him that it would get easier, I knew he wouldn't want to hear it right now.

"If you ever need anything, just get in touch, okay?" I

encouraged him. I gave his thigh a gentle tap and left him to mull over his grief.

Needing a breath of fresh air, I walked over to Robert, who was finishing up with another of Morgana's victims.

"Want to step outside?" I asked as he stood up on shaky legs.

Nodding, he gave me a faint smile and motioned for me to lead the way.

Moving away from the entrance we'd come through, I made my way across the cellar toward the stairs Matthew and I had used the last time I was here. Climbing out of the wine cellar and into the tool shed was like stepping back in time. Everything looked exactly the same. The memory of Matty showing me around the winery and into this shed filled me with a sense of appreciation for how simple life used to be.

Stepping out of the stuffy shed with Robert right on my heels, I sat down under the canopy of trees and looked out over the winery's rolling hills.

"Beautiful, isn't it?" I pulled my knees up against my chest.

"It sure is," Robert said, his eyes glued to me as he sat down.

"How're you feeling?"

"Drained. A couple of them were pretty worse for the wear." He leaned back on his elbows and stretched out his legs.

"Are you worried at all about paying a life for a life to save them?"

He shook his head, "No, none of them were close to death, so there's no balance to restore." he sighed. "They would've healed in time, broken and scarred, but they would have survived."

"Good." A small flock of birds dipped in and out of the vineyard below us. I hated the idea of anyone else dying to save the people we were trying to help here.

"And at least now we know your ability to heal isn't being hindered across the board."

"Yes, but that means they're doing something to their prisoners to make them immune." He laid down and threw his arm over his eyes. "If they learn how to weaponized whatever it is, they're doing to people, then healers across the globe may not be able to use their gift anymore."

I rested my head on my knees and said, "One problem at a time."

"How are you handling everything?" He must have picked up on the melancholy in my voice. "Seeing so much pain can take its toll."

"I'm alright. I just wish there was more I could do." I leaned back, laying on the cool earth, and stared up at the leaves. "They're all in pain, physically, emotionally, and all I can do is wrap a bandage around them. It's not enough."

"It's more than you realize. Your presence alone gives them hope."

"Still, I just wish I could be of more use. There's so many of them, I can't imagine you'll be able to heal them all." I turned my head to look at Robert, rustling the leaves under my hair.

"No, I won't." He picked a rogue twig out of my hair and my Magic hummed as his fingertips grazed my cheek.

"I wonder," I said, sitting up and thinking out loud.

"Wonder what?" Robert replied, matching my movement.

"Do you think we could use our *Artognou-Magic* to help more people?"

"I'm sure we could, but we're still inexperienced."

"We have to try," I pleaded. "If it can help *heal* more people, then we don't have a choice." I searched his eyes, waiting for a rebuttal, but instead, he smiled.

"You really are incredible." Robert stood up and reached out his hand for me to grab. "Shall we then?"

My nerves danced under my skin as I let him pull me to my feet. Just being close to him made my Magic bubble to the surface and as I looked up at him, I saw him through Zan's eyes for a brief moment. This feeling, my Magic, the Bond between us wouldn't exist without him.

"I almost forgot to tell you." I paused and laced my fingers through his. "I met an admirer of yours."

Robert's eyes narrowed as he looked down at me.

"His name's Zan and to him, you might as well be Superman," I laughed, as Robert pulled me toward the shed. "He asked if I would introduce you."

Robert chuckled and said, "Alright, we'll find him before we leave."

CHAPTER NINETEEN

Robert and I made our way back to the makeshift hospital corner with a renewed sense of purpose. We soon found the next person who needed our help and sat down next to them.

The gentleman lying in front of us had burns almost from head to toe. His glassy eyes tracked the movement around him and his lips stayed clenched together. My stomach bottomed out as I looked down at him. I couldn't begin to imagine the kind of pain he was in.

"We're here to help," I said softly, and his eyes feverishly held my own.

"You ready?" Robert gave my hand a squeeze.

"Ready." I closed my eyes and searched for the *Artognou* hidden deep within my own Magic.

"I need you to look at me, so I can connect." Robert said to the burn victim. "Good." He gave my hand another squeeze, and I pulled on the thread of our Bond with as much focus as I could.

It was faint at first, like tugging on a tightly wound ball of yarn. Taking a deep breath, I pulled on the Magic until it broke free and coursed through me. All the walls between Robert and I opened like a floodgate and his Magic poured into me, warm and inviting.

I opened my eyes, sweat starting to bead on my brow as I struggled to hold on to the connection. My eyes darted down the length of the burn victim as a red and angry patch of flesh faded to healthy, robust skin. All over his body the burns were disappearing as I dug my nails into Robert's hand, trying to hold on.

"Just a little longer," Robert grunted.

Digging deep, I focused on the unique feeling of the *Artognou* pulsing through me like a second heartbeat, but it faltered. The harder I tried to hold on, the faster it left me. It was like trying to hold the wind in my hands.

Letting out the breath I'd been holding, I slumped forward.

"I'm sorry," I said through a ragged breath. "I couldn't hold it."

A rough, calloused hand touched my arm, and I opened my eyes.

"Thank you," the burn victim said, although he was no longer covered in ruined skin. We hadn't healed him entirely, but we'd done enough to ensure he was no longer in danger.

Robert peeled my hand out of his and winced as my nails released his skin.

"Sorry," I said sheepishly.

"No, that was amazing. I wouldn't have been able to do half as much without you," Robert encouraged me, rubbing my back affectionately. "Do you think you can handle anymore?"

I wobbled my head from side to side. Of course, I wanted to help heal more people, but I wasn't sure if I'd be able to grab onto the *Artognou* again.

"All we can do is try." I gave him a tired smile. I thought I was tired after using my own Magic, but the combination of healing and connecting through the *Artognou* left me feeling weak and drained, like I'd been battling a nasty virus.

Robert waved over Scott, who rushed to our side and placed a hand on Robert's shoulder.

"You alright?" he asked.

"Fine," Robert replied, but the sweat on his brow told a different story. "Can you help him up and get him something to eat?"

"Mark, look at you." Scott reached down to help the formerly burnt man stand. "You're looking a fair sight better than this morning."

"Thanks to them." He bowed his head, and Scott helped walk him over to join the less critical patients.

"Robert," Meredith called out as she came running over. "Come quickly."

Robert and I stood and followed after Meredith toward the group of adults who were huddling together when we first came in. Now they were all crowded around a woman who was passed out on the floor.

"What happened?" Robert fell to his knees and checked for any obvious signs of trauma.

"I... I don't know," one of the men stuttered. "One minute we were all talking, the next she was on the ground."

Robert held his hand over her crumpled body and closed his eyes.

"She's bleeding internally," he announced. "Violet, come here." He reached for my hand. "I'm about spent, and I'm not going to get a good connection with her unconscious so you need to hold on as long as you can."

Nodding, I gripped his hand and mentally prepared to tap back into our connection. As I was about to close my eyes, I saw Zan's head poke through the crowd. His lips silently mouthed one word, "Mom."

My heart faltered as I closed my eyes and scrambled to pull

up my Magic. Recognizing the tenor of the *Artognou*, I let it spread through every nerve ending in my body. Fire ripped through me as Robert's Magic broke through the connection.

Taking a ragged breath through clenched teeth, I held on for dear life. I'd never felt anything so powerful, so primal in my entire life. The *Artognou* poured out of me, hungry and eager for an outlet. My heartbeat felt like it was in stereo, racing faster and faster toward the finish line. I wanted to scream, to let go, but I held on, pushing myself past what I thought was possible.

"Almost..." Robert grunted and squeezed my fingers so tightly I was sure my fingers were broken.

"Robert, I can't..." I muttered, the words barely audible.

"Just a few more seconds."

I began to shake my head as the *Artognou* exploded inside of me like a firework and then fizzled out, leaving me completely spent. Every muscle in my body turned to Jell-O, and I collapsed.

"Mom," I heard Zan yell, his voice sounding like he was in a tin can.

"She's going to be alright," Robert sighed, and then I felt his hand on mine. "We did it." Robert gave me a crooked smile as he kneeled next to me on the concrete floor.

"A life for a life?" My voice was barely a whisper.

Robert's lips formed a hard line, and he nodded.

"Let us through, let us through." Meredith's voice boomed over the bustle of voices surrounding us. Her hand went to my forehead. "You're burning up."

"I'm fine," I said as she helped me to a standing position. "I just need to rest a few minutes."

"We can get to the rest if-" Robert tried to plead.

"You're not healing anyone else," Meredith interrupted. "The both of you are exhausted and need time to rest and regain your strength."

"But the others?"

"We can manage the rest. You've done your part now it's time to take care of yourselves."

"Are you sure?" Robert asked as Scott helped support his weight.

Scott nodded. "You've done well."

"Let us get you something to eat and a quiet place to recharge." Meredith moved toward the exit while helping me keep my balance.

"Waker," Zan's small voice called after me. I turned toward him as he gripped me around the waist. "Thank you for saving my mom."

I smiled down at him, then looked at Robert. "I think he's the one you should be thanking." I nodded toward Robert.

Zan's eyes lit up.

Wincing, Robert knelt, so that he was eye level with Zan and placed his hand on the boy's good shoulder.

Zan's eyes grew into large disks and Robert's brow furrowed as he pulled on the last bit of Magic he had to heal Zan.

"I need you to do me a favor," Robert exhaled.

"Me?" Zan asked.

Robert nodded. "I need you to look after your mom for me. She'll need to rest since we weren't able to heal all the damage."

"Will she be okay, though?"

"She's going to be more than okay." Robert gave Zan a warm smile and rubbed his arm affectionately. "So you think you can do that for me?"

Zan nodded so furiously his hair fell into his eyes.

"Thank you," Robert said. He stood and held out his hand for Zan to shake.

Robert's hand engulfed Zan's tiny little fingers, but he didn't seem to mind. His smile stretched from ear to ear and I was glad that we were able to save his mother, no matter what the cost.

"Time for you two to take care of yourselves now," Meredith barked. She practically dragged me back to the Gator while Robert seemed to be walking of his own accord, if only barely.

"Was that *Artognou-Magic* that the two of you were using?" Scott whispered when the others were out of earshot.

Robert glanced at me as Scott pushed the heavy metal door open and a sense of wonder filled his eyes.

"It was," I answered.

I stared back at Robert, unable to believe we'd done it. We'd actually tapped into our *Artognou* and helped save people's lives.

"Merlin's beard." Meredith's eyes darting between the two of us. "We knew you got your Magic from Robert, but to be Bonded…" She trailed off and shook her head.

"What Meredith is trying to say is that it's an honor to know such truly magnificent people," Scott added.

"Right, anything you need, we're here, always." Meredith met my eyes and inclined her head ever so slightly. Right then, I realized that she no longer saw us as her peers.

"Thank you, Meredith, but you're already doing more than enough by helping all those people." Robert tried to refocus the attention onto them.

"It's the least we can do for the community," Scott chimed in, leading us to the Gator.

With more than a little help from Meredith, I hoisted myself into the bed of the four-wheeled vehicle.

"We'll take you to our private residence on the property. It's small, but it should more than suit your needs," Scott called over his shoulder and the Gator roared to life.

We took off across the unpaved gravel and rocks. Leaning against Robert for support, I couldn't help but think about how our *Artognou-Magic* would change not only our lives, but the lives of the people around us. We could do so much good in the world if only we could learn how to better control it. A small part of me wondered if Arthur had thought and felt the same. If his *Artognou-Magic* gave him the strength and courage to fight for what he believed in.

We slowed to a crawl, and I opened my eyes, not realizing that I'd closed them. A small cottage nestled under a grouping of trees in front of us. A pond, with white and purple flowers dotting the edge of the water, sat to the right of the front porch and light green shutters hung open on all the cottage windows.

"It's not much, but it's our home away from home." Scott gave me a small smile as he helped me out of the back of the Gator.

"It's beautiful," I sighed.

"It has everything you need," Meredith added, opening the front door. "Pantry's full and the bathroom and bedroom are around the corner." She pointed to the hall on our left.

Everything looked brand new, and I wondered if they ever really spent much time there.

"Thank you for this." Robert placed his hand on Meredith's shoulder and pulled her in for a hug. "I promise we won't be long."

"Don't be silly, take as much time as you need," Meredith cooed.

"We'll be back in the cellar if you need anything," Scott called from the front porch. "Think you can find your way back?"

Robert nodded and walked with Meredith to the front door.

"Thank you for coming so quickly today. Those people you saved…" Meredith said, turning in the doorway to face us. "I'm just grateful we didn't lose anyone else."

"As am I," Robert agreed, leaning against the door. He was hiding his exhaustion well.

"Meredith, come on," Scott urged from the Gator, "let them rest."

"You know where to find us if you need us," Meredith concluded and made her way down the porch stairs.

"Right back at you," Robert called after her and closed the door.

"I'm going to check in with the others real quick." He pulled his cell out of his pocket.

"Sure," I said, running my hand along the shelf filled with vinyl records.

Robert shuffled over to the kitchen and opened the refrigerator, ducking his head inside while waiting for someone to pick up the other end of the phone.

Wanting to explore the rest of the house, I made my way down the hall. One of the pictures I'd taken had been hung on the wall to my left. I touched the corner of the frame and a calmness washed over me at the memory of that day. What was only a few months ago felt like a lifetime, and I wondered if I could still capture the same tone of beauty and innocence now that I'd changed so much.

Moving a little further down the hall, I found a photo of Scott and Meredith on their wedding day and couldn't help but smile. They were the perfect complement to each other. Meredith's fiery red hair blew in the wind while Scott's darker features grounded them both.

I passed by the bathroom on the left and went to the bedroom door a little further ahead. The room was bathed in a soft afternoon glow and more than anything I wanted to lay down on the king size bed and recharge my batteries.

The floor creaked behind me and I looked over my shoulder. Robert stood in the doorway holding a couple bottles of water.

"Thought you might like something to drink." He extended the bottle for me to grab.

"Thanks." I moved closer to him. "How's everyone back home?" I sat down on the edge of the bed and cracked open the bottle.

"They're good." Robert stepped into the room and a secret smile pulled at the corner of his mouth.

"What is it?" I furrowed my brow out of curiosity.

"Apparently…" he started, and sat down next to me. "Becky has appointed herself general of the Maxwell family."

I laughed and rolled my eyes. "Of course she has. How does Brett feel about that?"

"Are you kidding? Those two are thick as thieves now." Robert took a sip of water and shook his head at the absurdity of it all.

"I'm glad Becky seems to be taking this all in stride." I fiddled with the wrapper on the water bottle.

"She would've made a good Promised One."

"You think so?" I looked at him, surprised.

"Of course. She's fiercely loyal to you and clearly an asset."

I smiled at the thought of Becky being a part of this world. As much as I wanted to keep her safe, having her in the know was a huge weight off my chest.

I leaned my head against his shoulder and asked, "Do you think there are others like Becky out there? You know, people who'd fall into the Magical world with open arms?"

Robert wrapped his arm around me, pulling me closer and letting his hand rest on my hip. "I'd imagine so, but it isn't the Becky's of the world you have to worry about."

Shifting my head, I looked up at him.

"There are far more people who would take advantage of it and use Magic for their own personal gain," Robert explained.

"It's kind of sad, isn't it? Having to hide such a big part of ourselves from the rest of the world."

Robert placed his fingers under my chin, lifting my head as he said, "Some things are only meant to be shared with the people you care about." His eyes softened with each word and the beat of my heart kicked up a notch.

A hunger I didn't know existed stirred in my abdomen as he leaned his forehead against mine.

"Violet," he continued, "I can't pretend to know how you-"

I pulled away from him so I could look him in the eyes. "Despite everything that's happened since Pacifica Pier…" My words faltered as I tried to catch my breath. "I never stopped caring about you."

His eyes searched mine for a long moment, a war waging within him, and then he tightened his hand around my hip and pulled me closer, placing his lips against mine.

The fire burning within me when we connected through the *Artognou* was nothing compared to this. Every nerve in my body called out to him as if seeking their other half. Pushing myself closer, I deepened the kiss and brushed my hand through his hair.

A small moan escaped my throat as he gently pushed me backward onto the bed. His body hovered above my own as he pulled his lips from mine to trace my collarbone with his mouth.

Every muscle in my body was sore, and each nerve fried from using our Magic but somehow his touch, his kiss, soothed the ache that had settled deep in my bones. He moved his mouth back to mine as his hand traced the curve of my body and settled on my hip. Pulling him closer to me, I pushed us both over the edge. The walls between us crumbled as the Robert I knew, the Robert I missed so desperately, pulled me tightly against him.

Each second chipped away at the emptiness I'd felt since he'd been taken, the heat of his body igniting a fire inside me that slowly filled in the broken pieces of my heart.

Pulling my mouth from his, I let my head fall back to try to catch my breath. His lips never skipped a beat as he kissed the tender skin of my neck, making my heart ache in their wake.

He lifted his lips from my skin and looked down at me as I let out a ragged breath. His endless, dark eyes bore into mine as he traced my lip with his thumb, undoing the last lock around my heart.

My fingers fumbled with the buttons on his shirt as I reached up to him, and he leaned in to kiss me once more.

"Damn buttons," I said against his lips. He chuckled and the warmth of his breath enticed me further as I pushed his shirt off his broad shoulders.

As his shirt fell to the floor, I ran my fingers lightly over his shoulders and down his arms, enjoying every inch of him. I'd seen him without his shirt on numerous occasions, but finally, I was able to appreciate him up close. Robert shivered ever so slightly at my touch as he pulled me against him. His lips lightly touched mine, but he didn't kiss me.

"You have always been more than just The Waker to me," he whispered. "Since the day we met, you stole my heart." He studied me as if he was trying to cement this moment in his memory.

He rolled over and pulled me on top of him, kissing me as if this was our last moment on earth. I let myself get lost in him. Every breath, every touch, a silent promise. With or without our *Artognou-Magic*, we were one, our bodies intertwined into a single being, our heartbeats echoing one another for all of time.

CHAPTER TWENTY

he sound of my phone vibrating woke me. The sun had long since faded and the bedroom had plunged into darkness. Rolling out of Robert's arms, I leaned over the edge of the bed and plucked my phone from the pocket of my jeans.

"Hel…" I said, then cleared my throat. "Hello," I tried again, and this time managed to not sound like I'd been smoking for fifty years.

"Hey." Becky's voice chiming through the phone. I had to hold the receiver away from my face. "We hadn't heard from you guys in a little while, so I said I would call. How's everything going?"

"What time is it?" I squinted at the bright screen on my phone. Eleven-thirty. We'd been sleeping for almost eight hours.

"Oh wow, it's late," I commented. "Everything's fine. We crashed pretty hard after healing a good majority of the people here."

"Everything okay?" Robert asked as he rolled toward me.

"Umm, excuse me, but are you two in bed together?" Becky sounded like she was speaking through a megaphone.

"Would you keep it down," I snapped under my breath.

"That isn't a no," Becky noted.

"Is there anything pressing you wanted to talk about or can we get back to sleep?"

"Oh, you bet your pretty little backside we have something to talk about." Even through the phone, I could tell she was foaming at the mouth for all the juicy details.

"Anything life threatening that we need to discuss?"

Becky let out a frustrated sigh. "No, but Brett wants to know when you'll be home. We think we've come up with a pretty solid plan, but apparently, they need your blessing."

I looked over at Robert and noticed his eyes were on me.

"I need to check on a few people before we leave, but other than that we can head back anytime," he said.

Robert traced my collarbone with his fingers and then followed the chain around my neck to the ring dangling over my chest.

"We'll be back first thing tomorrow morning," I said to Becky.

"Alright, see you then, *sleep* well," she teased.

"Night." I clicked the end button and plopped the phone down next to me.

I pulled Robert's fingers gently from the ring.

"I meant to ask you earlier, where'd you get this?" His finger traced the small circle of metal. "I've never noticed it before."

"Well, you wouldn't have, since I wear it under my shirt."

His eyes narrowed. "Don't evade the question."

Holding the cool metal between my fingers, I wrestled with the idea of telling him the truth. If I could trust him with my body, heart, and soul, could I trust him with this?

I searched his eyes as he propped himself up on his elbow.

"Violet, whatever it is, you can tell me," he urged.

He reached out and took my hand from the ring, holding my palm against his chest. The warmth of his bare skin and the steady beat of his heart undid me. He was the man who had saved my life, who had fought to keep me alive time and time again. The man I shared a Bond with both Magically and physically. If I couldn't put my trust in him, then surely Morgana had already won.

"Graham gave it to me." I looked toward the ceiling, knowing he would be hurt that I'd hadn't shared the truth with him earlier.

"Graham?" He reached for the delicate circle around the chain again, and this time I didn't stop him.

"It's The Ring of Dispel." I let out a heavy sigh.

When Robert didn't say anything, I shifted my head to look at him. His eyes were glued to the ring, turning it back and forth in his fingers.

"Robert, please say something."

His eyes touched mine for a brief moment before darting back to the ring.

"Why didn't you say anything before?" He gently placed the ring against my chest and draped his arm over me.

"Graham entrusted the ring to me and with everything that's happened I just thought it best to keep it quiet," I rambled. It felt good to tell him the truth, and I couldn't get the words out fast enough.

"So you haven't told anyone else?"

"Actually..." I bit my lip. "Brett knows."

"Well, at least you trusted someone with the truth."

"I'm sorry I didn't tell you sooner, I just wasn't..." I felt like an idiot and couldn't finish the sentence. The thought of not trusting Robert almost seemed absurd now, given our proximity.

"You never have to apologize to me. It's my own fault that you felt like you couldn't come to me with this." He rolled onto his back and I turned on my side, following after him. "Did Graham at least warn you about the power of the ring?" He held out his arm so I could tuck in next to him and lay my head on his chest.

"He did. That's why I kept it a secret. No one should have this kind of power." I touched the chain around my neck and my heart turned cold.

"We do need to tell the others. Matty at the very least."

"I know." I let my fingers dance around Robert's bare chest. "That's what Brett pulled me aside about. She wanted me to tell everyone about the ring."

"Why didn't you say anything then?" He moved his hand up and down my spine, leaving goosebumps across my skin.

"My aunt taught me to trust my intuition, and in that moment, it just didn't feel right."

"Is it Lila that's stopping you?" He moved his hand up my side and then brushed my hair behind my ear.

"It's definitely a factor. I know you trust her, but I still worry that she might be playing us."

"Whatever you're feeling, trust it. I've learned the hard way more than once what happens when you go against your own judgment." He kissed the top of my head and I curled in tighter.

"I just wish I could get a glimpse of something, anything, but every time I try looking into The Pieces of Three, nothing happens."

"Maybe you're coming at it from the wrong angle," Robert suggested.

"What do you mean?" I adjusted myself so I could look up at him.

"If Morgana has a way of blocking your visions, she'll be sure to block anything that might lead you closer to waking The Lady. You need to find a backdoor into your visions."

"I've never thought of that before," I admitted.

"You should speak with Bethany. She might have some insight."

I could feel his body start to relax under me and I let my eyes close.

"I'll call her in the morning." I sighed against his chest.

"Tomorrow'll be another long day. We should rest if we're going to use the *Artognou* again." He ran his hand along the length of my spine and settled on the small of my back.

"Mmm, yes, we should sleep." I pushed the length of my body against him.

In one fluid motion, he rolled me over so that he was lying on top of me. "Then again, sleep's overrated." He gave me a wicked smile before leaning in and kissing me full and hard.

The next morning came much too quickly and before I knew it we were on the road back to Pismo. Saying goodbye to the Deardon's was much harder than I thought it'd be knowing what was ahead of us. I would never forget the people we met at Caltome or the good we did while we could.

As we passed the city limit sign welcoming us to Pismo, it dawned on me that this might be the last time I'd return home if everything went to plan. I still had no clue what Graham meant when he said I'd be lost to The Lady, but I was pretty certain I wouldn't make it through this in one piece.

Robert pulled into the garage, but neither of us moved. It was like we both knew the moment we stepped out of the car, the bubble we'd been living in the last twenty-four hours would burst.

"You ready?" he asked, grabbing my hand.

"As ready as I'll ever be" I gave him a tight-lipped smile.

Kissing the top of my hand, he released his hold on me and we both stepped out of the car.

As if on cue, Lila burst into the garage. "Your sister is insufferable."

Robert let out a sigh, and I swore I could hear the faint pop of our perfect little bubble.

"What's Brett done now?" Robert asked. He moved toward Lila, and I followed behind them.

"It's about time you two showed up," Becky said as she came running down the hall, arms wide open. "Don't think you've gotten out of telling me what happened between you two," she whispered as she pulled me into a bear hug.

"I promise we'll talk later," I vowed, pulling her away from me as I made my way toward the others.

"How'd everything go at Caltome?" Brett asked, rising from the couch as we walked into the living room.

"We helped as many as we could," Robert reported.

"Everyone should make it through just fine," I added.

"From what I hear, they'll be more than just fine," Matthew remarked, standing in the doorway to the kitchen.

"How could you have possibly heard anything already?" Lila spat at him.

Robert and I shared a look. Clearly, we had missed something, because Lila was in an extraordinarily snarky mood.

"For your information," Matthew said patiently. "I talked to Scott last night. He said Robert and Violet were able to use their *Artognou-Magic* to help more than their fair share."

"So it's true then? You're really able to use *Artognou*?" Annabel asked as she waltzed into the room and settled herself onto the couch. Doing a double take, I noticed that Annabel was back to her normal self. The wounds that had been infected just a few days ago had all but vanished, and I wondered how that was even possible.

"Will you please just-" Jake caught sight of us and stopped pursuing Annabel. "Oh hey guys, how was the trip?" Jake asked as he walked in a moment later, shaking his head.

"It was productive," Robert replied.

I pinched the bridge of my nose. In the few hours Robert and I had been away, I'd forgotten how chaotic being around everyone could be.

"Well, if it isn't our very own Romeo and Juliet," Ethan called out, his voice booming through the room. "How was the honeymoon?" He wiggled his eyebrows suggestively.

Elodie entered the living room a moment later and smacked her brother up the backside of his head while Becky and Brett yelled, "Knock it off, Ethan," in unison.

"Ow." Ethan rubbed the back of his head. "Man, touchy crowd."

Just as Robert and I had found a rhythm, so had everyone else. An outsider looking in would never be able to guess the turmoil and history this group had endured.

"Now that everyone's here." I wrapped my fingers around the cool, metal ring, "I have something I need to share with all of you."

My eyes met Robert's, and he gave me a warm smile. I'd wrestled with the idea of telling everyone the entire way from Caltome, but in the end, I'd decided I needed to trust the people around me. After all, I'd only gotten this far because of the people standing in front of me, and if didn't trust them after everything we'd been through, then we'd already lost what was important.

"We're much closer to The Lady than any of you realize," I explained, and held the ring between my thumb and forefinger for everyone to see.

"Is that what I think it is?" Annabel asked with a shaky voice.

"The Ring of Dispel." I let the words roll off my tongue.

"Where'd you get it?" Matty asked as he stretched his fingers toward the circular beacon of hope.

"Graham gave it to me." I unlatched my necklace and slipped the ring into the palm of my hand.

"Graham?" Lila balked at the name and caught my attention.

"Did he tell you where he got it from?" Matty asked, wide-eyed.

"Not really. He said it was an old family heirloom, but that's about it."

Matty glanced at Brett almost too quickly for me to notice. Almost.

With everyone's perplexed gazes glued to me, I was starting to feel self-conscious.

"How can you be sure it's *the* ring?" Annabel asked, her skeptic voice pulling my attention toward her.

"I guess I can't be. But I believed Graham when he gave it to me," I replied.

"May I?" Matty stepped toward me with both of his hands held out, ready to inspect the relic should I grant him access.

I nodded, and he gingerly lifted the ring from my fingers, placing it flat on his palm. Turning the thick stone over in his hand, he closed one eye to get a better look at the inside of the band and the underside of the stone.

We all watched Matthew inspect the piece of jewelry. I wasn't sure what he was looking for exactly or how he thought he could confirm its authenticity, but still, I waited like the others for his final say.

"The inscription looks valid, but we won't know for sure until someone recites the spell," Matthew concluded.

"Absolutely not." I snatched the ring from his fingers. "Graham explained what this ring does. If it is real, and I've got a pretty good feeling about that, then I'm not letting anyone recite any spell."

"There is something else we can try," Matty started. He raised his eyebrows as if he was asking me to hear him out. When I didn't protest, he continued. "The Lady of the Lake's enchantments are some of the most powerful ever created. Even Merlin himself struggled to overcome some of her charms." He paced back and forth, one arm behind his back, the other moving wildly with each word. "It's more than likely that even if someone tried to destroy the ring, they wouldn't be able to."

"Violet?" Robert asked. My name rolled off his tongue like a caress. As I glanced over at him, he said, "Put the ring on the coffee table."

Confused, I looked between him and the ring in my hand. His eyes were gentle and warm, the eyes of the man I trusted.

I placed the ring on the table and took several steps away from the living room.

Understanding fell on the rest of the group and they each backed away from the table.

"Here goes nothing." Robert exhaled as a multicolored electric sphere formed in his hand.

A shock wave rippled through us as Robert's Magic connected with the ring and an explosion of wood and dust rained down on us.

Swatting the dust away, Robert knelt into the rubble of what used to be a coffee table and picked up the perfectly intact ring.

"I would assume that Graham was correct in telling you that this…" Robert held out the ring for me to grab, "is, in fact, The Ring of Dispel."

"Well, this changes things," Annabel coughed as the smoke cleared. "All we need now is the sword."

"And we already have a plan for that," Matthew beamed.

"So what'd you guys come up with?" I asked, taking the ring back from Robert.

"Jake, help me with the table?" Brett asked, motioning her brother over.

"I was able to narrow down the type of physical security the compound has," Becky said. Her eyes landed on Matthew, who nodded encouragingly. "But I need to be there to take it down."

"What? No way, it's too dangerous," I protested. The image

of Zan and the others crossed my mind. There was no way I was going to put Becky in the cross-hairs with Morgana.

"Told you she wasn't going to like it," Brett said under her breath as she and Jake raised their hands above the pile of rubble. Bits of wood and powder swirled into a waist-high tornado, and with little effort the coffee table reformed in front of them.

"We don't have any other options," Matthew tried to reason.

"Can't you show one of us how to disable the system?" I asked.

"I could, but if something goes wrong on the spot, you won't know how to fix it," Becky pointed out.

"Can't you just relay commands to one of us?" Robert suggested.

"It won't work. All radio signals in the area are monitored. We wouldn't be able to say one word without being flagged," Lila informed us.

"Or so she says," Annabel added. She looked Lila up and down like an insect she wanted to crush.

Lila threw her hands in the air. "Why would I lie about that?"

"Alright." Matthew stepped forward. "The point is, we need Becky to take the system down if we want any chance of getting Excalibur."

"Backup a second," I said. "How exactly are we all getting there in the first place? Annabel's still on the mend."

"We've got that figured out too," Lila chimed in. "Since Annabel isn't strong enough to orb all of us. I'm going to make another round of orbing potion."

"I thought we needed a full moon for it to work?" I crossed my arms, hating every step of this insane plan.

"The moon works best, but any other large, natural force will work too," Lila said.

"And it just so happens, Mercury and Jupiter will be visible at dawn starting next week.," Matty waved his hand to the roof and stars above. "It should be enough to give us the boost we need."

"Alright, go on," I said through gritted teeth.

"Once she takes down the physical security, what do we do about the Magical ward?" Robert asked.

"As long as we abstain from using Magic, we shouldn't set off any alarms," Lila said with a shrug.

"Is this seriously the best you guys could come up with?" I looked around the room.

"Violet's right, not using Magic isn't really an option," Robert agreed.

Brett scoffed and said, "I told you they weren't-"

"Oh, shut it, Brett," Lila snapped. "We've all heard your opinion."

Brett shot daggers at Lila but kept her mouth shut, which had my mouth nearly on the floor. Brett wasn't one to take lip from anyone and especially not Lila.

"Just hear me out," Lila continued in a pleading voice as she turned to me.

"The floor is yours," I conceded.

She let out a sigh and said, "We only have to get so far without Magic. It won't be long until they realize something's wrong and once they do, we'll have already slipped inside and Magic will be an option again."

"Okay, but how are we going to make it past the patrols you talked about?" I asked.

"That's where we come in," Elodie chimed in, and Lila motioned for her to take the reins. "Ethan, Jake, Brett, and I will create a diversion by freeing the prisoners. Hopefully the commotion will lead as many of Morgana's men away from the house as possible."

"It should give you, Robert, Annabel and Lila enough time to get in and out before anyone notices," Brett finished.

"Once we have the sword, we'll hightail it out of there." Annabel shrugged like it would be the easiest thing in the world.

"And what about everyone else?" I asked.

"We'll meet at the rendezvous point where Matty will be waiting with a boat." Lila nodded in Matty's direction.

"Brett, you're okay with this?"

She shrugged, "Apparently I don't get a say in the matter."

I looked between Brett and Matty, who were on opposite sides of the room. Neither of them looked at the other, and by the scowl on Brett's face, I'd bet they'd been arguing about it all night.

"Let's say this plan works and we get away with Excalibur," Robert said, playing devil's advocate. "Do we even know where to find The Lady?"

He was right, I'd been so worried about collecting The Pieces of Three that I never once stopped to think about where we might actually find The Lady of the Lake.

"Of course," Matty said, his smile stretching from ear to ear. "The Lady resides at none other than Dozmary Pool in Cornwall."

CHAPTER TWENTY-ONE

We spent the next week getting ready for our trip overseas. Lila finished brewing another batch of vomit-inducing orbing potion, and Becky and Matthew spent most of their time researching as much information as they could about Avalon. The two of them were a perfect match, Matthew with his book smarts and Becky with her technical know-how. There wasn't a doubt in my mind that the two of them could take over the world if they wanted to.

As for the rest of us, we trained, and we trained hard. No more punches were pulled, no spells were held back as we prepared for the battle waiting for us. Jake split us into teams and we attacked one another over and over again until the sun gave way to the stars and our bodies collapsed onto the mats. Not one of us escaped unscathed, and while Robert could heal our wounds, he couldn't wash away the exhaustion that had settled deep in our bones.

Every night, while the others rested, Robert and I worked on connecting to our *Artognou*. It was getting easier and easier to tap into the Magic, but it still drained us pretty quickly and left us needing more rest than the others.

On our last day in Pismo, I woke up to early afternoon sunlight and made my way downstairs. As I navigated through the house, I could hear Ethan's deep voice and Annabel and Becky's laughter. There would be no training today, no more research. Today we would spend time with the ones we loved. Without saying it, we all knew there was a chance we wouldn't come out of this unscathed. This was war after all, and death was a natural side effect.

"I thought you'd never wake up. How're you feeling?" Robert asked as he came up behind me and wrapped his arm around my waist.

Turning in the circle of his arms, I leaned against the wall. "I'm okay, still a little sore, Ethan really took me down yesterday." I picked a piece of lint off his shirt, and the kitchen erupted into a roar of *whoops* and laughter.

"Come on." He grabbed my hand. "You should be with them."

Robert pulled me along and we wandered into the kitchen where everyone was eating and trading stories.

"I never thought I'd see the day you'd sleep past noon," Becky teased me as we entered.

A smorgasbord of food had been laid out on the counter.

"Are those donuts from Java Beach?" I looked to Becky for confirmation.

"You bet'cha," Becky replied. She smiled and pulled the box closer.

I picked up a perfectly glazed donut. "I haven't had one of these in ages."

It was like taking a bite of heaven. The sugary goodness melted on my tongue and the dough was light and airy. If someone didn't stop me, I would eat the entire box.

Pulling up a seat at the island, I filled a plate with a little of everything while the others continued their conversation. Lila was telling everyone what it was like to grow up on Avalon, and without any sort of resentment, we all listened. She had become part of our little group without anyone realizing it. Annabel seemed to be the only one still openly hostile toward her.

I hadn't forgiven Lila for everything she'd done to me, but I no longer harbored the hatred for her I once had. It was incredible how things could change so much in such a short amount of time. Graham had said change was inevitable and looking around the room, listening to everyone sharing stories and laughing at one another, I realized it couldn't be more true.

"Can I steal you for a minute?" Becky asked when Ethan finished telling us a story about the first time he met Robert.

"Sure." I pushed away from the counter and we made our way toward the backyard.

"They're all pretty amazing," Becky said as she closed the French door behind her.

"I'm so glad you're getting to know them. The Maxwells, they've become like family to me."

"I can tell." Becky gave me a playful smile as we both sat down on a pair of pool chairs. "Do you remember when we were here for Jake and Annabel's wedding?"

"Yeah. Man, that feels like another life." I thought back to that day, Robert in his suit, Annabel and Jake dancing through the night and Ian who almost cost me my life.

"So much has changed. Are you sure you're ready for this?" Becky asked, her voice suddenly soft.

"No, but I don't really have a choice. Morgana has to be stopped. She's already caused so much damage and pain." I thought about the gentleman I'd helped at Caltome, who blamed himself for the loss of his Ava. How many more people would have to suffer, how many more people would lose their Ava's if I didn't wake The Lady?

"She's really, real, isn't she?" Becky turned her head to look at me.

"As real as either of us. And she's a force to be reckoned with."

"It's kind of surreal if you think about it," Becky mused.

"What do you mean?"

"Magic, Morgana, you? It's like you're the star of your very own fairy tale."

I laughed. "It sure doesn't feel like a fairy tale."

"Maybe not. But at least you got the guy."

I could hear the smile in her voice.

Sighing, I said, "For now at least." A sharp pang shot through my heart. She didn't know what Graham had told me about being lost to The Lady and if it was true, I would lose not only Robert but everyone I cared about.

"What's that supposed to mean?" Becky sat up and looked down at me.

Sitting up as well, I said, "There's no guarantee that we'll make it out of this alive."

"Stop it right now," Becky warned. "You are not going to go into this thinking about dying.

"Beck-"

"No. You will make it out of this and you will live happily ever after."

I eyed her. "Since when did you become a hopeless romantic?" Christy was usually the one spouting tales of white knights and happily ever after's.

"It's not that. It's just… after everything you've been through, losing your parents, almost dying, and now this. Don't you think you deserve to ride off into the sunset?"

"Becky, life is messy, and it's not a guarantee. We can only do the best with the time we have."

"Look, I know what you're about to do is dangerous and I get that there's a chance things could go wrong."

"A big chance," I amended.

"I just don't want you going into this thinking you're a lost cause. You're not the only one who's worried about losing the people they love."

I pulled Becky into a tight hug. "You're right. I'm sorry."

"I know we're not family, family. But you're like a sister to me." She pulled back so that we were looking at each other. "I can't lose you."

"You won't." I gave her my best smile as my heart broke.

"Good, now that's settled, you can finally tell me what happened between you and Robert at the winery." She laid back down on her pool chair. "And don't skimp on the details.

I sat down beside her and told her about everything that happened at Caltome. From Zan, to using our *Artognou-Magic*, to spending the night with Robert. She hung on my every word, only interrupting when she wanted me to elaborate in greater detail.

The sun moved across the sky as we chatted about everything that had happened over the last week. Magical conundrums aside, it was almost like old times. Just the two of us, talking and sharing every detail of our lives. I'd missed this so much, and it warmed my heart that I no longer had to lie to her. I took solace in the knowledge that if something did happen to me, Becky would at least know the truth.

The rest of the evening was a quiet affair. Everyone scurried off to their own corner of the Maxwell house to prepare for the next day. A calmness washed over the house that left me anxious. It wasn't like the Maxwells to act subdued, which only added to the overwhelming anxiety pumping through my veins. Tomorrow would change everything, and as sure as I was about my role in all of this, I feared following the path that just might end with my death.

Crawling into bed next to Robert, I laid my head on his chest and said, "Do you think our plan is going to work?"

"Honestly, I don't know." He ran his fingers through my hair. "It's a big risk going after Excalibur like this."

"What choice do we have?"

"That's the problem, we don't have any other options. It makes us desperate, and Morgana knows that."

"It still bothers me that she went after the tokens at all. It just doesn't make sense why she would want them."

"Whatever the reason, after tomorrow it won't matter." He kissed the top of my head and I adjusted myself so that I could look up at him.

"Promise me something?"

He eyed me. "Depends."

"Promise that no matter what happens, Becky will be taken care of."

He reached up to touch my face. "Nothing's going to happen to you."

"But Graham-"

"I don't care what Graham said." His arm squeezed me to him. "You will make it through this."

"Just promise me." I placed my hand on his chest. I could feel his heartbeat under my fingers and more than anything I hoped he was right.

Robert nodded once, and I bent to kiss him.

"Thank you," I said against his lips.

Pulling me into his arms, he deepened the kiss. He may not want to believe it, but deep down he knew this could be our last night together.

The next morning, we all met downstairs. Not much was said as Lila handed out the tiny vials of orbing potion to each of us. Matthew gave me the necklace, and I packed it neatly away in the bag he'd given me to carry the sword. Fingering the ring around my neck, a small tremor of panic rose in my throat as we made our way down to the beach.

The early dawn sky pressed down on me as I caught a glimpse of the two planets that would help us make the trip to Avalon.

"Everyone ready?" Annabel asked as she walked into the surf.

"Remember, we need to land here," Matthew advised Lila, pointing to a location on a map. "It's just outside their range. Once Becky does her thing, you'll be free to make the trip across the channel." He followed Annabel into the water.

"I got it," Lila snapped. We'd all gone over the plan a dozen times over the last week, but Matthew was clearly anxious.

"You okay?" Robert whispered as he pulled me into his side. The cold ankle deep water stung my skin and sent goosebumps across my arms. "You look a little pale."

"Fine, just didn't sleep well." I forced a smile and looked up at him, wishing we could go back to Caltome and live in our little bubble.

"We've got this." He laced his fingers through mine as the rest of the group linked hands as well. "I won't let anything happen to you, I swear it." His eyes met mine and I could feel our Magic bubbling just under the surface.

The ten of us stood in the shallow water, our linked hands forming a closed circuit as the salty ocean air filled my lungs. Never in a million years did I think I would find a family I could call my own, but as I looked around at the faces of the Maxwell family, Becky, Ethan and Elodie, I'd never felt more a part of something. Whatever happens now, at least I knew what it felt like to have a family I could call my own.

"Alright, hold on everyone. Becky, this is going to rock your world," Lila said.

We each drank the potion and Lila began to recite the spell. I caught a glimpse of Becky, her eyes wide with excitement just before we were hurtled through oblivion.

My knees buckled as I landed, and I rolled until I hit something rough and solid.

"Holy Batman, that was insane." Becky laughed as she got to her feet.

"Insane is one way to put it." I winced.

"Right, Becky, you're up." Matthew moved to help her unpack the gear she'd brought with her.

Pulling her laptop from her bag, along with a small antenna, Becky got straight to work.

"So that's Avalon?" I stepped next to Robert and looked across the water. The island was fairly small and tucked neatly behind a sheen of mist.

Robert nodded and kept his eyes on the distant shoreline. I couldn't help but wonder what he saw in his mind's eye.

"Alright, let's split into our teams," Brett announced. "When Becky gives the go ahead, we'll need to cross as quickly as possible before they notice anything's amiss. Jake, the boats."

Jake turned to the nearest grouping of trees and raised his hands. The sound of earth churning and roots snapping filled the air as a small cluster of trees rose from the ground, dirt clinging to their roots. Rolling them onto their sides, Jake recited a spell, and the trees began to buckle in on themselves. Bark and dirt flew in every direction as the wood reshaped itself into two canoe-like boats.

"No one said he was going to go all Dumbledore." Becky stared at Jake as he gently laid the boats to rest on the shore in front of us.

"Becky, focus," Brett ordered.

"Right, sorry." She shook her head in disbelief and who could blame her? Even I was impressed. I'd never seen Jake do anything like that before.

"We need to get in and out quickly," Lila blurted, her nerves clearly getting the better of her.

"It's not going to be that easy," I said, looking at the ominous island.

"I know. But the longer we're in there, the more at risk we become."

"I'm in," Becky announced. "When I say go, you'll have five minutes before the system reboots."

Ethan, Elodie, Jake, and Brett got into their boat while Lila and Annabel settled into ours.

"Violet, come on," Robert called to me.

I knelt down and placed my hand on Becky's rapidly moving fingers.

Pausing, she looked up at me and I wrapped my arms around her.

"Thank you, for everything," I said, trying to hold back tears.

"You come back in one piece, alright?"

Nodding, I stood and placed my hand on Matthew's shoulder.

"Get her out of here the second we're in," I told him.

Matthew nodded. "Go. We'll be fine."

Robert grabbed my hand when I made it back to the others and pulled me along to our boat.

"Fifteen seconds," Becky yelled from her place among the trees. Settling next to Annabel, she gave my shoulder a squeeze. "Ten, nine, eight…"

Robert pushed our boat into the water at the same time Jake's hit the cold Atlantic Ocean.

"Seven, six, five…"

"Here goes nothing," Lila whispered under her breath as we each grabbed a paddle.

"Four, three, two, one."

We shot off into the choppy water. Jake's boat veered to the right, shooting for a small beach that would allow them to get in before us and create the distraction we needed.

Digging my paddle into the water and pushing as hard as I could, I worried that it wasn't going to be enough, that we wouldn't make it before our time ran out.

"Push," Robert encouraged. "It's not that far."

Lila dug in front of me and we sailed across the dark ocean. Seagulls flew overhead, their wings spread wide as they coasted toward the shore. If only it were as easy for us. I huffed as a small spray of water flew into the air and brushed my skin.

Another minute ticked by and I was sure we'd never make it. Our destination still looked too far away, and there wasn't much time left. Searching for the other half of our group, I saw them pulling their boat onto the beach and disappearing into the trees.

"Almost there," Robert called out like a ship's captain.

I put my head down and pushed even harder, thankful for all the training we'd put ourselves through. A few months ago, there'd be no way I would have been able to get across that channel without a break.

We smacked into something solid and the boat creaked. I looked up and realized we'd made it to Avalon.

The water came up to my ankles when I jumped out of the boat and climbed onto a rock.

"We need to keep moving," Lila called to all of us. "We aren't inside the barrier yet."

Hurrying after her, we climbed the rocks leading to a narrow plateau. Lila pulled herself up first and then helped Annabel and me over the edge. Robert picked up the rear and then we made a run for it through the trees.

"We just need to make it past that grouping of trees," Lila huffed as she pointed ahead.

Dodging rocks and fallen trees, we followed Lila without a word. There was a charge to the air that had my skin prickling with each step. It might not have been the mythical island from the stories, but there was definitely something sinister about this place.

Lila slowed to a walk and then crouched behind a bush. Just

up ahead I saw a break in the trees and the outline of a building came into shape.

"We should be good here for a minute," Lila said, breathing heavily.

"Hopefully the others will be able to create enough of a distraction so we can slip in," I said as I searched the outline of the house for any sign of a patrol.

"They'll do their part, we'll do ours," Robert vowed, looking over his shoulder at me.

"My father's vault is on the second floor." Lila pointed to a window about halfway up the house. "We should start there."

"How're we supposed to crack the vault?" Annabel asked.

"I can get in." Lila smirked like a child who knew where the cookie jar was kept.

"Well then, I guess there's no time like the present," Annabel chimed in.

Lila took a deep breath. "Alright, follow me and stay alert." She took a step and then turned back to us. "And try not to use Magic until we have to."

Tiptoeing out of the cover of the trees, we made our way across the lawn. The only sound came from the birds squawking overhead and shoes squishing through the damp grass. If we weren't breaking into the enemy's house and trying to steal a Mythical sword, I might have actually enjoyed the scenery. The grass was a shade of green I thought only existed in crayon form, and the stone of the house reminded me of a castle. Even from this distance, I could tell the place was built to look like a fortress.

Lila turned to the left, and we followed behind. A part of me still wasn't sure we should be letting her lead us into the mouth of the devil, but what other choice did we really have? She knew this place intimately, and while Robert and Annabel had both spent time here, they were kept in a prison almost the entire time.

Lila came to a stop and held out her arm for us to follow her example. Pressing myself against the stone walls, I could feel how cold the rock was through the layers of clothing. I was about to ask what we were waiting for when I heard voices.

Robert pulled Lila behind him by her arm so that he was in front of all of us. Squaring his shoulders, he tensed his body. The moment someone turned the corner, Robert sprang into action and landed a punch on the guy's jaw.

His companion looked around confused for a moment and then recognized Lila. "What're you-" he began but was cut off when Lila swung her leg out. Stumbling backward, he lost his footing and fell in a heap of limbs. Straddling him and placing her legs on his arms, she pressed her forearm down on his neck.

The guy Robert was fighting took a swing at him, and Robert ducked out of the way. With quick feet, he circled around and got him in a chokehold. The man's eyes bulged, and he pulled at Robert's arm until he slumped forward.

Robert let him go and the guy fell forward. Grabbing his arms, Robert dragged him and propped him up against the wall.

Lila stood, panting. Robert walked over to her and dragged the body of the unconscious guard next to the other.

"He knew you," I said, nodding to the guard Lila had disabled.

"Yeah, he used to have a crush on me. Followed me everywhere." Lila looked down at him and almost seemed remorseful.

"He'll be following you for a different reason now," Annabel said and kicked the guard's shoe.

Shaking her head and snapping back to reality, Lila took the lead again. "It won't be long until someone finds them. Come on." She tapped Robert on the shoulder like a football player congratulating another player on a job well done and rounded the corner without another word.

We skirted around the back of the house until we came to a

door. Checking the handle, Lila pulled gently, and the door cracked open.

She held her finger up for us to wait and then disappeared inside. Wings flapped overhead and the sound of critters jumping through the bushes made me more and more anxious with each passing second. I was about to go after Lila when she poked her head through the door and motioned for us to follow.

I stepped into the house behind Annabel, and Robert closed the door. We were in a huge modern kitchen. It was the complete opposite of what the exterior looked like. Stainless steel appliances, a huge island in the middle, and beautiful polished white stone counters. It was a dream kitchen, and I looked at Lila with more than a little surprise.

"Come on," she whispered, and we followed her through another door that led to a large walk-in pantry.

"Are we hiding from someone?" I asked.

Lila shook her head. "There's an old hidden passageway." She started taking food off the shelves in search of something. "As a kid, I used to play hide and seek with a few friends. I found this tunnel, and I was able to run back and forth so they couldn't find me." She pushed on one of the slates of wood holding up the shelving and the wall came away with a creak.

"Does anyone else know about this?" Robert asked.

"I doubt it. It's not like anyone would think to look for a secret passage in the pantry."

"Where does it lead?" I asked.

"To the front of the house, behind a coat closet. It's the closest I can get us to the stairs without being detected. We'll have to wing it after that." She hunched her shoulders and her brows rose.

"Lead the way." I motioned for her to take the lead.

Ducking her head, she disappeared into the hole. Annabel followed with a scowl, and Robert and I picked up the rear. He closed the door behind us and nudged me forward once it was secured.

"Never in my life have I walked through so many secret passageways," I whispered over my shoulder.

Robert chuckled. "I would bet this isn't your last, either."

Swatting a cobweb out of the way and wiping the sticky web on my pants, I followed Annabel closely. Voices echoed on the other side of the wall, and we all froze. Did they know we were here? Did they find the guards Lila and Robert had taken out?

"We're almost there," Lila said as softly as she could.

Slowly and carefully, we crept through the walls. Footsteps rushed passed us and someone shouted somewhere in the house. They had definitely been alerted to our arrival. How we were going to get upstairs, unlock a safe and escape with an ancient sword was beyond me. By then the tunnel ended and we found ourselves right behind the coat closet.

"I thought we'd have more time," Lila cursed.

In the small space, Robert's body was pressed against mine. In any other situation, I wouldn't have minded, but it was not the time for distractions. I pushed myself closer to Annabel, who gave me a weird look over her shoulder.

"What do you suggest now?" Annabel's snarky attitude was coming off her in waves.

"Let me check, wait here," Lila suggested. She held up her hand as a stop sign and then pushed through the back of the closet.

We waited in silence, the house coming to life around us as Morgana's men rushed to find the intruders. My heart accelerated in my chest and I could feel the blood pumping throughout my entire body. My Magic, catching the tenor of my emotions, began to bubble to the surface, ready for a fight. I wiggled my fingers and prepared to run out of here firing on all cylinders when I felt it. The hum of our *Artognou* slowly crawling through my blood, heightening all my senses. Robert must have been just as charged as I was if our Bond was coming to the surface so easily.

I turned to look at him and his eyes lit up in the dark. My skin tingled, and I shivered as another dose of raw energy filled me.

"Can you-" he started.

"Yeah," I cut him off, a little breathless from the power humming just under my skin.

Lila came back into the passageway, bringing a gust of fresh air with her.

"They don't know we're here yet," she revealed. "It's the others they're after. The distraction's working. Everyone is rushing out of the house like madmen."

I let out a sigh of relief and my Magic retreated, taking the electricity of the *Artognou* with it.

"Just a few more seconds and we can make a run for it," Lila advised.

"Do you want to tell us where we're headed in case we have to split up?" Annabel asked.

"Good idea." Lila tried giving her a smile. "When we exit the closet, we'll turn left and head straight up the staircase. Once we get to the second floor, turn right and it's the first door on the right. Simple."

"Something tells me it's not going to be that easy."

"With mostly everyone gone, it won't be too difficult. Besides, now that they know someone's here, we can use Magic." Lila raised her eyebrows suggestively.

"It's gotten quiet. I say we go," Annabel urged.

"Let's do it," Lila agreed. She pushed through the back of the closet again and we all filed in behind her.

I didn't know what I was expecting, but the entire thing was empty, not even a coat or umbrella. Suddenly I felt very exposed. Lila turned the handle and cracked the door slightly. Peeking out, she pushed the door another inch.

We all braced ourselves and she threw the door open. After a quick turn to the left, we ran up the stairs. We spotted not another soul until we reached the landing. At the end of the hall to our left stood Morgana. Catching her eye as we all turned right and into the first room, I felt the air in my lungs turn to ice.

"Lila, Go. Morgana's coming," I yelled the second the door was closed.

Grabbing Robert's hand, I looked up at him and said, "Are you ready?"

"More than ready," Robert replied. He gave my hand a tight squeeze, and the *Artognou* flared to life, nearly knocking the wind out of me.

Lila ran to one of the bookshelves and started throwing the thick volumes to the floor. I heard a loud click and then she said, "I'm almost in."

Letting my Magic take over, my breathing became ragged and my heart tried to break through my rib cage. I felt alive and on the brink of death all at the same time.

The double doors swung open and smacked against the walls with the force of a hurricane. Morgana stood before us with an amused expression on her face.

"We meet again," she said.

Without having to communicate, Robert and I raised a shield. It was stunning, like a galaxy colliding with another as it swirled before us.

"And you've learned a few tricks since the last time too," Morgana noted. "You know, I didn't really appreciate your little trick with the necklace." She moved back and forth like she was stalking her prey.

"This can end now, Morgana," Robert barked.

She laughed and leaned against the door frame with her arms crossed. "You may have learned how to tap into your *Artognou-Magic*, but you still don't have the power to kill me."

She actually looked shocked that we could be so bold as to even try.

"It isn't here!" Lila yelled, running out of the wall safe.

"Did you really think it would be that easy?" Morgana stepped into the room and the shield Robert and I had created pulsed.

"Where is it, Morgana?" I growled.

"You mean this?" Morgana flicked her wrist and Excalibur appeared out of thin air. "Beautiful, isn't she?" Morgana cooed. Holding the sword by the hilt, she turned the blade side to side.

"What do we do?" I asked under my breath as I kept my eyes on Morgana.

"Arthur never deserved it," she said through gritted teeth and her eyes shot toward me. "And neither do you."

Morgana's fingertips crackled with Magic. The air in the room felt heavy as Robert and I barely managed to hold on to our *Artognou-Magic*.

"Back off," I managed to say.

"Do you really think you can stop me?" Morgana looked closer to yawning than stepping away.

Robert squeezed my hand tighter. The Magic rolling through us was almost unbearable.

"Take another step and find out," I challenged, the words spilling out of my mouth.

Morgana squared her shoulders and faced us. Straightening her arms at her side, one palm turned up, the other gripping the sword with white knuckles. Taking another step, she threw her arms toward us, the tip of the sword pointed directly at the center of our shield. Hot white electricity struck our defense with such force that I had to take a step back to keep my balance.

"We're leaving here with that sword," I vowed.

"Wanna bet?" She growled over the roar of our shield blocking her Magic. When I lifted my other hand in

Morgana's direction, Robert looked at me, unsure of what I was doing.

"Just keep the shield up," I said. "*Mortem*," I called out. The word formed on my lips and my entire body filled with Magic. A blueish-green orb formed in my hand as the power of the *Artognou* poured into me. For the first time since I'd become Magical, I felt invincible.

Cocking my arm like I was throwing a baseball, I wound up and hurled the orb directly at Morgana. Lifting Excalibur in front of her, the orb ricocheted off of the blade, hitting the bookshelf instead and exploding. Books flew into the air, their pages ripped from their binding as fire and smoke took hold of the room.

Fury, like I'd never seen, filled her cold blue eyes, and she rushed us, placing her hand against our shield. White sparks formed on her fingers, penetrating the barrier, keeping her at bay.

"Hit her again," Robert grunted.

I summoned the spell again and flung the orb at Morgana. Throwing the sword behind her, she kept one hand on our shield, trying to break through while the other froze my spell just inches from her.

"Again," Robert yelled. Our connection erupted, Magic pouring through every cell in my body as Robert reinforced our shield.

Beckoning another Orb of Demise, the ball of Magic vibrated on my palm as I pitched it directly at Morgana's chest.

Her reflexes were quick, but not quick enough. The spell hit her square in the chest and she flew across the room.

"Lila, the sword," I yelled.

Lila darted across the room and reached Excalibur as Morgana got to her feet.

"Hurry," Annabel yelled over the now blazing fire.

Lila mumbled something under her breath and by the time

Morgana took one step, Lila was standing behind our shield, sword in hand.

"How'd'you? Never mind. Get Excalibur out of here," I ordered.

"No, Violet. You need to take the sword and you need to wake The Lady," Lila said, handing me the last token.

"She's right, get out of here," Robert grunted. Sweat was starting to bead off his brow and I could feel our Magic start to waver.

"Not without you," I huffed as I struggled to hold on.

"You have to." Lila stepped forward. Green sparks flickered on her fingertips. With a nod of her head, she shot a Galvin spell toward Morgana.

Raising her shield Morgana blocked the spell, but Lila didn't let up and as I let go of Robert's hand, I could feel him summon his Arcane Magic through the Bond. Between his Magic and the *Artognou,* I collapsed to my hands and knees.

"Annabel, get her out of here!" Robert yelled.

"What about you two?" she called back as the hot, smoky air began swirling around us like a tornado.

"We'll be fine, just get Violet out of here!"

"Robert, no." I looked up at him. He held my gaze for a fraction of a second, then turned to face Morgana.

"Lila, on my count," Robert called to her as Annabel lifted me from the floor.

"Let's go," Annabel said, pushing the window open.

"Can't you orb us?" I asked.

She shook her head, "I'm still too weak, I don't know where we'd end up!" She yelled over the roar of the fire.

"Here goes nothing then." I threw one leg over the window sill. We were only on the second floor and while I knew I could easily make the jump, butterflies flapped fervently in my stomach. Flipping my other leg over the sill, I hurtled myself over the ledge.

CHAPTER TWENTY-TWO

My feet hit the grass, and my legs buckled under me. I rolled to the side and out of the way so Annabel could make the jump. Propping myself up on all fours, I looked around for any sign of a threat, but everything looked serene. If I didn't know any better, I could easily be fooled into a false sense of security.

I ripped my bag off of my back and shoved the sword inside, zipping it up as Annabel landed next to me, her feet finding their mark perfectly.

"Come on, let's get you out of here." She pulled me to my feet.

As we ran toward the west side of the property, an explosion sounded from the second floor. Looking over my shoulder, the window we'd just jumped through and half of the exterior wall had been blown apart.

Terror, like I'd never felt, gripped me and I stumbled to a halt.

"Violet, we can't stop," Annabel pulled me. My feet moved without me telling them too, and as we reached the cover of trees, I fell to my knees and threw up.

Annabel kneeled next to me and grabbed me by the shoulders. "You can't fall apart, not here and not now, do you hear me?"

Looking up at her, I knew she was right. We needed to keep moving no matter what happened to the others or this would all be for nothing.

"Okay." I stood up and took a deep breath. The cool, damp smell of earth cleansed the odor of fire and Magic from my nose as we made a run for it.

Annabel disappeared into the brush. Stepping over fallen logs and pushing through thorny bushes, I tried to keep up with her, but step by step she was slowly disappearing.

"Annabel, wait," I called after her quietly.

Ducking under a low hanging branch, the bag strapped to my back hit a limb and knocked me backward. Losing my balance, I hit the ground with an audible thud. My entire body vibrated from hitting the damp, packed soil of the forest floor.

Huffing, I stood and wiped the dirt off of my pants as Lila burst out of the bush to my right, scaring me half to death.

"Where's Robert?" I barked.

"I don't know. We got separated," she huffed and leaned over with her hands on her knees.

If Lila made it out safely, then Robert could be okay too. I thought, trying to keep myself from assuming the worst.

"Where's Annabel?" Lila looked from side to side.

"Just up ahead." I pointed in front of us, but there was no sign of her anywhere.

"Right, well come on. We don't have much time." Lila pushed me forward and followed behind me.

Our shoes crunched through the fallen leaves and twigs as we pushed forward. Within just a few short minutes, I could hear the sound of waves crashing on the shore. Eagerness welled up inside me and I pushed forward with a new found strength.

Lila kept up with me, her footsteps just over my shoulder and her heavy breathing matching my own. The trees began to thin and I could see Annabel at the edge of the water with Matty at the helm of a small fishing boat. Keeping my eyes on them, I pushed one foot in front of the other. Just a few more steps and we'd be safe.

I blinked and in the breath of a second Annabel's face changed from determined to terrified, her eyes wide and her mouth yelling a warning. Two hands strung my back, and I fell face forward into the dirt. Lila tumbled to the ground next to me and our eyes caught as a Galvin spell flew over our heads.

She saved me, pushed me out of harm's way. I studied her expression a moment longer, and then a stunning spell flew from her hand.

"Go," she yelled.

Scrambling to my feet, I summoned my shield and ran the last few yards to Annabel. She grabbed my arm and pulled me into the boat.

Looking back toward the beach, Lila squared off with a burly man and a lanky woman. I knew we couldn't leave her to fend for herself, not after she just saved me.

Summoning the strength I had left, an electric charge coursed over my skin and a wave of energy bounced off of me toward the beach.

"Lila, get down!" I yelled, and she hit the sand just before my Magic reached her.

The others weren't so lucky. The blast hit them and they flew backward, disappearing into the trees.

"Run," I called over the thrum of the engine.

Lila got to her feet and ran toward us, kicking sand up all around her.

Just as she reached the water, Jake and the other's came running up the south side of the island.

Helping Lila over the edge of the boat, I turned to Matty. "We're not leaving without everyone."

He nodded once, but the tension in his shoulders and his grip on the wheel made me wonder if someone had given him other orders.

"Let's go," Jake said as he effortlessly jumped into the boat.

"They're not far behind us." Ethan grabbed the railing and hoisted himself over the edge.

"Not until Robert's on board," I said.

"He's not with you?" Brett looked around for her brother.

"We got separated," Lila said.

Elodie climbed into the boat and said, "Robert knows what he's doing. He'll make it back."

"Elodie's right, we need to go, Robert will find another way," Annabel argued.

"You don't under-"

I was cut off by the loud boom of an explosion in the distance. Smoke billowed from the trees in front of us and without thinking, I threw off my bag and jumped into the shallow water.

"Violet, wait!" I heard someone yell as I ran up the beach.

To my right, I saw a group of Morgana's men running toward the boat as I ducked behind a group of bushes.

"Are you insane?" Lila grabbed me by the arm as she took cover with me.

"I'm not leaving him." I held her glassy blue eyes, daring her to stop me. "You can either help me, or get out of my way." I ripped my arm from her grasp as someone went flying across the beach in front of us.

"They won't be able to hold them off for long," Lila said, moving further into the trees. "Let's do this quickly."

Smoke and the *crackling* of burning trees surrounded us as we moved further away from the shore.

A group of Magical flaming arrows shot through the leaves toward a small grouping of rocks and exploded on impact.

Through the dust and debris, I saw a figure run from the rocks, taking cover behind a large fallen tree. An Arcane orb rounded the top of the trunk and flew across our field of vision, giving us a direct path to Robert.

"It's him," I whispered to Lila.

"You get to Robert, I'll circle round and take care of whoever's hiding in the bushes."

Splitting up, I summoned my shield and made a dash through the burning trees and leaves toward Robert. The normally vibrant, golden hue of my shield was muted, and I knew my Magic wouldn't last much longer in a fight.

To my left, I heard a loud *whoosh* and ducked just as a freezing spell whizzed by me.

"Robert, are you there?" I took cover behind a tree trunk.

"Violet?" Robert's voice sounded just in front of me. "What the hell are you doing here?" he seethed.

I looked around the truck and spotted Robert just a few feet ahead. Looking in the distance, there was no sign of Lila or the attackers, so I ran for it.

Kicking up dirt and dodging a low-hanging branch, I slid next to Robert and ducked down behind the tree.

"Thought I'd come save you." I gave him a wry smile.

He rolled his eyes. "I've got it under control."

Just then the tree truck keeping us hidden shattered into a million pieces. Bark and leaves rained down all around us and we made a run for it.

"Yeah, it really looks like you have it all under control," I yelled as we ran toward the beach.

A bolt of electricity shot ahead of us and we stopped in our tracks, ducking behind a boulder. Robert raised both hands and purple smoke and sparks formed into disks above his palms.

"Get ready to run when I tell you."

He shot upright and threw the disk-like Frisbees in the direction the bolt of electricity had come from.

"Run." We both bolted from our hiding place.

The forest started to thin and I could just make out the beach in front of us.

"We're almost there," I called behind me as another explosion erupted from somewhere behind us.

I faltered, but Robert was right behind me, guiding me the rest of the way. The scene on the beach was pandemonium as we broke through the curtain of branches and leaves.

Brett stood in the boat, her hands raised to the sky as she pulled lightening from the clouds. Electricity crackled across her skin as bolts of hot white light flew from her hands, picking people off one by one.

A shower of blue sparks rained down on Jake's shield as an invisible puff of air blew the attackers around him backward.

Angry red light shot across the shore toward Ethan and Elodie as their blades cut Morgana's men down. Lila leapt in front of them at the last moment and threw up her shield to save them.

"Come on, let's get this over with," Robert grabbed my hand and ran straight for the boat.

Barreling through the sand, cinder orbs, lightning and Devils flames shooting past us, we made it to the boat unscathed.

"Everyone back to the boat," Robert yelled and took the wheel.

"Where's Matty?" I looked around, frantic something might have happened to him.

"I told him to take cover," Brett yelled over her shoulder as an Orb of Demise shot across the beach toward her.

Jumping in front of her, I summoned my shield, and the orb bounced off of me and back toward the shore.

"Thanks." She leaned over to help Annabel into the boat.

Robert fired up the engine as a spell hit the side of the vessel and rocked us back and forth.

Ethan, Elodie, and Lila jumped into the boat next, followed closely by Jake, who was still throwing spells at the shoreline.

"Get us out of here," Jake yelled.

The engine sputtered, and we slowly moved into deeper water.

"Forget this," Lila shoved her way to the back of the boat.

Holding both hands up she said, "*Citius.*" Jets of water flew from her hands and the boat shot forward away from Avalon.

"Now that's more like it," Lila smirked.

"Everyone okay?" Robert yelled over the roar of the engine and Lila's spell.

"A little battered and bruised, but we're alive." Brett clapped her brother on the shoulder.

"The sword?" Jake asked.

Picking up the bag with the tokens I said, "we got it."

"Cornwall, here we come," Matty said.

CHAPTER TWENTY-THREE

We made it back to the mainland of Scotland as the sun started to dip below the horizon. With the time change and orbing around the world, my internal body clock was pretty much screwed. Matthew arranged for us to stay with a Magical family, who ran a small Inn on the edge of Loch Ness. The moment we arrived, Becky shot up from the picnic table sitting near the entrance and tackled me into a bear hug.

"Thank God, you're alright." She held me at arm's length and then pulled me in for another hug. "I was starting to worry, you guys were supposed to be here hours ago." She released me and her eyes landed on each person in our merry band of misfits.

"We ran into a few complications," I mumbled, barely able to keep my eyes open.

"The sword?"

I tapped the strap of the bag. "We got it."

"We should head inside," Matty said, taking the lead.

Following behind him, I took in the scenery. The landscape was stunning and unlike anything I'd ever seen. The midnight black water of the loch was surrounded by lush green hills covered in a carpet of golden leaves. A low fog hung over the water, giving the loch a mystical quality that did wonders for the Loch Ness Monster business.

Exhaustion settled deep in my bones as we filed into the Inn. Soft yellow light bathed the wooden interior, making everything feel quaint and homey. If I ever got the chance to have a real vacation, I'd love to come back here and enjoy the ambiance.

"I've got an extra bed in my room if you want," Becky said as the front desk clerk handed out the rest of the keys.

"Sounds good, just give me a minute, okay?"

She nodded.

Pulling Robert to the side, I said, "I'm gonna bunk with Becky. She shouldn't be alone."

"Of course." Robert nodded and kissed the top of my head. "I'll just be down the hall if you need me." The corner of his lips turned up and I couldn't help but reach up and kiss his lips.

"Finally." Ethan clapping loud enough to draw everyone's attention.

"Shut up, Ethan," I said, rolling my eyes.

Robert gave my hand one last squeeze before I bid goodnight to the rest of the group.

"I need to shower, then sleep for a week," I said as Becky led the way to our room.

"Are you sure you don't want to stay with Robert tonight?" She wiggled her eyebrows at me.

"I'm sure," I said, fighting the lump in my throat.

If Graham's prophecy came true, then tomorrow I would be lost to The Lady. I cared a great deal for Robert, but Becky was my family and I wanted to spend one more night with her, just in case the worst happened.

The next morning came much too quickly. Leaving a note on the nightstand, I snuck out of my room while Becky slept and I met the others at the back of the property.

The sun glistened off of the loch and I could see my breath in the cool morning air. Mercury and Jupiter hung in the early dawn sky, and I shivered under Robert's arm.

"Violet, Robert," Matty nodded in our direction. "You know what to do."

"We've got our marching orders," Robert said.

"Thank you, for everything. We wouldn't be here without you," I said, inclining my head toward Matty.

"Just wake The Lady and come home to us in one piece, all of you." He looked around our group and draped his arm over Brett.

"It's time," Lila said, and she handed us one last vile.

Matty gave Brett a kiss, then took a few steps away.

Downing the potions, I linked hands with Ethan and Robert as Lila began to recite the spell.

Streaks of light sped past me as we swirled through a vortex meant to transport us to Dozmary Pool.

I must've been getting used to Lila's putrid orbing potion because this time, I landed on my feet without feeling like I was going to hurl everywhere.

Looking around, we were in an empty field. The grass just about knee high and in the distance I spotted a small lake with a willow tree in the middle.

"Everyone make it in one piece?" I asked, taking stock of our group.

"We need to get Violet to The Lady. Morgana won't be far off," Annabel suggested.

"Let's go then," I agreed, adrenalin pumping through my veins.

"Everyone keep an eye out," Robert warned.

We all ran toward the lake, the sword in my hand and the necklace and ring safely tucked in my pocket. We got about one hundred yards from the edge of the water when a dozen or so of Morgana's followers appeared out of thin air.

"Here we go," Brett said under her breath as storm clouds began forming overhead and everyone circled around me.

"What're you waiting for, an invitation?" Ethan roared at Morgana's minions.

Without further ado, half of them charged while the others began shooting spells from every angle. We each raised our shields, creating a barrier around us and protecting Ethan and Elodie.

I dropped to the ground, slipping the ring on my finger and fastening the necklace around my neck. Picking up the sword, I readied myself to run at a moment's notice.

"Violet, you ready?" Brett called back to me before one of the men burst through her shield. Lila released a thread of Devil's Flame and the attacker crumpled to the ground, screaming in pain as his flesh burned from the inside out.

"Thanks," Brett said, nodding toward Lila. "Violet?"

"Yeah, I'm good!" I yelled. "On your mark."

At that moment a hailstorm of cinder orbs rained down on us and Annabel lost hold of her shield.

"Anna, move!" Jake yelled as a Galvin spell struck Annabel in the torso, immobilizing her.

"Change of plans!" Robert shouted. "Lila, you're with me. We need to get Violet to the lake, now."

"Give me a few seconds and I'll cover you," Brett called over her shoulder.

As a cinder orb came flying at Annabel, Jake stepped in front of her, shielding her from being incinerated. Still feeling the effects of the Galvin spell, she twitched on the ground next to me as the battle continued around us.

"Hang on, Annabel," I urged, patting her arm and trying to soothe her.

Lightning crackled overhead, catching everyone's attention.

"On my mark!" Brett yelled. A thick vine of raw electricity struck Brett's fingertips as she yelled for us to run. She threw her arms out, sending bolts of lightning in every direction.

Robert, Lila and I broke into a sprint, heading for the lake just ahead of us.

"There she is," Lila said as the three of us ran through the clearing.

"How do we get to her?" I huffed, out of breath.

"You see that boulder?" She pointed to the far side of the lake where a cluster of rocks led from the willow to shallow water.

"Yeah?"

A loud explosion behind us shook the ground, and we came to a halt. Looking over my shoulder, black smoke rose from where we'd left the others.

"We don't have much time." I started to run toward the rocks. The weight of what we were about to do hung heavy on my heart and for the first time since we started this journey I could see the finish line.

Robert threw down his bag the moment we reached the rocks. "Alright," he began. "Matthew said we would have to connect first and then say the spell together. Are you ready?"

"As ready as I'll ever be," I said, and gave him a half-hearted smile.

"Well, aren't you three resourceful." Ian crept out from the other side of the boulders.

"Ian, what're you doing here?" Lila asked, gaping with surprise.

He clicked his tongue. "I'm disappointed in you, Lila. Did you really think she would leave this place unguarded?"

"Of course not, I'm just wondering why she sent you."

He chuckled. "Nice try, but you're not getting under my skin."

"I suggest you leave while you still have legs to walk on," Robert threatened.

"You don't scare me, you filthy Healer." Ian spat in Robert's direction.

"You can't expect to take us on all by yourself," I said, holding my nerve.

"Oh, how right you are," Ian agreed and smiled at me. "Boys!"

Half a dozen men and women rose from the knee high-grass and surrounded us.

"You know, I always liked you. Right to the point, no foreplay," Ian mocked. He winked at me and I honestly had to stop myself from throwing up.

"Bite me." I let a blast of energy explode off me towards Ian.

All hell broke loose. Two guys ran at me as Robert made a beeline for Ian. Ducking and summoning my shield, the first bolt of magic ricocheted and hit a nearby rock. I let the Magic build up inside me like I'd practiced and focused on the closest attacker. Orange light erupted from the palm of my hand and struck him dead in the chest. Stunned and his chest smoking, his legs gave out and he crumpled to the floor.

The attacker beside him paused for a moment and then charged at me. I quickly switched my feet, holding the sword tightly in one hand, I braced for impact. His fist came at me as he ran, and I was able to duck out of the way. When I turned to keep him in my sights, he slammed his foot into my chest, knocking the breath out of me as I fell to the ground. In an instant, he was on top of me, but I was prepared. I shoved my legs against his sternum and he flipped over my head. Picking up Excalibur, I got to my feet and saw Ian rearing up to take a shot at Robert.

"Robert, look out," I yelled.

Caught off guard, Robert looked in my direction and Ian's bolt of electricity caught his left shoulder.

My attacker was on me again, trying to rip the sword from my hands, but this time I summoned my Magic to handle him. A pulse of hot light flashed off of me and threw my attacker twenty feet into the air. Watching him fall, I ran toward Robert, who was on the ground and holding his shoulder as it healed.

Lila had already dispatched one of her attackers and from the looks of it, she was about to lay the final blow on another one of Ian's goons.

I reached Robert in a few short strides and knelt down beside him. The field had been cleared and Ian was nowhere in sight.

Lila kicked one of the fallen guys once more and looked around her. When she spotted us, she started jogging in our direction.

Ian shimmered out of thin air in front of Lila and she slammed into him, falling to the ground.

"I'm going to enjoy this," Ian said stalking toward Lila.

"Come on, Ian, you're not going to hurt me," Lila said, inching away from him.

"I wouldn't be too sure about that." Ian brandished his knife.

"You and I have history." Lila stood and took a hesitant step towards him.

"You think my history with you outweighs what I have with Morgana?" Ian seethed.

"Lila," Robert warned, but she ignored him and took another step in Ian's direction.

"What you have with Morgana isn't real, she's manipulating you," Lila said.

Ian chuckled, then grabbed Lila by her arm and yanked her toward him.

"The only one manipulating anybody is me," Ian growled. "You think your father would have ever been able to wake

Morgana without me?" Ian moved his blade to Lila's neck. "He was weak, pathetic, clinging onto every word I said. I enjoyed slitting his throat."

"You killed Aiden?" I asked, my brow furrowed.

Robert took a step next to me, his muscles coiled and ready for a fight as Ian yanked Lila's head back by her hair.

"Not another step, *Healer.*" Ian leveled his eyes on Robert.

"You have a decision to make," Ian warned, struggling with Lila in his arms.

"Ian, don't do this," Lila pleaded, pulling at his arm.

Robert took a step toward Lila but caught himself.

"What'll it be, your precious Waker or your whore?" He smiled, and in that moment I could see just how evil he really was. He liked making Robert choose who would live and who would die.

I stepped forward, deciding to take action. "He won't have to choose," I said, and sauntered toward Ian.

"You're right, he won't." Annabel stepped out from behind the rocks. She sauntered up behind Ian and Lila and forced Ian's hand to pull the knife across Lila's neck.

Lila crumpled to the ground, trying to cover her wound with her hands. Blood spewed through her fingers as she collapsed into the grass.

"Lila!" Robert yelled and took a step in her direction.

"Annabel, how could you?" I recoiled. Never in a million years did I think that she was a sheep in wolfs clothing.

She chuckled and her image shimmered. Annabel's short blonde hair turned wavy and red. Her nose widened and her crystal blue eyes turned a muddy brown.

"What've you done with Annabel?" Panic rose inside of me as I looked between Lila and the redhead in front of me.

"Annabel's been dead since the moment I took her," Ian smirked.

"No... no you're wrong!" I shouted. "I saw her-"

"You saw what Morgana wanted you to see," the fake Annabel spat.

Robert circled behind me, trying to get to Lila and heal her.

"But why?" I asked.

"Plan's changed once Morgana returned, and we needed someone on the inside.

"Not so fast, Robert," the redhead warned, snapping her head in his direction. "You won't be healing Lila today. She needs to pay for her betrayal."

Ian placed himself between Lila and us, daring someone to come near her.

Angry tears gathered in my eyes, but I refused to let a single drop spill over. My body shook with anger as I looked at Robert, who shared my look of horror. This whole time I'd been blaming Lila for leaking information, but it was the woman standing in front of us. She knew our every move because she was a part of them.

"Why do any of this? What's the point?" Robert asked.

"We needed to make sure you collected the tokens," fake Annabel explained.

"Great, and then what?" Robert sneered at her.

In a split second, everything clicked. They were there for The Lady and we'd led them right to her.

Brett ran up next to me and quickly summoned another round of lightning as Robert threw himself toward Ian.

Summoning my own shield, I quickly moved over to Lila. There wasn't much I could do for her, but I had to try.

A loud grunt caught my attention and Ian was on the ground, Robert on top of him and pummeling him with his fists.

"I'm here, Lila, I'm here," I told her. I tore my sweater off and held the arm to her neck, trying to stop the bleeding.

Her mouth opened to speak, her teeth covered in blood, but no words came out.

"Shh, don't try to talk. Just stay calm, we'll get you out of here," I reassured her.

I looked up, desperate for Robert to heal her when Ian blasted Robert across the field. Ian took one step toward us before Jake was able to shoot a bolt of blinding light at him, making him yell out in pain and stumble backward.

Lila's cold, bloody hand touched my face and the horrifying realization hit me. This was the vision I'd had playing out in real time. Her eyes pierced through me as I looked at her, and I realized I could try to save her. I could try to tap into our *Artognou*.

Searching for the connection to Robert, it was faint. Closing my eyes, I pulled on the thread of Magic hiding deep inside me, but it faltered the moment I got a grip. As much as we'd trained over the last week, we still struggled to connect without touch.

"No, no, just hold on." I looked down at Lila dying in my arms.

"Everything he did, he did out of love for you," Lila choked out, her hand falling from my face as a stream of blood poured out of her mouth. "I don't deserve it, but I hope you can forgive the pain I caused you." Her eyes closed, and I wasn't sure if they would open again.

"Lila, stay with me, Lila." I shook her and her eyes popped open.

"For what it's worth, I don't hate you," I said.

Her eyes closed again and frantically I searched for Robert.

Dodging an orange stunning orb, bright blue electricity sparked from his fingers, catching Ian in the leg.

"Get to The Lady, we'll hold them off," Brett said as a cinder spell flew past us.

I looked down at Lila. Her body gone limp.

"Lila?" I shook her, but she didn't move. "Lila, wake up." I tried again, but she was gone. Grief I didn't know I'd feel filled my heart. Laying her down in the grass, I rose to my feet and my eyes caught the redhead as she blinked out of existence.

Grabbing Robert's arm and the sword, I yelled, "We need to go, now!"

"I'll be right behind you," Robert said. He pulled his arm free and stalked after Ian.

"No, you're coming with me and we're ending this," I ordered. "Now."

Summoning my shield, we started to walk across the boulders. My whole life had been leading up to this moment, and I wasn't going to let anything get in my way. Not once did I look back as Robert and I clambered toward my destiny.

CHAPTER TWENTY-FOUR

My legs burned as we reached the larger rocks and began to climb. I pushed myself forward and my heart ached at the loss of Annabel and Lila. Tucking the sword under my arm, it was hard to navigate the stone's smooth surface. Pulling myself up over the last boulder, I stood atop the large cluster of rocks. The willow tree and what looked to be an altar was just a few feet away.

"We made it," Robert said, sweat beading on his forehead.

Closing the gap between the altar and myself, I held the sword in one hand and cut my palm. The blood pooled in my fist and as I held my hand out, pebble-sized drops of blood dotted the surface of the altar and a groove for the sword appeared.

Robert placed his hand on my shoulder and nodded. Taking a deep breath, I found the familiar thread of our *Artognou*, and this time I was able to connect. I pulled on our Magic and it burned through me, hot and eager.

Grabbing the spell from my pocket, I recited the words written on each token. The *Artognou* flared inside me and the opening of the rock pulsed with anticipation.

I raised the sword with both hands, ready to plunge the blade into the stone when a cold breeze touched my skin. Robert flew away from me as if he was a puppet on strings. Reaching after him, I watched in horror as he flew over the side of the rocks into the lake below. A woman dressed in all black appeared in front of me. Her long, dark hair swirling around her as bright blue eyes stared at me like a hawk.

"Hello, Violet," she purred, watching me with a curious smile.

"Morgana," I said, still holding the sword above my head. "You can't stop me. I will wake her." I lifted the sword a little higher, ready to plunge it into the stone.

"You speak of her as if she's an actual person." Morgana paced back and forth, her dark dress trailing behind her. She looked like someone who had just stepped out of a Grimm's fairy tale.

This was a trick, it had to be. "Regardless of what she is, I will wake her and she will send you back to hell."

A low chuckle shook her shoulders. "You really don't know, do you?"

"Stop playing games, Morgana." I inched the sword toward the stone. My hands vibrated as raw power bubbled from the altar. Excalibur pulled toward the opening like a magnet, aching to find its sheath.

"The Lady," Morgana sneered, "is not a woman. She's an entity that you must take within yourself. She'll destroy you the second you release her." Her eyes held mine, and she cocked her head as if she was studying me.

"You're lying." The sword shook in my hand and I hesitated. Graham's words echoed back to me. *The Waker will be lost to The Lady.* Could Morgana really be telling the truth?

"You know something, don't you?" Morgana stepped closer to me. "Someone warned you." Her eyes focused on mine and she reached her hand toward me.

"That's close enough." I lifted the sword and pointed it at her. "What do you care if waking her does kill me?"

"Do you really have no regard for your own life?" Morgana took a step back, unphased by the sword pointing at her.

"Again, I don't see how that's any of your concern."

"You've done your part, played out your destiny beautifully," Morgana beamed. "But I'm afraid this is the end of the line for you."

The redhead who fooled us all into believing that she was Annabel, appeared in front of us. Bowing her head to Morgana, she faced me. "I'll take it from here," she said.

I blinked in disbelief. "Why do you want to wake The Lady? I thought she was meant to destroy you?"

"Whoever said I was going to wake *her*?" Her left eyebrow rose, and she smirked.

"If not The Lady, then who?"

"Nimue. the other half of her soul, of course."

The vision I'd seen so many times of myself with amethyst eyes flashed across my mind. I was meant to wake The Lady and nothing Morgana said would stop me.

"Yeah, well, I was born for this."

I lifted the sword and plunged it into the rock. Bright yellow light erupted from the stones and I could feel raw, hot Magic course up the blade and into my hands. I tried to let go, but my hands were glued to the hilt. The magic burned as it entered my body, and I felt like I was being set on fire from the inside out.

The redhead burst through the light. A disarming spell hitting me square in the chest and I was thrown backward, away from the altar.

Relief filled me as the heat of the Magic instantly disappeared. I got to my feet and saw her reach for the sword. Reciting a different spell from the one I did, the redhead closed her fingers around the hilt. The brilliant light that had surrounded me turned dark as her hair flew around her face.

"No!" I yelled, but it was too late.

She let out an ear-splitting scream and fell to her knees, her hand still tightly wrapped around the hilt of the sword.

I couldn't let this happen. I couldn't let Morgana win. I ran toward the altar and Morgana appeared in front of me.

Summoning a stunning spell, I threw it at Morgana, but she deflected it.

"Your part is done, Waker," Morgana spat. A quiet anger replaced the calm, even demeanor she had before. She wasn't going to let me anywhere near Excalibur.

"Morgana, please!" the woman screamed. Her voice was ragged and deep.

Morgana and I both turned to look at the redhead. Her eyes had turned red and her hair had turned completely white.

"No!" Morgana shouted and ran to her side. "Fight it, you can do this." Morgana lifted her head.

The Magic was too much for her, and if she held on any longer, she would die. Steeling myself for what had to be done, I took a stepped toward Morgana.

I summoned a disarming spell and threw the orb at the limp body hanging off of the sword. Hurtling away from the sword, her body skidded across the smooth surface of the stones and she came to a stop, unconscious, in a heap of legs and arms.

Morgana rose and placed herself between me and the altar. Summoning a cinder orb in each hand, I ran directly at her.

She threw her arms to the side and black smoke crawled out of her. Pulling my shield up around me, I threw the first Cinder orb at her. The orb vanished into thin air and passed right through the spot Morgana had been standing before crashing into the rocks, turning them to dust.

I ran toward the sword and just as I was about to reach for it a force hit me square between my shoulders and I fell over, the wind knocked out of me.

Rolling onto my side, Excalibur towered above me. I lifted my hand, still gasping for air, and reached toward the blade.

Something heavy landed on my chest. It was Morgana's boot. She pressed down on me with all of her weight and I felt my shoulder pop out of place.

"I am so sick of people getting in my way," Morgana growled at me over the roar of the wind and Magic flowing out of the stone.

I grabbed her foot with both hands, trying to dislodge her.

Summoning every last bit of Magic I had in me, I focused all my energy into throwing Morgana off of me. A volcanic rush of energy erupted deep inside me, light exploded from every pore on my body, and Morgana tumbled across the boulders.

The light faded as quickly as it had come, and I dragged my exhausted body to the sword and stood up. Wrapping my fingers around the hilt, it was like a plank had been shoved up my spine. Every muscle in my body flexed and my body went rigid as The Lady took over. Fire erupted inside my body again, and although I felt like my flesh was being wrenched from my bones, I felt powerful.

Something foreign began to take shape inside of me. My heart raced as a voice came to life in my head. The light from the crevice slowly began to fade, and I faded with it. My body felt less and less like my own as something alien took hold, shoving me aside. I was barely conscious as my hands lifted the sword out of the stone.

My legs moved without me telling them to, and I realized that The Lady really had taken over. I was trapped in my own body, but at least I wasn't dead. That was a relief.

"Hello, Morgana." My voice sounded different, stiff.

Morgana slowly got to her feet and dusted herself off.

"Vivian," Morgana sneered. She paused, looking me up and down with utter contempt.

"You shouldn't have come back to the land of the living." Vivian's voice echoed in my head.

A menacing chuckle came from deep within Morgana. "And what are *you* going to do about it? Merlin's been dust for centuries. Without him, you'll have a hard time stopping me."

Vivian smiled, and all at once I knew exactly what she was going to say. All of her memories, her knowledge flooded into my head, our head.

"Merlin is bound to this universe until the day it ceases to exist. I will find him and we will send you back beyond the veil," Vivian said with my voice.

Morgana's talon-like fingers balled into angry fists. Her eyes snapped up, and she stared right into mine. Or should I say Vivian's? She threw her hands up and a wall of fire flew at us. Without even flinching, Vivian lifted the sword, and the flames deflected around us. Raising the other hand, she shot a pulse of white light at Morgana. The flames and the light hit each other and exploded.

Flying backward, we landed in the thick grass below. I didn't feel the impact, but I knew my body would be bruised in no time. Vivian was going to have to get used to a mortal body if she planned on staying alive long enough to kill Morgana.

Morgana stood next to us and said, "Mark my words, I will send you back to your realm and make sure you're never able to return again." With that, the wind picked up, and she vanished.

I need to get back to Robert. I thought.

"Who's Robert?" Vivian asked as she picked us up off the ground.

You can hear me?

"Of course. We're both inhabiting your body."

Why can't I feel anything? I asked.

"You're lucky to be alive at all. Most can't handle the transition."

That woman?

"She's still alive, but barely."

Vivian turned and looked at the cluster of boulders, sword in one hand, blood still dripping from my palm.

My vision.

"Vision?"

Before I could answer, I heard Robert yelling my name. "Violet."

"Violet, are you alright?" Robert called as he came running around us, just like he did in my vision. "Oh God." He reached a tentative hand toward us.

This is your Robert? Vivian asked inside our shared mind.

Yes.

"Violet, please talk to me, say something," Robert pleaded.

He cares for you a great deal, it would seem.

He does. I thought about the night we'd shared at Caltome and understanding lit up in Vivian.

"Robert, correct?" Vivian asked.

Robert took a step back at the sound of her voice. She still sounded like me, but there was a cadence to my voice that was entirely Vivian.

"Yes. What have you done with Violet?" Robert asked.

Vivian touched our torso and said, "You need not worry, she is still alive."

"Who are you?"

"My name is Vivian, but you would call me The Lady of The Lake."

ENJOY THIS BOOK? YOU CAN MAKE A BIG DIFFERENCE

Reviews are the most powerful tool in my arsenal when it comes to getting attention for my books. It's reader like you, who share their love for a story that helps, authors like me get their stories out into the world.

Only about 1% of readers actually leave a review, good or bad. So all I ask, is that you join the 1% of readers who have already left reviews and share your thoughts with other readers!

Curious what others wrote, check it out below and get inspired to write your own Magical review!

"I was completely captivated while reading."

"Great story! I've been a fan of this series ever since I first fell in love with Soothsayer."

"Two thumbs way up! I'm aching to find out what happens next!"

With your support, we can share *Trivium* with the world!

THANK YOU!

I hope you enjoyed *Trivium*. I have been with these characters for many years and it's such a privilege to share them with you. Violet is in for a rough ride as we go into the finale. I can't wait for you to see what happens.

I'm sure you're wondering what happens next, is Violet really lost to The Lady forever? You'll have to wait until the final book to see what happened to Violet and The Lady. It's definitely not what you might expect, but I really hope you'll love it when you get to Elysium.

In the meantime you can start reading Morgana's novella on the next page, r you can go ahead and buy the next book at your favorite retailer or directly from me on my website, allison-sipe.com

I wanted to give you the opportunity to experience Morgana's POV from the moment she comes back to the land of the living up until the events at the end of Trivium.

THANK YOU!

I love to hear from my readers, so please feel free to email me any questions or just drop me a line and say hello on my website, allisonsipe.com And again, thank you for taking this journey with Violet and Robert!

Until next time, Embrace Your Magic!

ABOUT THE AUTHOR

Allison Sipe lives in Southern California with her boyfriend and two Pomeranians. She has a degree from California State University Northridge in English Literature and is very proud to have gone to school for something she loves.

She published her first novel, *Soothsayer* in 2015 and has been writing like a mad woman ever since.

When she's not reading and writing, she loves to travel. She's been around Europe and London is one of her favorite cities. Hawaii is also near and dear to heart, since she wrote most of her first book while vacationing on Kauai.

www.allisonsipe.com

ACKNOWLEDGMENTS

First and foremost, I must thank my family and friends for their support on this journey. Without their encouragement and love, I wouldn't be able to keep sane while writing these Magical stories.

Jessica, first and foremost, thank you for coming up with the title for this one! Trivium, truly is your book. I seriously can't thank you enough for putting up with my crazy plot lines. Knowing that you'll read through my books with a fine-tooth comb over and over again, always putting a smile on my face! You truly are a writer's best friend.

Eric, you always say that you feel lucky when I'm 100% present with you and I have to thank you, for all the times I'm in LALA Land. I know I tend to stare off into space, or look at you and say crazy things, but it's nice knowing you're always there when I return to earth. I couldn't ask for a better PIC and I'm incredibly thankfully to have you by my side for this crazy ride. #powercouple

Katie (KA-BOOM)! What would I do without you constantly harassing me for the next book? It's incredibly encouraging that you always want more. I'm sorry for torturing you for so long. And of course, thank you for being such an amazing friend and sharing this series with the world. Your support is so incredibly amazing and I don't know how I got so lucky to have you as my friend.

To all the indie authors out there who've shared their knowledge along the way. I wouldn't be where I am today without such an amazing and supportive community. I am so proud to be a part of a group of people who are constantly encouraging and supporting one another. You all ROCK!!

Last but certainly not least, I want to thank my fans and loyal readers. Whenever I'm having a rough day creatively, I look at all the cards and emails you've sent me and it gives me the strength to keep writing. The fact that even one person out there in the world has enjoyed one of my books, makes me so, unimaginably happy. You guys are the absolute best and I couldn't ask for a more amazing fan base.